About the Authors

Cat Schield lives in Minnesota with her daughter, their opiniated Burmese cats and a silly Doberman puppy. Winner of the Romance Writers of America 2010 Golden Heart® for series contemporary romance, when she's not writing sexy, romantic stories for Mills & Boon Desire, she can be found sailing with friends on the St. Croix River or in more exotic locales like the Caribbean and Europe. You can find out more about her books at www.catschield.net

USA TODAY bestselling author **Jules Bennett** has penned more than fifty novels during her short career. She's married to her high school sweetheart, has two active girls, and is a former salon owner. Jules can be found on Twitter, Facebook (Fan Page), and her website julesbennett.com. She holds contests via these three outlets with each release and loves to hear from readers!

Annie West has devoted her life to an intensive study of charismatic heroes who cause the best kind of trouble in the lives of their heroines. As a sideline she researches locations for romance, from vibrant cities to desert encampments and fairytale castles. Annie lives in eastern Australia with her hero husband, between sandy beaches and gorgeous wine country. She finds writing the perfect excuse to postpone housework. To contact her or join her newsletter, visit www.annie-west.com

Royal Scandals

Royal Scandals:
His Royal Heir

CAT SCHIELD

JULES BENNETT

ANNIE WEST

MILLS & BOON

First Published in Great Britain 2021
By Mills & Boon, an imprint of HarperCollins*Publishers,* Ltd
1 London Bridge Street, London, SE1 9GF

www.harpercollins.co.uk

HarperCollins*Publishers*
1st Floor, Watermarque Building,
Ringsend Road, Dublin 4, Ireland

ROYAL SCANDALS: HIS ROYAL HEIR
© 2021 Harlequin Books S.A.

Royal Heirs Required © 2015 Catherine Schield
What the Prince Wants © 2015 Jules Bennett
The Desert King's Secret Heir © 2016 Annie West

ISBN: 978-0-263-30304-9

MIX
Paper from
responsible sources
FSC™ C007454

This book is produced from independently certified FSC™ paper to ensure responsible forest management.

For more information visit: www.harpercollins.co.uk/green

Printed and Bound in Spain using 100% Renewable electricity at CPI Black Print, Barcelona

ROYAL HEIRS REQUIRED

CAT SCHIELD

For Delores and Jerry Slawik.
Thank you for making me feel
like part of your family.

One

"She's the perfect choice for you," Gabriel Alessandro's brother joked, nudging his shoulder.

The two princes were standing at the edge of the dance floor watching their father, the king, sweep Gabriel's future bride through a series of elegant turns while their mother concentrated on keeping her toes from beneath the prime minister's clumsy feet.

Gabriel released an audible sigh. With his future bride's father building a high-tech manufacturing plant just outside the capital, Sherdana's economy would receive the boost it badly needed. "Of course she is."

Lady Olivia Darcy, daughter of a wealthy British earl, was just a little too perfect. While she exuded poise and warmth in public, in private she never relaxed, never let down her guard. This hadn't bothered him at all in the days leading up to their engagement. From the moment he'd begun looking for a wife he'd decided to listen to his head and not his heart. Past experience had demonstrated losing himself in passion led to nothing but heartache and disappointment.

"Then why are you looking so grim?"

Why indeed? Even though Gabriel didn't have to pretend to be besotted with his fiancée in front of his brother, he wasn't about to admit his regret that his personal life would have less passion and drama once he was married.

Until the wedding planning had begun in earnest, he'd considered himself well and thoroughly lucky to have found a woman who wouldn't drive him mad with her theatrics and demands. It was in sharp contrast to his affair with Marissa, which had been a tempestuous four-year romance with no future.

Gabriel was not a world-famous musician or a dashing Hollywood actor or even a wealthy playboy. He was the heir apparent of a small European country with strict laws that dictated his wife must be either an aristocrat or a citizen of Sherdana. Marissa had been neither.

"How happy would you be if you were marrying a virtual stranger?" Gabriel kept his voice soft, but there was no hiding his bitterness.

Christian's grin was positively wicked. "The best part about being the youngest is that I don't have to worry about getting married at all."

Gabriel muttered an expletive. He was well aware that neither of his brothers envied him. In many ways that was a relief. In centuries past Sherdana had seen its fair share of plots against the crown both from without and within. It would have been awful if either of his brothers had schemed to keep him off the throne. But that was highly unlikely. Nic lived in the US, building rocket ships that might someday carry regular—wealthy—citizens into space while Christian was very happy buying and selling companies.

"...hot."

"Hot?" Gabriel caught the final word his brother had spoken. "What's hot?"

"Not what." Christian shot him a wry glance. "Who. Your future bride. I was just remarking that you should spend some time getting to know her. It might be more enjoyable than you think. She's hot."

Lady Olivia Darcy was many things, but Gabriel wouldn't label her as hot. A gorgeous package of stylish sophistication, she had the fashion designers competing to dress her. Her features were delicate and feminine, her skin pale and unblemished. She was slender, but not boyish, with long legs, graceful arms and an elegant neck. There was a serene expression in her keen blue gaze.

And it wasn't as if she was a frivolous socialite, spending her days shopping and her nights in clubs. She worked tirelessly for almost a dozen charities all focused on children's causes. The perfect future queen of Sherdana.

Gabriel shot his brother a narrow look. "You just referred to your future sister-in-law and queen as hot. Do you think Mother would approve?"

"I'm her baby boy." The youngest of the triplets, Christian had played the birth-order card all his life. "She approves of everything I do."

"She doesn't approve of your antics, she simply feels bad for all those times she had to leave you to the nanny because she could only carry Nic and me."

Ignoring his brother's gibe, Christian nodded toward the queen. "She's hot, too, you know. She'd have to be to keep Father interested all these years."

Gabriel had no interest in discussing his parents' love life. "What has you so determined to stir up trouble tonight?"

Christian's expression settled into severe lines. "Now that Mother has you all settled, she going to turn her sights to Nic and me."

"Nic is more interested in fuel systems than women," Gabriel said. "And you've made it clear you have no intention of giving up your bachelor ways."

In the five years since his car accident, Christian had become guarded and pessimistic when it came to his personal life. Although the burn scars that spread down his neck and over his shoulder, chest and upper arm on the right side were hidden beneath the high collar of his formal blue tunic, the worst of Christian's hurts were below the skin, deep in his soul where no healing reached. The damage was visible in those rare moments when he drank too much or thought no one was watching.

Gabriel continued, "I don't think either of our parents hold out any hope that the two of you will settle down anytime soon."

"You know Mother is a romantic," Christian said.

"She's also pragmatic."

But Christian didn't look convinced. "If that was true, she'd accept that you will father all the heirs Sherdana could ever want or need and leave Nic and me alone. That's not the impression she gave me earlier this evening."

A knot of discomfort formed in Gabriel's chest as he thought of his future bride. Once again his gaze slid to Olivia, who was now dancing with the prime minister. Although her smile was lovely, the reserve in her blue eyes made her seem untouchable.

His days with Marissa had been sensual, wild and all-consuming. They'd awaken before dawn in her Paris apartment and make love in the quiet hush of the early morning. After which they'd sit by the window, gorge themselves with pastries washed down with strong coffee and watch the sun paint the rooftops with golden light.

"Your Royal Highness."

Gabriel turned to his private secretary, who'd appeared out of nowhere. Usually Stewart Barnes was the calm eye in the middle of the hurricane. At the moment, sweat shone on his forehead.

The hairs on the back of Gabriel's neck rose. "Problem?"

Stewart's approach had caught Christian's attention, as well. "I'll deal with it," he said, stepping away from his brother's side.

"No, sir." The private secretary moved to block Christian. He gave a small shake of his head and met Gabriel's hard gaze with a look that conveyed the seriousness of the issue. "I know the timing is bad, but a lawyer has arrived with an urgent message for you."

"A lawyer?"

"How did he get into the palace?" Christian snapped, eyes blazing.

Gabriel barely registered Christian's words. "What could possibly be so important?"

"Did Captain Poulin give you a reason for granting this man entrance at such an inappropriate hour?"

"Can't it wait until after the party?"

Stewart's attention bounced between the two men as they fired questions at him. "He wouldn't tell me what it's about, Highness, only the name of his client." Stewart's tone was low and urgent. "I think you'd better speak to him."

Unable to imagine what could have rattled his unflappable private secretary, Gabriel shared a glance with Christian. "Who is his client?"

"Marissa Somme."

Hearing his former lover's name aroused a hundred emotions Gabriel would have preferred not to feel. He was a little surprised that Marissa had waited so long to contact him. He'd expected her to pull a stunt five months ago when he'd announced his engagement. To say she had a flare for the dramatic was like describing the Himalayas as tall hills.

"What mischief is she up to?" Gabriel demanded.

Christian cursed beneath his breath. "Something newsworthy, no doubt."

"I can't afford anything to interfere with the wedding." Sherdana's future was riding on the deal he'd struck with Lord Darcy. A deal that wouldn't be sealed until Olivia became a princess.

Gabriel glanced around to see if anyone had noticed their exchange and met Olivia's level gaze. She was beautiful, his future wife. But he'd chosen her for more than her appearance. She had a purity of spirit he knew would charm the Sherdanian people and her efficient, calm way of handling problems would see her through the hectic days ahead.

Beside her his father was laughing at whatever story she was telling him, looking years younger. Recent economic difficulties had taken their toll on the king. Once vibrant and strong, he'd begun to tire faster in recent months. It was why Gabriel had taken on more and more of the day-to-day running of the country.

Although she returned her attention to the king, the slightest lift of her delicate eyebrows let Gabriel know her curiosity had been aroused by his exchange with Christian and Stewart. Awareness surged through him. It was the first time that they'd connected at a level deeper than politeness. Anticipation sparked. Perhaps they would be able to share something more than a bed.

"Please, Your Highness."

Glancing toward Christian, he said, "Will you go entertain my fiancée while I discover what's going on?"

"Don't you mean distract?" Christian countered, his expression sour.

"Just make excuses for me until I can get back."

And then he was slipping through the multitude attending the ball honoring Sherdana's independence from France back in 1664, smiling and greeting the guests as if nothing in the world was wrong. All the while two words pounded in his head: *Marissa Somme.* What could this be about?

Since it first declared itself a principality, Sherdana had survived as an agrarian economy. But Gabriel wanted his country to do more than survive, he wanted it to thrive.

Tucked between France and Italy on a verdant plane resplendent with grapevines and fertile fields, Sherdana
needed an active technological culture to move the economy into the twenty-first century and beyond. Olivia's father, Lord Edwin Darcy, held the match that would light
the fuse. Nothing must interfere with that.

Entering the green salon, Gabriel strode over to greet
the man who'd barged in unannounced. The lawyer wore
his gray hair short, making no attempt to hide the bald
patch that caught the light from the wall sconces behind
him. His clear gray eyes had few lines at the corners. This
was not a man who smiled often. Dressed in a navy suit
and black overcoat, the only spark of color about him was
a thin line of yellow in his striped tie.

"Good evening, Your Royal Highness," the gentleman
said, bowing respectfully. "Forgive me for interrupting,
but I'm afraid the matter is quite urgent."

"What mischief is Marissa up to now?"

"Mischief?" The man looked dismayed at Gabriel's
harshness. "You misunderstand the reason I'm here."

"Then enlighten me. I have guests waiting. If you have
a message from Marissa, then deliver it."

The man straightened his shoulders and tugged at his
coat lapel. "It's a little more complicated than a message."

"My patience is wearing thin."

"Marissa Somme is dead."

Dead? Gabriel felt as if he'd been clobbered with a
poker. For a second he couldn't process the man's words.
Brilliant, beautiful, vivacious Marissa dead? His gut
twisted.

"How?"

The older gentleman nodded in sympathy. "Cancer."

Even though he hadn't spoken with her in a very long
time, the news rocked him. Marissa had been the first
woman he'd ever loved. The only one. Their breakup three

years before had been one of the most painful experiences of his life. But nothing compared to knowing she was gone for good. Wounds he'd thought healed were reopened, the pain as fresh as it had ever been. Never would he see her again. Hear her laugh.

Why hadn't she called him? He would have helped her out.

"You came all this way to deliver the news of her death to me?" Had she still cared about him? Despite her final angry words? Impossible. She'd never once tried to contact him.

"And to bring you something she said you should have."

"What?" Gabriel demanded. Had she returned the diamond heart pendant he'd given her for their first anniversary? He'd been a romantic fool in those days. Young. Rebellious. Caught up in a passionate affair that had no future. And a fool. "What did you bring me?"

"Your daughters."

"Daughters?" *As in more than one?* Gabriel wondered if he'd heard the man properly.

"Twins."

"Marissa and I had no children together."

"I'm afraid that's not true."

The man pulled out two birth certificates and extended them. Gabriel gestured to Stewart to take them and watched as his private secretary scanned the documents. Stewart's blue eyes were awash with concern as he glanced up and met Gabriel's gaze.

"They bear Marissa's last name, but she listed you as the father," Stewart said.

"They can't be mine," Gabriel insisted. "We were careful." Perhaps not careful enough. "How old are they?"

"They will turn two in a month."

Gabriel quickly did the math. They'd been conceived in the week he'd been in Venice shortly after their breakup.

Marissa had come and thrown herself at him in one last attempt to make him abandon his duty. They'd made love all night, their kisses frantic, embraces feverish. When she'd awakened to find him departing the room before dawn, she'd lashed out, claiming that he'd led her on, accusing him of indifference. Despite her antagonism, regret had stuck with him for months afterward.

They'd had no future. His duty was to his country. She couldn't accept that and he'd let the relationship go on too long. She'd begun to hope he would give up everything for her and he'd enjoyed shirking his responsibilities. But it couldn't last. Sherdana always came first.

What would he have done if he'd known she was pregnant? Set her up in a villa nearby where he could visit? She would never have put up with that. She'd have demanded his complete and total devotion. It was what had torn them apart. He belonged to the people of Sherdana.

"This could all be a huge hoax," Stewart said.

"Marissa might have loved drama, but pulling a stunt like this goes beyond anything she'd do."

"We'll know for sure after a DNA test," Stewart said.

"And in the meantime? What am I to do with the girls?" the lawyer asked impertinently.

"Where are they?" Gabriel demanded. He crackled with impatience to see them.

"Back at my hotel with their nanny."

He didn't hesitate to ponder the consequences. "Get them."

"Think of your upcoming wedding, Highness," Stewart cautioned. "You can't have them brought here. The palace is crawling with media."

Gabriel aimed a disgusted look at his secretary. "Are you telling me you're not clever enough to transport two toddlers here without being seen?"

Stewart's spine snapped straight as Gabriel knew it

would. "I will see that they are brought to the palace immediately."

"Good."

"In the meantime," Stewart said, "I suggest you return to the gala before you're missed. I'm sure the king and queen will wish to discuss the best way to handle things."

Gabriel hated every bit of Stewart's sensible advice and the need to play host when his attention was shackled to reckless urges. He didn't want to wait to see the girls. His instinct demanded he go to the lawyer's hotel immediately. As if by taking one look at the toddlers he could tell if they were his. Ridiculous.

"Find me as soon as they're settled," he told Stewart.

And with those parting words, he exited the room.

Knowing he should return immediately to the party but with his mind racing, Gabriel strode into the library. He needed a few minutes to catch his breath and calm his thoughts.

Twins. His heart jerked. Did they have their mother's clear green eyes and luxurious brown hair? Had she told them about him? Was he insane to bring them into the palace?

A scandal could jeopardize his plans for stabilizing Sherdana's economy. Would the earl still allow Olivia to marry him if word got out that Gabriel had illegitimate twin daughters? And what if Olivia wasn't willing to accept that her children wouldn't be his only ones?

Gabriel left the library, burdened by a whole new set of worries, determined to make sure his future bride found him irresistible.

From her place of honor beside the king of Sherdana, Olivia watched her future husband slip through the guests assembled in the golden ballroom and wondered what was so important that he had to leave the Independence Day gala in such a hurry.

It continued to bother her that in less than four weeks, she was going to become a princess, Gabriel's princess, and she had very little insight into the man she was marrying. Theirs was not a love match the likes of which Kate had found with William. Olivia and Gabriel were marrying to raise her father's social position and improve Sherdana's economic situation.

While that was great for everyone else, Olivia's London friends wondered what was motivating her. She'd never told anyone about the dream conceived by her three-year-old self that one day she'd become a princess. It had been a child's fancy and as she'd grown up, reality replaced the fairy tale. As a teenager she'd stopped imagining herself living in a palace and dancing through the night with a handsome prince. Her plans for the future involved practical things like children's charities and someday a husband and children of her own. But some dreams had deep roots that lay dormant until the time was ripe.

Before Olivia considered her actions, she turned to the king. "Excuse me."

"Of course," the handsome monarch replied, his smile cordial.

Released, she left the king and headed in the direction her fiancé had gone. Perhaps she could catch Gabriel before he returned to the ballroom and they could spend some time talking, just the two of them. She hadn't gone more than a dozen steps before Christian Alessandro appeared in her path.

His gold eyes, shadowed and wary around most people, warmed as he smiled down at her. "Are you enjoying the party?"

"Of course," she replied, bottling up a sigh as the youngest Alessandro prince foiled her plan to speak to his brother alone.

She'd encountered Christian several times in London over the years. As the wildest Alessandro brother, in his university days, Christian had spent more time partying than studying and had barely graduated from Oxford. He'd earned a reputation as a playboy, but had always treated her with respect. Maybe because Olivia had recognized the clever mind he hid beneath his cavalier charm.

"I noticed Prince Gabriel left the party in a hurry," she murmured, unable to conquer the curiosity that loosened her tongue. "I hope nothing is wrong."

Christian had an impressive poker face. "Just some old business he had to take care of. Nothing important."

"He looked a bit shaken up." She stared at her future brother-in-law and saw the tiniest twitch at the corner of his eye. He was keeping something important about Gabriel from her. Olivia's pulse skipped. Seemed she wasn't the only one with secrets.

Since Gabriel had opened negotiations with her father a year ago, Olivia hadn't had much opportunity to get to know the man she would marry. The situation hadn't improved since she'd arrived in Sherdana a week ago. With the wedding only a month away and parliament in session, they'd barely spent an hour alone together and most of that had been divided up into one- to five-minute snippets.

A stroll in the garden the day after she'd arrived, cut short when they'd met the queen's very muddy vizsla. Gabriel had commended Olivia's nimbleness in dodging the dog and retreated to the palace to change his trousers.

A moment in the carriage before the parade yesterday. He'd complimented her hat.

A whole five minutes during the waltz this evening. He'd told her she looked lovely.

Their exchanges were polite and cordial. At all times

he'd been the perfect prince. Courteous. Gallant. Cultured. And she'd been seized by the absurd desire to muss his hair and shock him with outrageous remarks. Of course, she would never do that. The daughter of an earl, she was acutely conscious of her image and position.

Christian refocused her attention on the crowd around them and began filling her ear with all sorts of salacious gossip about the local nobility. Normally she'd be amused by his outrageous slander of Sherdana's wealthy and powerful, but with each new dance the air in the ballroom grew stuffier and she wanted to spend time getting to know her fiancé.

What did Gabriel expect from her? A political partner? Or an attractive figurehead that he could trot out for state occasions? She hoped it was the former.

Firstborn, he'd won the right to inherit the throne by a mere forty minutes. But there was no question in anyone's mind that he was utterly and completely suited to the role.

His commitment to Sherdana was absolute and apparent to all. He'd been educated here and rarely left, except on official business. While in contrast, his two younger brothers had both chosen to spend as little time in their native country as possible.

Drawn by a magnetic pull too great to resist, her attention returned to the ballroom doors that Gabriel had passed through. What could have taken him away in the middle of the party? As if her thoughts had summoned him, she spied the prince coming through the crowd toward her.

Her gaze traced the sculpted breadth of his shoulders, the way his white jacket stretched across his broad chest, providing an abundance of room for the medals pinned there. A blue sash cut diagonally from shoulder to hip.

"Forgive me for neglecting you," he said as he came to a stop before her. "I hope my brother has kept you sufficiently entertained."

"Christian has been filling me in on your guests."

For the first time in her company, Gabriel's courteous mask slipped. He shot his brother a hard look. "What have you been telling her?"

"Things most people, including you, wouldn't. If she's going to be Sherdana's princess, she needs to know where the bodies are buried or she'll be no help to you at all."

Gabriel shook his head. "She doesn't need to know all the ins and outs of our politics to help out the country or me."

Olivia's heart sank. Now she knew what he expected from her. There would be no partnership, no working together. She would attend ceremonies and support charities while he ran the country and dealt with its problems alone.

"She's smarter than you're giving her credit for, Gabriel. You should use her to your best political advantage."

"Thank you for your opinion, brother." And his tone said that was the end of the conversation.

With a mocking bow, Christian retreated. While part of Olivia regretted his departure, she was glad for a moment alone with Gabriel. Or she was until he began to speak.

"I know you haven't seen much of Sherdana since your arrival," he said, his polite formality pushing her to greater impatience. "But maybe that can change in the next week or so."

"That would be lovely." She bit back her thoughts on how unlikely it was. With the wedding only a month away she would scarcely have the opportunity to sleep, much less take a tour of the countryside. "I'm eager to visit the wine country."

"Sherdana takes pride in its wine as you well know."

"As it should," she murmured, her boredom coming through in her tone. "I'm glad you were able to get your business resolved so you could return to the party so quickly."

"Business?" There wasn't the least suggestion of understanding in his manner.

"I saw your private secretary approach you with some news. It seemed to be something unpleasant. And then you left. Christian explained it was old business you needed to take care of."

"Ah, yes. Just a misunderstanding with Stewart. It was nothing."

"I'm glad." But her mind was busy cataloging all the nuances of his tone and expression. Her future husband was skilled at deflection.

"Would you care to dance?" he asked, his deep voice rumbling through her like distant thunder.

Not really. She was tired and her shoes pinched. But she smiled. "Of course."

A waltz began to play as Gabriel took her hand and led her onto the dance floor. Keeping her expression pleasant and neutral was torture as his palm slid against her back. The gown she wore had a modest cut, showing no cleavage or bare shoulders, but the material was silk and the heat of Gabriel's hand burned through the fabric and set her on fire.

"Are you feeling compelled to marry because your father wishes it?"

The abruptness of his question was so unexpected, she almost laughed. "Why would I need to be compelled by my father? You're rich, handsome and going to be king one day. What girl wouldn't wish to be queen?"

"You didn't answer my question."

"I'm not being forced to marry you. I have been given an opportunity many would envy." She assessed his expression, curious where this line of questioning originated. "Are you worried that down the road I'll regret my choice?" She cocked her head and regarded him intently. "Or are you looking for an excuse to break our engagement?"

"Nothing like that. I am just wondering if perhaps you'd have preferred a different life."

"I'm sure many people wish every day that they'd done something different. Mostly, we must play the hand life deals us. For some, it's struggling with poverty. For others raising a child on their own or dedicating themselves to their career and forgoing a family." She pitched her voice into sympathetic tones for the next example. "For you it's ensuring your kingdom's economic security. I get to marry a prince and someday become a queen."

For some inexplicable reason, he grew short with her. "But is that what you want?"

"To marry you and become a queen?" She let her surprise show. "Of course."

Gabriel didn't appear convinced. "We haven't had much time to get to know each other," he said. "I hope that will change over the next month."

"Perhaps we could begin now. What is it you'd like to know?"

"Let's begin simply. How do you come to speak French and Italian so fluently?"

"I had a whole army of tutors from the time I was small."

"Your accent is quite good."

"I've been told I have an aptitude for languages. I speak quite a few."

"How many?"

"Six, but I understand three more."

"That will come in handy when dignitaries visit us."

Once again it hit her that she would never return to her home in England for anything more than a short visit. As princess, she would be expected to spend most, if not all, of her time in Sherdana. At least she would see her father frequently because he would want to keep an eye on his investment.

"You don't smile much, do you?" His question was more reflective than directly aimed at her.

His observation caught her off guard.

"I smile all the time."

Gabriel's gaze slipped intently over her features, arousing a frantic thrumming in her chest. "Polite smiles. Political smiles, but I'm not sure I've once seen you smile because you're happy."

"I assure you, I'm quite happy."

"Stop telling me what you think I want to hear. That's not what Sherdana needs of its princess and definitely not what I expect from my wife."

The intensity of his tone and the nuances of his observation did not belong to the man she'd known up to this point. His frank speech loosened her tongue.

"Are you giving me permission to argue with Your Highness?"

He made a face. "Gabriel."

"Of course."

"Olivia." Tone commanding, he somehow managed to caress her name in a way that vibrated through her. "It would make me very happy if you would start thinking of me as a man and not a prince."

His demand sent a ripple of excitement up her spine. She decided to speak her mind.

"I will if you stop thinking of me in terms of economic gain or financial dealings and realize I'm a woman who knows exactly what she wants."

At her words, Gabriel blinked. Surprise quickly became curiosity as he regarded her. For the first time she believed he was seeing her as a person instead of the clause in the contract he needed to satisfy so her father would build a plant in Sherdana and create technical jobs to bolster the economy.

"I'm beginning to think there's more to you than I real-

ize," Gabriel remarked, executing a turn in the dance that
left her breathless.

"Thank goodness." It was an effort to get out more than
those two words.

Perhaps marriage might hold more of an adventure than
she'd first thought. She hadn't expected her husband to excite her. Even seeing how handsome Gabriel was, he was
always so in control. She never imagined passion. And
growing up sheltered from the experiences an ordinary girl
would have with boys such as dating or even just hanging
out, she'd never experienced desire. Until this moment,
she wasn't sure she could.

Relief made her giddy. Tonight she'd glimpsed a very
important and unexpected benefit this marriage would
have for her and for the first time in months, she faced her
future with a light heart.

Two

Olivia lay on the blue velvet chaise in the bedroom she'd been assigned at the palace, a heating pad taking away the discomfort of cramps. She stared up at the touches of gold leaf on the ceiling's ornate plasterwork twenty feet above her. From the tall, narrow mirrors between the wide cream silk-draped windows to the elegant chandeliers, it was a stunning, yet surprisingly warm, space.

It was a little after two in the morning. She'd felt the first twinge of pain not long after the king and queen left the gala and had taken the opportunity to slip away. The attack had been blessedly mild. A year ago, she would have taken a pain pill and retreated to bed. Thank goodness those days were behind her. A princess couldn't avoid public appearances because she wasn't feeling well. She must have a spine of steel and prove her value was more than the economic boost her father's new technology company would provide.

As if to mock her optimism, a fresh ache began. She'd first started suffering with sharp cramps and strong periods when she was fifteen. Frightened by the amount of blood she lost each month, Olivia had gone to see a doctor. She'd been diagnosed with endometriosis and had begun taking oral contraceptives to reduce the pain and shorten her periods. Yoga, massage and acupuncture had also helped her cope with her symptoms, but none of these could correct the problem.

She'd needed surgery for that.

Olivia couldn't explain why she'd been so reluctant to have the growths removed when the pain grew progressively worse in her early twenties. She couldn't share her fears with her mother—who'd died giving birth to her—so she'd hidden the severity of the problem from everyone, including her father. Only Libby, her private secretary, knew how debilitating the pain could get. Libby had helped Olivia keep her doctor visits out of the press and made excuses when she had bad days. Olivia wasn't sure what she'd have done these past eight years without Libby's help.

It wasn't until a year ago, when she'd confronted the connection between endometriosis and infertility, that she began to rethink her plans for coping with the disease. If she was marrying a wealthy businessman, a politician or even one of her own country's nobles, she could discuss this issue with him and together they could decide what to do about her potential barrenness. But she was marrying the future king of Sherdana and would be expected to produce an heir.

So, she'd had the surgery and had been living pain free for almost twelve months.

With a sudden surge of impatience, Olivia set aside the heating pad and got to her feet. Brooding over her medical condition was the quickest way to doubt herself and that wasn't the way she faced things. Despite the late hour, the luxurious king-size bed held no appeal. She needed some fresh air and exercise. Perhaps a walk in the garden.

Although she'd removed her ball gown upon returning to her room, she'd not yet dressed for bed. Slipping off her robe, Olivia pulled on a sleeveless jersey dress and found a pair of ballet flats that would allow her to move soundlessly through the sleeping palace.

The room she'd been given was in the opposite wing of the palace from the royal family's apartments and used for housing dignitaries and visitors. Her father slept next door, his room as expansive and substantially furnished as hers. Olivia tiptoed past his door, aiming for the stairs at the far end of the hall that would deposit her close to the pink receiving room and the side gardens beyond. With her limited time in the palace, Olivia hadn't had a great deal of time to explore, but she'd taken this route her second day to meet with the queen.

When she got to the end of the hallway, the high-pitched shriek of an unhappy child caught Olivia's attention. The sound was muffled and it came from somewhere above her. She reached the stairs and paused to listen. She waited no more than a heartbeat before the cry came again, only this time there were two voices.

In an instant Olivia's destination changed. Instead of going down to the ground level, she headed up to the third floor, following the increasingly frantic exclamations of the children and the no less agitated voice of an adult trying to quiet them.

At the top of the stairs, Olivia spied two shadows racing toward her down the darkened hallway. Curious as to what was going on, she'd taken several steps in their direction when a voice cut through the shadows.

"Karina. Bethany. Come back here this instant." The shrill command provoked the children to faster flight.

Worried that at the speed they were going, they might pitch down the stairs, Olivia knelt and spread her arms wide. With their path blocked, the children stopped abruptly. With eyes wide, arms around each other for comfort, they stared at Olivia.

"Hello." She offered them her gentlest smile. "Where are you two going so late?"

"You girls are nothing but trouble."

The scolding woman hadn't spied Olivia in the dimness or she wouldn't have spoken so rudely. The two little girls shrank away from their pursuer, obviously afraid, and sidestepped in Olivia's direction. Now that they were closer, Olivia could see them better. She blinked, wondering if she might be seeing double.

The two little girls, two frightened little girls, were mirror images of each other with long brown hair and large dark eyes in their pale faces. They were dressed in identical dresses and tears streaked their matching cheeks.

Olivia wanted to snatch them into her arms, but feared upsetting them still more. Although her childhood had lacked a loving mother, Olivia had developed a strong maternal instinct. Being warned by the doctor that unless she had surgery she might never have her own children had been a sharp knife in her heart.

"You'd better learn to behave and fast or the people who live here will kick you out and you'll have nowhere else to go."

Having heard enough, Olivia surged to her feet to confront the woman and was surprised when the girls raced to stand behind her. They gripped her dress with strength born of fear, and protectiveness surged through her.

"Stop speaking this instant," Olivia commanded without raising her voice. "No one deserves to be threatened like that, especially not children."

The nanny stopped dead in her tracks and sneered. "You don't know what they're like."

"Whom do you work for?"

The woman looked wary. "I take care of these two."

"Yes, yes." Olivia put one hand on each of the toddlers' heads. The hair was silky beneath her fingers and she longed to give the girls her full attention, but this woman must be dealt with first. "But who are their parents?"

"Their mother is dead."

Olivia sucked in a short breath at the woman's lack of compassion. "That's awful."

The woman didn't respond.

"In heaven," the child on her left said.

Olivia liked the girls' nanny less and less. Had the woman no heart? Did the father know how badly his daughters were being cared for? "Perhaps I should speak to their father. What is his name?"

"A lawyer hired me a week ago to take care of them." The woman stared at Olivia in hostile defensiveness.

"Well, you're not doing a very good job."

"They're terribly spoiled and very difficult. And right now they need to be in bed." Eyes on the children, the nanny shifted her weight forward and her arms left her sides as if she intended to snatch the little girls away from Olivia.

The little girl on her right shrank back. Her sister, emboldened by Olivia's defense, fought back.

"Hate you." She hung on Olivia's skirt. "Wanna go home."

Although she'd been too young to know the shock of losing her mother, Olivia remembered her lonely childhood and ached for the sadness yet to come for these girls. She wanted to wrap her arms around the toddlers and support them through this difficult time, but these were not her children and she shouldn't get attached.

With a heavy sigh, Olivia knew it was time to extricate herself from the situation. She would summon a maid to get the girls settled and return to her room. In the morning she would find out to whom they belonged and fill him in on his employee.

"If I make this mean lady go away," Olivia began, gazing down at the dark heads. "Would you go back to your room and go to sleep?"

"No." Only one of the pair seemed to be verbal. The

other merely gave her head a vehement shake. "Stay with you."

Oh, dear. Obviously she'd defended the girls a little too well. But maybe it wouldn't hurt for them to spend one night with her. There was plenty of room in her big bed and in the morning she could sort them out.

"Would you like to come to my room to sleep tonight?"

In unison, the two dark heads bobbed. Olivia smiled.

"You can't do this," the nanny protested.

"I most certainly can. I suggest you return to your room and pack. I will send someone to escort you out shortly." Olivia extended a hand to each girl and drew the children toward the stairs. Once they were settled in her room, she would send a maid up for their nightgowns and things.

It took time to descend to the second floor. The toddlers' short legs made slow work of the steps, giving Olivia time to wonder who in the palace would raise a cry that they'd gone missing. She looked forward to having a conversation with their father in the near future about the sort of person he'd employed to take care of his children.

When Olivia entered her room, she was surprised to find it occupied by a maid. The girl looked up in surprise from the desk items she was straightening as the trio entered. Although the palace had provided Olivia with maids to tidy up and assist with whatever she needed, she hadn't expected to find one in her room during the middle of the night. And from the expression on the woman's face, she wasn't expecting to be caught at it.

"Lady Darcy, I was just tidying some things up for you."

"At two in the morning?"

"I saw your light on and thought you might be needing something."

Not wanting to make a huge scene in front of the little girls, Olivia scanned the maid's face, confident she'd be able to recognize her again from the hundred or so servants that maintained the palace. She had a small scar just below her left eye.

"Could you run down to the kitchen and get glasses of warm milk for these two?"

"Hate milk," the talkative one said. "Ice cream."

Recalling the nanny's assessment that the girls were spoiled, Olivia hesitated a moment before giving a mental shrug. Again she reminded herself they weren't her responsibility. She could indulge them to her heart's content. "With chocolate sauce?"

"Yeah!"

Olivia nodded. "Please fetch two bowls of ice cream with chocolate sauce."

"Of course, Lady Darcy."

The maid scooted past her, eyeing the odd group before disappearing through the doorway.

Olivia half sat, half collapsed on the sofa near the fireplace and gestured to the girls. "Let's get acquainted, shall we? My name is Olivia."

They hesitated for a moment before coming toward her. Olivia kept her warmest smile fixed on her face and patted the seat beside her.

"Please sit down. The ice cream will take a little while. The palace is very big."

The girls held hands and stared about the enormous room in wide-eyed silence. Now that she could see them better, Olivia noticed the Alessandro family resemblance. In fact, they looked like the pictures she'd seen of Gabriel's sister, Ariana, at a similar age. Were they cousins? She frowned. Her extensive research on Sherdana had included all the royal family. She recalled no mention of young cousins.

"I've only been here a few days and I've gotten lost a dozen times already," she continued, her voice a soothing monotone. "I was very scared when that happened. But I also discovered some wonderful places. There's a library downstairs full of books. Do you like stories?"

They nodded at her, their movements identical as if choreographed.

"So do I. My favorite stories when I was a little girl were about princesses. Would you like to hear one?" She took their smiles as assent. "Once upon a time there were two princesses and their names were Karina and Bethany."

"That's us."

Gabriel paced his office, impatient for Stewart to arrive with news that the twins had been settled into the palace. In his hand was the single photo he'd kept of Marissa after they'd broken up. He'd sealed it in an envelope and shoved it in the back of a drawer. Why he'd kept it was a question he was brooding over now.

After a long, unproductive strategy session with Christian regarding Marissa's daughters, he'd sent his brother home. Although he had rooms for his use in the palace, Christian liked his privacy and only rarely stayed in them. Sometimes Gabriel suspected that if either of his brothers had a choice they would give up their titles and any claim to Sherdana's throne. As it was they spent almost no time in Sherdana. Nic had gone to university in the US where he'd met his business partner and only returned when he absolutely had to, while Christian spent most of the year out of the country pursuing his business interests.

As close as the triplets had been growing up, the distance between them these days bothered Gabriel. While he'd known, as eldest son, that he'd be in charge of running the country someday, he'd never expected that his brothers wouldn't be around to help.

Stewart appeared as Gabriel was returning Marissa's photo to the envelope. Glancing at the clock he saw it was almost three in the morning. He'd sent his private secretary to check on Marissa's daughters half an hour earlier.

"Well?" he demanded, pushing to his feet.

"They arrived at the palace a couple hours ago and I arranged to have them escorted to the nursery in the north wing." It had seemed prudent to squirrel them away at the opposite end of the palace, far from where the royal family was housed.

"Have you seen them?" He wanted to know if the girls bore any resemblance to him, and could scarcely restrain himself from asking the question outright. Christian had cautioned that a DNA test would have to be performed before Gabriel let himself get emotionally involved. It was good advice, but easier agreed to than acted upon.

"Not yet."

Gabriel's temper flared. "What have you been doing?"

The private secretary wasn't fazed by his employer's impatience. "I went to the nursery, but they appear to be missing."

"Missing?" He couldn't imagine how that had happened. "Didn't the lawyer say they had a nanny? Did you ask her where they are?"

"She's gone. Apparently she was escorted from the palace by one of the guards an hour ago."

"Escorted…? On whose authority?"

"Lady Darcy's private secretary."

Unable to fathom how she'd gotten involved, Gabriel stabbed his fingers through his hair. This business with Marissa's daughters was fast spiraling out of control. "Have you spoken with her?"

"It's three in the morning, sir."

And if two little girls weren't missing, he might be inclined to leave his questions until morning. "Tell her I want to speak to her."

"Right away."

His private secretary wasn't gone more than five minutes. "Apparently she's in Lady Darcy's room, sir." Stewart paused. "With the girls."

Dismay shouldered aside irritation as Gabriel headed for the wing that housed his future bride. An encounter between Olivia and Marissa's daughters was a problem he hadn't anticipated. No doubt she would have questions about them. She was proving more troublesome than he'd expected based on their limited interaction before he'd proposed. Christian had warned him there was more to Olivia than a pretty face and polished manners, but she'd done an excellent job keeping her agenda hidden. The question was why.

Gabriel knocked on the door of Olivia's suite, agitation adding sharpness to the blows. His summons was answered more quickly than he expected by a pretty woman in her early thirties, wearing a classic blue dress and a frown. Her eyes widened as she spied him standing in the hall.

"I'm here looking for two little girls who've gone missing from the nursery," Gabriel said, his tone courteous despite the urge to push past her. "I understand they are here. May I come in?"

"Of course, Your Highness." She stepped back and gestured him in. "Lady Darcy, Prince Gabriel is here to see you."

"If you'll excuse us," Gabriel said, gesturing her out before entering the dimly lit suite and closing the door behind him.

His gaze swept the room in search of his fiancée. He spied her by the fireplace. She looked serene in a simple cotton dress, her hair in the same updo she'd worn to the gala. So she hadn't yet gone to bed. This thought made his attention shift to the large bed where he spied a lump beneath the covers.

"Sorry for the late visit," he told her. "But two children have gone missing."

"Bethany and Karina."

She knew their names. What else had she found out?

"What are they doing here?" he asked the question more sharply than he'd intended and saw her eyes narrow.

"They each had a bowl of ice cream and fell asleep." Her sweet smile had a bit of an edge. "They were terrified of that horrible woman who'd been hired to look after them and refused to sleep in their own beds. So I brought them here."

"And plied them with ice cream?"

"Their mother just died a few days ago. Strangers tore them from the only home they'd ever known and brought them to this big, scary place. Do you have any idea how traumatic all that was for them?"

"The nursery is not scary."

"It was for them. And so was that awful woman who was taking care of them."

"Is that why you had her escorted out of the palace tonight?"

Olivia's eyes flashed. "I suppose you're going to tell me it wasn't my place to fire her, but she reminded me of the villain in every children's story I've ever read."

Her outrage was charming and Gabriel found his annoyance melting away. "How did you come to meet them?"

"I couldn't sleep so I thought I'd go for a walk. When I got to the stairs I could hear their cries and the nanny's scolding. They were running down the hall away from that woman and the things she said to them." Olivia's lips tightened. "I would like to speak to their father about her. First thing tomorrow morning if at all possible."

"The situation with them is a little complicated," Gabriel told her, his gaze once again drawn to the lump in the center of the mattress.

"Then explain it to me."

This was what Gabriel had been wrestling with all evening. What he was going to tell the world about Marissa's daughters was a small issue compared to how he would explain things to his parents and the woman he would soon marry.

"Some matters need to be cleared up first."

Olivia's hard stare searched his expression for a long silent moment before she spoke. "What sort of matters?"

He couldn't tell her that the girls were none of her business when she'd already taken their care upon herself. At the same time, he didn't want to claim the girls before the matter of their heritage was cleared up.

"Perhaps you're referring to a DNA test." She laughed at his surprise. "They look like your sister when she was young."

"They do?"

"Didn't you notice?"

"They only just arrived. I haven't seen them yet."

Heart thumping hard against his ribs, Gabriel moved toward the bed. Since finding out about the twins, he'd been impatient to see them, but abruptly his feet felt encased in concrete. Caught between dread and hope that the girls belonged to him, Gabriel stared down at matching faces, peaceful and so innocent in sleep.

The breath he'd taken lodged in his chest as recognition flared. Marissa hadn't lied. They were his. He traced each of the children's delicate cheeks with his finger and his muscles slackened as relief washed over him.

"They're yours, aren't they?" Olivia's voice swelled with emotion, but when he glanced at her, her expression was as serene as if they were discussing the weather. "I had hoped they belonged to Christian."

"I just learned about them tonight."

"Their mother never told you?" Olivia sighed. "And now she's dead."

"Things ended badly between us." He couldn't face Olivia with his emotions this raw, so he kept his gaze on his daughters. "I didn't know she was ill." For a moment he was consumed by despair. He pressed his lips into a tight line. Then, feeling her watching him, he settled his features into an impassive mask.

"You loved her."

He and Olivia had never spoken of love. Their marriage was about politics, not romance. But if she suspected he'd given away his heart to another woman, she might not be so happy.

"We were together a long time ago."

"Karina and Bethany aren't even two. It wasn't that long ago."

Despite her neutral tone, Gabriel suspected she wasn't thrilled to have his past thrown so fully in her face. If the truth about the twins got out the press would speculate and create drama and controversy where there was none. Olivia would become the unwitting victim of their desire for ratings.

"This has to remain a secret," he told her.

"Impossible. The minute you brought them to the palace you risked word getting out."

"Perhaps, but I'd like to postpone that as long as possible so we can strategize how we're going to control the damage."

"If you're worried about my father's reaction, don't be. He's committed to opening a plant here."

"And you?"

"They're two precious little girls. I'll support whatever decision you make, but I think you should proudly claim them as yours."

Her eyes were clear of hesitation or deceit. Did she

realize this would make her a stepmother to his former lover's children? Would another woman have been so understanding?

"I can't figure you out."

"Your Highness?"

"Gabriel," he growled, amused rather than annoyed. "I'll not have you calling me Your Highness in bed."

The underlying heat in his voice reached her. Her cheeks flared pink.

"Gabriel," she echoed, her soft voice low and intimate in a way that warmed his blood. "I promise to remember never to refer to you as Your Royal Highness, or Prince Gabriel, while we're making love."

For the first time he glimpsed the Olivia beneath the enigmatic, cultured woman he'd decided to marry. Impish humor sparkled in her eyes. Intelligence shone there, as well. Why had she hidden her sharp mind from him? Gabriel considered how little time they they'd spent together and shouldered the blame. If he'd gotten to know her better, he'd have seen the truth much sooner.

"All of a sudden, it occurs to me that I've never kissed you." He took her hand and dusted a kiss over her knuckles.

"You kissed me the day you proposed."

"In front of a dozen witnesses," he murmured. He had asked her to marry him in front of her father and close relations. It had been a formality, really, not a true proposal. "And not the way I wanted to."

"How did you want to?"

She'd never flirted with him before and he discovered he liked the challenge in her gaze. Anticipation lit up the room as he set his finger beneath her chin and tilted her head, bringing her lips to a perfect angle to align with his. He watched her long lashes drift downward.

Her breath caught as he stopped just shy of brushing Olivia's lips. The disturbed rush of air awakened his senses with fierce urgency. He longed to crush her against him and feast on her soft mouth. Instead, he concentrated on the scent of her, a delicious floral that reminded him of a spring evening when the roses were in full bloom, while he reined his urges back under control.

What was happening to him? Her body's tension communicated across the short distance between them, the trembling of her muscles, a siren call that demanded he claim her. He was a little startled how compelling that desire was.

Ever since they'd danced, he'd been preoccupied with investigating the chemistry that had sparked between them. He hadn't expected to find passion in his marriage. But now that the sexual chemistry had flared, he couldn't wait to explore her every sigh and moan.

From the start she'd intrigued him. Every time they shared the same room, she'd claimed and held his attention. But he'd chosen her because of what her father's investment could mean for Sherdana rather than for any emotional connection between them. And then tonight she'd revealed that her tranquil exterior camouflaged a quick mind and determined nature.

"This might not be the best place for our first kiss," he told her, his voice raw and husky. Body aching in protest, Gabriel stepped back.

"I understand." She glanced toward his sleeping daughters.

But he doubted that she did because he barely understood his own actions.

No woman before or after Marissa had made him feel like losing all control, and it was logical to assume that no one ever would. Earlier he'd thought of Olivia as cool and untouchable. He'd been very wrong.

This abrupt and overwhelming craving to make love to her long into the night until she lay sated in his arms wasn't part of the plan. He needed a woman who would grace his side in public and warm his bed at night.

The operative word being *warm*.

Not set it on fire.

"I think they should stay here tonight," Olivia murmured, her words wresting him back to the other complication in his life. "In the morning, we can get them settled upstairs." She must have seen a protest building because she shook her head. "They're staying put. They've been through enough for one night. I want to make certain someone familiar is with them when they wake."

Gabriel's eyebrows rose at her adamant tone. "And you're that someone familiar?"

"I fed them ice cream," Olivia said, her expression lightening. "They'll be glad to see a friendly face."

"You certainly have that." He glanced toward the sleeping girls. "And a very beautiful one, as well."

Three

Olivia didn't sleep well on the couch. But she wasn't sure she'd have slept any better in her bed alone. She kept running through her evening. Rescuing the twins, discovering they were Gabriel's illegitimate children and finally, the kiss that had almost happened.

Why had he hesitated? Had she imagined the desire in his eyes as they'd danced earlier that night?

Doubts had begun to plague her as soon as Gabriel left. Her experience with men wasn't extensive. Indulging in lighthearted affairs wasn't something she'd ever done. Her friends accused her of being overly conscientious about her reputation, but in fact, she hadn't been attracted to the men in her social circles. She might have worried about her inability to feel physical desire if she hadn't experienced something magical her first year of university.

She'd attended a masquerade party with one of her friends. The event's host was one of London's most notorious bachelors, and it was the last place she should have shown her face. Fortunately, the costumes and masks had enabled her to remain anonymous. The crowd had been racier than she was used to. Drinking and drugs had led to some boisterous behavior and Olivia had made the mistake of getting cornered.

The man had used his size and strength to pin her against the wall and run his hands beneath her skirt. She'd struggled against the hateful press of his moist lips against her throat, but couldn't free herself. And then it had been over and he'd ended up sprawled on the floor some distance away, the hands he cupped over his bloody nose muffling the obscenities he launched at the tall stranger who'd stepped in.

The hallway was too dark for her to see her rescuer clearly and she was still shaken up by the violence of the encounter, but she managed a grateful smile. "Thank you for helping me."

"You don't belong here," the stranger had told her, his English lightly accented. "It isn't safe for someone as young as you are."

Her cheeks had grown hot at his words because he was right and she had felt foolish. "When is it safe for any woman when a man won't stop when she says no?" She peered through the guests, searching for her friend. "Next time I will carry a stun gun instead of lipstick in my purse."

He'd smiled. "Please don't let there be a next time."

"You're right. This isn't my crowd." She had spotted her friend halfway across the room and decided it was time to leave. "It was nice to meet you," she had told him. "I wish the circumstances had been different." Impulsively she rose up on tiptoe and touched her lips to his cheek, before whispering, "My hero."

Before she moved away, he had cupped her cheek and dropped his lips to hers. The touch electrified her and she swayed into his solid strength. His fingers flexed against her skin, pulling her closer. The kiss had been masterful. Demanding enough to be thrilling, but without the roughness that would make her afraid.

Magic, she remembered thinking, as she'd indulged in a moment of reckless daring.

Olivia released a long slow exhale at the memory. Seven

years later it continued to be the most amazing kiss she'd ever had. And she'd never even known his name. Maybe that's why it dwelled so vividly in her memory.

Lying with her forearm across her eyes, Olivia pushed aside the emotions stirred by that singular event. No good would come from dwelling on a romantic moment. The man who rescued her was probably as vile as the rest of the guests and had merely suffered a momentary crisis of conscience. She was marrying an honest, good man and needed to stay focused on the here and now.

As the room began to lighten, Olivia gave up on sleep and pulled out her laptop. During her research into Gabriel and his family, she'd focused on all things Sherdanian. Now she searched for his past romance and discovered a couple articles that mentioned him and Marissa Somme, a half American, half French model he'd dated for several years.

Olivia scanned the news stories. A few mentioned rumors that Gabriel had been considering abdicating the throne to one of his younger brothers, but ultimately, the affair ended instead.

Awash in concern, Olivia went looking for images of the couple. What she saw wasn't reassuring. The news outlets had gotten it right. The couple had been very much in love. Olivia stared at Gabriel's broad grin and Marissa's blinding smile and guessed if she hadn't been a commoner and an unsuitable candidate to give birth to the future king of Sherdana, they would have married and lived happily ever after.

Obviously Gabriel had chosen his country over his heart. And Marissa had vanished.

Hearing soft whispers coming from the bed, Olivia rose from the sofa. Sure enough, the twins were awake. They'd pulled the fluffy cream comforter over their heads, encasing themselves in a cozy cocoon.

For a moment, Olivia envied them each other. An only child, she'd always longed for a sister to share secrets with. If her mother had lived, she could have had a second child and Olivia might not have grown up so isolated from other children. Because her world had been filled with adults—nannies and various tutors—she'd never had a best friend her own age to play with. In fact, playing wasn't something she'd been given much freedom to do.

Multiples obviously ran in the Alessandro family. Did that mean she could expect a set or two of her own to be running around the palace in the years to come?

Olivia tugged on the comforter, pulling it down little by little to reveal the twins. They lay with noses touching, intent on their communication. Their first reaction as the comforter slid away was fear. Olivia saw their hands come together, as they took and received reassurance from each other.

Then, they recognized her and smiled.

"Someone's been sleeping in my bed," she teased, her words bringing forth giggles. "And they're still here."

Then she growled like a big bad bear and reached down to tickle them. Squeals and laughter erupted from the girls, a vast improvement over last night's terrified protests.

Olivia sat down on the bed. The prince would be back soon and the girls needed to be prepared to meet him. No doubt he'd informed the king and queen and they would be interested in meeting their grandchildren. It would be an overwhelming day for the girls and Olivia wanted to prepare them.

"Today you are going to meet many new people," she told them. "I know you might be scared, but you don't need to be."

"A party?"

"Sort of." If that was what it took to keep the twins from being afraid, then so be it.

"A birthday party?"

"No."

"Mommy said."

Bethany's mention of their mother reminded the girls that she was dead. Olivia saw Karina's lip quiver and rushed to distract them.

"Are you this old?" She held up two fingers and was rewarded with head shakes.

"We're this old." Bethany held up one finger.

"But you're too big to be one. I'll bet you have a birthday coming up soon."

"Get pony," Bethany said with a definitive nod.

Olivia rather doubted that, but clever of her to try to sound convincing. "I'm not sure you're old enough for a pony."

Karina spoke for the first time. "Puppy."

That seemed more doable.

"Pony," Bethany repeated. "Mommy said."

"There might be a pony in the stables," Olivia said, aware she was already caving to their demands. She hadn't pictured herself the sort of mother to give in to her child's every whim.

Bethany nodded in satisfaction. "Let's go."

"No." Karina shook her head. "Puppy."

"Oh, no. It's too early to go to the stables. We have to get dressed and have breakfast. Then we have to get you settled in your own room."

"No." Karina's large green eyes brimmed with anxiety.

Immediately Olivia realized what was wrong. "It's okay," she assured them. "The mean lady is gone. You will have really nice people taking care of you."

"Stay here." Bethany had an imperious tone well suited to a princess.

"I'm afraid you can't do that."

"Why not?"

"This is my bed and you two take up way too much room."

"Slept with Mommy."

Somehow they'd circled back to Marissa again. Olivia held her breath as she watched for some sign that they would get sad again, but the girls had discovered the mattress had great springs and they started bouncing and laughing.

Olivia watched them, amusement taking the edge off her exasperation. The challenges confronting her were coming faster than she'd expected. She wasn't just going to become a wife and a princess, but now she was going to take on the role of mother, as well. Not that she couldn't handle all of it. Maybe it was just her sleepless night and her anxiety about marrying a man who might not be over his dead former lover.

While the girls jumped off the bed and raced around the room, looking out the window and exploring the attached bathroom, Olivia heard a soft knock. Assuming it was Libby, she opened the door. To her intense surprise, Gabriel stood there, looking handsome and elegant in a charcoal pinstripe suit, white shirt and burgundy tie.

"I hope it's not too early," he said, entering the room. His gaze slid over her hair and silk-clad body.

Several maids followed, one pushing a cart loaded down with covered plates. Delicious smells wafted in their wake.

Olivia smoothed her hair, acutely aware of her makeup-free face, knowing she wasn't looking her best after such a rough night. She hadn't even brushed her teeth yet.

"No, of course not. You're eager to meet the girls."

"I am." His gaze went past her shoulder, golden eyes intense and a little wary.

Olivia's heart gave a little start as she realized he must be thinking about their mother. Chest tight, she shifted her attention to the twins. "Bethany. Karina. Come meet…" She wasn't sure how to introduce the prince.

Gabriel supplied the description. "Your father."

Beside him, Gabriel felt Olivia tense in surprise. In the hours since leaving her room, he'd contemplated what the best political move would be regarding his daughters and decided he didn't give a damn about the fallout. He intended to claim them.

Olivia held out her hands to the girls and they went toward her. She introduced them one by one, starting with the little girl on her right. "This is Bethany. And this is Karina."

Gabriel could discern no difference between their features. "How can you tell?"

"Bethany is the talkative one."

Neither one was verbal at the moment. They stood side by side wearing matching nightgowns and identical blank stares.

Deciding he would appear less intimidating if he was at their eye level, Gabriel knelt. "Nice to meet you." As much as he longed to snatch them into his arms and hug the breath from their bodies, he kept his hands to himself and gave them his gentlest smile.

The one Olivia had introduced as Bethany eyed him suspiciously for a moment before declaring, "We're hungry." Her imperious tone made her sound like his mother.

"What would you like for breakfast?" he asked them. "We have eggs, pancakes, French toast."

"Ice cream."

"Not for breakfast," he countered.

Olivia made no effort to hide her amusement. Her grin and the laughter brimming in her blue eyes transformed her from an elegant beauty to a vivacious woman. Gabriel felt his eyebrows go up as her charisma lit up the room.

"Wit' chocolate."

Bethany's demands forced Gabriel to refocus his attention. "Maybe after lunch." He'd met some tough negotiators in his time, but none had shown the sort of determination exhibited by his daughters. "If you eat everything on your plate."

"Want ice cream."

"How about waffles with syrup?" He tried softening his words with a smile. The twins weren't moved.

"Olivia." Bethany's plaintive, wheedling tone was charming, and Gabriel found himself struggling to restrain a grin.

"No." Olivia shook her head. "You listen to your father. He knows what's best." She gently propelled the girls toward the table the maid had set for breakfast and got them into chairs. "There aren't any booster chairs so you'll have to kneel. Can you do that?"

The twins nodded and Gabriel pulled out the chair between them, gesturing for Olivia to join them, but she shook her head.

"You should spend some time alone with them. I'm going to shower and get dressed." With one last smile for the twins, she headed toward the bathroom.

As the door shut behind her, Gabriel turned his full attention to the toddlers. "Have you decided what you want to eat?"

Their green eyes steady on him, they watched and waited for some sign that he was weakening. Gabriel crossed his arms over his chest and stared back. He was not going to be outmaneuvered by a pair of toddlers.

"Pancakes."

The word broke the standoff and Gabriel gestured the maid forward to serve pancakes. Having little appetite, he sipped coffee and watched them eat, seeing Marissa in their gestures and sassy attitude.

The girls ate two large pancakes before showing signs of slowing down and Gabriel was marveling at their appetite when the bathroom door opened and Olivia emerged. Her long blond hair framed her oval face in soft waves and she'd played up her blue eyes with mascara and brown eye shadow. She wore a simple wrap dress in seafoam that accentuated her tiny waist and the subtle curves of her breasts and hips. Nude pumps added four inches to her five-foot-six-inch frame and emphasized the sculpted leanness of her calves.

Gabriel felt the kick to his solar plexus and momentarily couldn't breathe. Her beauty blindsided him. Desire raged in his gut. He hadn't expected to feel like this when he proposed. She'd been elegant, poised and cool, inspiring his admiration and appreciation.

In a month she would be legally his. But he was no longer content to wait until his wedding night to claim her. Such had been the heat of his desire for her last night that if the twins hadn't occupied her bed, he would have made love to her.

The strength of his desire gave him a moment's pause. Wasn't this feeling what he'd hoped to avoid when he chose her? Craving something beyond reason was what had gotten him into trouble with Marissa. But desire wasn't love and didn't have to become obsession. He should feel a healthy desire for his future wife. Surely, he could prevent himself from getting in too deep with her and repeating his past mistakes.

He'd sunk into a black depression after his breakup with Marissa. Knowing they couldn't have a future together hadn't prevented him from letting himself be lured into love. He'd come through the other side of losing Marissa, but the fight to come back from that dark place wasn't something he wanted to go through ever again.

"Coffee?" he asked, shoving aside his grim reflections.

He just needed to be certain that he kept a handle on his growing fascination with her. He'd lost his head over Marissa and look what it got him. Two beautiful, but illegitimate, daughters.

"Yes." she gave a little laugh, seeming more relaxed with him than ever before. "I'm afraid I'm in desperate need of the caffeine this morning."

"Rough night?"

"The couch is not as comfortable as it is beautiful."

"Did you get any sleep?"

"Maybe an hour or so." She dished up scrambled eggs, fruit and a croissant. She caught him watching her and gave him a wry smile. "Your pastry chef is sublime. I will need plenty of exercise to avoid becoming fat."

"Perhaps after we speak to my parents about the girls we could take a walk in the garden."

"That would be nice, but I don't think there's time. My schedule is packed with wedding preparations."

"Surely if I can let the country run without my help for half an hour you can delegate some of the wedding preparations to your private secretary. We haven't really had a chance to get acquainted, and with our wedding less than a month away, I thought we should spend some time alone together."

"Is that a command, Your Highness?"

He arched an eyebrow at her playful tone. "Do you need it to be?"

"Your mother is the one who determined my schedule."

Suspecting his fiancée needed no help standing up to the queen, he realized she was chiding him for his neglect during her first week in Sherdana. "I'll handle my mother."

"A walk sounds lovely."

"Go see pony," Bethany declared, shattering the rapport developing between the adults.

"Pony?" Gabriel echoed, looking to Olivia for an explanation.

"Apparently Bethany wants a pony for her birthday. I told her she was too young, but I thought maybe there was a pony in the stables they could visit."

"None that I know of." He saw the bright expectation in their faces vanish and couldn't believe how much he wanted to see them smile again. "But I could be wrong."

He made a mental note to have Stewart see about getting a pair of ponies for the girls. He and all his siblings had all started riding as soon as they could sit up. Ariana was the only one who still rode consistently, but Gabriel enjoyed an occasional gallop to clear his mind after a particularly taxing session of cabinet.

"Do you ride?" he asked Olivia.

"When I visit our country house."

A knock sounded on the door. Olivia's private secretary appeared, Stewart following on her heels. They wore duplicate expressions of concern and Gabriel knew the morning's tranquillity was about to end.

"Excuse me a moment." He crossed the room and pulled Stewart into the hall. "Well?"

"The king and queen are on their way here."

He'd hoped to be the one to break the news to his parents. "How did they find out?"

"The arrival of two little girls in the middle of the night didn't go unnoticed," Stewart told him. "When your mother couldn't find you she summoned me."

"So, you felt the need to spill the whole story."

"The king asked me a direct question," Stewart explained, not the least bit intimidated by Gabriel's low growl. "And he outranks you."

"Gabriel, there you are. I demand to see my granddaughters at once." The queen sailed down the hallway in his direction, her husband at her side. Lines of tension bracketed the king's mouth. After nearly forty years as a queen, nothing disturbed her outward calm. But discovering her son had fathered two illegitimate girls was more stress than even she could graciously handle.

"They've been through a lot in the last few days," Gabriel told her, thinking she would upset the twins in her current state of agitation.

"Have you told Olivia?"

"Last night." He held up a hand when his mother's eyes widened in outrage. "They spent the night with her after she stumbled upon them fleeing their nanny."

The king's light brown eyes had a hard look as they settled on his son. "And how does your future bride feel about it?"

As diplomatic as his parents were with the outside world, when it came to family, they were blunt. It wasn't like them to dance around a question. Of course, they'd never come up against something this enormous before.

"What you want to know is if she intends to marry me despite my having fathered two children I knew nothing about."

"Does she?"

The king's deep frown made Gabriel rein in his frustration. As much as he disliked having his carelessness pointed out, he had let passion overwhelm him to the exclusion of common sense. Marissa had made him wild. She was like no other woman he'd ever met. And because of that their relationship had made his parents unhappy.

Gabriel exhaled harshly. "So far it appears that way."

"Does her father know?" the king asked.

"Not yet. But the girls are living in the house. It won't be long before the truth comes out."

His mother looked grim. "Will Lord Darcy back out on the deal?"

"Olivia doesn't think so. He wants his daughter married to royalty."

"Have you figured out what we're going to say to the press?"

"That they're my daughters," Gabriel said. "We'll send out a press release. Anything else would be a mistake. Olivia noticed the resemblance immediately. They look exactly like Ariana did at that age. Coming clean is a good offensive and hopefully by doing so we can minimize the scandal."

"And if we can't?"

"I'll ride it out."

"We'll ride it out," the king said.

"Have you considered that Olivia might not want to raise Marissa's children?"

Gabriel had already entertained those doubts, but after what he'd seen of Olivia, he'd discovered layers that might surprise everyone. "I don't think that will be an issue. She's already very protective of them and they trust her."

The queen sighed and shook her head. "It *will* be wonderful having children in the palace again. Let's go see your girls."

Four

Olivia was standing with her hands relaxed at her sides as the door opened to admit the king and queen. Libby had warned her they were coming and she'd made sure the girls' hands and faces were clean. The arrival of more unfamiliar people had revived the toddlers' shyness and they hid behind Olivia.

"This is your father's mother," Olivia explained to them, using gentle pressure to nudge them into the open. "She's come to meet you."

Karina shook her head, but Bethany peered at her grandmother. The queen stopped dead at the sight of the girl and reached out a hand to her husband.

"Gabriel, you were right. They look exactly like your sister at that age." She took a seat nearby and gestured Bethany toward her. "What is your name?"

To Olivia's delight Bethany went to the queen.

She stopped just out of arm's reach and studied the queen. "I'm Bethany."

"It's nice to meet you." The queen looked toward her sister. "And what is your name?"

Bethany answered again. "Karina."

"How old are they?" the king asked.

"They'll be two in a few weeks," Gabriel answered.

"Puppy." Karina had finally spoken.

"I have a puppy you can meet. Would you like that?"

The queen smiled as Karina nodded. "Mary," the queen said to the maid who'd brought the twins' clothes from upstairs. "Go get Rosie." The Cavalier King Charles spaniel loved people, especially children, and was a great deal calmer than the queen's vizsla.

In five minutes the maid was back with the dog and both twins were laughing as Rosie licked their cheeks. "Gabriel, why don't you and Olivia make yourself scarce for a while. I'll see the girls are settled."

Recognizing an order when she heard one, Olivia let Gabriel draw her from the bedroom and down the stairs.

"Let's get out of here while we can," he murmured, escorting her through a side door and into the garden.

The late May morning had a slight edge of coolness, but when he offered to send someone upstairs for a sweater, Olivia shook her head.

"Let's walk in the sunshine. I'll warm up fast enough."

He took her hand and tucked it into the crook of his arm. Olivia gave herself up to the pleasure of his strong body brushing against her side as they strolled along the crushed granite pathways.

"Thank you for all you've done with the girls," he said. "It breaks my heart that they'll grow up without their mother, but I'm glad they have you."

"You never knew yours, did you? She died when you were born?"

She'd never told him that. "I guess we both did our research."

"I've treated our engagement like a business arrangement. For that I'm sorry."

"Don't be. I knew what I was getting into." She heard a touch of cynicism in her tone and countered it with a wry smile.

Gabriel didn't smile back. "I don't think you have any idea what you're getting into."

"That sounds intriguing." Olivia waited for more, but the prince didn't elaborate.

"Starting now I intend to learn everything there is to know about you."

While she was sure he meant to flatter her with the declaration, Olivia froze in momentary panic. What if he found out she hadn't come clean about her past fertility issues? Even with the problem solved, he might be angry that she hadn't disclosed such an important fact.

"A girl needs to keep a little mystery about herself," she countered, gazing up at him from beneath her lashes. "What if you lost interest once you discovered all my secrets?"

"It never occurred to me that you'd have secrets," he murmured, half to himself.

"What woman doesn't?"

"I'd prefer it if we didn't keep secrets from each other."

"After the surprise you received last night, I understand why. So, what would you like to tell me?"

"Me?"

Olivia congratulated herself on turning the conversation back on him. "Getting to know each other was your idea. I thought you'd like to show me how it's done."

Gabriel's eyes gleamed with appreciation. "What would you like to know?"

"Why did you pick me?"

"Your passion for issues relating to children and your tireless determination to make their lives better." Gabriel stopped and turned her to face him. "I knew you would be exactly the sort of queen my country would love."

As his words sank in she stared at the pond, watching the ducks paddle across the still water. "Your country."

At times like this it amused her to think of how many girls longed to be her. If they knew what her life was like, would they still want that? Marriage to a prince might seem like a fairy tale come true, but did they understand the sacrifices to her privacy or the responsibility she would bear?

But marriage into Sherdana's royal family would offer her the opportunity to focus on things near and dear to her heart and to advocate for those who needed help, but who had no one to turn to. Earlier in the week she'd had an opportunity to speak with a local hospital administrator about the need for a more child-friendly space to treat the younger patients. The woman had a lot of ideas how to change the children's ward to make a hospital stay easier on the children as well as their families.

Olivia was excited about the opportunities to help. Sherdana would find her an enthusiastic promoter of solutions for at-risk and underprivileged children. She was proud of the money she'd raised in London and loved the hours she'd spent visiting with children in the hospitals. Their courage in fighting their illnesses always inspired her. She intended to inspire others to help.

As Sherdana's princess and future queen, she would be in the perfect position to bring children's issues to the forefront of public awareness.

"I will do my best to never let your country down."

"I knew you'd say that."

Her knees trembled as he slid his hand beneath her hair, fingertips drawing evocative circles on her nape.

Cupping her cheek in his palm, Gabriel turned her head until their eyes met. Her heart skipped a beat. He wanted her. The expanding warmth in her midsection told her so and she basked in the certainty.

His gaze held her entranced until the second before his lips skimmed hers. Wrenched free of anticipation, relief rushed through her like a wildfire. A groan built in her chest as his tongue traced the seam of her lips. Welcoming the masterful stroke of his tongue into her mouth, she leaned into him, pressing her breasts against his chest, needing his hands to cup their weight and drive her mad.

A throat cleared somewhere behind them. "Excuse me, Your Highness."

Gabriel stiffened and tore his mouth free. Chest heaving, he drew his thumb across her lower lip. "We will continue this later," he promised, his voice a husky rasp against her sensitized nerve endings.

"I look forward to it."

She received the briefest of smiles before he turned to face his private secretary. Released from the compelling grip of his gaze, Olivia had a hard time maintaining her composure. The kiss, although cut short, had been everything a woman craved. Passionate. Masterful. A touch wicked. She locked her knees and moderated her breathing while she listened to Gabriel's conversation with his secretary.

Stewart cleared his throat again. "Sorry to interrupt, but the media found out about your daughters and Lord Darcy is meeting with your parents."

Distantly, she became aware that Stewart was filling in Gabriel rapid-fire style about what had been on the television this morning.

"How did they get wind of it so fast?" Gabriel demanded.

Not even the ice in his voice could banish the lingering warmth Olivia felt from his kiss.

Stewart came up with the most obvious source. "The lawyer might have gone to them."

"Unlikely. He had nothing to gain."

"Someone in the palace, then."

"Who knew last night?"

"The maids who were tasked with preparing the nursery," Stewart said. "But they've worked for the palace for over a decade."

Olivia considered the one who'd been straightening her room at two in the morning. The strangeness of it struck her again, but surely the palace staff was carefully screened and the woman had merely been doing as she said.

"The nanny." Olivia knew with a sinking heart that this had to be the source of the leak. "The one I had escorted off the property."

Stewart considered this. "The lawyer assured me she'd been kept in the dark about the twins' parentage."

"But that was before they'd been brought to the palace," Gabriel said.

"I'm sorry," Olivia murmured, aware she'd committed her first huge mistake as Gabriel's fiancée. "I shouldn't have taken it upon myself to remove her."

"She was the wrong caretaker for the girls and you had their best interests at heart." Gabriel offered her a reassuring nod. "Besides, it was going to be impossible to keep the twins hidden for long."

Although she was accustomed to life in the public eye, she'd never been the focus of such frenzied interest on the part of the media, and the upcoming wedding had stirred them like a cane striking a wasp nest.

"If we present a united front," Olivia said, feeling like his partner for the first time, "I'm sure everything will blow over."

Gabriel took her hand and scorched a kiss across her knuckles. "Then that's exactly what we'll do."

Hand in hand, Olivia and Gabriel entered the salon most often used by the family for its proximity to the back garden and the views of the park beyond. They found Christian and Ariana there. Gabriel caught sight of the television and heard the reporter. The amount of information the news channel had gleaned about the twins' arrival late last night revealed that someone inside the house must have been feeding them information. Gabriel went cold as the reporter speculated on whether or not the powerful Sherdana royal family had paid Marissa to go away or if all along she'd hidden her daughters to keep them from being taken away from her.

"They may be painting us as the bad guys," Christian commented, "but at least they're not claiming we're weak."

Gabriel didn't reply to his brother's remark as Marissa's face came on the screen. As the narrator gave a rundown of her career, Olivia moved as if compelled by some irresistible force, stepping closer to the television. Dismay rose in Gabriel as one after another, the photographs of his former lover on the covers of *Vogue, Elle* and *Harper's Bazaar* flashed on the screen. Her legs looked impossibly long. Her face, incredibly beautiful.

Gabriel knew his daughters would be as exquisite. Would they follow in their mother's footsteps and pursue careers in fashion? Photographers would stand in line to take their picture. They'd make an incredible pair. But was that any way for an Alessandro to make a living?

The question forced Gabriel to consider his daughters' place in his household. They were illegitimate. With their mother's death, that situation could never be rectified. An ache built in his chest for Bethany and Karina. At their age they would retain few memories of their mother. They'd never again know her love.

When the television began showing images of Gabriel and Marissa together, laughing, arms around each other, looking happy and very young, he realized Olivia had gone still. Picture after picture flashed on the screen, and many of them weren't paparazzi shots. There were photos taken of them in private at friends' homes, even a couple when they'd vacationed on a private island in the Caribbean.

Gabriel's disquiet grew as Olivia's attention remained

glued to the news footage that recapped his turbulent years with Marissa. Naturally the reporters made their relationship sound more dramatic, the end more tragic than it actually had been.

While he watched, Olivia's private secretary approached her and spoke softly in her ear. She nodded and came to stand before Gabriel.

"My father wishes to speak to me."

"I'll walk with you."

"You should stay and discuss what is to be done now that the story is out."

Her suggestion made sense, but he wasn't sure it was good to let her leave without clearing the air. "I'd like a moment alone to speak with you."

"I have a fitting for my wedding dress at ten. I should be back a little before noon."

Once again their schedules were keeping them apart. "I have a lunch meeting with my education adviser."

"Perhaps Stewart and Libby can find us a moment to connect later this afternoon."

Gabriel wanted to proclaim they should make time, but had no idea what he was committed to for the rest of the afternoon.

"This shouldn't wait until later. Let's go to my office and discuss this situation in private."

"Whatever you wish."

Disliking the polite calm of her tone, he guided her from the room with a hand at the small of her back. Beneath his palm, her spine maintained a steady inflexibility that marked the change in her mood from their earlier interlude.

As pointless as it was to resent the timing of recent events, Gabriel couldn't stop himself from wishing he and Olivia had been given a month or two to form a personal connection before their relationship had been tested to this extent. But that wasn't the case and as he escorted her into his sanctuary and shut the door, he hoped they could weather this storm without sustaining permanent damage.

His office was on the first floor of the palace, not far from the formal reception room. Originally the space had been one of the numerous salons set aside for visiting guests. Five years ago, he'd appropriated it for his own use, tearing down the lavender wallpaper left over from the late 1970s and installing wood paneling and bookshelves that he'd filled with his favorite authors. The room was his sanctuary.

"You're upset."

"Just concerned about the twins." Her quiet voice and dignified demeanor were at odds with the passionate woman who'd melted in his arms a little while ago. Gabriel felt something tighten in his chest. "I think it might be a good idea to have them in the wedding. I thought I would talk to Noelle Dubone. She's creating my wedding dress and I'm sure she would be happy to design matching flower-girl dresses for Bethany and Karina to wear."

Gabriel leaned back so he could stare into her eyes. "Are you sure?"

"Completely. The world knows they're here. Hiding them would be a mistake."

"I agree. I'll speak with my parents about it." He could tell that Olivia's anxiety over the twins' welfare had been sincere, but surmised more than that was bothering her. "The news coverage about my relationship with Marissa—"

At his slight pause she jumped in. "You looked very happy together." She seemed to have more to say, but remained silent.

"We had our moments." Gabriel drew a deep breath. "But much of the time we fought."

"The paparazzi must not have caught any of those moments on film."

She sounded neutral enough, but Gabriel sensed she

wasn't as tranquil as she appeared. "We fought in private." And then made up in spectacular fashion.

His thoughts must have shown on his face because her eyebrows rose.

She moved toward the French doors and looked out. Gabriel stepped to her side. For a moment he wanted nothing more than to take her in his arms and relive the kisses from earlier. The compulsion to be near her tested his composure.

Her gaze slid in his direction. "Passion can be addictive."

How would she know that?

He knew of no serious romances in her life. Her private life was without even a whiff of scandal. No boyfriends. No lovers.

"Do you have firsthand knowledge of this fact?" Lord in heaven, he sounded suspicious. And yet, he couldn't stop himself from probing. "Have you…?" Realizing what he'd almost asked, he stopped speaking.

"Taken a lover?"

Damn the woman, she was laughing. Oh, not outwardly where he could see her mocking smile and take offense. But inwardly. Her eyes sparkled and her voice had developed a distinct lilt. Had his expression betrayed an unanticipated flare of unfounded jealousy? Or was she reacting to the revelation that for all his sources, he knew nothing about her?

Gabriel turned her to face him, but she wouldn't meet his gaze. "Have you?"

"No." She shook her head. "You'll be my first."

Desire exploded as she met his gaze. Wild with satisfaction that she would be completely his, Gabriel lost touch with his rational side. Surrendering to the need to kiss her senseless and show her just how addictive passion could be, he cupped her cheek in his palm, slid his other hand around her waist to hold her captive and brought his lips to hers.

He gave her just a taste of his passion, but even that was enough to weaken his restraint. Breathing heavily, he set his forehead against hers and searched her gaze.

"Your only." He growled the words.

"Of course."

Her matter-of-fact tone highlighted just how fast he'd let his control slip. His hands fell away, but his palms continued to burn with the heat of her skin. He rubbed them together, determined to banish the lingering sensation.

The need to spend some time alone with her had just grown more urgent. He was concerned that the media storm surrounding the arrival of the twins would make her father consider changing his mind about letting his daughter marry Gabriel. No wedding. No biotech plant on the outskirts of Caron, Sherdana's capital. Gabriel needed to hedge his bets with Olivia.

As long as she still wanted to marry him, everything would proceed as planned. He just needed to reassure her that marrying him was a good idea. And he knew the best way to convince a woman had nothing at all to do with logic.

Some private time should do the trick, just the two of them. A chance to present her with a small token of his affection. Thus far her engagement ring was the only jewelry he'd given her. He should have had a gift ready to present on her arrival in Sherdana, but he'd been preoccupied. And if he was honest with himself, he hadn't been thinking of Olivia as his future bride, but as a next step in Sherdana's economic renaissance.

"I'll arrange for us to have a private dinner in my suite."

"I'll look forward to it," Olivia said, her expression unreadable. Gabriel had chosen her partly because of her composure when dealing with reporters and her public persona. Now, he wasn't happy at not being able to read her.

Shortly after she departed, Gabriel summoned Stewart and had him reschedule his morning appointments so Gabriel could meet with his jeweler. Half an hour later, he entered the reception room where Mr. Sordi waited with two cases of sparkling gems. Despite the wide selection, Gabriel wondered if he'd have trouble selecting the perfect piece for his bride-to-be. In the end, he chose the first bracelet that caught his eye, believing the fanciful design of flowers rendered in diamonds and pink sapphires would please her.

Business concluded, he let Stewart show the jeweler out while Gabriel slipped the bracelet into his office safe. He dashed off a quick note to Olivia, inviting her to dinner, and got one of the maids to deliver it. Then he went off to his lunch meeting with his education adviser, but his thoughts were preoccupied with the evening to come.

After a short conversation with her father to assure him that she'd already known about the twins and was perfectly happy that they'd come to live with their father, Olivia went to change her clothes, but ended up standing on the stone terrace outside her room, staring at the garden below. The euphoria of those passionate moments in Gabriel's arms were misty memories.

Olivia's heart sank to her toes. Caught up in the romance of kissing Gabriel in the beautiful garden, she'd been on the verge of doing things in public she'd never even done in private. While on a subconscious level she'd begun to think in terms of love. In reality she was embarking on an arranged marriage.

Being told Gabriel had loved the mother of his children and being confronted by the hard truth of it were very different animals. The pictures playing across the television screen had complicated her emotions. She'd been besieged by thorny questions.

Had he been thinking of Marissa as he kissed her? Had he been wishing that the woman he'd loved wasn't dead? Or that her ancestry had permitted them to be married? Marissa had been every man's fantasy. Vivacious, sexy, breathtakingly beautiful. In her eyes danced promises she might or might not keep. A man could spend a lifetime wondering which way she would go. How could Olivia hope to compete?

She couldn't.

But she wasn't marrying Gabriel because he loved her. She was marrying him because as a princess her voice advocating for children would reach further and she could fulfill her dream of becoming a mother. Her children would be the next generation of Alessandros. Still, it hurt to see the way Gabriel had stared at the screen as his former lover's face was shown in photo after photo. Her heart had ached at the way his expression turn to stone while his eyes looked positively battered.

Suddenly Olivia wasn't sure she could do this. Sucking in a sharp breath, she glanced down at her engagement ring. Sunlight fell across her hand, lighting up the large center diamond like the fireworks at a centennial celebration. She'd come to Sherdana to marry a prince, not a man, but after tasting passion and realizing she wanted more, she didn't think she could settle for marrying a man with a past that still haunted him.

A man still in love with the mother of his illegitimate twin girls.

Maybe this marriage wasn't meant to be.

But so much was riding on it. So many people were counting on the jobs her father's company would bring to Sherdana. And the wedding was less than a month away. She had a fitting for her dress in less than an hour. Olivia stared at the slim gold watch on her arm, her mother's watch.

A short time later, Olivia stepped out of the car that had driven her and Libby to the small dress shop in Sherdana's historic city center. She'd pushed aside her heavy heart, averse to dwelling on something over which she had no control. She was her father's daughter. Raised as a pragmatist, she knew it was impractical to indulge in pretty dreams of falling in love with her prince and living happily ever after.

The shop door chimed as Olivia entered. Wide windows provided a great deal of light in the small but elegant reception room. The walls had been painted pale champagne to complement the marble floors. There was a gold damask-covered sofa flanked by matching chairs in the front room. The glass-topped coffee table held a portfolio of Noelle Dubone's previous work. Some of her more famous clients were not featured in the book, but on the walls. Stars, models, heiresses, all wearing Noelle's gorgeous gowns.

Almost before the door shut behind them, Noelle was on hand to greet her. The designer offered Olivia a warm smile and a firm handshake.

"Lady Darcy, how delightful to see you again."

Noelle had a lilting Italian accent. Although Sherdana shared borders with both France and Italy, it had chosen Italian as its official national language. With her dark hair and walnut-colored eyes, Noelle's lineage could have gone back to either country, but from earlier conversations Olivia knew the designer's ancestry could be traced back to the 1500s. Noelle might not be one of Sherdana's nobility, but the church kept excellent records.

"It's good to see you, as well," Olivia said, warming to the willowy designer all over again. Choosing to have a dress made by Noelle had been easy in so many ways. Although her London friends had counseled Olivia to go with a more famous designer and have an extravagant gown made, Olivia had decided she much preferred Noelle's artistry. Plus Noelle was Sherdanian. It made political sense for Olivia to show her support of the country where she would soon be a princess, especially taking into consideration how hard-hit Sherdana's economy had been in the past few years.

"I have your dress waiting in here." Noelle showed Olivia into a dressing room.

For her more famous clients, Noelle often traveled for fittings. She would have brought the dress to the palace if Olivia had requested. But Olivia liked the shop's cozy feel and wasn't eager to entertain anyone's opinion but her own.

The dress awaiting her was as beautiful as she remembered from the sketches. It had stood out among the half dozen Noelle had shown her six months ago; in fact, the rendering had taken her breath away.

With the help of Noelle's assistants, Olivia donned the dress. Facing the three-way mirror, she stared at her reflection, and was overcome with emotion. It was perfect.

From the bodice to her thighs, the dress hugged the lean curves of her body. Just above her knees it flared into a full skirt with a short train. Made of silk organza, embroidered with feathery scrolls over white silk, the gown's beauty lay in its play of simple lines and rich fabrics. Although Noelle had designed the dress to be strapless, Olivia had requested some sort of small sleeve and the designer had created the illusion of cap sleeves by placing two one-inch straps on either shoulder.

"What are planning to do for a veil?" Noelle asked.

"The queen is lending me the tiara she wore on her wedding day," Olivia said. "I'm not sure I want to use a veil with it."

"Good. When I designed the dress, I didn't picture it with a veil." Noelle stepped back to admire her handiwork.

"You have lost a little weight since we measured you. The waist needs to be taken in a little."

Olivia turned sideways to peer at the way the short train looked behind her. "I will try not to gain before the wedding."

For the next hour, Noelle and her staff worked on minor alterations to the fit. While Olivia thought the dress fit well enough that she could have worn it as is, Noelle was obviously a perfectionist.

"I have another project that I'd like to talk to you about," Olivia said as Noelle handed off the dress to her assistant.

Ever since arriving, she'd been thinking about including the twins in the wedding. While Gabriel seemed okay with the idea, she wasn't sure how his family would react, but after this morning's media coverage of the girls' arrival at the palace, hiding them from public scrutiny would be impossible and counterproductive.

"Come into my office," Noelle said. "Tell me what you have in mind."

Sipping the coffee Noelle's assistant had provided, Olivia contemplated the best way to begin, then decided to just dive in.

"Did you happen to see the news this morning?"

"About Prince Gabriel's daughters?" Noelle pressed her lips together. "The royal family hasn't given them much fodder for stories in the last few years. I'm afraid the level of coverage on this particular item so close to your wedding is just too huge for them to use restraint."

"Dealing with the media comes with the territory," Olivia said. "You'd know that."

Noelle looked startled for a second. "I only design for the stars," she demurred. "I'm not one of them myself."

"You are making a name for yourself. Don't be surprised when you become as big a story as your clients."

"I hope that doesn't happen. I like my quiet little life."

Noelle's gaze touched a silver frame on her desk. It held the photo of a small dark-haired boy. The angle didn't offer a very good view of his face, but Olivia could tell from Noelle's expression that he was very special to her.

"Is he your son?"

"Yes. Marc. He was two in that picture. The same age as the prince's daughters."

Olivia felt a clenching low in her abdomen. A cry from her empty womb. "He's beautiful. How old is he now?"

"Almost four."

Olivia didn't ask about the boy's father. She knew Noelle wasn't currently married and wasn't sure if the question would arouse difficult memories.

"I would like to include Prince Gabriel's daughters in the wedding and want you to make dresses for them."

"I'll work on some sketches and send them over to the palace. Did you have a color in mind?"

"White with pale yellow sashes. To match Princess Ariana's gown." The color suited the dark-haired princess and would her nieces, as well.

"I'll get to work immediately."

At the sound of a light knock, both women looked toward the door. Noelle's assistant hovered on the threshold.

"I just wanted to let you know that there are media outside."

Although the announcement of her engagement to Gabriel had briefly made Olivia newsworthy in England, the future princess of a small country hadn't interested the British press for long.

In Sherdana, however, it was a different story. She'd found the citizens were very curious about her. When she'd visited three months ago, she'd been besieged by requests for interviews and followed wherever she went. Numerous public appearances had filled her daily schedule from ribbon-cutting ceremonies to attending sessions of parliament.

But when Olivia emerged into Noelle's reception room, she understood the assistant's concern. At least a hundred people crowded the streets, most of them armed with cameras. Surely not all these people were reporters. David, her driver, and Antonio, the enormous man Gabriel had assigned to accompany her whenever she was out in public, had called in five others from palace security to create a corridor of safety between the front door of the wedding shop and the car.

Olivia shot Libby a look. "I think life as I knew it has come to an end." Then she turned to Noelle. "Thank you for everything. The dress is perfect."

"You're welcome."

Squaring her shoulders, Olivia put on her public face and stepped toward the front door. Noelle held it open for her with a whispered, *"Bon courage."*

"Olivia, how are you dealing with the discovery of the prince's illegitimate children?"

"Lady Darcy, can you tell us if the wedding is still on?"

"How do you feel about raising another woman's children?"

"Do you think the prince would have married Marissa if he'd been able?"

The questions rained down on Olivia as she headed for the car, smiling and waving as she walked, but responding to none. She slipped each query into its own special cubbyhole for later retrieval and didn't realize she was holding her breath until the car had pulled away from the curb. Libby watched her in concern.

"I'm fine."

"You look...unhappy."

"I'm just tired. The twins slept in my bed and I wasn't able to get comfortable on the couch. That's all."

The excuse pacified her secretary and gave Olivia the space to sort through the highs and lows of the last twenty-four hours. While she wasn't naive enough to think that Gabriel was marrying her for anything other than business, Olivia had hoped that he'd grow fond of her. But while they'd kissed in the garden, she'd let herself believe that their future could be filled with passion and romance.

The photos of him with Marissa that the media had broadcast this morning had been a wake-up call. That was love. Olivia stared out the window at the old town slipping past.

She needed time to adjust to sharing him with a ghost.

Five

When Olivia returned to her room after the fitting, she discovered an invitation and a small, slender box wrapped in ribbon. Heart pounding, she opened the envelope and recognized Gabriel's strong handwriting.

A quiet dinner, just the two of them. In his suite. She clutched the stationery to her chest and breathed deep to calm her sudden attack of nerves. Except for the brief time last night and this morning, they hadn't been alone together. Did he intend to seduce her? Olivia certainly hoped so, but what did she wear to her deflowering? Something demure that matched her level of experience in all things sexual? Something that bared her skin and invited his touch?

Her fears that he didn't find her attractive had melted beneath the heat of this morning's kiss. But he was accustomed to women with far more experience than she possessed. Apprehension made her nerves buzz like a swarm of angry hornets.

Leaving her worries to sort themselves out, she tugged at the ribbon holding the box closed. The pale blue silk fell away. Her fingers brushed the hinged lid as she savored the anticipation of her first gift from Gabriel. From the box's shape, she knew it was a bracelet.

Olivia took a deep breath and opened the lid. Lying on a bed of black velvet was a stunning free-form emerald an inch and a half wide and almost two inches long that dominated the design. The rest of the band was diamonds, set in a diamond-shaped pattern. Bold and contemporary, it wasn't the sort of thing she'd wear, being a little too trendy, but she couldn't fault Gabriel's taste.

Ignoring a pang of disappointment that he'd chosen something so not her taste, she draped the wide cuff over her wrist. As she admired the sparkle, she couldn't shake a nagging sense of familiarity. It was a unique piece, something one-of-a-kind, yet she was certain she'd seen it before. But where? The answer eluded her and she set aside her musings as Libby arrived and helped Olivia decide on the perfect outfit to highlight Gabriel's extravagant gift.

Around midafternoon she went up to the nursery and found the twins eager to visit the stables. But she listened with only half her attention as Bethany chattered on the short walk to the stables. Olivia was having a hard time thinking about anything except her dinner with Gabriel and the hope that they could forget all about Marissa and begin their lives together. Comparing herself to Gabriel's former lover would only lead to trouble down the road. She'd be smarter to put that energy into keeping Gabriel's mind fixed on the present.

While a pair of grooms took Bethany and Karina to look at the ponies their father had ordered to be delivered to the stable, Olivia drifted along the barn's center aisle, stroking a soft nose here and there, lost in a pleasant daydream. The soothing sounds of the barn wrapped her in a cocoon of stillness that allowed her ample privacy to relive the moments in the garden that morning.

Her blood heated and slowed, flowing into the sensitive area between her thighs that Gabriel's fervent kiss had awakened earlier. She leaned her back against a stall and closed her eyes to better relive the delicious caress of his hands against her back and hips. Her breasts had ached for his possession. She'd never felt anything like the powerful craving his kiss aroused. She'd been seconds away from begging him to touch her everywhere. He'd been her master. Her teacher. And she, a very willing student.

The memories disturbed the smooth rhythm of her breathing. How was it possible that just thinking of Gabriel aroused her?

"Are you okay?"

Olivia's eyes snapped open. A groom peered at her, concern in his brown eyes.

She offered a weak smile, feeling heat in her cheeks, put there by her sensual daydreams. Had she really been standing in the middle of a barn, imagining how it would feel to have Gabriel's large, strong hands roaming over her bare skin?

"Fine." The word came out a little garbled. What magic had he wrought to make her forget her surroundings so completely? "I'm fine."

From outside came the twins' high-pitched voices lifted in childish delight. Olivia pushed away from the wall and went in search of them. In the stable yard, beneath the watchful eyes of the grooms who'd taken charge of them, they each stood on a mounting block in order to better acquaint themselves with their new pony.

Olivia fought anxiety as she watched the girls, but soon she calmed down. These ponies had obviously been chosen for their placid demeanor; otherwise the excited movements of the twins would have startled them. The geldings were well matched in size, color and markings. Bethany's had a long, narrow blaze that stretched from forehead to right between his nostrils. Karina's had a wider stripe of white that spread out as it reached the nose. Both ponies had two white front socks and one back.

Bethany was the first to notice Olivia. She threw her

arms around the pony's neck and said in an excited voice. "Look at my horse. Her name is Grady."

Olivia started to correct Bethany on the gender of her new pony, but Karina jumped in before she could speak.

"Peanut." The quieter twin looked so delighted that Olivia wondered if she would still demand a puppy for her birthday.

"They're lovely," Olivia said. "But I think they're both boys."

The girls were too excited to listen and went back to petting and chattering to their ponies. The head groom came over to where Olivia stood.

"They will make fine horsewomen."

"I believe you're right."

"Would you like to see the mount His Highness chose for you?"

It had never occurred to Olivia that she would receive a horse as well when she told Gabriel how she loved to ride whenever she spent time at Dansbrooke. The park around the palace wasn't as extensive as the lands surrounding her family's country estate, but she welcomed the opportunity to get whatever exercise she could.

"I'd love to see him." She laughed. "Or her."

"It's a mare. A Dutch Warmblood. I heard you've done some eventing. You'll find Arioso is a wonderful jumper and an eager athlete."

The beautiful chestnut had large, soft eyes and a gentle disposition, but before she had time to do more than stroke the mare's long neck, the twins had finished with their ponies and joined her at the stall.

Deciding they'd had enough for one day, Olivia gathered them together and bid the grooms goodbye. After depositing them with a pair of maids in the nursery, she returned to her room to bathe and dress.

Olivia took a long time preparing for the evening. She

played with hairstyles for an hour before settling on a softly disheveled updo that required only a couple of pins to keep it in place. The gown she'd chosen was a simple black sheath that bared her arms and appeared demure in the front but dipped low in the back.

Anticipation began to dissolve her calm as she zipped up the dress and fastened simple diamond dangles to her earlobes. Boldly eschewing panty hose, she slid her feet into elegant patent leather pumps.

She wanted everything about her to say "touch me."

And surveying her appearance in the full-length mirror, Olivia felt confident she'd done just that. That left only one more thing to do. Olivia popped the top on the jewelry box and laid the wide bracelet across her wrist. Libby helped by securing the clasp.

"Is this all for my brother's benefit?" Ariana had slipped into the room after a soft knock.

Olivia felt her cheeks heating. "Do you think he'll approve?"

Ariana smiled. "How could he not?" Her gaze slipped over Olivia, stopping at the diamond-and-emerald bracelet. She reached for Olivia's hand, as the color drained from her face. "Where did you get that?"

"Gabriel sent it to me." Concern rose in Olivia. Why was Ariana looking as if she'd seen a ghost? "Why? Do you recognize it?"

"Gabriel sent it?" Ariana echoed. She shook her head. "I don't understand."

"You recognize it?" Olivia felt her heart hit her toes. "It's cursed, isn't it?"

"You might say that."

"Tell me."

"It's none of my business."

There was no way she was letting Ariana get away

without an explanation. "If there's something wrong, I need to know."

"Really, I shouldn't have said anything." Ariana backed toward the bedroom door. "I'm sure everything is fine."

It wasn't like Ariana to hedge, especially when it came to things that distressed her. And seeing the bracelet had obviously upset the princess.

"What do you mean everything is fine? Why wouldn't it be? What aren't you telling me about the bracelet?"

Olivia caught Ariana's wrist in a tight grip. Startled, the brunette looked from the hand holding her, to the bracelet on Olivia's wrist and finally met her gaze.

"I don't want to upset you."

"And you think that's going to persuade me to let you walk out of here without spilling the truth?" Olivia tugged her future sister-in-law toward the wingback chairs flanking the fireplace. She didn't let go until Ariana sat down. "Tell me what about the bracelet upset you."

Releasing an audible sigh, the princess leveled her pale gold eyes on Olivia. "The last time I saw that bracelet was the night before Gabriel broke things off with Marissa."

Pain lanced through Olivia, sharper than anything she'd experienced this morning as she'd watched the pictures of Gabriel and Marissa on the television.

"He bought it for her."

"Yes. It was…for their second anniversary."

The cool platinum burned like acid against Olivia's skin. She clawed at the clasp, blood pounding in her ears. Her excitement over having dinner alone with Gabriel vanished, replaced by wrenching despair. The first gift he'd given her had been the bracelet he'd bought to celebrate two years with Marissa?

The clasp popped open beneath her nails. Olivia dropped it on the mantle and sat in the chair opposite

Ariana, unsure how much longer her shaky legs would support her.

"How did he get it back?"

"I don't know. Maybe she returned it when they broke up."

Olivia felt sick. It was bad enough that Gabriel had given her the trinket he'd bought for another woman, it was worse that it was a returned gift. "I thought I'd seen it before," she murmured.

Ariana leaned forward and placed her hand over Olivia's. "I'm sure this is all a huge misunderstanding. Maybe I'm thinking of a different bracelet."

Olivia drew comfort from Ariana for a moment, before sitting up straight and bracing her shoulders. "The only misunderstanding is mine. I thought tonight was supposed to be the beginning of something between us." She offered Ariana a bitter smile. "I forgot that our marriage is first and foremost a business arrangement."

"I don't believe that's true. I saw the way Gabriel watched you this morning. He was worried by how you reacted to the press coverage of the twins' arrival and all the scandal it stirred up."

"He's worried about losing the deal with my father."

"Yes, but there's more to it than that. He had other opportunities to secure Sherdana's economic future. He chose you."

Ariana's words rang with conviction, but Olivia shook her head. The sight of the bracelet made her long to hurl it into the deepest ocean. She felt betrayed and yet she had no right. She was marrying Gabriel because he was handsome and honorable and she would one day become a queen. Her reasons for choosing him were no more romantic than his.

"Ask him to tell you about the first time you met."

"The party at the French embassy?" Olivia recalled

his stiff formality and their brief, stilted conversation, so different from their exchange in the garden this morning.

"Before that."

Olivia shook her head. "We didn't meet before that."

"You did. You just don't remember."

How was that possible? Every time he drew near, her stomach pitched and her body yearned for his touch. His lips on hers turned her into an irrational creature of turbulent desires and rollicking emotions. If they'd met, she'd have recognized the signs.

"Your brother is very memorable," she argued. "I'm certain you are mistaken."

Ariana's eyes glowed. "Just ask him."

Abruptly filled with uncertainty, Olivia looked down at her gown and noticed the brush of cool air against her bare back and arms. She'd dressed to entice Gabriel. She'd wanted his hands to go places no man had ventured before. Even after learning that he'd given her a bracelet that once belonged to his former lover, she still wanted him. She ached with yearning. Burned with hungers unleashed by an hour in the bath tracing her naked skin with her fingertips, imagining Gabriel doing the same.

"Damn it." The curse shot out of her and startled Ariana.

"Oh, I've really done it," the princess muttered. "Please don't be mad at Gabriel. That was five years ago. I'll bet he doesn't even remember the bracelet."

Olivia's gaze sharpened into focus as she took in Ariana's miserable expression. "You remembered."

"I'm a woman. I have an artist's eye for detail." Ariana shook her head. "Gabriel is a man. They don't notice things like fashion. Now, if he'd given you a set of antlers off a buck he'd shot, that he'd recall."

Olivia recognized that Ariana was trying to lighten her mood, but the damage had been done. She wasn't half as angry with Gabriel as she was with herself. For being a fool. For not realizing that she never would have agreed to marry Gabriel unless she was already emotionally engaged.

But it was too late. She was already in too deep. The only thing she could do now was keep her wits about her and not allow herself to be disappointed again.

To his intense shock, Gabriel was second-guessing himself.

As he towel-dried his hair. As he shaved for the second time that day. As he dressed in gray slacks and a black collarless button-down shirt.

All he could think about was what a mistake he'd made with the bracelet he'd chosen for Olivia's first present. As beautiful as the item was, he couldn't help but think she'd appreciate something more romantic with a little history attached.

He was grimly amused with himself. Since when had he devoted this much time and energy to a gift for a woman? In Marissa's case, he'd always zeroed in on the most flamboyant piece available, the more expensive the better, and been richly rewarded for his generosity.

Gabriel slid a watch onto his wrist and checked the time. He had half an hour before Olivia was due to arrive if he wanted to fetch a particular piece from the vault. "I have a quick errand to run," he told Stewart. "If Lady Darcy arrives before I return, serve her a glass of champagne and assure her I won't be long."

With that, he exited his suite and headed to the vault, his mind on the perfect thing to present to his fiancée. It took him exactly ten minutes to find the necklace and return. Stewart was alone when Gabriel returned.

"Dinner is set to be served at eight."

"Perfect." Gabriel had no interest in rushing. At the

same time, he wanted plenty of the evening left over for getting to know Olivia thoroughly. "You ordered all her favorites?"

"Of course." Stewart's head turned at the light knock on the door. "That must be Lady Darcy. I'll let her in, then make myself scarce."

Gabriel grinned, glad she was as eager to begin their evening as he. Stewart went to answer the door. With his pulse kicked into overdrive, Gabriel found himself holding his breath in anticipation. Realizing what he was doing, he exhaled, wondering how long it had been since the idea of spending time alone with a woman had excited him. But Olivia wasn't just any woman.

She aroused him faster and more intensely than anyone since Marissa. To look at her, it made no sense. She was elegant, cool and poised. Not the sort of sultry, lush temptress that turned men's heads. But today he'd discovered an inner core of vibrant, sensual woman hiding within her. The little he'd sampled explained his craving for a more prolonged taste.

A tense conversation was taking place near the door. Gabriel frowned as he spied the petite woman standing in the hall. Not Olivia. Her private secretary. Although curious about the content of their discussion, Gabriel made no attempt to listen in. He would learn what it was about soon enough.

The exchange at the door came to an end. Stewart came toward him, wearing a frown.

"What's wrong?"

"Your Highness." Stewart looked as if an elephant had stepped on his toes. "Lady Darcy has declined your invitation."

Dumbstruck, Gabriel stared at his assistant. Declined his invitation? Outrageous.

He'd anticipated their evening alone and the chance to learn more about her. "Is she ill?"

Stewart hesitated. "I didn't…get that impression."

"What impression did you get?" he demanded, impatient at his secretary's caginess.

Stewart squared his shoulders. "That perhaps she was unhappy…with you."

"With me?" When they'd parted this morning she'd been all dreamy eyes and feminine wiles. What could have possibly happened in the past twelve hours?

Without another word to Stewart, Gabriel exited his suite. Long, determined strides carried him down the hall toward the rooms assigned to Olivia. He barely noticed the maid scurrying out of his way as he passed her. He did, however, notice Ariana stepping out of Olivia's suite.

"Gabriel, what are you doing here?"

"I'm here to collect Olivia for dinner."

Ariana's gold eyes widened. "Didn't you get the message? Olivia's not up to having dinner with you tonight."

He leaned down and pinned his sister with a steely glare, wondering what mischief she had been up to. "What's wrong with her?"

Ariana set her hand on her hip and regarded him with annoyance. "She's not feeling well."

"Then I'd be remiss in not checking on her," Gabriel intoned, sounding as suave as he could through gritted teeth. "Step aside."

But his sister didn't budge. "Leave it tonight, Gabriel," she coaxed. "Give her a little time."

"Time for what?"

"Honestly," his sister fumed. "You can be so insensitive sometimes."

What was he missing? "Enlighten me."

Ariana pressed her lips together, but Gabriel kept up his

unrelenting stare and she finally sighed. "She's had your affair with Marissa thrown in her face all day."

He remembered the expression on Olivia's face while the footage of him and Marissa had played on the television. But he thought they'd cleared the matter up in his office. Why was she letting the past bother her? Gabriel nudged his sister aside and reached for the door handle.

"Gabriel—"

"This is none of your concern. It's between me and my future bride."

"Fine." Ariana tossed up her hands. "But don't say I didn't warn you."

With her dire words ringing in his ears, Gabriel entered Olivia's suite. Some impulse prompted him to slip the lock before scanning the space. His fiancée was not in the bedroom. After his encounter with Ariana, he'd expected to find Olivia sulking over some perceived slight. Then he noticed a slight billowing of the sheer curtains over the French doors leading out onto the terrace.

Olivia stood near the terrace railing staring out over the pond and the park, her gaze on the path where they'd walked and kissed this morning. She wore a black dress that bared her back in a plunging V. She'd knotted her hair on top of her head, exposing the nape of her neck. The sight of all that bare skin did unruly things to his body. He'd always been a sucker for a woman's back, finding the combination of delicacy and strength an intoxicating combination.

Gabriel shoved aside desire and refocused on the reason he'd come here in the first place.

"We're supposed to be having dinner in my suite."

"I don't feel up to it," she replied in a cool tone, not bothering to turn around.

"Then you're not upset."

"Of course not."

He didn't believe her. For the briefest of moments he wondered if she was trying to manipulate him with some feminine trickery. He almost laughed at the notion. Marissa was the only other woman who'd tried to best him with her wiles. He'd quickly set her straight.

Time to set Olivia straight, as well. "I thought this morning you understood that whatever was between Marissa and me has been over for three years."

"What sort of evening did you have in mind for us tonight?" She turned around and faced him and he got his first glimpse of her expression. Genuine anger shimmered in her gaze. "Were we to sip champagne and become lovers or did you plan to educate me on Sherdana's upcoming social and economic challenges?"

What had gotten into her? This morning she'd been like warm honey in his arms. Tonight she'd become an ice sculpture. All this because a few reporters dredged up old news from three years ago?

"I'd hoped we'd spend some time getting to know each other tonight, but I had no intention of rushing you into bed." Tired of sparring with her, he stepped within touching distance. "I thought that we'd reached an understanding this morning."

"So did I," she murmured, the fire fading from her tone.

"Then what's wrong?"

"Our marriage is an arrangement."

"Yes." He grazed his fingertips up her sides from her hips, letting them coast along the side of her breasts. The hitch in her breath told him the fight was over. "But it doesn't have to be all business between us."

"And it isn't," she agreed. "It's just that I'm not really sure what's happening."

So, he wasn't the only one struggling to find his way. Ever since last night, he'd found himself drawn to her as never before, but he wasn't sure she felt it, too. And now that he knew she did, he wasn't about to let her run away from it.

"We have strong sexual chemistry," he told her, and then in a softer voice confessed, "I wasn't expecting that."

Her scent flowed around him, feminine and enticing. As desire began to assert itself, he noticed the details his anger had blinded him to. For a woman intent on denying him her company, she'd dressed with care. He dipped his head and drank in the feminine scent of her. She'd dabbed a light floral perfume behind her ears. His lips found the spot and made her shiver.

"Gabriel, please." Her hand on his chest wasn't going to deter him now that he'd gotten wind of her imminent surrender.

"Please, what?" he inquired. "Stop?"

Knowing it was what she had in mind, he tugged the pins from her hair and tossed them aside. The golden waves spilled around her face and shoulders.

"Yes." But the word lacked conviction.

"You're lying," he pressed. "And badly. This is what you wanted when you dressed tonight." He took her stiff body in his arms and immediately the fight began to drain from her muscles. "My hands on you." He dipped his head and drew his lips across her cheek, finishing his thought with his breath puffing against her ear. "My mouth tasting your skin."

Her body was limp against him now, all resistance abandoned.

"We're meant to be together." He was more convinced of that than ever. "You know it as well as I do."

She'd closed her eyes to hide from him, not realizing how futile her actions were. "Yes."

Six

Without sight, all her other senses came to life. The unsteady rasp of Gabriel's breath told her he too was disturbed by the attraction between them. But was it enough? Hadn't she discovered less than an hour ago that she wanted more from him? So much more.

His fingertips grazed along the sensitive skin inside her arm, from the hollow behind her elbow to the pulse jerking frantically in her wrist. Gently he laced their fingers and began to pull her along the terrace. Her eyes flew open.

"Where?" Her gaze found his and she saw feverish hunger blazing in the bronze depths.

"To bed, of course," he teased, but there was nothing lighthearted about the determined set of his mouth or the tension that rode his muscles. Tension that communicated across the short distance between them.

"What about dinner?"

Inside the suite once more, he drew her close, sliding a hand over her hip to pull her against the hard jut of his erection, and bent to whisper in her ear. "You made me hungry for something besides food."

His lips dropped to hers, lingering at the corner of her mouth for too long. His unproductive nuzzling wasn't getting the job done. She wanted a kiss. A real, hard, deep kiss with no possibility of interruption. Growling low in her throat, she lifted on tiptoe and framed his face with her hands, holding him still while she pressed her mouth to his. Her tongue tested the seam of his lips as she flattened her breasts against Gabriel's broad chest, eager to convey her desire, letting her hunger shine through.

Gabriel captured handfuls of the dress near her shoulder blades and pulled the edges forward and down, baring her torso to the waist. Olivia gasped at the sudden rush of cool air over her breasts.

He slid his hands up over her rib cage until his fingers reached the undersides of her breasts. Smiling with male satisfaction, he cupped her and kneaded slightly.

She arched into the pressure of his hands, offering herself to him. Reaching behind, she found the dress's zipper and slid it down. With a determined stroke of her palms against her hips, the dress pooled at her feet, leaving her wearing nothing but her black pumps and a white lace thong.

He had tracked the progression of the dress to the floor, his gaze sliding over her legs as the falling black fabric bared her to him. Liking the way his nostrils flared at the sight of her nakedness, Olivia stepped out of the dress and kicked it aside.

Pressure built inside her as she hooked her fingers in the thong, determined to rid herself of it, as well. Gabriel's hands covered hers, halting her actions.

"This is your first time." His voice sank into rich, warm tones that did little to equalize her pulse or diminish her hunger. "I want to take this slow."

"I don't."

His lips moved into a predator's smile, slow and lazy. "You'll thank me later."

And with that, he swept her feet off the floor.

Placing her in the center of the big bed, Gabriel stepped back to rid himself of his clothes. Olivia raised herself on her elbows to better catch the unveiling of all that amazing bronze skin. From the little contact she'd had with his body, she knew he was lean and well-muscled, but nothing prepared her for the chiseled perfection of his torso as his shirt buttons gave way. She goggled at the sheer beauty of his broad shoulders and the sculptured magnificence of his chest.

He raised his eyebrows at her obvious curiosity, his hands going to the belt buckle. As he unfastened the top button, he kicked off his shoes. His pants hit the floor, followed by his socks.

He left on his boxers, but Olivia's eyes were drawn to the way they bulged in front. Her obvious curiosity and lack of concern turned him on and sped even more blood to his groin. Making this the most amazing night of her life might prove challenging. She certainly wasn't playing the part of nervous virgin.

He climbed onto the bed.

"What's this?" His finger grazed a black Chinese character in the hollow beside her hip bone and her stomach muscles twitched.

"A tattoo."

His elegant British fiancée had a tattoo? And in a very sexy spot, he might add. He frowned.

"What does it say?"

"Hope." She bent the leg opposite him and braced her foot on the mattress so she could cant her hips toward him. "I got it in college. My one wild act freshman year."

He imagined her baring her body for the needle, sliding down jeans and underwear. And the thought of another man touching her there made him want to roar in outrage.

His emotions must have shown on his face because she rushed to say, "It was done by a woman."

His shoulders relaxed at her words. She was his, or would be soon. And he wasn't the sort of man who cared to share. Living with two brothers had turned him into a possessive madman when anything encroached on what he believed was his.

"In that case, it's very sexy."

She grinned at how grudging his words sounded. It continued to both infuriate and delight him that she was not even remotely close to the type of woman he thought he'd chosen to make the next queen of Sherdana and his wife.

He hadn't anticipated surprises. He'd expected gracefulness and composure, not this wanton creature with her disheveled hair, bare breasts and body marked by the word *hope*. But now that he had her, she turned him inside out with wanting. She fired his imagination and his blood in the span of a heartbeat. Life would not be dull with her.

Which was the problem. He'd had passion once, crazy desire. It had consumed him and compelled him to think with every part of him but the one that mattered for the future king of Sherdana: his head. He didn't need a wife who made him feel out of control. He needed someone sensible, who kept him focused on matters of state.

Yet deep down he knew Olivia would do that.

And then, behind the closed doors of their private suite, she would make him forget everything but the sweet rush of carnal pleasure.

The best of both worlds.

What was there to worry about?

Taking her leg in his hand, he caressed upward from her knee to the place where her thighs came together.

"That's…" Her voice faltered as he slid one finger beneath the scrap of lace hiding her hot, wet center from him. She balled her fists into the coverlet, holding her breath as the tip of his finger grazed her warmth.

"You are incredibly wet," he said, delighted by the quickness of her arousal.

"Stop talking and touch me."

"Like this?" Stripping off her underwear, he did as she

asked, dipping between the folds that concealed her core and riding the river of wetness toward the knot of nerves. He circled it slowly, listening to her pant, smelling the waves of her arousal. Her hips rose off the mattress, pushing into his hand.

Gorgeous.

With her eyes closed, her knuckles whitening as she held on to the bed linens for dear life, she was as deep into the throes of sensual pleasure as any woman he'd ever known. She writhed against his hand, mindless in her pursuit of her ultimate goal. He watched her face, absorbing each tremble and jerk of her body as he carried her closer and closer to orgasm. Her brow knit as she concentrated. He picked up the pace and watched her mouth open, her back arch.

It was the sexiest thing he'd ever seen.

And it was his name that escaped her lips as she climaxed.

Panting, she opened her eyes. "That was incredible."

He grinned. "It gets better."

"Better?" She sounded doubtful. "I can't imagine that it could get better than that."

He loved a challenge. "Hold your opinion for another hour or so."

"An hour?" She stared at him, her eyes wide with uncertainty. "I don't think I could possibly survive that long."

He didn't think he would survive that long, either. But he was determined to try.

Forking his fingers into her hair, he brought his mouth to hers. Desire continued to claw at him, and tasting her eagerness only made it that much harder for him to maintain control.

He wanted to claim her, make her his. The notion that he was the first man to put his hands on her made him wild. The uncivilized part of him that had run wild with

Marissa roared within its cage, demanding to be free. Gabriel turned his back on those impulses.

Making this first time perfect for her was the only thing that mattered. And for him to do that, he must stay in control.

Her hands left the mattress and moved up his sides. Caresses like fire swept over his skin as she explored the contours of his shoulders and back.

His tongue delved between her parted lips, tasting her passion, capturing the soft cries she made as his fingers found her breasts, nails raking lightly over her taut nipples. Her legs tangled with his. Her wet curls dampened his boxers. He rocked against her heat and broke off the kiss to take her nipple in his mouth.

Her head fell back as he suckled her. Cupping her butt in his hand, he guided her undulating rhythm until they were in sync. A groan collected in his chest as her fingers speared beneath the waistband of his boxers and found him.

Olivia gasped at the first contact with Gabriel's erection. The silken feel of his skin. The steel beneath. The sheer size of him made her whimper with fear and excitement. How was she supposed to take all of him inside her?

"It's okay," he murmured, easing her fingers away. Somehow he'd understood what was in her mind. "I'll take it slow. You'll get the chance to get used to me little by little."

"But you aren't little, so little by little isn't how I see this happening," she retorted, twisting one hand free so she could touch him again.

A groan burst from him as she wrapped her hand fully around his length and measured him from tip to base.

He pulled her hand away and pinned it on the pillow by her ear. "It certainly isn't going to happen that way if you don't stop touching me."

"But I like touching you," she countered, lifting up to kiss his chin. She'd been aiming for his lips, but with his chest pressed against hers, she couldn't lift up that high. "Kissing you." She could barely gain the breath she needed for speech as his body slid down hers. "I've been waiting a long time for this."

"Then let's not delay."

Further conversation became impossible as Gabriel kicked off his boxers and slid between her thighs. Olivia felt his erection against her skin and wiggled her hips to entice him to bring their bodies together in the way they both wanted. Her entire focus consisted of this powerful man and the ache only he could satisfy. Despite her inexperience, she knew exactly what she wanted. Gabriel inside her. She needed to be connected to him on that elemental level and she needed it now.

"Gabriel, please," she murmured, her body shuddering as his mouth slipped over her skin, licking, nibbling, kissing. He seemed determined to investigate every inch of her when there was only one place she wanted his attention focused. "Take me."

Her voice broke on the plea. But it had its effect. He kissed her one last time on the hollow beside her hip bone and settled the tip of his shaft at the entrance to her core. The feel of him there was so amazing. She lifted her hips and took him a little way in.

"We'll get there," he murmured, framing her face with his hands.

Surrendering to the ride was part of the excitement. Forcing him to move faster would get her to satisfaction quicker but wasn't the journey worth some patience?

"You're extremely tight." Capturing her lips in a hot, sizzling kiss, Gabriel flexed his hips forward, sliding into her a little deeper. "It will go easier the first time if you relax."

She was a mass of anticipation and tension. How the hell was she supposed to relax? Olivia gripped his wrists and focused on his expression. His rigid facial muscles and intense concentration told her that this slow loving was taking its toll on him, as well.

"I have no idea how to do that." The heavy throb in her womb grew more powerful as she held her breath and waited for him to join with her completely.

His low chuckle sounded near her ear.

"Breathe."

"I can't." Her words were garbled, starved for air.

His teeth nipped her throat and she gasped. Then he was sucking on the spot where he'd administered the love bite, his tongue laving the tender area. Her mouth fell open as an electric charge shot from where he'd placed his mouth to the place where he was claiming her in the most elemental way possible. Her body stretched as he rocked against her again, his movement driving him a little deeper into her.

The sensation was incredible. She focused on the joy of being filled by him and her muscles unwound. Relief swept through her and she gave herself over to wonder with a murmur.

"Or maybe I can."

"That's it," he coaxed, withdrawing with the same deliberate motion only to move into her again.

The sensation was incredible. She loved the way he filled her.

It took a moment of concentration before she shifted her hips into sync with his slow rhythm. Which was too slow as it turned out. He might have all the patience in the world, but she didn't. His gentleness wasn't getting him where she needed him most. So, as he began his next measured, torturous thrust into her body, she arched her back, drove her hips forward and sunk her nails into his tight rear, accepting all of him. They cried out in unison. If she hadn't been so shattered by the feel of him so deeply buried in her, Olivia might have giggled. Utterly possessed, she had no breath to laugh or speak.

Gabriel licked his lips and slowly his gaze refocused. The transformation of his features from rigid concentration to outright shock magnified the pleasure inside her.

"What happened to slow?" he murmured, fingertips grazing her cheeks with reverent gentleness.

Olivia's body had adjusted to his. A contented purr rumbled in her chest. She ran the soles of her feet down his calves and drifted her hands along his spine.

"You were taking too long."

"It's your first time," he grumbled. "I was trying to be gentle."

"What happens now?" Her inner muscles flexed as he rocked his hips against hers.

"Watch and see."

With those cryptic words, Olivia turned herself over to the dazzling display of fireworks in Gabriel's eyes as he began to move against her, gauging her every response. Then he thrust back inside her and pleasure began to build once more.

He captured her hips in his hands and helped her find his rhythm. To her astonishment her body caught fire. Pleasure radiated outward from her core, spreading in waves of sensual hunger that climbed higher and higher, reaching outward with an intensity that made her feel as if she was on the verge of splintering into a million pieces.

And then it began, the breaking. Yet this time, unlike the last, she had Gabriel with her, climbing beside her. She held on to him, glorying in his strength and the power of the pleasure he gave her.

Her breath caught as the sun exploded behind her eyelids. Ecstasy blasted through her, detonating with all the power of a volcano. She cried out and clung to Gabriel as his movements increased. Everything went dark for a second, then she heard her name on Gabriel's lips and he thrust one last time, shaking with the power of his orgasm, before collapsing on her.

Olivia tunneled one hand through his hair while her other unlocked from his shoulder. His chest heaved against her, as he dragged air into his lungs in great gulps. Their hearts thundered in unison, as matched in the aftermath as they'd been during their loving.

She scrambled for words, but nothing could describe her emotions at the moment. Instead, she settled for silence and let her fingers talk for her. She ran them soothingly across his skin, conveying her profound thanks.

"Are you okay?" Gabriel asked, rousing himself enough to slide out of her and roll onto his side.

The loss of him from her body hit her like a sledgehammer. The connection they'd had, now severed, made her realize just how intimate the act of making love was. For those few minutes, she'd not just taken him into her body, into her womb, but into her heart, as well. He'd possessed her body and soul.

"Never better," she replied, unable to mask the smile in her voice.

He gathered her close and dropped a chaste kiss above her brow. Beneath her palm, his heartbeat returned to normal.

"That makes two of us." His thumb moved against her shoulder in an absent fashion as if his mind was somewhere besides the two of them naked in this bed. "You're sure that wasn't too rough?"

"Since I have nothing to compare it to, I'm going to say it was just rough enough."

He stopped staring at the canopy overhead and sliced a sharp look her way. His mouth tightened for a second until he realized she was teasing him.

"I had hoped to initiate you in a more civilized manner."

"There's a civilized way to make love?" Despite her best intentions, she giggled. "Do tell." Lifting onto her elbow, she walked her fingers down his stomach. "Better yet, why don't you show me?"

Gabriel growled and captured her fingers in a tight grip, placing their clasped hands on his chest. "Behave."

"Or what?" She had no idea what demon had possessed her but suddenly she felt more free and alive than any time in her life. Keeping her virginity intact all these years had obviously created a powder keg of trouble. Like a genie in a bottle, once released, her sexuality was ready to cause as much mischief as possible before she stuffed it back in and replaced the cork. "You'll spank me?"

Gabriel's eyes widened at her outrageous suggestion, but temptation danced in their bronze depths. His pupils widened, a sure sign of sexual arousal, and his erection flared to life again.

And shockingly enough, she felt herself awakening, as well. What did this man do to her?

"You led me to believe you were cool and composed," he complained as she wiggled around until she got a thigh on either side of his hips. His erection prodded her from behind. He looked pained as she extricated her hand from his grasp and raked her nails down his chest and over his abdomen, smiling as his muscles twitched beneath her touch. "What's gotten into you?"

She leaned forward to grin at him. "You."

His hands bracketed her hips as she poised herself over his shaft and slowly lowered herself downward. Taking him deep, adjusting the angle to give herself the most pleasure, she watched his face contort with delight and his eyes glaze over.

When she sat on him, savoring the feel of him buried inside her once more, she watched his gaze come back into focus. He reached up to capture her breasts in his hands, kneading gently, pulling at her nipples while she rose off him, mimicking the slow way he'd tortured her.

For a while he let her control the action, and she appreciated the chance to learn how the feel of him sliding in and out of her could be different if she leaned forward or backward. She liked taking him deep until the tip of him nudged against her womb.

But her education would not be complete without a little tutoring, and Gabriel's patience couldn't last forever. His fingers bit into her hips, changing her cadence. He began to move powerfully, driving himself into her. The bite of her nails created half-moons in his shoulders as his hand slid between their bodies and touched the knot of nerves hidden in her hot wet lips. Sparks exploded behind her eyes as her body began to pulse with ever stronger pleasure. She threw her head back and her mouth fell open in a keening cry as pleasure spun through her like a cyclone.

Gabriel thrust into her, his pace frantic, his own mouth open to expel a groan of acute pleasure. Olivia watched him climax, watched him become completely hers. Panting, she trembled in the aftershocks of her orgasm, her inner muscles clenching around his shaft as he poured his seed inside her and she welcomed this essence of him she could keep.

For the past two hours, Gabriel had lain beside Olivia and listened to her deep regular breathing while his thoughts retraced the evening. As morning light began to come in through the windows, he rolled out of bed, moving carefully to avoid waking Olivia. While he dressed he kept his eyes off her to avoid succumbing to the temptation to return to bed and wake her. Again. A full-fledged grin engaged every muscle in Gabriel's face. He couldn't help it.

Making love with Olivia had demonstrated his life would be spectacularly entertaining from here on out.

As he exited her room, he wondered if she'd done it on purpose. Picked a fight with him that ended in spectacular lovemaking. It was something Marissa had done often enough. Sex with her had been mind-blowing, hot, passionate, animalistic. She'd scratched long welts on his back and marked his shoulders with love bites. She'd possessed him as much as he'd possessed her.

But although their sex had been out of this world, it had many times left him feeling empty. And in typical male fashion, he'd ignored the emotional vacuum because what did he care if his carnal needs were satisfied.

Then, last night, he'd discovered what he'd been missing all those years. Spectacular sex and a deep emotional connection that left him more than a little rattled. With her curious innocence and startling sensuality, Olivia had slipped beneath his skin as if she'd been there all along. As if she was the answer to a prayer he hadn't even realized he'd breathed.

He hadn't liked the sexual power Marissa had held in her delicate hands. He liked Olivia's ability to influence his emotions even less.

Which was why he was heading for his suite of rooms rather than face her in the moments before dawn.

An hour later, Gabriel found Stewart in the office on the first floor. His private secretary had a cup of coffee at his elbow and wore a troubled frown.

"You're up early," Gabriel commented, settling himself behind the intricately carved cherry desk.

"I think you might be interested in seeing this." Stewart extended a jewelry box in Gabriel's direction.

He frowned at it. "What is that?"

Stewart nudged his chin at the box. "When Lady Darcy's secretary delivered her message that she wasn't joining you for dinner, she gave me this. You left before I had a chance to open it."

With an impatient snort, Gabriel cracked open the box. The hairs on the back of his neck lifted as he stared at the contents.

"Where the hell did this come from?" he growled, staring in shocked dismay at the bracelet he'd given Marissa for their second anniversary. "Why did Olivia have it?"

Stewart shook his head. "I spoke with her secretary this morning and apparently it was waiting in her room when she got back from her fitting."

"No wonder she was so angry." He closed the box with a snap. "Ariana must have told her I'd bought this for Marissa."

"Who would have done this?" Stewart asked, refocusing Gabriel on the real trouble spot.

"Whoever it was wanted to create trouble between Olivia and me." Gabriel sat back and steepled his fingers.

"Someone could have entered her suite and left it for her. Staff is coming and going all the time."

"That means someone in the palace is playing a dangerous game." Gabriel poked at the box with a pen. "Time to give Christian a call. This sort of intrigue is right up his alley."

Seven

Finding Gabriel gone when she awoke didn't surprise Olivia. A quick glance at the clock told her it was past eight. He had probably been up for hours. She eased into a sitting position, taking inventory of every strained and aching part of her. Nothing a hot shower wouldn't cure.

When she stepped from the bathroom a short time later, she discovered a visitor. Gabriel sat beside a table laden with an array of breakfast offerings. With his long legs stretched out in front of him and his hands clasped around a steaming cup of coffee, he hadn't yet noticed her.

Olivia leaned her shoulder against the door frame and let her gaze drift over his strong features and muscular torso clad in a tailored midnight-blue suit, white shirt and shimmering burgundy silk tie. For the moment his powerful energy was banked. But Gabriel in a contemplative state was no less arresting than him fully engaged.

Some small sound, probably a dreamy sigh, alerted him to her presence. He straightened and came toward her, his movement fluid, and before she knew it, he'd wrapped her in a snug embrace and given her the lusty morning kiss she'd been hoping for when she'd first awakened.

Desire stirred at the firm press of his mouth against her. He tasted of coffee and raspberries. Olivia dipped her tongue in for a second taste, murmuring approval.

"Good morning," he said, breaking the kiss, but not

ceasing the slow advance of his hands up her spine. "I'm sorry I left without doing that earlier."

"Why didn't you wake me?" She snuggled her cheek against his chest, savoring the unsteady pace of his heart and the hoarse timbre of his voice.

"Because I would have wanted to pick up where we left off last night," he retorted, his voice soft and deep. "And the palace would have been fully awake by the time I left your room."

That wrenched a laugh out of her. "You don't think everyone knows what happened last night?" Her cheeks heated despite herself. She'd always known there would be no privacy for her in the palace, but facing his parents and siblings when she knew they'd be apprised of what had happened between them last night would take a little getting used to.

"Perhaps, but I'd prefer to at least give the appearance of propriety until we're married." Gabriel gave her a wry smile that enhanced the devilry in his eyes. "Are you hungry?"

Her hands snaked around his waist, to tug his crisp white shirt from his pants. "Starving."

With a deep, rumbling laugh he caught her wrists. "I meant for breakfast. We missed dinner last night."

She waited until he'd dusted a kiss across her knuckles before answering. "I'd quite forgotten about dinner."

His eyes glowed with fierce delight as he drew her toward the table and poured a cup of coffee. "I didn't know what you liked for breakfast so I ordered some of everything."

"Usually I have an egg-white omelet with mushrooms and spinach, but today I think I want pancakes with lots of syrup."

To her astonishment, Gabriel served her himself. Olivia found it quite difficult to concentrate on her delicious breakfast while he watched her through eyes that danced with fondness and desire.

"Aren't you eating?" she asked.

"I had something an hour ago." He glanced at his watch. "The girls are going for their first ride this morning. I thought we should go watch. I already checked with your secretary and she said you're available until ten."

Considering his busy schedule, Olivia was delighted that he'd made time for such an important event. "They'll be thrilled. I took them to the stables yesterday afternoon. They loved the ponies. I predict they'll be enthusiastic equestrians."

"I have something for you." He pulled a small box out of his pocket and set it on the table between them.

Olivia eyed the black velvet case on the crisp white linen and shook her head. "I don't want it." The memory of yesterday's gift had made her more blunt than polite.

Gabriel didn't look at all surprised or insulted by her refusal. "You don't know that until you open it."

More of his mistress's leftovers? Olivia heaved a sigh. "You really don't need to give me anything."

"I need to explain about the bracelet."

She did not want to hear about the wretched thing ever again. "There's nothing to explain. It was beautiful. It was rude of me not to accept something you put so much thought into."

Gabriel leaned back in his chair, his expression a mask. But his eyes glittered like sunlight on water. "I'm not certain whether to be appalled or delighted that you are such a skillful diplomat."

She kept her lashes down and her lips relaxed. All her life she'd been watched for any sign of reaction or weakness. She'd mastered her facial muscles well before her fourteenth birthday. And she'd needed to. Her stepmother had enjoyed poking her with emotional sticks. Any reaction was sure to displease Lord Darcy, who wanted nothing more than for his two girls to get on. He was fond of reminding the women that he loved them both. And wished with all his heart that they would get along.

"You are marrying me because of my diplomacy and public image."

"In part." Gabriel turned over her hand and set the box on her palm. "I'm also marrying you because of your impeccable breeding and the fact that ever since the day I met you, I haven't been able to stop thinking about you."

Stunned by his admission, she stared at Gabriel's gift, knowing no expensive bauble could compare to the gift of knowing he was smitten with her. "That's lovely of you to say."

"Now back to the bracelet. Do you know where it came from?"

His question confused her. "From you."

He shook his head. "This is what I selected for you."

"Then where did the bracelet come from?"

"That's what I'd like to know."

Relief swept through her. "Then you didn't give me Marissa's bracelet."

"No." He gave her a stern look. "And I'm a little bothered by the fact that you think I'd be so cruel."

Olivia opened her mouth but had no ready response. Since dancing with him at the Independence Day gala she'd become foolish and irrational where he was concerned. With her hormones overstimulated and her emotions swinging from one extreme to the other, she shouldn't be surprised her brain was producing nothing but gibberish.

"Someone in the palace with access to my room played a cruel joke on me."

"Whoever it is, I don't think they are playing. This is a very serious breach in security. One that I will address." The determination in his voice matched the steel in his expression. After a second his gaze softened. "Please open my gift."

Olivia did as she was told.

Unlike the previous evening's trendy, emerald bracelet, this necklace was exactly something she would have chosen for herself. Olivia touched her fingertip to the large teardrop-shaped aquamarine, set into a frame of diamond-lined branches and suspended from a chain of faceted aquamarine beads and diamond-encrusted platinum balls. Gabriel had picked out the perfect, unique gift.

"The necklace belonged to my great-aunt Ginnie. Her husband gave it to her as an engagement present. I believe it came from his mother who received it as her engagement present."

"I love it." And she did. More than any million-dollar diamond necklace he could have found in the treasury. It represented tradition and love. And it demonstrated a sentimental side she would never have guessed Gabriel possessed. Feeling bold, she picked up the necklace and sat down on her fiancé's lap. "Can you help me put it on?"

She lifted her hair off her neck and held still while his knuckles brushed her nape. The casual touch sent shivers spiraling along her nerve endings. As the drop settled against her skin, she turned and planted a sweet kiss on Gabriel's cheek.

"Is that the best you can do?" he questioned, laughter in his voice.

Veiling her eyes with her lashes, she peered at him. "If I do much better we run the risk of not leaving this room in time to take Bethany and Karina for their first ride."

His response was to capture her lips in a sizzling kiss. Olivia sagged against him, surrendering to the firestorm of desire that had not burned out even after last night's lovemaking. She groaned beneath his lips as his hand found her breast, thumb coaxing her nipple to a hard point.

With a low growl, he broke off the kiss. "Perhaps you were right to be cautious." And with that, he stood with her in his arms and carried her to the bed.

In the end, they were in time to watch the twins circle the ring on the docile, well-mannered ponies, each led by an attentive groom. Although both were equally delighted by the ride, their individual personalities shone through. Bethany chattered incessantly as she rode, her every thought voiced. Karina was more circumspect and her seat was more natural. Of the two, Gabriel suspected she'd be the better rider.

Soon the twins' first riding lesson was done, leaving Gabriel free to turn his thoughts to the woman beside him and all that had transpired in the past twelve hours.

Since discovering last night how swiftly Olivia became aroused, he'd taken full advantage of her ardent responses and made love to her with fierce passion. Already his lust for her was dangerously close to uncontrollable. Telling himself making love to Olivia was a novelty that would soon wear off wasn't cooling his ardor one bit. Even now, as he watched her smile as her gaze followed the twins, he felt heat rise in his blood.

It shocked him to realize that he'd happily forgo the rest of his appointments to spend the time alone with Olivia in her suite. This was how he'd been with Marissa. Preoccupied. Distracted. Obsessed.

Then again, it was early in their relationship. The time of exploration when all things were fascinating and new. Their lust would eventually burn itself out and they could settle into companionable monotony. But even as he entertained this possibility his instincts rejected it. More than his blood hummed when she was near. This was a feeling he'd never known before. Besides being beautiful, Olivia was intelligent and caring. He'd been right the first time he'd pronounced her perfect. But he'd underestimated how deep that flawlessness went.

"Gabriel?" Olivia said, returning him to the here and now. "I was just explaining to Bethany and Karina that we can't have dinner with them tonight."

"Because we are…" He had no idea what was scheduled that evening. How was that possible? He usually knew his itinerary backward and forward.

"Going to the ballet," Olivia prompted.

"That's it." He smiled at her.

"But perhaps we could visit before we leave to read you one quick bedtime story."

"That we can do."

The twins' chorus of happiness sent a bird winging off through the trees from a few feet away.

"I think it's time to head back to the palace," Olivia said, shaking her head as the girls began to protest. "Your father has work to do."

Gabriel was impressed how well she managed the toddlers. The twins were darling but rambunctious. Marissa had done a fine job of blending discipline with love for they seemed to take direction well and had none of the fits of temper he had grown accustomed to with their mother. Despite losing Marissa recently, they were adjusting nicely to life in the palace. Of course, they had each other, something he could relate to with two brothers of his own. Sometimes it had seemed as if it was him, Nic and Christian against the world when in truth it was probably more reasonable to say it had been the three of them against their parents.

After leaving the twins in the hands of two young maids, Gabriel walked Olivia to her meeting with the wedding planner and bussed her cheek in a chaste kiss goodbye. He had fifteen minutes before his first meeting of the day and went in search of Christian.

His brother was nowhere near the palace. Christian had an office in the city that he usually preferred to work out of, claiming fewer distractions. Gabriel suspected he liked working without the king's or queen's "subtle" influence. With two brothers ahead of him for the throne, Christian had always enjoyed a lot of freedom. So had Nic. The middle brother didn't even live in Sherdana. He'd gotten his education in the States and resided in California while he pursued his dream of privatizing space travel.

Gabriel envied them both.

And he wouldn't trade places with, either. He'd been born to rule and had never wished to do anything else. But being king came with a price. He belonged to the people of Sherdana and owed it to them to do what was best for the country, even at the expense of his own desires. Breaking off his relationship with Marissa was only one of many sacrifices he'd made for Sherdana, but it had been his hardest and most painful.

It was why he was marrying a woman he admired instead of one he loved. And yet, hadn't last night and this morning proved that life with Olivia at his side would be the furthest thing from hardship?

Grinning, Gabriel headed into his father's office where the energy minister had come for a briefing.

Olivia yawned behind her hand as she surveyed Noelle's drawings for the twins' dresses for the wedding. It was almost midnight. She'd just returned from another event, this one raising money for an arts program for underprivileged children.

She wasn't insensible to the irony that what she intended to pay for these two dresses could probably fund the program for a year.

Behind her the door to her suite opened and closed. Her skin prickled in anticipation as muted footsteps advanced toward her. The faint scent of Gabriel's aftershave tickled her nose a second before his hands soothed along her shoulders.

"Waiting up for me?"

Gabriel placed a kiss on her neck, his lips sliding into a particularly sensitive spot that made her tremble.

Was it possible that less than a week ago their every private encounter had been stilted and awkward? Now she spent her days as a tightly wound spring of sexual anticipation and her nights in Gabriel's arms soaring toward the stars.

"Of course," she answered, setting aside the sketches and getting to her feet. She'd already dressed for bed in her favorite silk pajamas. They covered her from neck to toe. Not exactly seductive, but Gabriel never seemed to care.

"I'm leaving early in the morning," he explained, pulling her into his arms and dropping a sweet kiss on her lips. "And I will be gone for four days. I wanted a private moment with you before I left."

Four long days. And nights. She'd gotten accustomed to cuddling against his side, her cheek on his bare chest, his heartbeat lulling her to sleep.

She adored his intensity—making love with Gabriel was like being consumed by the sun—but these moments of stillness had their own rewards.

"Just a moment?" She tipped her head to grant him better access to her neck and ran her nails along his nape the way he liked.

"Did I mention I'm leaving very early in the morning?" Tender mockery filled his voice. He nudged his hips into her, letting her feel his erection. She smiled, no less turned on despite wanting to do nothing more than stretch out on her mattress and sleep for twelve hours.

"Of course," she murmured. "I just thought that perhaps you could give me a few minutes to say goodbye properly."

"Just a few minutes?"

Olivia's bones turned to water as he drew his tongue along her lower lip, tasting, but not taking. With his hands warm and strong on her lower back, she leaned into his powerful chest and savored the tantalizing slide of his mouth against hers.

"Take as many as you need."

She'd grown accustomed to sharing her bed with him and hated the thought of sleeping alone these next four nights. Every morning, after he woke her with kisses and made love to her in the soft light before day, she fell back to sleep wondering if once they were married, once she became pregnant, if he would share her bed every night. She already knew that a suite of rooms was being prepared for them in the family wing. They would each have their own space. Their own beds after the wedding. That wasn't what she wanted.

Olivia wasn't surprised when Gabriel swept her off her feet and carried her to the bed. The chemistry between them had skyrocketed in the days since they'd first made love. With their clothes scattered across the mattress, Olivia clutched at Gabriel as he brought her to orgasm twice before sliding into her. Being filled by him was a pleasure all its own and Olivia wrapped her thighs around his hips and held him close while he thrust into her.

He stayed for several hours, his large hands moving with such gentleness up and down her spine. Snuggled against his chest, with their legs intertwined, Olivia let herself drift. When she awoke several hours later, Gabriel was gone and she was already lonely.

Exhausted, but restless, Olivia left the bed and slipped into a robe. Her suite faced the gardens behind the palace so she had no hope of catching a final glimpse of Gabriel, but she opened the French door that led to the terrace and wandered across to the railing. At night the garden was lit up like a magical fairy tale, but dawn was approaching and the garden had gone dark. A cool breeze carried the scent of roses to her. Olivia leaned her arms on the cool stone. Vivid in her thoughts was the night Gabriel had found her out here and demonstrated that resisting him was a pointless exercise.

And now she knew it had been all along. When she'd agreed to marry him, she'd fooled herself into believing that sexual desire and mild affection would make her happy. After several nights in his arms she'd completely fallen under his spell. It was as if all her life she'd been moving toward this man and this moment.

Recognizing that her motivation for marrying Gabriel had changed, she had to ask herself if she was no longer concerned whether one day she'd become a queen...what did she really want?

Love.

The thought made her knees weak. Olivia braced herself against the stone railing. Deflated, she stared at her hands. At the engagement ring sparkling on her finger.

She couldn't be falling in love with Gabriel. He certainly wasn't falling in love with her.

This was an arranged marriage. A practical union for the good of his country. A sensible bargain that would lead to stability and children. She hadn't expected to fall madly in love with her husband or be deliriously happy. She expected to be content. To feel fulfilled as a mother and someday as a queen.

Sexual satisfaction hadn't entered into her plans—not until Gabriel had kissed her.

Olivia turned away from the softly lit garden and returned to her suite. As she closed and locked the glass door, her gaze fell on her desk and the locked drawer where she'd placed copies of important paperwork, including a file with some of her medical information. Had those

scratches always marred the lock's brass surface? The idea
that someone in the palace could have tried to break into
her desk was ridiculous. And then she recalled the night
the twins arrived. There'd been a maid at her dresser in
the middle of the night. When nothing was missing she'd
seen no reason to pursue it.

A few hours later, when Libby entered the suite, Olivia
was still seated at the desk. She'd opened the locked drawer
and hadn't found anything disturbed, but with the twins' arrival at the palace having been leaked to the press and the
mysterious appearance of Marissa's bracelet, Olivia had
checked each page of her thick file to make sure it was intact.

"Why are you looking through your papers?"

"I might be mistaken, but I thought I spotted fresh
scratches on the lock and wanted to make sure my medical file hadn't been rifled." Olivia glanced up when Libby
didn't immediately comment. "What's wrong?"

"Prince Christian is systematically interviewing the
staff about the leaks to the press."

A chill chased across Olivia's skin. "He thinks someone
inside the palace is providing information?" She remembered the photos of Gabriel and Marissa. Those hadn't
been paparazzi shots. They had been taken among friends.

Olivia touched the lock again, wishing she could determine if the scratches were recent. If someone had gotten
their hands on her medical records it could have cata-
strophic results. "Keep me updated on the investigation,"
she said, "and see if you can find a more secure place for
these."

Gabriel was having a hard time keeping his mind on today's biotech plant tour. For the past several days he'd been
touring manufacturing plants in Switzerland and Belgium
in search of other businesses that would be interested in
moving their operations to Sherdana. He probably should

have sent Christian to do this. His brother had made a significant amount of money investing in up-and-coming technology. Christian would have been interested in the product lines and the way the manufacturing facilities were organized. Gabriel was finding it as dry as overdone toast.

That's probably how both his brothers felt about what went into the running of the country. These days, they had little in common. It often amazed Gabriel that three people could share a womb for nine months, communicate among themselves in their own language until they were teenagers and participate in a thousand childhood adventures together yet be so completely different in their talents and interests as they entered their twenties.

Nevertheless, this trip couldn't have come at a better time. The past few nights with Olivia had been some of the most passion-filled of his life. She'd slipped effortlessly beneath his defenses with her eager sensuality and curious nature. He'd become obsessed with the soft drag of her lips across his skin and the wicked suggestions she whispered in his ear as he entered her.

His constant craving for her company warned him he was fast losing touch with why he was marrying her. Cool, sophisticated elegance and a warm heart. Not feverish kisses and blazing orgasms.

Gabriel cleared his throat and tugged at his collar as the head of the factory droned on. He definitely needed some space from her. Unfortunately, the distance wasn't having the effect he'd hoped for. Being apart was supposed to cool him off. That was what he'd anticipated, but that wasn't the result.

He daydreamed about her at the oddest moments. Him. Daydreaming. Like some infatuated fool. He'd never expected her to preoccupy him in this way. She was supposed to be a sensible mate, an able partner in governing the country, not a hellcat in bed.

Hope.

The tattoo drove him crazy. Its placement. Its message.

It awakened him to possibilities. He wanted to throw sensible out the window and take chances. Because of Olivia he wanted to shake up the established way of doing things. She'd awakened his restless spirit that he'd believed he'd conquered after ending things with Marissa.

Every day he was finding out that Olivia was more than he'd expected.

And he'd be a fool not to worry about the power she now had over him. Yet he was helpless to stop what was developing between them. The best he could hope for was to slow things down until he shaped the relationship into something he was comfortable with.

But was *comfortable* going to make him happy in the long run? Was he really going to shortchange his future all for the sake of feeling safe and in control?

A few days after Gabriel left on his trip, Olivia was scheduled to have a private lunch with the queen. Ten minutes before the appointment, she slipped pearl earrings into place and stepped in front of the mirror to assess her appearance. She'd chosen a sleeveless pink dress edged in white with a narrow white belt to highlight her waist, and accessorized with a pair of floral pumps. The feminine ensemble required a soft hairstyle so she'd left her hair down and coaxed out the natural wave with a light blowout.

This morning she'd awakened to some discomfort in her lower abdomen and wasn't feeling on top of her game, but wasn't about to cancel on the queen.

Drawing a fortifying breath, she entered the private dining room that only the immediate royal family used. Pale blue had been chosen for the chairs as well as the curtains framing the large windows. It was the only splash of color in a room otherwise dominated by white walls and lavish plasterwork painted gold. More intimate than many of the other rooms on the first floor, it nevertheless didn't allow her to forget that this was a palace.

"You look lovely," the queen said as she breezed into the room. She wore a classic suit of dusty lavender and a stunning choker of pale round Tahitian pearls. Noticing Olivia's interest, she touched the necklace. "An anniversary gift from the king," the queen explained, her smile both fond and sensual.

"It's beautiful."

"Matteo has exceptionally good taste."

The queen gestured toward the dining table, capable of seating twelve, but set for two. As the two women sat down, a maid set a glass of soda on the table before the queen.

"Diet cola," she, sipping the fizzy drink with pleasure. "I got a taste for it when we visited the States two decades ago. It's my indulgence."

Olivia nodded in understanding. She wasn't much of a soda drinker herself, but she understood how someone could come to crave a particular item. Like a tall, bronze-eyed prince for example.

The servers placed plates of salad in front of the two women and the queen launched a barrage of questions to determine what Olivia knew about Sherdana's current political climate and their economic issues. Although Olivia had been expecting to discuss the wedding preparations, she was just as happy to share what she knew about the country she would soon call her own.

"Does my son know how bright you are?" the queen asked, her expression thoughtful as the maids cleared the main course and served dessert. She frowned at the plate in front of her and sighed. "Oh, dear. The chef is experimenting again."

Olivia stared at the oddest fruit she'd ever seen. About

the size of her fist with a leathery hot-pink skin, it had been sliced in half to reveal white flesh dotted with tiny black seeds. A hollow had been carved out of the center and filled with yogurt and sliced strawberries.

"Dragon fruit," the queen explained. "And from what I understand quite delicious."

Olivia took her first bite and was surprised at the wonderfully sweet flavor. It had a texture like a kiwi with the seeds adding a little crunch to each bite.

"You look pale." The queen pointed at Olivia with her spoon. "I expect you'll get more rest with my son away."

Olivia's entire body flushed hot. The queen had just insinuated that she knew where Gabriel had been spending his nights.

"Oh, don't look so mortified," the queen continued. "You are to be married and my son was determined to have a short engagement. Besides, there are no secrets in the palace."

"No, I suppose there are not." Olivia knew better than to think her nights with Gabriel were something between just the two of them. She'd grown up surrounded by servants who knew most everything about her daily habits.

"How are the twins' dresses coming for the wedding?" The queen had taken a few days to approve the idea of Bethany and Karina being a part of the ceremony, but Gabriel had at last persuaded her.

"They should be finished later this week. The lace Noelle has chosen is beautiful. I think you'll be pleased."

"Noelle is very talented. You will all look beautiful." The queen nodded in satisfaction. "I must say, you've accepted this situation with Gabriel's children much better than most women would in your position."

"It's hard to imagine anyone not adoring those precious two," Olivia admitted, but she understood what the queen was getting at. "I love children. Helping to make their lives better is the foundation for all my charity work. I would be a wretched person and a hypocrite if I turned my back on Bethany and Karina because of who their mother was." And what Marissa had meant to Gabriel.

"They certainly have taken to you," the queen said. "And you seem to have everything it takes to be an excellent mother."

"Thank you."

The queen's praise should have allowed Olivia to relax, but the tick of her biological clock sounded loud in her ears.

Eight

"How was the trip?" Christian asked as he and Gabriel crossed the tarmac toward the waiting limo. "I hope you brought me a present."

"Naturally." Gabriel hoisted his briefcase and deposited it in his brother's hands. "It's filled with all sort of things I'm sure you'll find vastly interesting."

"Unlike you?"

"Technology is more your and Nic's thing." Gabriel was aware that the trip had been less productive than he'd hoped. Mostly because he'd had a hard time concentrating. Thoughts of Olivia had intruded with a frequency he'd found troubling. "You probably should have gone instead of me, but it was something I needed to do. I want to encourage more technology firms to move to Sherdana. The best way for me to do that is to speak to companies that might be looking at expansion."

"I'll bet you hated it."

Gabriel shot Christian a quelling look. "I can't expect to enjoy every aspect of my position. Some things must be done no matter how painful. This was one of them."

"Is your future wife another?"

This time Christian laughed out loud at his brother's sharp look.

"How I feel about my future bride is none of your business."

"Come on, you've got to be a lot happier about having to get married these days. From what I hear, you two have been acting like a couple kids in love."

Gabriel growled in displeasure, but couldn't ignore the electric charge that surged through him at the mere thought of seeing Olivia again and feeling her soft lips yield beneath his. Each of the past four nights he'd gone to bed alone and found himself unable to sleep. Plagued by memories of Olivia's smiles and her sassy sensuality, he'd lain with his hands behind his head, staring up at the blank ceiling and doing his best to ignore his erection.

Cold showers had become his 2:00 a.m. ritual. How had she bewitched him in such a short time?

"Neither one of us is in love," Gabriel muttered. "But I won't deny we're compatible." He leveled a hard gaze at his brother, warning him to drop the matter.

"Not in love?" Christian cocked his head. "Maybe you're not. But are you sure about her?"

Christian's question roused a memory of the last evening before his trip. He'd almost succumbed to Olivia's plea to spend the night. She'd seemed so vulnerable, her characteristic confidence lacking. But that didn't mean she was in love with him.

"Ridiculous," he said. "We've only spent a couple weeks in each other's company."

"You don't believe in love at first sight?"

Gabriel regarded his brother's serious expression with curiosity. "Do you?"

"Absolutely."

"Is that why you do your best to chase every woman away who gets too close?" Gabriel wondered if his brother was taunting him or if he was offering Gabriel a rare glimpse into his psyche. "Have none of them made you feel as if you were clobbered by something beyond your understanding or control?"

Something flared in Christian's gaze but was quickly gone. His mocking smile returned. "Who wants to settle down with one woman when there's a banquet of lovelies to sample?"

"One of these days someone will appeal to your palate and you'll find that you can't get enough of that particular delicacy."

"Is that what happened to you?"

"I'm getting married because I have to." Gabriel was well aware that he'd dodged the question and not with any finesse.

Christian's eyes narrowed. "And if you didn't have to?"

"Since that's never been an option, I've never really thought about it."

And he didn't want to think about it now because it opened old wounds. Would he have stayed with Marissa if marriage to her had been possible? Had he loved her or had he inflated his feelings for her because circumstances made it impossible for them to have a future?

"Well, I certainly stirred you up," Christian taunted.

"Wasn't that your intention?" Gabriel countered, staring past the hedge that bordered the driveway to the palace. For a moment he glimpsed a pair of ponies and the two little girls riding them. Despite his tumultuous thoughts, he couldn't help but feel joy at the appearance of his daughters and feel sorry for Christian. His cynical attitude would undoubtedly prevent him from experiencing the wonder of holding his own children in his arms and feeling their enthusiastic kisses all over his cheek.

"God," Christian exclaimed, "you are smitten."

"I caught a glimpse of my angels out riding."

Christian snorted. "They're not exactly angels. In fact, they've been turning the palace upside down with their version of hide-and-seek, which entails them finding some tiny nook and not coming out until every servant is called upon to look for them. It's been worse these last few days with Olivia feeling unwell."

Gabriel frowned. "What did you say about Olivia? She's ill?"

"Didn't you know?"

"I spoke with her last night. She said nothing." Gabriel rubbed at the back of his neck. "How bad is it?"

"I don't know. She hasn't been out of her suite for the last two days."

"Has she been in bed that whole time?"

"I don't know," Christian sounded amused. "But if you'd hinted that you'd like me to check on your English flower in her bedroom, you should have said something."

Gabriel didn't even look at his brother as he exited the car and strode into the palace. Tension rode his shoulders as he entered the foyer, barely hearing the greetings from the staff on duty. Why hadn't Olivia told him she wasn't doing well? He took the stairs two at a time and turned in the direction of his fiancée's suite. His knock was answered by a maid.

"I'm here to see Lady Darcy," he told her, his scowl compelling the young woman to step back.

Three women occupied the room. Olivia sat on the couch with her feet up, her back to him while Ariana sat opposite her facing the door. Olivia's private secretary was by the desk. His sister's lilting laugh broke off as he entered.

"Good afternoon, ladies." He forced himself to approach Ariana first. His sister looked splendid as always in an evening-blue dress. The color flattered her golden skin and dark brown hair. She wore a simple gold bangle at her wrist and gold hoop earrings.

"Welcome back, Gabriel," she said, standing as he drew near and making her cheek available for a kiss.

"We missed you," Olivia echoed, turning to gaze up at

him. Her normally pale complexion lacked its customary healthy glow and there were shadows purpling the skin beneath her eyes.

Concern flared. He sat beside her on the sofa and touched her cheek with his fingertips. "Last night on the phone, why didn't you tell me you've been ill?"

"It's nothing."

"You're too pale. I demand to know what's wrong."

Olivia sighed and cast her gaze toward Ariana. Her eyes widened, causing Gabriel to turn his head. Ariana had vanished. The door to the bedroom was shut. They were alone.

Gabriel refocused on Olivia. "Answer me," he growled.

Red patches appeared on her formerly dull cheeks. "I've been having a particularly difficult period," she murmured.

Relief flooded him. She was embarrassed to discuss her body's natural process? Was that why she'd kept silent the night before? Amused, Gabriel dipped a finger beneath her chin and raised it.

"I'm going to be your husband. You better prepare to discuss all sorts of things like this with me."

"Be careful or you may live to regret those words," she muttered, but her lips were soft and eager beneath his. "Welcome home."

An endearment hung between them, unspoken. She'd promised not to call him Prince Gabriel or Your Highness as they made love, but she had yet to find a pet name for him. What would it be? Darling? Dearest? Sweetheart?

My love?

"Did you have a successful trip?" she asked.

"It was very long." He leaned forward and kissed her neck below her ear, smiling as she trembled. "And lonely."

She framed his face with her hands. "I missed you so much. In fact—"

A knock sounded on the door, interrupting her. Heaving

a weary sigh, Gabriel kissed Olivia on the nose and then raised his voice to be heard in the hall. "Come."

Stewart poked his head around the door. "The king wondered if you'd gotten lost on your way to the meeting with the prime minister."

Gabriel stood and bent over Olivia's hand. "Duty calls."

"Of course." The bright smile she gave him didn't quite reach her eyes. "Perhaps we can have dinner together?"

Regret pinched him. "I'm afraid I can't tonight. I already have an appointment."

"Of course."

He'd grown familiar with the micro expressions that belied her thoughts and could see she was disappointed. He hated being the one who robbed her eyes of their sparkle, and the intensity of his desire to see her smile caught him off guard. Falling in love with his fiancée wasn't what he'd had in mind when he decided to marry Olivia.

"I'll stop back to check on you later," he said.

Her gaze clung to his face. "I'll be waiting."

The morning after Gabriel returned from his business trip, Olivia caught herself smiling almost as often as she yawned. True to his word, he'd returned after his dinner to check on her and they'd snuggled on the sofa until almost three in the morning while Olivia filled him in on the twins and he spoke of what he'd seen in Switzerland and Belgium.

In addition to talking, there'd been a fair amount of kissing, as well. Lighthearted, romantic kisses that left Olivia breathless and giddy. He'd treated her with tender patience, not once letting passion get the better of him. Olivia had found his control both comforting and frustrating. Four days without him had aroused her appetite for his hands roaming over her skin and she cursed her cycle's timing.

On the other hand, there would be nothing to get in the

way of their magical wedding night. Unless there wasn't going to be a wedding.

This was her first period since discontinuing the birth control pills that regulated her cycle. At first she'd been down because as amazing as her nights with Gabriel had been, she hadn't gotten pregnant. Soon, however, she began to worry as old, familiar symptoms appeared. Assuring herself everything was going to be fine became harder each day as her period stretched out. For the past two days fear had begun to sink deep into bone and sinew. She began to confront the very real possibility that her surgery might not have cleared up her problem. She had to face that getting and staying pregnant might be more difficult than she'd assumed.

Then, after seeing Gabriel yesterday, it became clear what she had to do. She needed to tell him the truth. Despite the connection they shared, she wasn't sure how he was going to react to her news. She could only hope he would act like his father and work with her to solve any issues that came up.

"Olivia?"

A soft voice roused her. With the paparazzi hungry for their first glimpse of Gabriel's daughters, Olivia had requested that Noelle bring their flower-girl dresses to the palace to be fitted. Blinking, she refocused on the slim, dark-haired woman.

"Sorry, Noelle. With the wedding two weeks away my mind tends to jump around a great deal these days. What were you saying?"

"I asked if you wanted me to bring your dress here next week for the final fitting rather than have you come to my shop."

"It would help me if you brought the dress by. I'm drowning in wedding preparations and that would save me time."

"I'd be happy to."

A moment later the twins appeared in their new finery. They looked like angels in their matching sleeveless white dresses with full lace skirts and wide satin sashes in pale yellow. Noelle's assistant had pinned up their hair and attached wreaths wrapped in pale yellow ribbons.

"These are merely to demonstrate one possible look for the girls," Noelle explained. "If you like it, I'm sure the florist could create beautiful wreaths with yellow roses."

"The dresses are perfect," Olivia breathed. "Thank you so much for making them on such short notice."

"I'm happy you like them."

While Noelle and her assistant made little adjustments to the dresses, Olivia distracted Bethany and Karina by explaining to them what their role in the wedding would be. They seemed to understand the seriousness of the event because they listened to her with wide eyes and their full attention.

An hour later, Noelle had left, taking the dresses with her, and Olivia was reading the twins a story when the door to her suite swung open without warning. Startled, Olivia swiveled on the sofa to face a very unhappy Gabriel.

"What's wrong?"

"It's time for the twins to head back to the nursery," he answered, his voice level and cool as he gestured to the nanny who jumped to her feet. "I think it's time for their lunch."

Olivia set the book aside and got to her feet to urge the girls over to their father for a kiss and a hug. His manner softened for them, but a minute later they were gone and Gabriel was back to scowling.

"Is it true?" he demanded.

Her stomach twisted at the hard suspicion in his eyes. "Is what true?"

"That you're infertile?"

Of all the things that had raced through her mind, this was the last thing she'd expected. How had he found out? Libby was the only person who knew about her condition and Olivia knew her private secretary would never betray her.

"Where did you hear that?"

He stalked across the room toward the television and snatched up the remote. Dread filled Olivia as he cued the power button. She'd not imagined he could look so angry.

"Sources inside the palace confirm that the future princess has little to no chance of producing an heir for Sherdana's throne. With her medical condition you have to wonder what the prince was thinking to propose."

The words blaring from the television were so horrifying that Olivia would have crumpled to the floor at his feet if Gabriel hadn't seized her arms in a bruising grip.

His gaze bore into hers. "Tell me the truth."

"I had a condition," she began, and at his dark scowl, rushed on. "But I had surgery to correct the problem. I should be able to get pregnant." But after these past few days and the return of her old symptoms, her confidence had waned.

"Can you or can't you?"

"Six months ago when you proposed I thought I could. At this moment I honestly don't know."

"You should have told me." He set her free as if the touch of her was distasteful. "Did you think you could keep this a secret forever?"

"I really didn't think it was going to be a problem." Olivia clasped her hands to keep them from shaking and looked up at Sherdana's crown prince, who stood there like a granite statue. Little about his current demeanor encouraged hope that he might listen to her with a rational ear. "I would never have agreed to marry you if I believed I couldn't have children."

"But your doctor warned you the chances were slim." It wasn't a question.

She didn't ask him how he knew that. The reporter on the television was divulging her detailed medical records. Her privacy had been violated and yet she was being treated like a villain.

"He never said slim. He said there was a good chance I could get pregnant, but to do so I had to stop taking the pill and he wasn't sure how my body would react since I've been on it almost ten years."

"But you were a virgin. I can attest to that. Why were you on birth control?"

"I had severe cramps and bleeding. It helps control those problems." Olivia wrapped her arms around herself. "I quit taking the birth control before I left London. I wanted to get pregnant as soon as possible. Provide you with your heir. I knew that's what you all would expect."

Gabriel's expression didn't change, but his lips tightened briefly. "We expected you to be truthful, as well."

She flinched at his sharp words.

"I intended to tell you tonight. I haven't felt right these last few days and thought I needed to discuss the situation with you."

"I need an heir, Olivia." His harsh tone softened.

"I understand completely." Their marriage was an arrangement, an exchange of her hand in marriage for her father's business. But she was also expected to be a mother. "I never would've agreed to marry you knowing I might not be able to have children."

He needed to marry someone who could provide the next generation of Alessandros. At the moment she wasn't completely convinced she could do that.

A sharp pain lanced through her and she winced. Her cramps had been a dull ache all through the morning, but now they gained in strength.

"Are you okay?"

She shook her head. "It's been a hectic morning and I've done too much. I should probably take something and lie down for a while. Can we continue later this afternoon?"

She barely waited for his agreement before heading toward the bathroom and the bottle of pain medication she hadn't needed earlier in the day. She shut the bathroom door, hoping that Gabriel wouldn't come to check on her, and braced her hands on the vanity top. The woman in the mirror had dark circles beneath her eyes and white around her mouth.

The pain in her body was vivid and icy, very unlike her usual cramps. The difference scared her.

Forcing herself to take deep, even breaths, she fought back nausea and swallowed her medication. Within minutes, the sharp edges came off the ache in her pelvis and she was able to return to the bedroom. There she found Libby waiting for her with the queen. Helpless tears filled Olivia's eyes. She blinked them away.

"Have you tried pineapple juice?"

The queen's suggestion confused Olivia. "No."

"There's something in it that will help with your cramps."

Olivia clasped her hands as her stomach flipped sickeningly. Why was the queen being nice, given the news?

"Thank you. I'll try pineapple juice."

"You aren't the first woman in this palace to grapple with reproductive issues. I was young when I came to marry the king and eager to give him the heir he needed. Unlike Gabriel, Matteo had no male siblings to take over the throne if something happened to him."

"You had trouble getting pregnant?"

"There's a good reason why Gabriel has two brothers so close in age." The queen gave a fond smile. "I wasn't able to get pregnant without help. We did in vitro fertilization twice before the procedure was successful. Gabriel, Nicolas and Christian are the result."

"And Ariana?" The princess was six years younger than her brothers, close to Olivia's own age.

"My miracle baby."

Olivia liked the sound of that. She hoped her own miracle baby was on the horizon. Because the way she felt at the moment, a miracle might be exactly what she needed.

"Do you love my son?"

She rolled the engagement ring around and around on her finger. "Yes."

"Good, then you'll do what's best for him."

And leaving Olivia to ponder what that was, the queen took her leave.

When the door opened a short time later, Olivia looked up, expecting Libby, and saw a maid instead. "I really don't need anything right now. Perhaps you could check back in later this evening."

"I thought you'd like me to pack your things. I'm sure you'll be heading back to England now that the prince knows you can't have children."

The woman's snide tone wasn't at all what Olivia was expecting and she sat up straighter, adrenaline coursing through her veins. Of average height and appearance with brown hair and hazel eyes, the woman looked like any of a dozen palace maids. But there was a frantic energy to her movement that made Olivia apprehensive.

"Don't be ridiculous," she said, feeling at a disadvantage as the maid stalked toward her. "I'm not leaving."

Olivia pushed to her feet. The sudden movement sent pain stabbing through her. She swayed and caught the back of the chair. Her breath came in labored gasps. Something was very wrong.

"Of course you are." The woman's hazel eyes burned

with a crazy zeal. "The prince won't marry you now that he knows you're damaged."

"That's for him to decide." It was hard to keep her mind on the conversation when it felt as if hot pokers were being driven into her lower abdomen. "Get out."

"What makes you think you can order me around?" the woman spat. "Because you have a title and your father has money?"

Step by deliberate step, Olivia backed away from the maid's furious outburst. It was then that she recognized the woman's face. She'd been the one who'd been searching the desk the night the twins arrived.

"Who are you?" she asked.

"My sister was twice the woman you could ever hope to be."

The woman made as if to rush at her and Olivia stumbled backward.

"Marissa was your sister?" Impossible. This woman was as plain and dull as Marissa had been beautiful and vibrant.

"My younger sister. She was beautiful and full of life. Or she was until Prince Gabriel destroyed her."

"What do you mean?"

Olivia knew she had to keep the woman talking. Somewhere behind her was the bathroom with a solid door and a lock. She just needed to get there.

"In the months following her trip to visit him in Venice, she grew more and more depressed. She couldn't live with the fact that he wanted nothing more to do with her." The sister glared at Olivia as if she'd been the cause of Marissa's heartache.

"I'm sorry your sister was upset—"

"Upset?" The woman practically spat the word. "She wasn't upset. She was devastated. Devastated enough to try to kill herself. I was the one who found her bleeding to death. She'd slit her wrists. It was at the hospital that she found out she was pregnant. She loved her girls. They were everything to her."

Olivia reached her hand back and found the bathroom door frame. "Bethany and Karina are wonderful."

"He doesn't deserve them. He doesn't deserve to be happy. And now he won't because you can't have children. He won't want you anymore." Marissa's sister was shouting now, her voice rising in unbalanced hysteria.

Another wave of pain made Olivia double over. She backed into the bathroom and clawed at the door. Blackness pushed at the edges of her vision. By feel alone she shut the door and slid the lock into place. The door rattled as Marissa's sister beat against it in fury and Olivia staggered back.

With her strength failing, Olivia slid to the floor and set her back against the vanity, hoping that the door would hold. Hoping that someone would come find her. Hoping that Marissa's sister was wrong about Gabriel.

Nine

Gabriel leaned forward in the saddle and urged his stallion to greater speed. Wind lashed at his face, and he focused on the thrum of hoofbeats filling his ears to slow his racing mind. He'd gone for a ride after leaving Olivia because he needed to sort through the conflict raging in him.

Although the powerful Warmblood had stamina enough for a longer run, Gabriel slowed him to a walk after only a mile. He passed the lake where he and his brothers had swum during the hot summers of their youth and wished he could go back to those innocent times.

Accusing Olivia of lying had been unfair. She wouldn't do that. If he'd learned anything about her, it was that she had a great deal of integrity.

What woman, when faced with the prospect of never becoming a mother, wouldn't deny the possibility? Especially someone who adored children the way Olivia did. He'd watched her with the twins. He'd seen how his daughters had bonded with Olivia. She'd won them over with her generous, kind heart. They'd been as helpless against her sweetness as he'd been.

By now his parents would be discussing damage control. And debating how to proceed. Olivia had understood the position this news report had put him in. They would advise him against marrying a woman whose fertility was in question. But he wouldn't make any decisions until he knew the extent of her problems.

And if she could never have children?

He would need to address the bargain he'd struck with her father. The deal with Lord Darcy was contingent on Olivia becoming Gabriel's wife.

Talk about being stuck between a rock and a hard place. No matter what decision he made, he would fail Sherdana.

Two hours later he entered the salon in the family section of the south wing and found everyone assembled.

His sister came forward to give him a hug. "Did you check on Olivia?"

"I went for a ride."

His father regarded him with a frown, his opinion clear. Gabriel ignored him and went to sit beside his mother. He'd come to a preliminary decision and knew it wouldn't meet with everyone's approval.

"I needed some time to think."

The king fixed Gabriel with a hard stare. "How do you intend to handle this?"

"Handle?" Gabriel hadn't considered how they should approach the press about this latest bombshell. "We could start by sending out a press release downplaying the serious nature of Olivia's problems, but I'm not sure with her doctor's records as proof, this is going to do us much good."

"I meant with Olivia," the king said, his voice a low rumble.

Gabriel became aware that his entire family was watching him and waiting for his answer. It was as if the occupants of the room had stopped breathing.

"What do you mean?" Gabriel asked, certain he knew where his father was going with the question, but needing to hear it asked out loud.

"You need a wife who can bear children."

In other words, he must break his engagement with Olivia and reexamine the dozen or so women he'd rejected when he chose her.

"And what am I to say to Lord Darcy? That his daughter's only value to me lies in her ability to produce heirs?" His father's glower told Gabriel he'd stepped into dangerous territory with his sarcasm. At the moment, Gabriel didn't care. What could his father do? For a moment, Gabriel reveled in rebellion. As a teenager, he'd been the best behaved of his siblings, getting into trouble rarely and then never with anything serious.

Nic had started a fire in his room at fifteen experimenting with rockets. Christian had "borrowed" their uncle's Ferrari when he was fourteen and gone joyriding. The expensive sports car had ended up half submerged in a ditch and Christian had been disciplined, but that had only temporarily slowed him down, not stopped him completely.

Gabriel had shouldered his future responsibility like a dutiful son and the newspapers had been filled with photos of him accompanying his mother on her visits to the hospital and various other charitable events and headlines about how lucky Sherdana was to have such a shining example of youth for their next monarch.

"I had fertility problems, as well," the queen reminded her husband, breaking the tension between father and son.

"But neither of us had any idea before we married," the king said, sending his wife a stern look.

"Yet despite your need for an heir, you didn't set me aside when my troubles came to light."

"We'd been married two years. How could I have let you go?"

Gabriel saw the unspoken communication that passed between his parents and felt a flare of envy. The emotion didn't surprise him. He'd felt twinges of it before when watching his parents in private. They were so in sync with each other. He'd hoped for just a little of that depth of intimacy in his own marriage and had begun to believe he'd find it with Olivia.

"Olivia and I will talk later this afternoon."

"You are intending to break off the engagement."

"I'm not sure that's necessary." He saw his father's brows come together. "She claims she had surgery to correct the problem. We need to discuss the situation in more depth and consult a doctor before I make such a radical decision."

The door flew open without a warning knock, catching everyone's attention. Stewart stood in the open doorway, his face stark with concern.

"Forgive my interruption," he said, bowing in apology. "Something has happened to Lady Darcy."

Gabriel's heart jumped in his chest. He surged to his feet and crossed the room in three strides. "What's wrong?"

"I don't know. Miss Marshall said she's locked herself in the bathroom and won't answer the door."

"What makes you think something has happened to her?"

"Her clothes are all over the suite and they've been shredded."

Cursing, Gabriel lunged past his secretary and raced down the hallway. Stewart's long legs usually made him a match for Gabriel, but he had to resort to jogging to keep up.

When Gabriel entered the suite, he registered the destruction in passing but didn't stop. He rushed over to join Olivia's private secretary, who was at the bathroom door, knocking and calling for her to answer. Shoving her aside, Gabriel kicked in the door.

When the door frame gave and the door shot open, the metallic tang of blood immediately hit him. Olivia lay on the cold tile, a large crimson patch on her pale blue skirt. Panic tore through him.

"Call an ambulance!" He dropped to his knees beside her and was relieved to see her chest rise and fall. "When did you enter the suite?" he demanded of her private secretary.

"Perhaps ten minutes ago. I called to her but she didn't open the door or answer. And from what had happened to her clothes I knew something had to be wrong."

How long had she been bleeding like this? Gabriel clenched his teeth and fought the fear rising inside him. She couldn't die. He wouldn't let that happen.

"Get me a blanket off the bed. We're going to take her to the hospital."

Libby did as she was told. "What about the ambulance?"

"There isn't time." Besides, he didn't think he could sit around and watch Olivia slowly bleed to death without going crazy. He'd always prided himself on thought before action, but right now, he was thinking of nothing but saving the woman he'd been yelling at no more than three hours earlier.

Forget that. Focus on getting Olivia to the hospital.

He wrapped her lower half in the blanket and scooped her into his arms. His family had arrived in the hallway just outside the suite. He brushed past his father and brother without answering their offers of help. Olivia was his fiancée. His responsibility.

And he blamed himself for her current crisis. Somehow he knew that if he'd been more approachable, if so much pressure hadn't been brought to bear on her, Olivia might have talked to him about her fertility problems and a safe solution might have been reached.

The limo was waiting at the bottom of the stairs. He settled her into the backseat and cradled her body in his lap. Only then did he become aware of the thundering of his heart. The painful pounding in his chest wasn't caused by carrying her through the palace, but by the sight of her utter stillness and pallor. As the car raced through the palace gates, it finally hit home just how bad this situation was.

"Faster," he growled to the driver as he hooked his finger around a strand of her blond hair and pulled it away from her lips.

The car's powerful engine roared as they sped through the city, but the fifteen-minute drive had never felt so long.

Gabriel brushed his lips across Olivia's forehead and silently pleaded with her to hang on and fight. *Like you fought for her?* Gabriel tried to tune out the mocking inner voice, but guilt sliced at him.

At the hospital's emergency entrance, five people in scrubs crowded the car as soon as it stopped. Stewart must have called ahead and warned them he was coming. They got Olivia situated on a stretcher and took her away before he had a chance to say a word. He rushed toward the glass doors in their wake, catching bits of medical jargon as they sped the unconscious woman inside.

He'd expected to be allowed into the treatment room with her, but a nurse blocked his way.

"Let the doctors work," she said, her voice kind but firm.

He might have ten inches and eighty pounds on her, but Gabriel sensed that the nurse could stop him if he tried to go past.

"How soon will I know something?"

"I'll make sure someone keeps you informed."

"She's lost a lot of blood," he said.

"We know."

She herded him into a private waiting room and offered coffee. Gabriel stared at her, unable to comprehend why this woman was behaving in such a mundane manner while Olivia was down the hall struggling for her life.

"No," he snapped, and then moderated his tone. "Thank you. All I need is information."

She nodded and headed off.

Left alone, Gabriel dropped his head into his hands and surrendered to despair. She couldn't die. She couldn't leave him. He wasn't sure how to step into the future, to become king without her by his side. They would figure a way around her infertility. He recalled his mother's words. She, too, had struggled to produce the heir her husband so desperately needed. When natural methods had failed, she'd gotten help from specialists. And now, she had four children to show for it.

He and Olivia would find specialists, as well. They would have children together.

"Gabriel?"

A hand touched his shoulder. He lifted his head and stared up into his sister's face. She touched his cheek and her fingertips came away with a trace of moisture.

"Is she?" Ariana gasped, seeing his expression.

He shook his head, guessing what conclusion she'd leaped to. "They're working on her now."

"Any word how she's doing?"

"No. The nurse said they'd keep me informed, but she hasn't been back." He glanced at his watch. "That was thirty minutes ago."

What had been happening while he'd been lost in thought? Anxiety flared that he'd had no news. How bad had things gone since she'd been taken away from him?

"She's going to be all right, Gabriel," Ariana said, moving toward him.

Standing, Gabriel wrapped his arms around his sister. She pushed her body against his to offer comfort.

"Your Majesties. Prince Gabriel. Princess Ariana." A

solemn man of average height in pale green scrubs stood five feet away from the royal pair. "I'm Dr. Warner."

Gabriel felt Ariana's tight embrace squeeze his ribs even harder and appreciated her support. "How's Olivia?"

"I won't sugarcoat it. Not good. She's lost a lot of blood." The doctor looked even grimmer as he delivered the next bit of news. "She's still hemorrhaging. We've sent her up to the OR."

A primal cry of denial gathered in Gabriel's chest. "What aren't you telling us?" he demanded.

"The only way to save her may be a hysterectomy. Naturally we will do everything possible to avoid such a drastic procedure."

"Do whatever it takes to save her life." Gabriel pinned the doctor with his gaze, making sure the man understood. "Whatever it takes."

Ten

The first time Olivia opened her eyes, she was aware of nothing but pain. It stabbed at her like slivers of broken glass. Then, something changed. The hurt eased and she fell backward into darkness.

The next time she surfaced, she kept herself awake longer. But not by much. Voices reached her ears, but the speakers were too far away for her to catch individual words. And the pain was back. All she wanted to do was escape into numbness.

They said the third time's the charm. Olivia wasn't sure she agreed when next she regained consciousness. Her body ached. No. Not her body, her abdomen.

Breathless with fear, she stared around the hospital room. It was empty. She was alone.

She felt hollow. Like a balloon filled with air.

The last thing she recalled was fighting with Gabriel. Where was he? Did he know she was in the hospital? Did he even care? Her heart contracted.

"Good to see you awake," a nurse said as she entered the room. "How's your pain?"

"Manageable." Her mouth felt stuffed with cotton. "May I have some water?"

The nurse brought a cup close and placed the straw between Olivia's lips. She sipped gratefully, then sagged back against the pillow, exhausted by the simple movement.

"I feel so weak."

"You've been through a lot."

"What happened to me?"

"The doctor will be along in a little while to talk to you."

Without energy to argue, Olivia closed her eyes and let her mind drift. The silence pressed on her, heightening her tension. She fought to clear her head, sought her last memory. Her period had been heavier than ever before. And the cramping… She'd been afraid, depressed. Gingerly she sent her fingertips questing for the source of her discomfort. Pain shot through her as she pressed on her lower abdomen.

Just then, the door opened again and a handsome older man in scrubs came in. "Good afternoon. I'm Dr. Warner."

"I wish I could say it's nice to meet you."

"I understand. You've been through a tough time."

"What happened to me?" Her mind sharpened as anxiety filled her.

"You were hemorrhaging, and we had a difficult time stopping your blood loss." He plucked her chart out of a pocket attached to the foot of the bed and scrutinized it. "How's your pain?"

"About a six." She waited while he jotted something down on her chart before asking, "How did you stop the hemorrhaging?"

"Surgery." He met her gaze. "It was an extensive procedure."

He hadn't said anything specific, but his expression told her just how extensive the surgery had been.

"I'm never going to have children, am I?"

"I'm sorry. The only way we could stop the bleeding was to remove your uterus."

Olivia shut her eyes to escape the sympathy in the man's face. Denial exploded in her head. She clutched the bed rails, desperate for something to ground her as the world tipped sideways. A wail began in her chest. She clenched her teeth to contain it as a lifetime of discipline and order asserted itself. She would grieve later. In private.

"I know that this will be a difficult adjustment. You are very young to have undergone such a drastic change."

"Who knows?" she whispered.

He looked taken aback. "Your father. The royal family."

"The media?"

"Of course not." Dr. Warner looked appalled.

"Is my father here?"

"He's in the waiting room with Prince Gabriel. I spoke with him an hour ago."

"Could I see him, please? No one else, just my father."

"I'll have the nurse fetch him for you."

But the man who showed up next wasn't a sixty-year-old British earl with gray hair and a neat beard, but a tall, hollow-eyed man with a dark shadow blurring his knife-sharp jawline. Olivia's heartbeat accelerated as Gabriel advanced into the room, his clothes rumpled, his face a mask. He reached out to cover her hand with his, but she moved it away just in time.

"I'm sorry," she said, unable to lift her gaze higher than the open collar of his white shirt. "I should have told you about my medical issues. I just thought that everything was going to be okay."

"You gave us a scare." He pulled a chair beside her bed and lowered himself into it. This put him at eye level with her and made avoiding his fierce golden gaze that much harder. "When I found you on the floor of the bathroom unconscious." His tone made it hard for Olivia to breathe. "I thought…" He shook his head.

"I'm sorry. I had no idea that quitting the pill was going to cause this much…" To her dismay a sob popped out. Just like that. No warning. No chance to swallow it or choke on it. Then tears were streaming down her face and Gabriel was stroking her hair and squeezing her hand. His gentleness only made her feel worse.

"Olivia, I'm so sorry."

He placed her palm against his cheek. The warmth beneath her fingers spread up her arm and drifted through her entire body as she took in the aching sadness in his eyes.

"I'm going to be fine," she lied, hating how much she wanted to lean on him for support. Choking on her misery, she barreled on. "At least now there's no question whether I can have children. You'll never have to wonder if by marrying me you made a huge mistake."

"Marrying you would never have been a mistake."

But if she'd had difficulty getting pregnant, he couldn't help but blame her.

"That's a moot point." She willed herself to be strong and to make the break quick and final. "We can't marry now."

"I'm not giving up on us." He covered her hand with his and regarded her with somber eyes.

"There is no more us, Gabriel." She tugged her hand free. "You are going to be king of Sherdana one day. You need to put your country's needs first."

"I have two brothers—"

"Please." She couldn't bear to hear any more. Anything he said would encourage her to be optimistic and the last thing she needed to do was hope everything was going to be okay. "I'm really tired. And I'm in pain. I just want to see my father."

He looked as if he wanted to argue with her. She shook her head and closed her eyes. Another tear trickled down her cheek, but she ignored it.

"And I think it would be better if you don't visit me again."

"I can't accept that."

"Please, Gabriel."

He exhaled harshly. "I'll get your father."

She waited to open her eyes until his soft footfalls receded. Her fingers tingled from contact with Gabriel's cheek. It brought to mind all those times when her hands had roamed over him, exploring his masculine contours, learning all the delightful ways his body differed from hers.

Reaching toward a nearby box of tissues exhausted her. The weakness was frustrating. Before she had the chance to lose herself in the black cloud of misery that hovered nearby, her father entered the room. His embrace stirred up emotions again and Olivia began to cry once more. This time, however, she didn't feel the need to hold back. His shirt was soaked by the time she ran out of tears.

"I want to go home," she told him, making use of the tissue box once again.

"The doctor wants to keep you in here for at least a week."

"Can't I be transferred to a hospital in London?"

"You are in no shape to travel." He patted her hand. "It's just a week. Then I'll take you home."

A week. It was too long. More than her body needed to heal and that wouldn't be possible until she was miles and miles from Sherdana and its prince.

Shortly after speaking with Olivia, Gabriel returned to the palace alone, his emotions in turmoil. Staff scattered as he crossed the expansive foyer, heading for his office. The way they disappeared he must have looked like the devil himself had come calling.

It had shocked him that after she'd survived her brush with death, her first act would be to end their engagement. She'd done it gracefully, shouldering the responsibility, leaving him free to move on with a clear conscience.

"Move on."

He spat out the words like the foulest curse. No matter how angry he'd been when he found out about her medical condition, he'd not really considered ending things. How could he ever replace Olivia in his life after making love with her? Watching her with his daughters? Seeing that damned tattoo. *Hope.* He could sure use some right now.

Entering his office, he flung himself into a chair near the cold fireplace. He'd been up all night. Exhaustion should be eating into his bones and muscles, but rage burned white-hot in his veins. He massaged his temples where a headache had begun the minute he'd walked out of Olivia's hospital room. Or perhaps it had been there all along. Up until that moment, he'd been completely focused on Olivia.

But after leaving her bedside, he realized that his role in her life was over. As was her role in his. From now on they would be nothing more than familiar strangers. He would probably not exchange a dozen words with her before she left for England and her old life.

God, his chest ached.

"Your Highness?" Gabriel's secretary had poked his head in the door.

"Not now, Stewart."

He needed some time to adjust. How much time, he didn't know. He'd never imagined having to live without Olivia and he wasn't going to pretend that he could just shake off this tragedy and continue on.

"Your Highness," Stewart persisted. "Your father, the king, wants to speak with you."

"I know my father is the king," Gabriel said, taking his annoyance out on his private secretary. He pushed out of the chair, deciding to face whatever his father had to say now rather that make the king wait until he'd showered and changed.

He found his father on the phone in his office and went

to pour himself a shot of scotch while he waited for him to conclude the call.

"A little early for that, isn't it?" the king demanded as he hung up.

"I think a man's entitled to a drink after his fiancée breaks up with him, don't you?"

The king shot him a hard glance as he rose to his feet and crossed to the tray with the coffeepot and cups. Pouring a cup, he plucked the crystal tumbler from Gabriel's finger and replaced it with bone china.

"I just got off the phone with Lord Darcy. He told me you and Olivia ended things."

Ah, so the old man was pulling his offer to set up a company since his daughter was no longer going to be Sherdana's queen. Gabriel shrugged. He didn't really blame the earl for changing his mind.

"She ended it," he said. "But don't worry. Christian will find us some other prospective investors." He sipped the coffee and regarded his father over the brim. "Perhaps one of them will even have an eligible daughter since apparently I'm back on the market."

The king let Gabriel's bitter comment pass unanswered. "Naturally, I would like to continue pursuing other companies, but the need isn't urgent. Darcy is going forward with his plans."

Gabriel's cup hit the saucer with a clatter. From his contact with Lord Darcy, he knew the man was a hardheaded businessman. Sherdana was a good choice for expansion, but not his only and not necessarily his best.

Olivia.

This was her doing.

The exhaustion he'd expected to feel earlier washed over him now. Gabriel wavered on his feet. "Olivia must have told him to honor the commitment. There's no other reason for Darcy to proceed."

"But if she knows you're not getting married, why would she persuade her father to honor his commitment to us?"

"Because that's the sort of woman she is," Gabriel said. "Honorable. The sort who doesn't go back on a promise. Unlike me," he finished in an undertone.

This time, his bitterness was too much for his father to ignore. "You are not reneging on a promise to Lady Darcy," the king said. "She understands she will never be able to give you an heir and has graciously ended your engagement."

That's when it hit him. He didn't want their engagement to end.

Olivia had promised to marry him. And if she was as honorable as he'd just described, she still would.

After six endless days in the hospital, with pain and grief her constant companions, Olivia was an empty shell in both body and soul. For the majority of her stay she'd lain with her eyes closed, floating on a tide of pain medication that dulled the ache in her lower abdomen but couldn't blunt the agony in her heart. With her ability to bear children ripped from her, she shrank from her future. Abandoned by optimism, tears filled her eyes and ran unheeded down her cheeks. Her losses were too much to bear.

On the third day of her incarceration, Libby had smuggled in her favorite chocolate. Olivia had put on a show of courage for her private secretary, but left alone once more, she'd retreated to the dark place where she contemplated what her life had become.

Then, this morning, twenty-four hours before she was scheduled for release, she instructed Libby to bring her files so she could compile a list of all the things she'd committed to in the past month.

"Are you sure you should be taxing yourself with this?" Libby protested, a dozen files clutched to her chest.

Olivia indicated that she wanted the files placed on the rolling tray positioned over her bed. "I've got to find something to keep my mind busy, or I'll go completely mad."

Libby did as she was told and then retreated to the guest chair with her laptop. "Prince Gabriel…" the private secretary began, breaking off when Olivia shook her head.

"How are Bethany and Karina?"

"They miss you." Libby opened the laptop and stared at the screen. "Everyone at the palace misses you."

Not wishing to go down that path, Olivia changed the subject. "Have they found Marissa's sister yet?"

"I'm afraid not."

The memory of the woman's attack had resurfaced a couple days after Olivia had woken up. It hadn't struck her as odd that no one asked about the incident because she'd assumed Marissa's sister had fled the palace with no one being the wiser.

When she'd shared the story with Libby, Olivia had learned what had happened after she'd passed out in the bathroom. She'd given herself a couple seconds to regret the loss of her wardrobe and then insisted on telling her story to palace security and the police.

"Her apartment in Milan is being watched," Libby continued, "but she hasn't returned there. From what I gather, she hasn't contacted her friends in six months. But I'm sure Prince Gabriel will not be satisfied until she's caught."

"I'll feel better when that happens," Olivia said, and opened the file sitting on top of the pile. It was a budget proposal for some improvements to a school she sponsored in Kenya.

The mundane work soothed her spirit. Nothing better for the soul than to worry about someone else's problems.

Ariana and Christian visited several times in the next

few days and brought regards from the king and queen as well as flowers. But Gabriel had been absent. She'd sent him away and asked Libby to make certain he understood that she wanted him to maintain his distance. Her grief was still too strong. She wasn't ready to face him. Not until she came to terms with the end of her engagement and her empty future.

"Prince Gabriel is desperately worried about you," Libby said.

As sweet as it was for Libby to say, Olivia doubted her use of the word *desperately*.

"I hope you've told him I'm recovering nicely."

"He might like to see that for himself."

Olivia's throat tightened and she shook her head. The words blurred on the sheet of paper she held in her hand and she blinked to clear her vision.

"He really cares for you. It's obvious." Libby sat forward, her eyes bright and intense. "I don't think I've ever seen a man so distraught as when we thought you might die. He commanded the doctor to do whatever it took to save you."

Joy dispelled Olivia's gloom for a moment as she let herself warm to Libby's interpretation of events. "Of course he cares," she agreed, wishing the situation was as simple as that. "We became…close these last few weeks. But he needs an heir. That's something I can't give him."

"But you love him. Surely that counts for more." Libby spoke quietly as if afraid of how Olivia would react to her audacity.

Olivia starting drawing circles on the notepad. She did love Gabriel, but he must never know. She didn't want to burden him with something like that. He already had enough guilt on his shoulders with Marissa. He didn't need to suffer even more regret because another woman entertained a desperate and impossible love for him.

"I love him, but please do not tell a soul," she rushed on as Libby's face lit up. "Prince Gabriel needs to find someone new to marry. I don't want him thinking of me at all as he goes about courting his future bride."

The thought of Gabriel with another woman made her heart ache, but she fought the pain.

Libby's delight became determination. "I really think he needs to know."

Olivia offered her friend a sad smile. "He can't. Sherdana deserves a queen who can have children."

"What about what you deserve?" Libby pushed. "Don't you deserve to be happy?"

"I will be," she assured her secretary. "My life isn't over. I'm just starting a new chapter. Not the one I expected to be starting, but how often do we get exactly what we expect?"

Eleven

Staring at pictures of women he'd rejected six months ago wasn't stimulating Gabriel's appetite for lunch.

"What do you think of Reinette du Piney?" his mother asked, sliding an eight-by-ten head shot of a very beautiful brunette across the table toward him.

"She's pigeon-toed," he replied, slipping his spoon beneath a carrot and lifting it free of the broth. "What exactly is it I'm eating?"

"Creamy carrot soup with anise. The chef is experimenting again."

"You really must stop him from inflicting his culinary curiosity on us."

"Gabriel, you cannot reject du Piney because she's pigeon-toed."

He wasn't. He was rejecting her because the only woman he wanted to marry had made it clear she was going to do the right thing for Sherdana even if he wouldn't.

In the meantime, his mother had persisted in starting the search for his future wife all over again, despite Gabriel's refusal to contribute anything positive.

"I'm only thinking of our children," he countered, setting his spoon down and tossing his napkin over it. "Imagine how they'd be teased at school if they inherited their mother's unfortunate trait."

"Your children will not be teased at school because

they will be tutored at home the way you and your siblings were." His mother sifted through the pictures and pulled out another. "What about Amelia? You liked her."

"She was pleasant enough. But I think her husband would take umbrage with me for poaching his wife."

"Bother."

Gabriel might have felt like smiling at his mother's equivalent of a curse if he wasn't feeling so damned surly. Olivia had left the hospital a few days ago and was staying at the Royal Caron Hotel until her surgeon cleared her for travel. By bribing the man with an enormous donation toward updating the hospital with digital radiology, Gabriel had succeeded in keeping her in Sherdana longer than necessary. He'd hoped she would let him apologize to her in person, but she adamantly refused to see him.

"Gabriel, are you listening to me?"

"I'm not going to marry any of these women."

His mother sat back and stared at him, her eyes narrowed and searching. "Have you decided on someone else?"

"Yes. The same person I've wanted all along."

"Olivia."

"You don't sound surprised."

"You take after your father. He's a romantic devil, too." Her eyes sparkled at Gabriel's doubtful expression. "Oh, not that anyone other than me would know it, but he wouldn't consider divorcing me when I couldn't get pregnant. Even after I left him and made him think that I'd fallen in love with another man."

"What?" This was a tale he'd never heard. "You fell in love with someone while you were married to Father?"

His mother laughed gaily. "Of course not. But I certainly convinced your father I did." A faraway look entered her eyes. "But he chased after me and discovered there was no other man. I finally admitted that the doctor told me I couldn't get pregnant the old-fashioned way and together we figured out a solution."

That sounded familiar. Except for the part where a solution was found together.

"I'm surprised," Gabriel admitted.

"Because your father counseled you to break your engagement with Olivia even before the hysterectomy? You need to understand how difficult those days were for us. The doubt, the worry. It was hard on us. Hard on our marriage. And we were deeply in love."

Her last words struck a nerve. "And Olivia and I are not." His mother's assumption annoyed him more than it should.

Given that he'd only just begun to get acquainted with the woman he had been planning to marry, it made sense that he couldn't possibly love her.

And if not love, then what emotion was at the root of his miserable existence without Olivia?

"He just wants to spare you." She reached across the table and laid her hand over his. "We both do."

Gabriel captured her gaze. "Would you change anything about the decision you made? Knowing the trials and heartbreak you suffered, would you walk away from the man you love and never look back?"

His mother withdrew her hand and sat back. Her expression was determined and sad at the same time. "No."

"Thank you."

He stood and circled the table to kiss her cheek. Expecting her to ask what he was up to, she surprised him again by staying silent.

Leaving his mother, he headed upstairs to await Olivia's arrival. She'd made arrangements through his mother to visit Bethany and Karina and bring them a special birthday present. Gabriel knew it was cheating to use his daughters to secure time with Olivia, but he was feeling a little desperate. If his daughters had taught him anything it was how to exist in the moment. There was no past or future with them. They lived for hugs, treats, mischief and pony rides. Every second in their company reminded him that wonderful things came out of less than ideal situations.

The twins weren't in the nursery. He'd arranged for them to have a picnic in the garden. In half an hour they would arrive for their nap. He hoped that gave him enough time with Olivia. While he waited, he sat on Bethany's bed and picked up the photo of Marissa on the girls' nightstand. A scrapbook had been among the twins' possessions. Olivia had chosen this particular picture to frame and place between the girls so they would remember their mother.

Marissa was pregnant in the picture. Not full-term, perhaps seven months, yet still huge. Had she known she was carrying twins? He traced her smile with his fingertips. She looked older than he remembered, aged by experience, not years, yet luminescent in motherhood.

Why hadn't she contacted him when she knew she was pregnant? Had she not wished to burden him? Had she feared his rejection yet again? He couldn't have married her. Wouldn't have married her. Even if Sherdana's laws hadn't dictated his bride needed to be a citizen of the country or of noble birth for his offspring to be able to inherit the crown, where Gabriel and Marissa had been most compatible was between the sheets, which was where they'd spent half of their time together.

Out of bed, her passionate nature had revealed itself in turbulent emotions and insecurity. He knew the latter had been his fault. He couldn't offer her a future and she'd deserved better. In the end, he'd let her go and part of him had been relieved.

He'd put Sherdana's needs before hers. He'd done the same with Olivia. Only this time there was no certainty that he'd made the right decision. No sense that a burden had been lifted from his shoulders. His daughters were the only bright spot in his future. His mother wanted him to consider who would become his princess, but he couldn't make that decision until he spoke with Olivia and saw for himself what was in her heart.

Olivia took on the challenge of the palace stairs at a sedate pace, but was uncomfortably short of breath by the time she reached the first landing. Several maids trotted past her, but none of the staff paid her undue attention. Still, she felt like an interloper in the place where she thought she'd spend the rest of her life.

Relaxing her grip on the gaily wrapped packages containing china dolls, Olivia forced herself to keep climbing. As beautiful as the dolls were, giving toddlers such delicate toys was probably a recipe for disaster. But Olivia wanted to share with the girls something special. The dolls were just like the one her mother had bought for her and not lived to present the gift.

In her heart Olivia knew it was selfish of her to want them to remember her. First their mother had died and now they faced the loss of someone else they relied on. It was too much change for ones so young. At least they would still have their father. Olivia was comforted by how much Gabriel loved his daughters.

In two days the twins turned two. The party Olivia had spent weeks planning had stirred the palace into new heights of frantic activity. As much as Olivia wanted to go, attending was out of the question. Even though she knew the twins would want her there, they were undoubtedly the only members of the royal family who would.

Who could blame them? Olivia knew the end of her engagement to Gabriel had driven the media into a frenzy of speculation about whom he might choose for his next bride. Social networks had blown up with news about the top two candidates. As long as Olivia remained in the picture, the news outlets would stir the pot. It was better if she disappeared from Sherdana. But she couldn't go without saying goodbye to Bethany and Karina.

Her slow rise to the second floor gave Olivia lots of time to remember how golden her future had seemed the first time she'd ascended these stairs and to brood about the handsome prince who'd never be hers.

Coming to the palace was a risk. She might run into Gabriel and lose the modicum of peace she'd made with her situation. At the same time, she was foolishly excited at the thought of running into Gabriel again. Even knowing they could never be together didn't stop her from longing to see him one last time.

It was irrational, but she'd been hurt that he'd heeded her desire for no further contact after her surgery. She'd broken things off. While part of her was relieved that he'd honored her wishes, her less rational side had resented Gabriel for taking her at her word.

But what truly upset her was, after everything that had happened, she continued to crave his company. She woke from dreams where he held her close and whispered she was his life, his dearest love, and discovered she was alone. And all along, her heart hung heavy in her chest. Emptiness lingered below the stinging incision in her abdomen. Depression coiled about her thoughts, threatening to smother her. A dozen get-well bouquets brightened her hotel suite but couldn't pierce the fog surrounding her emotions.

Olivia paused at the top step and leaned on the banister to catch her breath before proceeding down the hall to the nursery. She knew the twins would be finishing up lunch and had chosen this time to visit because it limited how long she would stay.

When she got to the nursery, she stopped just inside the

doorway, but didn't see the twins. Instead, Gabriel occupied the space. Her heart gave a giddy leap. He sat on Bethany's bed, a silver frame in his hands, fingertips tenderly resting on the face of the woman in the photo. Marissa.

His expression held such sorrow, his mouth drooping in regret as she'd never seen before. Her heart wept for his obvious grief, but the tears that sprang to her eyes weren't for Gabriel; they were for herself. She'd believed him when he claimed to be over Marissa, but three years later he continued to grieve for what could never be. Was that how she looked in those unguarded moments when she thought about all she'd lost? Was this what it looked like when a heart shattered?

Suddenly this errand didn't seem like a good idea. She should have let Libby bring Bethany and Karina to the hotel instead of returning to the palace. But the media had camped out in front of the hotel in the hope that she'd comment on her broken engagement. During the short walk from lobby door to car, Olivia had worn dark glasses and a wide brimmed hat to prevent the photographers from catching a newsworthy photo of her. Olivia couldn't put the girls in the middle of the chaos.

"Olivia!"

Gabriel's head snapped up at the enthusiastic cries coming from behind her. His gaze crashed into hers. She wobbled beneath the triple impact of the twins wrapping their arms around her hips and the raw emotion in Gabriel's eyes.

The twins' demands for attention offered her no chance to react to what she'd seen, but she was glad. Remaining upright as they pressed against her became that much harder thanks to the bulky, delicate bundles she carried.

Gabriel stepped forward and took the packages from her. "Girls, be gentle with Olivia. She's been sick and is very fragile."

The glow in his eyes warmed her head to toe as he extricated her from the twins' enthusiastic embrace. She had a hard time looking away.

"Don't like sick," Bethany proclaimed, her lower lip slipping forward.

Karina gave her head a vigorous shake.

"I'm much better now, but still a little sore. Like when you skin your knee how it takes a while to stop hurting."

Karina bent down to touch Olivia's unblemished knees. "Hurt?"

Olivia laughed. "No, angel. My knees are okay. My hurt is here." She pointed to her stomach.

"Can we see?" Bethany demanded.

Olivia gestured toward the packages Gabriel had set on their beds. "Why don't you open your birthday presents instead."

"Birthday."

Olivia smiled past her sadness at having to go home to England and never see these girls again. "They are very special. I hope you like them."

While the girls tore into the wrapping, Olivia watched them, but her attention was captured by the tall man who stood so close beside her. It seemed the worst sort of torture not to lean into his strength and forget about the past week. But the twinges in her abdomen kept her grounded in reality.

"That was a lovely gift," Gabriel said as the girls fell to exclaiming over the dolls' hair and wardrobe.

"Something for them to remember me by." Emotion seized her by the throat. "I didn't realize leaving them was going to be so hard."

"You could stay longer."

Olivia flinched at how her heart leaped with hope. "I can't, and it's not fair of you to ask."

Why would he even want her to stay? He knew as well

as she did that having her around would create problems for him both in the media and in his search for a bride.

"A lot of things haven't been fair lately." He brushed her hair off one shoulder, grazing her skin in the process.

To Olivia's immense shock, desire sparked. How was it possible after all she'd been through? She looked up to see if Gabriel had noticed her reaction and to her dismay, he had.

"Olivia." His deep voice rumbled in his chest, creating a matching vibration in her. "We need to talk." He found her hand with his.

The slide of his fingers against hers made her heart race. "I think we've said everything there is to say."

"Maybe you have, but I have a few things you need to hear."

Olivia's gaze shot toward the twins. To her relief, they were oblivious to the charged undercurrents passing between her and Gabriel. The girls had been through enough and didn't deserve to witness them arguing. She turned her back to them and pitched her voice to carry no farther than the foot that separated her from Gabriel.

"Don't do this. There's nothing you have to say that I want to hear. What I need is to leave this country and forget all about you."

"Can you do that?" he murmured, his free hand cupping the side of her face, his tender touch bringing tears to her eyes. "Can you forget me? Forget how it was between us?"

Harsh emotions sandblasted her nerves raw. "Would you want me to do otherwise?"

"Yes. Stay and fight—"

"Fight?" The word gusted out of her on a bitter laugh. "I have nothing left to fight with. It's gone, Gabriel. My ability to bear children. My chance to be a mother. I'm nothing more than a shell." An empty shell without him. "I just want to go home and forget."

Forget how his smile transformed her.

Forget how it felt to fall asleep in his arms.

Forget how much she loved him.

"Can you?" He cupped the back of her neck and pulled her gently against his powerful, muscular body. "Can you forget me?"

Her pulse danced with erotic longing. She tore her gaze away from the sensual light in his eyes that drew her like a candle in the darkness. How was it possible she could want him with such intensity when the parts that made her a whole woman were gone?

He lowered his voice to a husky murmur. "Because I will never be able to forget you."

It wasn't fair of him to tell her that. To tantalize her with longing for what could never be.

Contact with him seared her from breast to thigh. Her incision burned the way it had during those first few days, reminding her that she'd have a permanent mark on her body that would never let her forget.

"Maybe not forget," she told him, keeping her voice soft to hide its unsteadiness. "But you'll move on and be happy."

Before he could respond, they were struck from two sides by the twins. Sandwiched between them, Olivia had no way to escape Gabriel. He saw her predicament and a predatory smile curved his lips before they descended to hers.

Sweet sunshine washed through her body as she surrendered to the delicious drag of his mouth against hers. This was where she belonged. To this man. And these girls. The family she craved.

Her whole world contracted to Gabriel's kiss and the twins' hugs. A great rushing sound filled her ears, drowning out her inner voice and all the reasons why this couldn't be her future. Loving Gabriel had never seemed so easy.

Outside pressure didn't exist. She was free to express herself, to tell him what was truly in her heart.

I love you.

But she never uttered the words because the girls clamored for their own share of Olivia's attention as the kiss fell apart. Her lips tingled in the aftermath as Gabriel held her close a moment longer before letting her step back.

"Tea party. Tea party," Bethany called.

Karina seized her and pulled.

It took her a couple seconds to realize that the girls were referring to the small table set up near the window. She shook her head. "It's your nap time."

"Girls, Olivia is right. Hattie will read to you after you lie down."

While it hurt to kneel and give hugs and kisses to each of the toddlers, Olivia braved the pain for one last goodbye. By the time they had been persuaded to let her go, Olivia's sorrow had rendered her mute.

Gabriel seemed to understand her distress because he waited until they'd descended to the grand hall before speaking. "When are you leaving?"

"My final doctor's appointment is later this week. I expect to be able to travel after that."

"You really should come to the twins' birthday party. You planned everything. It's only right that you be there."

Temptation trembled through her. It would be so easy to agree, to prolong the final parting for another day. But what good would that do? She'd have one more memory to keep her awake at night.

"I think it's better that we said our goodbyes now."

"I don't agree." He took her hand and stopped her from leaving. His gold eyes were somber as he met her gaze. "Bethany and Karina will be sad if you don't come."

His touch made her want to turn back the clock. If she'd not been so rash as to stop taking the pill against her doctor's order, she would be marrying Gabriel in a week. Then again, the burden of producing an heir to the kingdom would still be weighing heavily on her.

"And I'm not ready to say goodbye," he said, interrupting her thoughts.

She delighted at his words, until she recalled how he'd looked at that photo of Marissa. Three years ago he'd turned his back on her and chosen his country instead. Olivia had seen the way he'd been tortured by that choice every time he looked at his daughters. Was he hoping that putting his country's needs second this time would somehow redeem him for failing Marissa?

She eased her hand free. "You already have. The second the story of my fertility issues made it to prime time any chance of us getting married was gone." She touched his arm in sympathy. "People in our positions don't belong to themselves."

"That's true," he murmured, seizing her chin and forcing her to look at him. "You belong to me."

She jerked away and took a step back. "I don't." But her blood sang another tune. She was his, heart and soul. There would be no other.

"Deny it all you want, but I was the first man who made love to you. The first man you loved. That sort of bond may stretch but it will not break."

Her pulse rocked at his use of the word *love*. Did he know the depth of her feelings for him? She'd not been particularly careful to guard her emotions during those long hours in his arms. Had he figured out the truth or was he simply referring to the physical act of loving?

"Why are you saying these things? Do you think leaving is easy for me?" She spied the front door and knew her reprieve was mere steps away, but she had a few hard truths to deliver first. "I was planning on making my life here with you. It hurts more than I can say that I can't marry you. Asking me to stay is completely—"

"Selfish," he interrupted, lifting her palm to his lips. "You're right. I am selfish."

When he released her hand, Olivia clenched her fingers around the kiss. His blunt admission had dimmed her frustration. This impossible situation was of her making. If only she'd told him of her fertility issues. He never would have proposed. She never would have fallen in love with him.

"You have a right to be selfish sometimes." Her smile wobbled, and then steadied. "You are a prince, after all."

"And yet it's not gaining me any ground with you, is it?"

She shook her head. "I'll come to the twins' birthday party."

It wasn't what she'd intended to say, but her heart had a mind of its own. Knowing she would never be able to take it back, Olivia remained silent as Gabriel escorted her to the waiting car and handed her into the backseat.

As the car rolled down the driveway, Olivia knew she'd been a fool to come here today. Obviously she hadn't learned anything these past few weeks. Gabriel held a power over her that was nothing short of dangerous. Thank goodness he would never know how unhappy she was without him because she had a feeling he might do something incredibly foolish.

Twelve

For the next two days leading up to his daughters' birthday party, Gabriel worked tirelessly to bring Christian up to speed on all the things that might come up in the next two weeks. After his last encounter with Olivia, he'd decided to take himself off the grid for a short time. Olivia's stubborn refusal to continue their relationship had forced Gabriel into a difficult position. Sherdana needed a royal heir. He needed Olivia. The opposing forces were tearing him apart.

On the morning of Bethany and Karina's birthday, Gabriel put his signature on the last report requiring his approval and went to have breakfast with his daughters. As usual they were full of energy and he smiled as he listened to their excited conversation.

It pleased him that Karina spoke more often now. Maybe she'd never be as talkative as her sibling, but as her confidence grew, she demonstrated a bright mind and a sly sense of humor. He had Olivia to thank for the transformation. She'd coaxed the younger twin out of her shell with patience and love. As attached as the trio had become, Gabriel was worried that Olivia's leaving would give rise to the girls' feelings of abandonment.

Scooping Karina onto his lap, he tickled her until she whooped with laughter. Could he make Olivia understand that there was more at stake than an heir for Sherdana?

Perhaps today's party would be the perfect opportunity to impress upon her how much she was needed and loved.

The festivities began at three. A large tent had been erected on the expansive lawn just east of the palace. A band played children's songs nearby and a dozen children jumped and twirled to the music in the open space between the stage and the linen-clad tables. Beyond that was a balloon bouncer shaped like a castle. The structure swayed as children burned off energy. On the opposite side of the lawn, their parents enjoyed more sedate entertainment in the form of an overflowing buffet of delicacies and free-flowing alcohol.

The crowd was a mix of wealthy nobility and leading businessmen. Gabriel stayed close to Bethany and Karina as they ate cake and played with the other children, keeping an eye out for Olivia as the afternoon progressed. She didn't arrive until almost five.

Looking pale and very beautiful in a light pink dress with short fluttery sleeves, she moved through the crowd, smiling politely when she encountered someone familiar, but otherwise avoiding eye contact with the guests.

Gabriel snagged a pair of wineglasses off the tray of a passing waiter. It was a chardonnay from one of Sherdana's finest wineries and he remembered how Olivia had wanted to tour the wine country. He added that to the list of things he'd promised and never delivered.

She caught sight of him when she was thirty feet away and very much looked as if she'd like to run away. Besieged by the memory of the kiss they'd shared in the nursery and the longing he'd tasted on her lips, Gabriel knew the only way to circumvent her stubbornness was to demonstrate the power of their passion for each other.

"I'm glad you came," he told her, as he drew close enough to speak. "I was beginning to worry that you wouldn't."

"I almost didn't." Her expression was rueful as she accepted the glass of wine he offered. "But I promised that I would."

"Bethany and Karina will be very glad."

Her gaze moved to where the twins were running with several children close to their age. "They look like they're having fun."

"All thanks to you. The party is fantastic."

"Libby did most of the work."

"But you are the one who came up with the concept and organized everything. You have quite a knack for party planning."

"In London I was on committees for several charities. I've done several large events, including children's parties. And speaking of children, I should probably say hello to Bethany and Karina. I won't be able to stay at the party long."

He inspected her face. Shadows beneath her eyes gave her the appearance of fragility. "Are you in pain?"

"Just tired." Her wan smile held none of her former liveliness. "My strength is not coming back as quickly as I'd like and I'm not sleeping well."

Gabriel tucked her hand into the crook of his arm and led her on a slow, meandering journey toward the twins, extending the amount of his time in her company. The tension in her slim frame troubled him and Gabriel wished he could do something to bring back the happy, vital woman she'd been two weeks earlier. He'd never felt so helpless.

Before he could bring her to where the twins were holding court, his daughters saw them coming and ran over. As they threw their tiny arms around her, Olivia's smile grew radiant. But there was sadness, as well. Sadness Gabriel knew he could banish if only she'd let him.

Hyped up on sweets and attention, the twins didn't linger long. After they'd raced back toward the other children, Olivia sidestepped away from Gabriel.

"I've taken up enough of your time," she said. "You have guests to attend to and I need to go."

He caught her wrist, preventing her from departing. "You're the only one I care about."

"Please don't," she pleaded in a hoarse whisper. "This is already so hard."

"And that's my fault." This wasn't a discussion he wanted to have in the middle of his daughters' birthday party, but he had to try one last time to reason with her. "Let me at least walk you out."

She must have seen his determination because she nodded.

Instead of leading her around the palace, he drew her through the doors leading to the green salon where they could have a little privacy.

"I'm sorry I didn't handle things better between us."

When he stopped in the middle of the room and turned her to face him she sighed. Looking resigned, she met his gaze. "You handled everything the way a future king should. I was the one who was wrong. I should have told you about my past medical issues before you had a chance to propose."

"What if I told you it wouldn't have mattered?" Gabriel lifted her hand and placed her palm over his heart.

"Then I would have to insult the crown prince of Sherdana by telling him he's a fool." She tried to pull her hand free, but he'd trapped it beneath his. Her tone grew more impatient. "You need an heir. That's something I can't give you."

"Unfortunate, yes. But that doesn't change the fact that I chose you and I'd committed to building a life with you. I'm not ready to give that up."

"That's madness," she exclaimed. "You have to. You must marry someone who can give you children."

Gabriel scowled at her response. "That's what the country needs me to do. But I'm not a country. I'm a man. A man who is tired of making everyone else's priorities his own."

"You don't have a choice," she whispered, blinking rapidly. "You are going to be king. You must do what's right. And so must I." With surprising strength, she wrenched her hand free and turned to flee.

"Olivia." He started after her, but realized nothing he could say at that moment would persuade her to change her mind.

Releasing a string of curses, Gabriel pulled out his cell phone and dialed. When the call connected, he said, "She won't budge."

"I'm sorry to hear that, Your Highness. The arrangements you asked for are complete and awaiting your arrival. Are you still planning on traveling the day after tomorrow?"

"Yes."

With the upheaval of the past several weeks, this was probably not the best time for him to leave the country, but he'd let the impossible situation with Olivia go on too long. She'd been right to say he didn't have a choice about his future. Fate had set him on a path and he needed to follow it to the end.

He found his parents together in the garden. They were strolling arm in arm, pausing here and there to greet their guests and enjoying the warm afternoon. He almost hated to spoil their peaceful moment.

"It was lovely of Olivia to come today," his mother said.

"She wanted to wish Bethany and Karina a happy birthday."

"You spent a lot of time with her." The queen's voice held a question.

Gabriel wondered how much his mother knew about his intentions. "It was her first social appearance since our engagement ended. I thought she could use the support."

"Of course. What happened with her was tragic and we cannot be seen turning our backs on her." Although the queen had spoken sympathetically about Olivia's plight, her priorities were her family and the country. "But you must not encourage her."

A bitter laugh escaped him. "She's well aware that I need a wife who can have children. If you think anything different, you don't appreciate her character."

The queen gave Gabriel a hard look. "Of course."

Gabriel shifted his gaze to his daughters. A trio of pre-teen girls were chasing the twins through the gardens. They laughed as they ran and Gabriel's heart lightened at the sound.

"I wanted to let you know," he began, returning his attention to his parents, "that in a couple days, I'm going out of town for a week or so."

"Is this the best time?" his father asked, echoing what Gabriel had been thinking minutes earlier.

"Perhaps not, but I have the future to think about and Sherdana still needs a princess."

The king frowned. "What about the state dinner for the Spanish ambassador?"

"Christian can take over while I'm gone." Gabriel forced his shoulders to relax. "I'm not the only prince in this family, you know. It's about time my brothers remembered that."

"I'm glad to hear you're ready to move forward," his mother said. "Can you give us some hint of your plans?"

"I'd rather wait until everything is finalized before I say anything."

"Very sensible," his father said and Gabriel wondered if the king would feel that way if he had any idea where his son was going and why.

Two days after the twins' birthday party, Olivia sat in an examination room, awaiting the doctor and fighting sadness. She was flying back to London in the morning. Back to her flat and her friends.

Her return would be far from triumphant. She'd been stripped of the ability to have children and because of that lost the man she loved. Thinking about the future only intensified her grief, so she'd spent the past few days finishing up the tasks she'd left undone such as the finalization of the menu for the hospital's children's wing gala taking place the following month and writing to cancel the invitations she'd accepted when she was still Gabriel's fiancée.

After ten minutes of waiting, Dr. Warner entered the room and interrupted her thoughts. Olivia was glad he accepted her assurances that she was getting along just fine in the wake of her hysterectomy and didn't voice the concern hovering in his expression. If he'd encouraged her to talk about her emotional health she might have burst into tears.

"Everything looks good," the doctor announced. "No reason you can't travel whenever you want."

"I'm leaving tomorrow," she said.

"Make sure you check in with your regular doctor within a week or two. He should be able to assist you with any side effects from your procedure and recommend a fertility specialist."

"Fertility specialist?" she echoed. "I don't understand. I can't have children."

"You can't bear children," the doctor agreed. "But your ovaries are intact. It might be possible to harvest your eggs and freeze them in case you decide to pursue motherhood in the future."

"I could be a mother?" Olivia breathed, overcome by the possibility that something she'd longed for with all her heart could still come to pass.

"You'd need to find a surrogate," the doctor said, his eyes twinkling. "And of course, you'd need a father, but it's certainly a possibility."

"I never imagined…" Her voice trailed off.

"Medical science is making miracles happen every day."

The doctor left her alone to dress and Olivia went through the motions in a daze. Her first impulse was to call Gabriel and tell him her news. Then she imagined how that call would go.

Gabriel, I have great news, I might be able to be a mother, after all. It's chancy and it will involve another woman carrying the baby, but it would be my egg.

Could a country as traditional as Sherdana accept a prince conceived in a test tube? And raised by a mother who hadn't actually carried him inside her for nine months?

Could Gabriel?

When Olivia returned to her suite at the hotel, she couldn't stop pacing as her mind spun through her options. Possible scenarios crowded her like desperate beggars in need of coin. Staring out the window at the river, she held her phone against her chest and searched for the courage she needed to dial Gabriel's number and tell him that she loved him and find out if he was willing to take a risk with her.

The sun had set by the time she dialed. With her heart pounding against her ribs, she counted rings, her hope fading as the number grew larger. When his deep voice poured through the receiver, telling her he was unavailable and asking her to leave a message at the tone, she held her breath for five seconds, then disconnected the call. She really didn't want to share her news with his voice mail.

Next, she tried Stewart. This time, she got through.

"I was trying to get ahold of Gabriel," she told his private secretary. "Do you know if he's in the palace?"

"No. He left two hours ago."

"Do you know where he went?" A long pause followed her question. Olivia refused to be put off by Stewart's reluctance. "It's important that I speak with him."

"I'm sorry, Lady Darcy. He has left the country."

"Did he go to Italy?"

Stewart paused before replying. "All he would tell me is that he had something he needed to do that would impact the future generations of Alessandros."

Olivia's stomach plummeted as she pictured Count Verreos and his beautiful daughter from the twins' birthday party and recalled the familiarity between her and Gabriel. Had they reached an understanding already? Was she Olivia's replacement?

"Is there any way to reach him?" she asked, desperation growing as she suspected where Gabriel and gone and why.

"I've left him several messages that he hasn't returned," Stewart answered, sounding unhappy.

"How long was he planning to be gone?"

"A week to ten days. Before departing, he left instructions that you should be given use of the royal family plane. It will be available to take you back to England tomorrow."

"That's kind of him." Although disappointed that Gabriel had at long last accepted their relationship was over, Olivia wasn't deterred. "But when you speak with him, would you tell him I intend to stay in Sherdana until we can speak face-to-face."

She hadn't believed Gabriel when he'd insisted this wasn't over between them. If only she'd known how right he was a couple days earlier.

After hanging up with Stewart, Olivia called her father and gave him the news that she was staying another week, but didn't share the real reason. To her relief, he didn't try to talk her into coming home immediately.

With nothing to do but wait, Olivia had an early dinner and took a walk in the private walled garden behind the hotel. Instead of enjoying the picturesque charm of the boxwood hedges and urns filled with cascades of bright flowers, Olivia grew more anxious with every step. What if Gabriel was proposing to Fabrizia Verreos at this very moment? A painful spasm in her chest forced Olivia to stop. Gasping for air, she sat down on a nearby stone bench and fought to normalize her breathing. She focused on the fat blossoms on the peach rosebush across the path from her. Closing her eyes would have allowed her mind to fill with images of another woman in Gabriel's arms.

A vibration against her upper thigh provided a welcome distraction. Pulling out her cell phone Olivia saw Stewart was calling. Her pulse hitched as hope bloomed.

"Prince Gabriel called me a few minutes ago," Stewart explained. "He is unable to return to Sherdana at the moment, but when I explained you intended to linger until he came home, he asked if you would fly to meet with him tomorrow."

It was what she wanted, but based on her panic attack a moment earlier, she was thinking that perhaps Gabriel intended to tell her in person that he was moving on.

"Of course." Afterward she could fly home.

"The plane will be waiting for you at ten. I'll send a car to pick you up."

"Thank you."

Olivia hung up and continued her walk, plagued by worries.

What if she didn't reach him before he proposed to Fabrizia? What if despite the passionate kiss he'd given her the day of the twins' birthday he wasn't willing to risk the unconventional method needed in order for them to conceive the next generation of Alessandros?

Pushing everything out of her mind that she couldn't control, Olivia concentrated on what she was going to say to Gabriel about the change in her circumstances. By the time Olivia returned to her room, she'd rehearsed and discarded a dozen ways to convince Gabriel they could have children. In the end, she decided the best argument was to tell him she loved him. And she was grateful she only had to wait hours instead of days before she could speak the truth of her heart.

The next morning saw her staring out the window with blurry vision as the royal family's private plane taxied down the runway. Plagued by uncertainty, she hadn't slept but an hour or so. Lulled by the drone of the engines, she shut her eyes and didn't realize she'd drifted off until the change in altitude woke her. Glancing at her watch, she saw that she'd been asleep for nearly two hours.

Stretching, she glanced out the window, expecting to see Italy's lush green landscape, but what greeted her eyes was shimmering blue water. The plane touched down smoothly and rolled toward a series of private hangers.

"Where are we?" she asked the copilot as he lowered the steps that would allow her to disembark into the foreign landscape.

"Cephalonia," the pilot answered, carrying her overnight bag down the steps to a waiting car. He handed her bag to the driver. "Greece."

"Thank you," she murmured to both men as she slid into the car's backseat. Although why she was thanking them, she had no idea. If they were kidnapping her, this was the oddest way to go about it.

"Where are we going?" she questioned the driver as he

navigated along a coastal road cut into the mountainside with a stunning view of the sea.

"Fiskardo."

Which told her absolutely nothing. The only thing she was certain of at this moment was that she was nowhere near Italy and Gabriel. What sort of trick had Stewart played on her? Was this some sort of plot to get her out of the way while Gabriel did his duty and secured himself a new fiancée?

If that was the case, Stewart better be the villain. If Gabriel had orchestrated this stunt, she was going to be even more heartbroken. Pulling out her phone, she dialed first Gabriel, then Stewart when the former still didn't answer. She had no luck getting through.

As soon as she arrived at her destination, she would figure out her next step. If this was Stewart's gambit, she would find another way to get in contact with Gabriel. Perhaps the queen would help.

With nothing to do for the moment, Olivia stared out the window as the car descended from the mountains and drove down into a seaside town. She'd never visited any of the Greek Ionian Islands before and acknowledged the scenery in this area was spectacular. At least Stewart had been kind enough to find a gorgeous place to squirrel her away. As the car navigated through town, she glimpsed the whitewashed houses with their flower-draped balconies and wondered if her final destination was one of the lovely hotels overlooking the harbor. Her spirits sank as they passed each one and came to a stop a short distance from the waterfront.

They were met by a handsome swarthy Greek in his midfifties who flashed blinding white teeth in a mischievous grin. Seeing his good humor restored her own. She followed him along the cement quay, lined with chartered sailboats, believing that there had to be a happy ending to all this adventuring.

"I am Thasos," he said as he helped her onto a luxurious thirty-four-foot cruiser.

"Where are we going, Thasos?" she questioned, accepting the glass of wine offered, glad for it and the tray of Greek food that awaited her.

"Kioni."

Another name that rang no bells. With a sigh, Olivia munched on bread, dolmas, cheese and olives while the boat sped out of the harbor. If she'd thought the water had appeared beautiful from the coast, it was nothing compared to the sparkling blue that surrounded her now. A short distance away, another island loomed, a great green hulk adorned with olive trees and cypress. Few houses dotted the mountainsides. She would have worried about being in such a remote area, but the bustle of the town they'd just left behind told her she hadn't been brought to the ends of the earth.

After polishing off a second glass of wine and taking the edge off her hunger, she stared at the coastline as it passed. Ninety minutes on the water brought them to another harbor, this one shaped like a horseshoe with three windmills on one side of its mouth.

"Kioni," Thasos explained with another wide grin.

Olivia sighed, wondering who was going to meet her here. Could she expect another taxi ride? Perhaps the plan was to keep her moving until she cried uncle. While Thasos maneuvered the boat toward the cement seawall that circled the harbor, Olivia gazed at this town. Smaller and less busy than Fiskardo, it nevertheless had the same charm. A few houses clustered close to the waterfront, but most clung to the side of the mountain that rose above this scenic harbor.

Everywhere she looked vivid purple and magenta bougainvillea vines brightened the whitewashed buildings or arched over the steps that led to the homes perched on the hillside. Silence descended as Thasos killed the motor and the light breeze brought the clank of cowbells to her ears. But she doubted the steep terrain was suitable for cows. More likely the bells she heard belonged to goats.

She stepped off the boat, helped by Thasos and another man, who claimed her bag for the next part of her journey. Olivia followed him for about thirty steps before she spied a tall, familiar figure coming down the street toward her.

Gabriel.

His white pants, pale blue shirt and navy blazer gave him the look of casual elegance. Her heart jumped in her chest as the wind tousled his hair. He slid his sunglasses up on his head as he approached and gave her a gentle smile.

He wasn't in Italy proposing to the daughter of an Italian count. He was here and from the expression on his face, he was very glad to see her.

Thirteen

The unguarded expression on Olivia's face when she spotted him made Gabriel the happiest man on earth. He was her white knight come to rescue her from the dragons. The fact that he was towing a donkey instead of a black charger hadn't made an impact on her yet.

"What are you doing here?" she demanded. "You're supposed to be in Italy."

He shook his head. "Italy? Where did you get that idea?"

"Stewart said you had gone to do something that would impact future generations of Alessandros. I assumed you meant to…propose to the daughter of Count Verreos." She touched the corner of her eye where a trace of moisture had gathered and a ragged exhale escaped her.

"No. I came straight here."

"Does Stewart know where you are?"

"No. I knew he wouldn't approve of what I intended to do."

"That's why I don't understand what are you doing here and why you dragged me all the way to Greece by plane, across an island by car and now here by boat."

"I needed some time to prepare." He grinned. "And I thought you might be less likely to argue with me if you were tired."

"Argue about what?" she demanded, her gaze drawn

toward the small donkey that stood beside him, ears flickering lazily forward and back. "And what are you doing with that?"

Gabriel patted the donkey's neck. "It's traditional for Greek brides to ride donkeys to their weddings."

"Bride? What are you talking about…?" Her voice trailed off as she noticed the donkey came equipped with a riding pad covered with flowers. "You can't be serious."

She sounded aghast, but hope glowed in her blue eyes.

"I'm utterly serious. The church and the priest are waiting for us. All you need to do is hop on." Seeing she wasn't fully on board with his plan, he caught her around the waist and pulled her body flush with his, taking care to treat her gently. "Marry me." He drew his knuckles down her cheek. "Please. I can't live without you."

Tears flooded her eyes. "You love me?"

"I love you. I adore you. You're my world." He peered down at her in surprise. "Haven't you figured that out by now?"

She took his hand and drew it away from her skin. Her grip was tight enough to make him wince.

"What of your parents' wishes? Have you considered the barrage of negative opinions you'll face when we return home?"

"None of that matters. No one matters but us. I have two brothers, both of whom are capable of getting married and having children. There's no reason why I have to be the one who fathers the next generation of Sherdana royalty. It was different when my father became king. He was the only direct male descendant. And besides, I think it's time my brothers took on a little royal responsibility."

A crowd of townspeople and tourists were gathering on the narrow street, drawn by the novelty of a decked out donkey and the argument between Gabriel and Olivia. The late-afternoon sun bathed the town in golden light, softening the scenery. The breeze off the harbor was gentle against Olivia's skin, soothing her anxiety.

"Neither one of them is going to be happy."

"I don't care. It's my turn to be a little selfish. We're getting married. Now. Today. And I'm not taking no for an answer."

That he was ready to marry her despite her inability to give him children thrilled her, and she could no longer wait to share her news.

"There's something I need to tell you."

"That you love me?"

"No."

"You don't?" he teased.

"Of course I do. But that's not what I need to tell you."

"But don't you think it's an appropriate thing to tell your groom on your wedding day?"

"Very well. I love you."

"When you say it like that, I'm not sure I believe you."

She leaned forward and slid her fingers into his hair, drawing him close for a slow, deep kiss. "I love you."

His response was almost a purr. "Much better."

"Now are you ready to hear what I have to say?"

"Yes."

Their impending nuptials had certainly brought out the mischief maker in Gabriel. Or perhaps it was getting away from the palace and all his responsibility. Olivia made a note to kidnap him at least once a year and bring him somewhere with no cell phones and no television so they could get reacquainted.

"When I spoke with the doctor yesterday—" she gathered a deep breath "—he gave me some rather startling news."

The wicked light died in Gabriel's eyes. He grew somber. He caught her fingers in a tight grip. "Is something wrong?"

"No. In fact, I think everything might be okay in time."

"How so?"

"He thinks that a fertility specialist might be able to harvest eggs from my ovaries." She watched Gabriel carefully, hoping he was open to what she had in mind. "It would require finding a woman willing to be a surrogate, but it's possible that you and I could still make babies together."

"This is the most amazing news."

Gabriel caught her around the waist and pulled her against his body. Dipping his head, he captured her lips with his for a long, slow kiss.

By the time he released her mouth they were both breathing heavily. Gabriel's eyes sparkled like the sun on the water behind them. Joy sped through her as she realized she was about to marry the man she adored.

"Come on, let's get you up on the donkey and get to the church."

"Are you sure it's tradition?" she protested, eyeing the creature doubtfully.

"Positive."

Their parade up the steep street to the church was not the formal affair it would have been in Sherdana. There was no gilded carriage pulled by six perfectly matched white horses. No thousands of people lining the streets to wave and throw rose petals at them. But there were smiles and hearty cheers as Gabriel lead the donkey through the heart of the town.

When they reached the church, Gabriel introduced his housekeeper, Elena, who took Olivia aside to help her into the modest knee-length wedding dress with cap sleeves and a large bow at the waist. A note from Noelle accompanied the dress, explaining that Libby had come to her a few days after Olivia went into the hospital because Gabriel was planning on marrying Olivia in a small island wedding and wanted a dress to suit the occasion.

So, despite his lack of contact during her hospital stay, Gabriel hadn't accepted that their engagement was at an end. He'd still wanted her as his wife, even though his family and political advisers would counsel him to move on.

Awash with joy, Olivia clutched the note to her chest and stared at her reflection. Although the design was much simpler than the lace-and-crystal-embellished gown she'd have worn to marry Gabriel in Sherdana, it was perfect. As was the man who awaited her at the front of the beautiful Greek church.

Gabriel's gaze never once wavered as she walked toward him, accompanied by the song of a single violin. There was no doubt, no restraint in his golden eyes, only possessiveness, and she reveled in his love.

He took her hand as she came to stand beside him and she tingled in delight. Elena and her husband were the only witnesses. The intimacy of the empty church allowed them the privacy to focus completely on each other and they exchanged vows in reverent tones. When they returned to Sherdana, there would be celebrations with family and friends. Until then, all they wanted was each other.

After the ceremony, they exited the church and encountered a small crowd. Apparently Gabriel and his brothers were well liked in the coastal town and when word got out that he had come to the island to get married, many had turned out to wish him and Olivia well.

They lingered for several minutes, greeting people and accepting congratulations until Gabriel insisted it was time he took his bride home. Laughing and shaking his head at good-natured invitations to stay in town and celebrate their wedding, Gabriel slipped his arm around her waist and began to edge out of the circle of people.

"My car is this way." He took her hand and began to lead her down the road.

"Oh, thank goodness, I was afraid you'd make me ride the donkey back to your house."

Gabriel laughed heartily. "It would take him too long to carry you that far and I can't wait that long to have you all to myself."

Once he got her settled in the passenger seat and slid behind the wheel, he sat sideways in his seat and regarded her intently.

After several seconds of his attentive silence, Olivia grew restless. "What are you doing?"

"Appreciating our first private moment as husband and wife. The circumstances of the last few weeks haven't given us any time together and when we leave here, there will be public appearances and meetings demanding our time. I intend to spend every possible moment until then showing my beautiful wife how much I adore her."

Being his wife was her dream come true. Olivia smiled. "If I'm beautiful, you have Noelle to thank for that." She gestured to her wedding dress. "Have you really been planning this romantic elopement since before I left the hospital?"

"It was your secretary's idea. She knows how stubborn you can be and came to me with a crazy plan that I should steal you away to someplace exotic and marry you."

"Libby?" Olivia considered her secretary's encouragement anytime Olivia had doubted her future with Gabriel.

"She helped me with the dress and arranged the church and the flowers."

"How were you planning to get me to agree to run off with you?"

"By offering you a ride home in our jet and then bringing you here. You made things a lot easier by asking to see me."

"Did Stewart have any idea what you were planning?"

Gabriel shook his head. "Stewart's loyalty is to Sherdana. Libby's loyalty is to you." He leaned forward and pressed a lingering kiss on her lips. "And so is mine."

Olivia contemplated her new husband during the short drive to his villa, a two-mile journey around the horseshoe-shaped harbor. Never again would she underestimate his determination or his loyalty to her. He'd been willing to go against his family for her. She couldn't ask for a better partner or soul mate.

Because they'd been delayed in town Elena had already arrived and was in the process of arranging a romantic table for them on the terrace high above the harbor. At Olivia's prompting, Gabriel gave her a brief tour of the villa. In the spacious bedroom they would share, Gabriel drew her toward the window and they stared out at Kioni, its lights glowing bright as dusk descended. With his arms wrapped around Olivia's waist and his chin resting on her head, he sighed.

Olivia chuckled. "Was that weariness or contentment?"

"Contentment. You will be hearing many more such sighs in the coming days while we enjoy some much-needed privacy."

"We will have to go back eventually."

His arms tightened around her. "I prefer not to think about that moment until it arrives."

"Won't the media come here looking for us?"

"In the past we've kept a low profile and the people who live on the island respect our privacy." His lips trailed of fire down her neck. "Now, let's go downstairs and enjoy our first dinner as man and wife."

They returned to the first floor and accepted glasses of champagne from Elena. She gestured them out onto the terrace and retreated to fetch the first course.

"This is beautiful," Olivia commented, admiring the simple but elegant scene.

With the sunset long past, the sky had deepened to indigo. A row of white candles stretched along the low terrace wall, pushing back the darkness, their flames protected by glass containers. More candles had been placed in the center of the table, their flickering glow making shadows dance over the fine white tablecloth, beautiful china and colorful flower arrangements.

Gabriel led her to the table and helped her into a linen-clad chair before taking his own seat beside her. The romantic lighting softened his strong bone structure and brought out the sensual curve of his lips as he smiled. "Here's to following our hearts."

Olivia smiled as she clinked her glass to his and marveled at her good fortune. She never would have guessed that she had to lose everything in order to gain the one thing she needed most.

Setting her glass down, Olivia reached for Gabriel's hand.

"A few weeks ago your sister told me to ask you something. I never did."

"Ask now."

"She said we'd met before six months ago. Is that true?"

"Yes."

"But I don't recall meeting you. And I assure you I would. Were we young children? Is that why I don't remember?"

"It was almost seven years ago at a masquerade party. Given the host's reputation I was a little surprised to discover the young woman I rescued was none other than Lady Olivia Darcy."

Gabriel had been her savior. The man whose kiss had set the bar for every other romantic encounter she'd had since. "You knew who I was?"

"Not until after you'd left and Christian informed me who I'd been kissing." Gabriel's fingertips grazed her cheek. "When I kissed you that night, something sparked between us. I wasn't ready to married and you were far too young, but something told me you were the woman I was destined to marry."

"But that was one kiss seven years ago." She couldn't imagine how a single moment in time could impact him so strongly. And yet hadn't she felt the magic between them? Compared his kiss to those that came after? "And my father approached you about building a plant in Sherdana."

"That's true, but Christian put the idea in his head. My brother is very clever when it comes to business dealings and had an inkling of how much you interested me."

"But you loved Marissa. You would have married her if Sherdanian law had allowed it."

"I never wanted to marry Marissa. She was my way of rebelling against duty and responsibility. I loved being with her, but I know now that I didn't love her. Not the way I love you."

His lips found hers and delivered a kiss that managed to be both incredibly arousing and spiritually satisfying at the same time. Olivia was weak with delight when he set her free.

"I can't quite believe all that has happened today," she murmured as his fingertips worked their way along her shoulder. "When I woke up this morning I was cautiously optimistic. Now I'm happier than I ever imagined I could be."

Gabriel gifted her with a smile of resolute tenderness. "And it's my intention to do whatever it takes to ensure you stay that way."

After disappearing from the radar for a week, and then reappearing with a glowing bride in tow, Gabriel had anticipated a media frenzy, but he hadn't expected the capital's streets to be lined with people.

In the back of the limousine, Olivia waved at the enthusiastic crowd, looking every inch a princess. But by the time the vehicle pulled up in front of the palace, her nerves had begun to show.

"Are we going to be taken to the gallows and shot?" she questioned. "Is that why everyone turned out to see us?"

"A member of Sherdana's royal family hasn't been executed in almost three hundred years."

"That's not as reassuring as you want it to be."

Gabriel squeezed her hand. "Everything is going to be fine."

"Since when are you such an optimist?"

"Since marrying you."

A footman stepped forward to open the limo's door. Olivia nodded toward a glowering Christian, who was striding through the palace's ornate main doors.

"He doesn't look happy."

"I think he's realized the trap has been sprung."

"You sound as if you're enjoying this far too much."

"Do you have any idea how many dossiers I looked through over the years, weighing my future happiness against what was right for the country, while my brothers ran around the United States and Europe following their dreams?"

"A hundred?" she offered.

"Try a thousand."

"Surely there weren't that many girls who wanted to marry you," she teased.

"Oh, there were at least three times that, but only one girl I wanted to marry."

"You really have become a smooth talker. No wonder I fell in love with you."

Christian extended a hand to assist Olivia as she exited the car and kissed her on each cheek before glowering at Gabriel over a perfunctory handshake.

"How are things?" Gabriel asked, overlooking his brother's surly mood. He kept ahold of Olivia's hand as they made their way into the palace.

"Sherdana's been doing just fine," Christian muttered.

"I meant with you. Has Mother come up with a list of potential candidates for your bride yet?"

"You really are a bastard."

"Don't let our mother hear you say that." He thumped his brother on the back. "But what do you have to worry about? Nic is next in line. The burden to produce an heir falls on him first."

"Mother's not taking any chances this time. She thinks both of us should be married."

"I agree with her. Nothing like marrying the woman of your dreams to know complete and perfect happiness."

Gabriel laughed heartily at Christian's look of disgust and followed Olivia up the stairs. As they entered the suite of rooms she and Gabriel would now be sharing, she leaned close and spoke in a low voice. "Why didn't you tell Christian there's a potential we can have children?"

He shut the door to the suite, ensuring their privacy, and took her in his arms. "I think we should keep this development our little secret for the time being."

"Are you sure?" Olivia reached up and threaded her

fingers through Gabriel's dark hair. "If it works, it will let your brothers off the hook."

"There's no reason to say anything until we have something definitive to tell."

"That could take months," she exclaimed, her eyes wide with uncertainty. "They could be engaged or even married by then."

"Making you my wife has been the best thing that could have happened to me. I think my brothers deserve to experience the same."

"You're going to force them into a situation where they have to find wives so that they'll fall in love?"

"Diabolical, isn't it?"

"They'll kill you when they find out the truth."

"I don't think so." Gabriel leaned down and silenced further protests with a deep, soul-stirring kiss. "I think they'll thank me for making them the second and third happiest men on the planet."

"You being the first?" She arched her eyebrows at him.

Gabriel responded with a broad grin. "Absolutely."

* * * * *

WHAT THE
PRINCE WANTS

JULES BENNETT

To the Gems for Jules Street Team!
Thank you for the encouragement, advice
and most of all for the support. I love you all!

One

The curves, the expressive green eyes, rich brown hair the color of his favorite scotch—all made for a punch of primal lust Mikos Colin Alexander hadn't experienced in years. This sure as hell was not the woman he'd expected to see on his doorstep.

Woman? No, she couldn't be more than twenty years old. She looked as if she'd just stepped out of a photo shoot for some popular American teen magazine. With her pink T-shirt, body-hugging jeans and little white sandals, this was not the image he'd had in mind when he'd gone online seeking a nanny.

Iris's angry cry drew his attention back to the point of this meeting. The lady at his door immediately shifted her gaze from him to the child on his hip.

"Aww, it's okay, sweetheart." Her voice, so soft, so gentle, got Iris's attention. "What's a beautiful princess like you crying about?"

Princess. He cringed at the term, hating how dead-on

this stranger was. But he was in LA now, not Galini Isle, a country so small that nobody here knew who he was. Which was just how he preferred it.

His wish to be free from his royal heritage had carried him through life, but the urge had never been stronger than after the accident that nearly took his life. Between that, his failed marriage, Karina's death and his being a widowed prince, the media was all over him. There wasn't a moment's peace back home and he needed to get away, to regroup...and maybe to never return.

Now more than ever he wanted independence—for him and his daughter.

"I'm sorry." Extending her hand, the lady offered him a wide, radiant smile. "I'm Darcy Cooper. You must be Mr. Alexander."

Darcy. The woman he'd emailed, the woman he'd spoken to on the phone. The woman he'd all but hired sight unseen to be his live-in nanny because of her impressive references and the number of years the agency had been in business.

Na pari i eychi. Damn it.

What happened to the short, round, bun-wearing grandmother type he'd seen pictured on the website? He'd been assured the woman coming to care for his daughter was the owner. No way could this curvaceous beauty be in charge of Loving Hands Childcare Agency. Perhaps they'd sent someone else at the last minute.

Colin shifted his irate daughter to his good hip. Damn accident still had him fighting to get back to normal... whatever normal was after nearly dying and then losing your wife. "You're not what I expected."

Quirking a brow, she tipped her head as a smile spread across her face. Her eyes ran over him, no doubt taking in his running shorts, T-shirt and bedhead.

"That would make two of us."

Her sparkling eyes held his. Was she mocking him? Of course she was. She had no idea who she was speaking to…not that anybody here knew of his royal status, but still. Nobody mocked him except his brother.

Iris's piercing wails grew louder, more shrill in his ear. Between lack of sleep and the constant pain in his back and hip, he was done trying to be Father of the Year. The fact that he'd had no choice but to find assistance still angered him. Iris was the only reason he was giving in. Her needs had to come before his pride—which is why he now found himself staring down at the petite, yet very shapely, nanny.

This is what he'd wanted, right? To be free from all the servants, the media, the people ready to step in and practically raise his child for him while thrusting her into the limelight? Hell, he'd even been running his own vacuum here. Among other domestic tasks like dusting and putting the trash out at the end of the driveway. His brother would die laughing if he saw Mikos wielding a dust mop.

Colin. He had to keep thinking of himself as Colin now that he was in the United States. His middle name would help him blend in so much better. He was here to see who he was as a man, not a prince. To rediscover a piece of himself he was afraid he'd lost.

He just wanted these next six months to be free of all things involving his royal status. He was tired of being home where pity shrouded the faces of everyone he came in contact with. Yes, he was a widower, but so many people didn't know he and his wife had been separated for months before her death. They'd had to keep putting up a good front for the sake of their reputations.

Pretenses. That word pretty much summed him up. He wanted this freedom, wanted to see how he and Iris could live without being waited on hand and foot. He'd promised his brother, King Stefan, that he would only be in the United States for six months, the maximum time a member of the royal family could be away from the island for personal reasons. Then Colin would have to decide whether to renounce his title of Prince Mikos Colin Alexander of Galini Isle or return to the island and resume his royal duties.

Colin was first in line to take over the throne if something ever happened to his brother. If he gave up his position, the crown would be passed to their oldest cousin, who'd rather chase skirts and make scandalous headlines than run a country. That fact had guilt coursing through Colin every time he thought about the situation.

He'd temporarily lost his title when he'd married Karina because she had been divorced once. Their land had archaic rules, but that was one he hadn't been about to fight.

Now that his wife had passed on, he was thrust back into the royal limelight whether he wanted to be there or not. And with his daughter being the next generation of royalty, that automatically made her a duchess. The entire situation was a complicated mess. Added to that, he faced years of ramifications if he chose to walk away from his title.

Colin was determined to be a hands-on father. Being in a new country, still adjusting to this lifestyle and trying to cope with this damn inconvenient handicap forced him to admit he might need just a bit of help. This short-term arrangement would give him good insight into whether or not he could fully care for Iris on his own and if he and his baby should stay here.

When Iris arched her back, screaming as if someone had taken her most prized possession, Darcy instantly reached for the girl.

Without asking, the woman swiped away Iris's tears and gently lifted her from his arms.

"Now, now," Darcy said, patting Iris's back and lightly bouncing his eighteen-month-old. "I'm not a fan of Monday mornings, either."

Colin crossed his arms over his chest as Darcy continued to speak in a calm, relaxing tone. Yeah, like that was going to work. Iris couldn't hear this woman for all the screaming. No way would Darcy's sweet, soft voice penetrate the power of a toddler's lungs.

Darcy stroked a finger across Iris's damp cheeks again. Little by little she started to calm as this virtual stranger kept talking in the same soothing tone, never raising her voice to be louder than Iris. Colin watched as his daughter stared at the stranger.

Within a minute or two, Iris had stopped fussing and was pulling Darcy's ponytail around. Strands of rich, silky hair instantly went to Iris's mouth as she sniffed, hiccupped and finally settled herself.

"Oh, no." He reached for the clump of hair that was serving as Iris's pacifier, but Darcy shifted her body away.

"She's fine," Darcy assured him in the same delicate voice she'd used moments ago to get Iris under control. "Babies put everything in their mouths. I promise it's clean."

Colin watched as Iris gripped the strands in her tight fist and gave a swift yank. Darcy only laughed and reached up to pat the baby's pudgy little hand. "Not so hard, little one. That's attached."

Colin couldn't believe this. Iris had cried off and on all night—more on than off—and had been quite angry all morning. How the hell did this woman calm his child in the span of a few minutes? With a ponytail?

Darcy tapped a fingertip to Iris's nose before turning her attention to him. "May I come in?"

Feeling like a jerk for leaving her on his porch, Colin stepped back and opened the door wider. As Darcy passed by him, some fruity scent trailed her, tickling his nose in a teasing manner.

If he thought she looked good from the front, the view from behind was even more impressive. The woman knew how to wear a pair of jeans.

Perhaps she was older than he'd first thought, because only a woman would be this shapely, this comfortable with her body. He'd assumed all women in LA wanted that waiflike build, enhanced with silicone as the perfect accessory.

Darcy Cooper was anything but waiflike and her curves were all natural.

Colin gritted his teeth and took a mental step back. He needed to focus. The last thing he needed was to be visually sampling a potential nanny. He had to blame his wayward thoughts on sleep deprivation. Nothing else could explain this sudden onset of lust. His wife was the last woman he'd slept with and that was before his near-fatal rock climbing accident two years ago. Between the accident, the baby, the separation from his wife and then her death…yeah, sex hadn't been a priority in his life.

Years ago he'd been the Playboy Prince of Galini Isle and now his life revolved around diapers, baby dolls and trying to walk without this damn limp. Oh, and his glamorous life now included housework.

Yet a beautiful stranger had showed up in his house only moments ago and he was already experiencing a lustful tug. He wasn't sure if he should be elated by the fact he wasn't dead and actually had hormones still ready to stand up and take notice, or if he should be angry because sex was the last thing he had time for.

He and Darcy had agreed on the phone two days ago that today would be a mostly hands-on type of interview. It was important that Iris connect with her potential caregiver. However, he had nobody else lined up because there wasn't another agency that had measured up to this one.

Darcy had been here for all of five minutes. How the hell did he expect her to live here for six months if his attraction had already taken such control of his thoughts? His life was already a jumbled mess without a steamy affair to complicate things further.

Colin watched Darcy as she walked around the open-concept living area, bouncing the baby on one hip as if they'd known each other for some time. Iris started fussing a bit, but just like moments ago, Darcy patted her back and spoke in those hushed tones.

He'd never seen anything like this. He'd tried all damn night to calm his daughter.

Karina would've known what to do. Even though he and Karina had been separated for nearly a year before she died of a sudden aneurism, he still mourned the loss. The rock-climbing accident had changed him, had him pushing her away due to his stubborn pride and fear of not being the perfect husband and father, but a part of him would still always love her. She'd been a loyal wife and an amazing mother.

When Darcy bent over the sofa and picked up a stuffed lamb, Colin clenched his fists at how the denim pulled across her backside. Why couldn't he tear his eyes away? Why couldn't he concentrate on something other than her tempting shape? No, she couldn't stay.

What he needed was someone old enough to be his grandmother, with many years of experience, a woman with silver hair in a bun and ill-fitting clothing. What he did *not* need was a woman who could kick-start his libido without even trying. But, damn it, she'd calmed Iris and had done so with the ease of an expert.

"What is her daily routine?"

Colin blinked as he stared back at the woman who

was trying to be professional when his thoughts had been anything but.

"Routine?"

Dancing the lamb toward Iris's nose and then pulling it back, Darcy simply nodded without even looking at him. "Yes. Naps, eating schedule, bedtime."

Since coming to LA only days ago, he did what worked best for them and he was still adjusting. As hard as this change was, he wasn't sorry he'd made the move.

Colin glanced at Iris's smile, the prominent dimple in her cheek that matched his own. Sure, she'd smile for the stranger, but not for him? He loved his little girl with every bit of his soul. He'd give anything to be able to care for her on his own without the fear of his handicap harming her, but he had to face his own limitations to keep her safe.

"Mr. Alexander?"

Colin returned his gaze to Darcy who was actually staring at him. Oh, yeah, she'd asked him a question. Unfortunately, he was going to have to end this trial before it started. Having someone like Darcy here would be a colossal mistake.

Holding those bright green eyes with his, Colin took a deep breath and said, "I'm afraid I can't use your services."

Darcy swallowed her shock. What had he just said? The very survival of Loving Hands was contingent on her landing this job. She refused to take no for an answer. She couldn't afford to.

She also couldn't afford to keep making eye contact with Mr. Alexander's baby blues. No, *blue* wasn't the right word. What was the proper description for a set of eyes that were so mesmerizing they nearly made her forget all her troubles? The power he possessed when he held her gaze was unlike anything she'd ever experienced, so she kept her focus on the sweet little girl in her arms.

Holding onto a squirming Iris was difficult enough without the added impact of desire. Though she'd certainly take a dose of lust over the ache in her heart from holding such a precious child. She'd avoided working with babies for years, giving those jobs to her employees. Unfortunately, the entire staff of Loving Hands had been let go and Darcy had to face her demons head-on if she wanted to save her grandmother's company. So, his "no" wasn't an option.

This would be the first job caring for a young child she'd taken on since having been told at the age of twenty-one she couldn't have kids due to severe endometriosis. She could do this…she had to do this. No matter the heartache, Darcy had to pull through.

But first she had to convince Mr. Alexander she was the one for the job.

Turning to fully face the sexy father, Darcy kept her hold on Iris, who was nearly chewing the ear off the poor lamb. A sweet smell wafted up from the child's hair, no doubt from whatever shampoo her father used for her.

Darcy had learned from the emails and phone conversations that Mr. Alexander was a single father and new to the area. She also knew his wife had died suddenly just a few months ago. What she didn't know was what he did for a living or where he was from. The sexy, exotic accent that made her toes curl in her secondhand sandals clearly implied that he wasn't American.

Honestly she didn't care where he was from as long as he was here legally and the job posting was legit. He'd offered her a ridiculous sum to live here for the next six months and care for his daughter, and that money would help her save her grandmother's dying agency…the agency

Darcy's ex had pilfered money from, nearly leaving Darcy on the street. Oh, wait, he *had* left her on the street.

Darcy didn't know what happened at the end of the six months, and with the amount of money he'd offered, she didn't need to know.

"You can't use me?" she asked, not ready to admit defeat. "Do you have another nanny service lined up?"

"No."

Shoulders back and chin up, Darcy used all of the courage she wished she possessed to cross the room. Closing the gap between them only made her heart pound even more. She would do whatever it took to pay tribute to the grandmother who'd given up everything to raise her.

Darcy's nerves had kicked into high gear before she'd even arrived here because so much was riding on this one job. Being turned away by the client hadn't been her biggest concern, either. Darcy had truly feared she'd take one look at the child and freeze…or worse, break down and start sobbing.

Yet here she was, holding it together and ready to fight for what her ex had stolen from her. Darcy had already given up her apartment and had slept in her car those first two nights until her best friend discovered what happened. Now Darcy found herself spending nights on the sofa in her bestie's overpriced, undersized studio apartment. This live-in nanny position would secure a roof over her head and a steady income to help get Loving Hands back up and running.

As if all of that weren't stressful enough, her would-be employer had opened his door and all coherent thoughts had completely left her mind. A handsome man holding a baby was sexy, no doubt about it. But this man with his disheveled hair and piercing eyes had epitomized sexy single dad. Those tanned muscles stretched his T-shirt in ways that should be illegal. Not to mention the flash of ink peeking from beneath his sleeve.

The man who all but had her knees trembling and her stomach in knots was trying to send her on her way. Not going to happen.

"So you have nobody else lined up," she repeated, praying she came across as professional and not pushy. "I'm here, your sweet little girl is much happier than when you answered the door, and you're ready to usher me back out."

When he continued to stare as if trying to somehow dissuade her, Darcy continued.

"May I ask why you're opting to not even give me a chance?"

His intriguing set of eyes roamed over her face, sending spears of tingles through her body just as powerfully as if he'd touched her. It was as though he was looking straight into her soul.

Iris squealed and smacked Darcy on the cheek with the wet, slobbery stuffed lamb's ear that had been in her mouth. Still, nothing could stop Darcy from trying to maintain some sort of control over this situation…if she'd ever had any to begin with. She had a feeling Mr. Alexander was a man who was used to being in charge. That thought alone had arousal hitting hard.

Focus, Darcy.

"Mr. Alexander?"

"Colin." That husky voice slid over her. "Call me Colin."

A thread of hope started working its way through her. "That would imply I'll be here long enough to call you by your first name."

The muscle clenched in his jaw, the pulse in his neck seemed to be keeping that same frantic pace as hers.

Before he could comment, she kept going, more than

ready to plead her case. "We discussed a trial period over the phone. Why don't we agree on a set time? That way if this arrangement doesn't work for either of us, we have a way out."

She'd care for Lucifer's kids to get the amount of money she and Colin had agreed upon.

"May I be honest?" he asked, taking a step back as if he'd just realized how close they were.

"Please."

Iris wiggled in Darcy's arms. Darcy set the toddler on the floor to play then straightened to see Colin's eyes still fixed on her.

"I wasn't expecting someone so young."

She was always mistaken for someone younger, which was normally a lovely compliment. "I turned thirty two weeks ago."

His eyes widened as he raked that gaze over her body once more. At one time she'd been self-conscious of her slightly fuller frame. Being surrounded by so much surgically enhanced beauty in Hollywood would wreak havoc with anybody's self-esteem.

She could still hear her grandmother's words on the subject: *Be proud of who you are, your body and your spirit. Nobody can make you feel inferior without you allowing it.* So Darcy had embraced her curves and her size twelve wardrobe, meager as it may be. Besides, who was in charge of dictating what was and wasn't socially acceptable?

Her ass of an ex had mentioned her weight. She should've known then he wasn't The One.

When Colin was done taking his visual journey, he rested his hands on his hips and shifted his stance. With a slight wince, he moved in the other direction. That was the second time she'd caught him moving as if he couldn't stand on one leg for too long.

"Are you okay?" she asked before she could stop herself.

"Fine," he bit off. "You don't look more than twenty-one."

With a smile, she shrugged. "It's hereditary and I'll take that as a compliment."

His eyes narrowed as he tilted his head. "It wasn't meant to be one."

Crossing her arms, Darcy glanced down just as Iris gripped Darcy's jeans and pulled herself up. The little girl with bouncy dark curls started toward the other side of the living area, which was immaculate.

Where were the toys? The random blanket or sippy cup? Other than that stuffed lamb, there were no signs a child even lived here. Even if they had moved in just a few days ago, wouldn't the place be littered with baby items?

Beyond that, from what she could see, the house was perfectly furnished, complete with fresh flowers on the entryway table and the large kitchen island she could see across the open floor plan.

"Perhaps you have an older, more experienced worker?"

The man was testing her patience. Withholding a sigh, Darcy focused her attention back on the sexy, albeit frustrating, guy. "I'm the only one available for the job at this time."

Not a lie. She was the only one—period. Just last month she'd had to lay off her final employee. Letting her grandmother's staff go had been heartbreaking, but the money simply hadn't been there after several of her clients had changed agencies. They had been like family and had all worked so well together. Fortunately, everyone understood Darcy's predicament and Darcy happily gave each of them glowing recommendations for other jobs. Hopefully she'd be able to get Loving Hands back on its feet and slowly bring her workers back.

"Listen," she told him, steeling herself against any

worry or doubt. She wasn't going to borrow trouble yet. "I realize I look young. I understand how you only want the best for your daughter. However, everything I do will be monitored by you since I'd be staying here. You see something you don't like or you believe her care is not up to par, let me know. That's what the trial period is for."

Colin glanced from her to Iris, who was now smacking her hands on the coffee table as if playing the drums. Darcy wasn't about to give him a chance to answer, because she might not like the one he gave.

"I'm here now and from the dark circles under your eyes, you need to rest." Darcy smiled, hoping he was not going to put up a fight. "I can take over while you take some time for yourself."

She waited a beat, her heart pounding. Would he send her away simply because she wasn't an old lady wearing an apron and sensible shoes?

Colin rubbed his eyes then raked a hand over his face, the stubble on his jaw bristling beneath his palm. Why was that sound so…erotic? His eyes settled on her again and she refused to look away, refused to step back or show any fear. This was her livelihood, her only option of getting out of the depths of hell she'd fallen into. Though being thrust into a lifestyle she'd dreamed about for years, a lifestyle that was completely impossible for her to have, was a whole other layer of hell.

When the silence stretched between them, hovering in the air like an unwelcome guest, Darcy was convinced he was going to show her the door. After what seemed like forever, Colin nodded.

"I'll give you today to prove yourself."

Two

Never before had he allowed someone to steamroll him into going against his instincts. Yet a determined woman with enough killer curves to fuel any man's fantasy for every lonely night had done just that.

Perhaps it had been her sensual body that had him caving and ignoring common sense. But Darcy had something else he admired—tenacity. She wasn't giving in and she made very valid points as to why he should keep her around.

Such as the fact that he would be monitoring her every move while she was here. Perfect, just what he needed. Watching her every move might very well be his undoing. He'd wanted to figure out who he was as a man while he was here in LA, but this unexpected lust was an angle he hadn't considered.

Colin clasped his hands behind his head and continued staring up at the vaulted ceiling in his master suite. Sunlight spilled in through the sliver of an opening in his blackout blinds. He hadn't even bothered getting beneath his navy duvet because he knew his mind simply wouldn't shut down, and getting too comfortable didn't really matter. Napping in the middle of the day really wasn't something he did, but he was exhausted.

Rest wouldn't be his friend for some time, he feared. He'd needed a nanny fast. Based on previous families his assistants had interviewed, Darcy was the best option. Unfortunately he hadn't had time to do a full background check on individual people, so he'd just placed a quick call to one of his assistants. Hopefully more information would come back within a few hours, but his gut said he could trust her.

When he told her she'd gotten the job, at least provisionally, she'd returned carrying one tattered old duffel bag. Didn't women have two bags just for makeup alone and another two for shoes? How the hell did she fit everything into one bag that looked as if it would fall apart if accidentally bumped the wrong way or dropped too hard onto the floor?

Before he'd come up to his room, Colin had offered to help her inside with her things, but she'd dismissed him. When she came in with so little, he'd assumed she had more in the car. She assured him she had it all under control and she only had the one bag. There was a story there, and if she was staying around he'd get to the bottom of it. Money was apparently an issue, so he'd be interested what her background check showed.

The cell on his nightstand vibrated. Glancing over he saw his brother's name lighting up the screen. Not what he needed right now.

With a grunt, he rolled to his side and reached for the device. "Yeah," he answered.

"I assume by your chipper greeting you're still on the nanny hunt and not resting?"

"I may have found someone," he replied, not adding that this someone would most likely keep him awake at night.

Stefan laughed. "As usual you're not going into details. Fine. I figured you'd have given up by now and be ready to return home."

"I've only been gone a few days. I think you know I wouldn't give up on anything that soon."

Returning home only meant going back to the life of status he'd never wanted, raising his daughter in a setting that would consume her and stifle her growth. As the current duchess, she'd be in the spotlight at all times. He remembered how irritated he'd been growing up when he couldn't just go out and spend a day at the beach. He'd always been escorted by bodyguards, which seriously put a damper on his teen years and his ability to sneak out to have some alone time with friends—not that he didn't invent some pretty creative ways to lose the guards.

His parents had been wonderful, but still they'd had duties to fulfill, which often kept them away for weeks at a time. Then his mother had passed away from a tragic car accident and his father had been even busier, pouring himself into work and serving the people of the island in an attempt to fill the void.

Colin wanted to be there fully for his daughter. He wanted to form a bond that was so strong she would know just how much he loved her and that he would always put her needs first. Even before the crown. Which reminded him, his brother was still on the phone.

"I know you've never wanted this title," Stefan continued. "You do realize that no matter where you live, you're still a prince, but if I die and you've renounced the title, our cousin will assume the position? He's the last person Galini Isle deserves."

Why couldn't he just have a simple life? A life without

the worry of an entire country on his shoulders? A small country, but still.

Again, it was times like this that he wished Karina were still alive. Colin knew his daughter needed a woman's guidance through life and he needed assistance with these major decisions.

"Listen, if an emergency arises, you know I wouldn't turn my back on you or Galini Isle. But I may have to renounce my title if I think that's the best decision for Iris." Colin sat up and swung his legs over the side of the bed. "Maybe I am making a mistake, but for now I need the distance. I need to figure out what the best plan is for Iris and for me. I'm all she has right now."

Stefan sighed. "If you came home, she'd have many people to love and care for her."

"I really need this time. Iris and I don't need to be surrounded by servants who look at us with pity. That's not what I want for myself or her."

"What about Victoria and me? We miss you guys."

Guilt had already eaten away at Colin's conscience, so Stefan adding another layer was pointless. He missed his brother, but they had their own schedules, their own lives. Years ago the two had been inseparable, often rock climbing or kayaking together. Stefan had stepped up when their father had passed from a heart attack and had scaled back his need for adrenaline rushes.

"When are you coming to the States for a visit?" Colin asked. "Isn't it time for Victoria to see her family?"

Colin's sister-in-law was from LA and was a member of the prestigious Dane family of Hollywood.

Stefan chuckled. "I knew you'd say that. Actually we're not coming for several months, but the annual royal celebration ball is in just over two months and we'd really like you here for that. No pressure, just throwing that out there."

Coming to his feet, Colin twisted from his waist in an attempt to loosen his back, which had wanted to tighten up and spasm a bit more lately. He'd slowed down on the therapy he was supposed to be doing at home. After this long he figured the prescribed exercises were a waste of time. Apparently not.

"I haven't even thought about the ball," Colin told his brother.

"The media will not be allowed inside the palace," Stefan assured him. "I can always smuggle you in via one of the underground entrances, just like when we were teens."

Colin laughed, remembering the numerous times they'd covered for each other so they could sneak out and meet up with their girlfriends at the time.

"Will you at least think about this?" Stefan asked. Colin knew he wasn't just referring to the ball. "Think about how hard life will be for you with no family and no one to help you with Iris."

Colin's mind flashed to the woman who had shown up earlier full of confidence and curves. She was helping his daughter, no doubt. It was what she was doing to Colin that had him questioning his judgment.

"I've got everything under control," Colin assured him. "I need to go check on Iris."

He disconnected the call and slid the phone into the pocket of his shorts. Stefan had wanted Colin to think about this decision to leave the royal title behind, as if Colin had thought of anything else. The moment he'd discovered his wife was pregnant he'd done nothing but try to get out of that damn wheelchair in order to live for his child and be the sole supporter and provider—not in the monetary way, but in the fatherly bonding way.

Growing up with maids, butlers, personal assistants and even people who picked out your daily wardrobe was a bit ridiculous. Just because his family happened to be titled, because they had a certain last name and were wealthy, they had every single material thing at their disposal.

But money could only do so much. Colin still worried about the pressure and responsibility that came with being a member of the royal family. He knew he was projecting his fears onto his daughter, but he was her main source of stability now and he'd rather be overprotective than to pass along something that would overwhelm her.

Raking a hand through his hair, Colin opened his door and stepped out into the hallway. The twelve thousand square foot home was large, not as large as the palace by any means, but big enough that he'd had video monitors installed in most rooms so he could watch the feeds from his bedroom. He'd also had sound monitors wired throughout the house so he could hear Iris no matter where he was. There were alarms on the doors and windows, so he definitely would've heard had Darcy tried to take Iris from the house. He might be paranoid, but he would never take a chance with the safety of his child.

Colin was headed for the steps when his back started twitching.

Damn it. He gripped the railing as he stood on the landing and breathed deeply, waiting for the crippling pain to pass. Total agony he could tolerate, but being in a wheelchair and rendered helpless he could not.

Immediately following the accident, the doctors had indicated he might not ever be able to walk again, but the moment he'd heard those words he'd made it his mission to prove them wrong. Granted, he was walking, but the spasms in his back and piercing pain in his hip and down through his leg would blast him at the most inopportune times. Another reason he needed a nanny. Back home he had a driver, but he needed someone for that task here, too. Damn it, he hated being dependent on others for help, but he couldn't risk his daughter's safety if his pain hit while he was behind the wheel.

Colin needed to start making use of that home gym he'd had put in before arriving. He couldn't put off the physical therapy any longer, because he refused to be at the mercy of this injury.

Once the pain ceased, Colin headed down the steps carefully, in case the sensations returned.

Just as he reached the last step, squeals carried through the foyer. Colin followed the sound and stopped short when he spotted the carnage that used to be his spotless living room. He'd seen Darcy and Iris on the screen in his bedroom just before Stefan had called, but he sure as hell hadn't see this disaster.

"What the—"

Darcy sat on the floor surrounded by toys. Her hair, which had been pulled back earlier, was now down and in complete disarray, as if her hands—or the hands of a lover—had been running through it. Dry cereal was strewn across his coffee table and had trickled down to the rug beneath. From the looks of things some of the pieces had been trampled on and ground into the carpeting. A sippy cup sat on its side, but, fortunately, no liquid appeared to puddle beneath due to the spill-proof lid. There was one blessing in this chaos.

While Darcy was smiling, her eyes on his, Iris was playing with the hair on a doll. Doll? That wasn't one of her dolls. Colin had only shipped her favorite things and this wasn't part of Iris's collection.

"Did we wake you?" Darcy asked, smiling as if this scene were absolutely normal. "We were trying to be quiet."

He'd turned the sound down in his bedroom, hoping sleep would come.

"You didn't wake me." He took a cautious step into the room, almost afraid to look for any more destruction. "Is this typically how you watch children? You let them destroy a house?"

Shoving her hair back, Darcy pulled a band from her wrist and secured the dark mass into a low, messy style. As she came to her feet, she wiped her hands on her pants.

"This is far from destroyed, Colin."

The second his name slid through her lips, his eyes locked onto that unpainted mouth. He'd been told numerous times how intimidating his stare could be, yet she hadn't blinked or even shied away from him. Granted, he didn't want to intimidate her, but he was pretty impressed by how strong she seemed to be. One more aspect of American women he found intriguing. So independent, so strong-willed. As if he needed another reason to be drawn to Darcy.

"Iris and I are playing, and when we're done we'll pick it up." Her arms crossed over her chest, sending the swell of her breasts up to the opening of her V-neck. "There were no toys in here at all so we quietly snuck to her room and I grabbed a few things. Then I wasn't sure what her eating schedule was and she was hungry. Took me a second to figure out what nack-nack was, but I figured it meant snacks when she tugged me toward the kitchen."

As she defended herself, Colin couldn't help but slide his gaze to the way the V of her shirt twisted toward one side, showcasing the swell of her breasts, all but mocking him. Then there was the way her rounded hips filled out her jeans in such a way that would make any man beg.

Prince Mikos Colin Alexander had never begged for anything in his life and he sure as hell wasn't about to start now because of some punch of lust to his gut that he couldn't get under control.

Darcy was quite a captivating woman. He still couldn't get over the fact she wore no jewelry or makeup whatsoever. The woman oozed simplicity and for some reason he found that to be utterly sexy and ridiculously arousing. She wasn't out to impress him in any way other than relating to the care of his daughter.

Iris squealed when she spotted him. With her little arms out wide, she ran across the hardwood, over the rug, crushing even more cereal pieces beneath her bare feet before she collided with his legs. Colin cringed when she reached for him. He wanted to scoop her up, but with his back just coming off a muscle seizure, he opted to take a seat in the closest armchair and pull her into his lap instead.

Iris's little hands smacked up and down his arm and he placed a kiss on top of her head, where her wayward curls always tickled his nose. The smile she offered him had him returning her five-toothed grin. How could he look at her and not smile instantly? She was his every reason for being, the motivation behind all decisions he made.

"How long will the living room be a war zone?" he asked, turning his attention back to Darcy.

She glanced around then back to him with a laugh. "You do realize you're raising a toddler, right? They will make messes, they will make memories and they will learn to clean up later. I assure you this area will be spotless once she lays down for a nap."

Iris wiggled right off his lap and headed toward the coffee table covered in a buffet of snacks. Weren't kids supposed to eat in high chairs? Had his assistants at the palace let Iris be so carefree when he hadn't been around?

"She's been playing in her room," Colin informed Darcy when she continued to stare at him. "That's why the toys are kept there."

A wide smile spread across Darcy's face, making her look even younger. "You really are a stickler for rules, huh? Children need room to grow, to flourish. Yes, they need schedules, but they also need to learn to be flexible."

Even though she stood above him, Colin met and held her stare. There was no way this nanny was going to come in here and wreck everything just for the sake of making memories or whatever the hell else she'd babbled about.

Colin wasn't stupid. He knew he owed his not-so-sunny disposition to the fact that he couldn't get a grip on his attraction. Why this woman? Why now? And why the hell were her breasts right at eye level?

"By flourish do you mean grinding cereal into the floor?" he asked, focusing on the mess. "Or maybe you mean throwing toys around the room without a care of what may break?"

"That was another point I was going to bring up." Darcy stepped over a stuffed animal and sank down on the edge of the sofa. Lacing her fingers over the arm, she brought her eyes back to his. "All of these breakables should probably be put away for now, or at least placed higher where she can't pull them down. She'll get used to what she can and can't touch, but for now I'd try to avoid unnecessary injuries."

The home had come fully furnished. Colin had simply paid a designer to get everything set up so he only had to bring their clothes and personal belongings. All the breakables and any other knickknacks sitting around meant nothing to him. He'd replace whatever was broken, if need be.

Colin glanced across the mayhem on the floor. Iris sat on her beloved lamb while playing with the new doll.

"Where did that come from?"

Darcy glanced over as Iris gripped the doll's long, dark hair and started swinging it around. "I brought it for her."

So in the single bag she'd brought, Darcy had managed to squeeze a doll in among her belongings?

"Is that something you normally do? Bribe potential clients?"

Darcy's eyes widened. "I've never had to bribe anybody. Your daughter was being introduced to a stranger and I used the doll as a way to talk to her and make her comfortable. I can take it back if it offends you."

Colin gritted his teeth. In the span of a few hours his house had been taken over by this free spirit who seemed oblivious to the mess surrounding them and was trying to tell him how to raise his child. She'd calmed Iris in a way he'd never seen and now his new nanny was stomping all over his libido. And he was paying her for every bit of this torture.

Iris started whimpering as she rubbed her eyes.

"Is this nap time?" Darcy asked.

"She tends to nap once a day." He smoothed a wayward curl from Iris's forehead and slid his finger down her silky cheek. "There's no set time. I just lay her down when she seems ready."

Darcy came to her feet, crossed the room and lifted Iris into her arms. "Come on, sweetheart. Let's get you down for a nap. I'll clean the mess today and you can help tomorrow."

Colin rose. Now that he didn't have to bend over and pick Iris up, he figured he could carry her to her bedroom. He hadn't felt even a twinge in his back since he'd been downstairs.

"I'll take her up." Colin took Iris from Darcy's arms, careful not to brush against any part of her tempting body. "You can work on this."

Holding his daughter tight, he headed up to the nursery. With her little arms around his neck, she still clutched the new doll and with each step he took it slapped against his back. Iris had taken to Darcy exactly the way Colin hoped his little girl would take to a new nanny. Yet some things about Darcy didn't add up. He'd picked her agency because of its reputation and level of experience. Okay, so she was older than he'd first thought. But why did she have so few belongings and why were her clothes a bit on the cheap, hand-me-down side?

With Iris nuzzling his neck, Colin stepped into the pale green and pink nursery. This was the one room he'd had painted before they'd moved in. Every other room had just been furnished as he'd requested. He'd wanted something special for Iris and the designer really went all out with the round crib in the middle of the spacious room, sheer draping suspended from the ceiling that flowed down over the bed and classic white furniture complete with all things girly, pink and just a touch of sparkle. The floor-to-ceiling window also had sheer curtains that were tied back with some pink, shimmery material, and toy bins were stacked neatly against the far wall.

A room fit for a princess...or duchess, as the case may be.

When he sat Iris in her bed, she quickly grabbed her little heart pillow, hugged her new doll to her chest and lay down. Colin watched until her eyes closed, her breathing slowed.

Darcy might be a bit of a mystery, but with his status, he had to be extremely watchful. She seemed trustworthy so far. If she just wanted privacy that was one thing. Who was he to judge? Wasn't he lying and pretending to be someone else right now?

The fact that there was more to figure out with the alluring, frustrating nanny left him no choice but to head back downstairs and talk with her now that they were alone.

Of course, he was hiding the fact that he was a prince, one who found her to be sexy as hell. Still, he needed help with Iris. For now he'd have to keep Darcy around, but that didn't mean she'd be here for the full six months. They needed to pin down a suitable trial period. In the meantime, he could be researching a backup in case Darcy didn't work out.

Regardless of the end result, he had to ignore how enticing she was. Romance, whether short- or long-term, was not on his agenda, and he sure as hell wouldn't be so trite as to fall into bed with his baby's nanny.

Three

Darcy had picked up the living room, piling all the toys and infant blankets neatly in the corner. The rogue cereal pieces were in the trash, except for the crushed bits. She'd have to ask Colin where the vacuum was kept to get the rug back in order. She'd work with Iris and her cleaning skills next time. The girl needed a nap more than she needed a lesson.

Playing with Iris, truly feeling a bond starting to form, was both a blessing and an ache she couldn't begin to put into words. For so long she'd had that little-girl dream of having her own family, but such things were not meant to be. Darcy hadn't thought this job would be so intense, yet maybe it was the combination of the baby and the man that had her stomach in knots. As grouchy as he was, Colin was still very sexy, there was no denying the obvious.

At first, the instant attraction to Colin had layered over her anxiety of working with an infant. The man was hot, hot, hot, and that was just the physical packaging. When he spoke with that accent he only rose another notch on the sexy scale. But there was nothing like seeing him holding his beautiful daughter, the way he looked at her with all the love in the world. Something about watching him with his guard down had Darcy melting even more.

As Colin's footsteps pounded down the steps, she stood at the kitchen sink rinsing the sippy cup. Quickly placing it on the drying mat, she wiped her hands on her jeans. She had no clue what mood Colin would be in or how he might react once they were alone.

Would he ask her to leave simply because of the mess? A good first impression was everything and she'd probably blown it. He'd told her she had until the end of the day to prove herself, but she may not make it that far. She stood to lose her pride and her grandmother's legacy. There was no plan B, there was no knight who would ride to her rescue. So if Colin was angry enough to ask her to go, she wouldn't have much choice.

Darcy couldn't get a good read on him. When he looked at her she couldn't tell if he was angry or turned on. Ridiculous to think a piece of eye candy like Colin Alexander would find her attractive, but he volleyed between being pissed and raking his eyes over her.

No way would she bring up the fact he turned her inside out. She'd always been a professional and this job was no different…except for the fact she needed this one more than any other.

Just as Darcy turned, Colin was rounding the large center island. Even in the openness of the kitchen, the man seemed to dominate the room. She stepped back, the edge of the counter biting into the small of her back.

"Is she asleep?" Darcy asked, trying to keep her voice steady, though she felt anything but.

"Yes." His eyes pinned her in place as he rested one

hand on the granite counter. "We need to talk while she's down."

Swallowing, Darcy nodded. This was like the equivalent of the breakup in a business setting. Still, she wouldn't go down without a fight.

"I need to clean the rug first," she told him, knowing he probably recognized the stalling tactic. "I wasn't sure where you kept your vacuum."

"There's a handheld one in the utility room. I'll get it later."

Oh, this wasn't good. An image of her grandmother flashed through her mind. Darcy had promised Gram before she passed that Loving Hands would stay up and running. Then love had entered the picture…or what Darcy had thought was love. How could she have been so naive as to trust a man with her life and her family business, and not see that he was a lying, greedy user?

Colin leaned against the island and crossed his arms over his broad chest. "Why only one bag?"

His question jerked her from her thoughts. That's what he'd initially wanted to talk about? Her luggage?

"How many bags do I need?" she countered.

A sliver of a tattoo peeked out from beneath the hem of his T-shirt sleeve. Darcy's belly clenched. She'd always been a sucker for ink. But shallow lust is what got her into a mess of trouble the last time. A sexy, smooth-talking man and tats over solid muscles…she refused to go down the same path again, when all she'd met at the end of her journey was a broken heart. Not that Colin was a smooth talker. He was more of a blunt, grumpy, irritable talker.

"Will you be sending for more belongings?" he asked.

Still stunned that this was what he'd wanted to discuss, she shook her head. "I have all I need. Does this mean I'm staying?"

When he raked a hand through his tousled hair, a masculine, woodsy scent slid across the gap and straight to her. How did the man positively reek of sex appeal when he looked like he'd spent days without sleep?

"I want to discuss the trial period," he told her, shifting his weight with a slight wince. "The contract we mentioned on the phone was for six months. I'll give you one month to prove that you're the right fit for the job. Anytime in that month we can decide to terminate the agreement."

Relief spread through her in waves. She would definitely win him over in a month. She was good at her job, she'd been raised helping her grandmother care for children and, honestly, raising kids was all she knew. The irony of the situation as it related to her personal struggles was not lost on her.

And, actually, caring for kids wasn't all she knew, just all she knew to pay her bills. Cooking was her hobby, her therapy, really, but it wouldn't keep her afloat financially no matter how much she enjoyed it.

"That sounds fair." She rested her hands on either side of her hips, gripping the edge of the counter with her palms.

"I know we agreed on compensation," he went on as if conducting a business meeting and not standing in his kitchen with sexual tension vibrating between them. "I'll give you half now and the other half at the end of the six months, if you stay. Between now and the sixth month, there may be incentives along the way. Bonuses, if you will."

"And if I leave at the end of this month?"

Colin's bright eyes held hers as he lifted a shoulder. "Then take the first half of the money and go. No incentives."

Half the money was better than no money. Still, she

needed the full amount to pay off Thad's debt and jump-start the agency again. This job would save her business and get her back where she needed to be so she would make sure she impressed him with her skills.

She was an excellent cook, if she did say so herself. Surely that would be another check in her favor. What single man wouldn't want someone who had hot meals ready for him every single night?

"I expect you to care for Iris during my working hours which I already went over with you on the phone," he went on. "I don't expect you to cook every meal, that's a duty we can share. I do need you to drive if we go out, as I'm still recovering from an accident that has limited my activities. If all of this is fine with you, then you can stay."

Darcy nodded, though she wanted to ask about his injury. But now wasn't the time and if she stayed on as nanny, she'd most likely discover what had happened to him.

"I'm fine with that deal."

She held out a hand to shake. He darted his gaze down to her hand, then back up to her face. With an emotionless expression, Colin slid his warm, strong hand into hers and an electric sensation shot straight up her arm. His eyes widened for the briefest of moments. The grip on her hand tightened.

This wasn't happening. No way could an attraction form so quickly, be so intense. She'd been convinced the tension and fascination was one-sided. Apparently not.

Darcy swallowed, wondering what he was thinking, feeling. She didn't want the awkwardness to settle between them. This was only day one, though, so she'd chalk it up to them getting a feel for each other...not the chemistry that was growing and already causing problems.

"Do you want to give me a tour of the house?" Darcy asked, needing to remove herself from temptation.

Colin blinked, dropped her hand and nodded. "Of course. I also wanted to let you know that if you need an evening off to go out or have some personal time, just give me notice. I don't expect you to put your life on hold and work twenty-four hours a day."

Laughter bubbled up and Darcy couldn't keep it contained. Colin's brows drew together.

"You find that funny?"

Waving a hand in the air, Darcy shook her head. "I have no social life. I won't require any time off."

He tipped his chin down slightly, causing a longer strand of dark hair to fall over his eye as he studied her. "You keep surprising me."

Besides his striking looks, Colin had a voice that would make any woman tremble with need. She didn't want to tremble, didn't want to have any type of unexpected attraction toward this man or any other. From here on out, until her agency was back in business, Darcy vowed to stay focused. No men, regardless of how lonely she was. She didn't need someone to complete her, not by any means. But there were those nights she missed being held, missed the powerful touch only a man could provide.

"I'm really pretty simple," she told him. "My work keeps me happy so I don't need anything else."

"What about friends? Boyfriends?"

Okay, that wasn't subtle. Was he asking as an employer or as a man?

Pulling her self-control up front and center, Darcy stepped away from him and headed out of the kitchen. "How about that tour while Iris is sleeping?"

Two weeks and a great deal of sexual tension later, Colin led Darcy down the hall toward the back of the house, well aware of her closeness behind him and even more aware of the unspoken attraction that seemed to be hovering between them. He'd been struggling to keep any emotions hidden. He didn't want her to look at him and see any sign of lust. Colin had no room for such things, not when he and his daughter were desperate for help.

But each time he'd seen Darcy with Iris, something had moved in him. Something he couldn't identify. He assumed at this point she had no boyfriend. She'd made no mention of one even though she'd never come out and answered him when he'd grilled her on the subject her first day.

She'd managed to put him in his place without a word. Fine. He didn't have time to get involved in her personal life and he sure as hell shouldn't want to.

Earlier today, when he'd mentioned working out, he'd seen a brief interest pass over her face. He figured if he showed her the gym and they both made use of it, maybe they could work through...whatever this was brewing between them. He couldn't speak for Darcy, but fourteen days of strain and sexual tension was taking its toll on him.

Colin headed toward the back of the house where the first floor bedroom had been turned into a gym. He'd specified to his designer all the equipment he'd need to continue his therapy on his own and to keep in shape. He had to keep his workouts inside now since his injuries prevented him from going out for a run or rock climbing. He'd never rock climb again. His one main passion in life had been stolen from him.

Shoving aside unwanted anger and frustration, Colin eased the French doors open and stepped inside.

"I know you're busy with Iris, but I wanted you to know this is available to you any time you want to use it. I have weights, a treadmill, elliptical, bike, all top of the line."

"Wow, you certainly take the meaning of home gym

to a whole new level." Darcy glanced through the room and smiled. "I've never had much time to devote to a workout before."

Colin didn't think she needed to work out at all, but he wanted to extend the offer since he'd been using the gym and he hadn't invited her to make use of the space yet. Darcy's shapely body was perfect from every angle... and he'd studied it at every opportunity since the moment she moved in.

"You're more than welcome to everything in here if you decide you'd like to try," he told her.

"I've never used any of these machines before," she muttered. "But I'm sure I could muddle my way through."

Or he could offer to show her.

Colin cursed himself. If they were both going to use this space, he knew they had to do so at different times. The last thing he needed to see was a sweaty, flushed Darcy because that would conjure up a whole host of other images and fantasies.

At this point, he had to get something out in the open. They'd gone two weeks with passing glances and innocent touching as they worked with Iris. Each day he found it more difficult to quash his desires. And Darcy was a damn good nanny, so getting rid of her was not an option.

"I need to be honest with you," he told her.

Tucking her long hair behind her ears, Darcy nodded. "Okay."

"You're a beautiful woman," he began, hoping he wasn't making a mistake. "There's a pull between us and I don't think I'm being presumptuous when I say that. However, I plan to remain single and I have every intention of keeping our relationship professional."

Darcy's mouth had dropped open. For a moment he wondered if he'd gone too far or if his imagination had taken over.

Upfront and honest was how he preferred everything. Okay, obviously there were exceptions since he was keeping a colossal truth from her. But his royal status wouldn't affect her life. She was a nanny, she'd get paid, they would part ways in less than six months and their personal lives could remain private, for the most part.

"Then I'll be honest, too." She laced her fingers in front of her and lifted her chin. "I won't deny the attraction. I mean, you have to know what you look like, but that's just superficial. I still don't know you very well because you're so quiet and brooding, but my main focus is Iris. I promise I'm not here looking for anything other than a job. I've had enough difficulties in my life the past few years. Does that help ease your mind?"

Part of him wanted to know what she'd been through, but the other part told him to shut up and deal with his own issues. Had she just called him brooding? He suppressed the urge to smile at her bluntness. Admiration for this woman who wasn't afraid to speak her mind mixed right along with his arousal where she was concerned. The combination of the two could prove to be crippling if he didn't keep a tight rein on his emotions.

Still, Darcy wasn't like any woman he'd ever known. She wasn't blatantly sexual, she wasn't throwing herself at him even though she'd admitted to being attracted, and she'd been in his house ample time to try her hand at seduction. Not once had she come out with skimpy pajamas or purposely been provocative to try to capture his attention. Perhaps that was just another reason he found her so intriguing and refreshing.

Would she be so controlled if she knew who he really was, how much he was worth?

Being a member of royalty had always made him an instant magnet for women. His late wife hadn't cared about his status, which was one of the things that had initially drawn him to her. But then reality had hit, and the accident that nearly claimed his life wedged between them at the same time she'd discovered her pregnancy. Months of stress and worry had torn them apart and for once in his life, money couldn't fix his problems.

"You okay?" Darcy asked.

Her delicate hand rested on his bare arm and Colin clenched his teeth, fighting away the memories. He couldn't live in the past, trying to pinpoint the exact moment his marriage went wrong. Like everything else, little things started adding up to bigger things and, slowly, the marriage had just dissolved.

Iris was his main concern now. He needed to relax, work on being a regular father giving his daughter the best life possible.

And to decide whether to renounce his title. The pressure of knowing that their wayward cousin, who didn't deserve the title, would have it if something happened to Stefan was overwhelming. He hated being in this position, but ignoring it wouldn't make the situation go away.

"Colin?"

Nodding, he let out a sigh. "I'm fine," he assured her, hating when her hand slid away. Those gentle fingertips trailed down his arm before leaving him wanting more than just an innocent touch. "Anything you want to ask about the equipment while I'm here with you?"

Her eyes roamed over the apparatus in the workout room. An image of her sweating with him flashed through his mind which led to other images of them sweating and he cursed himself. If he didn't get control over his libido he'd have more trouble on his hands than he could possibly handle.

"If I wanted to start working out, what would you recommend? The treadmill? I'm pretty out of shape."

Out of shape? Everything about her shape screamed

perfection. He never was one of those guys who needed his woman to be supermodel thin. He preferred having plenty of curves to explore.

When her eyes came back to his, he fought the urge to pull her inside and get that sweat going. He'd bet his royal, jeweled crown she would look even sexier all flushed, with a sheen of perspiration across her body.

"Do you really want to work out?" he asked. "I don't want you to feel pressured. I'm just offering the room to you."

Darcy shrugged. "I could stand to lose a few pounds."

Anger simmered beneath the surface. "Who told you that?"

Darcy entered the room and checked out the elliptical, the treadmill, the free weights. "He's no longer in the picture, but that's not what matters. What matters is that I've let myself go, and with all of this at my fingertips I don't see why I shouldn't take advantage of it while I'm here."

Colin stepped in and came up behind her, close enough to touch. He clenched his hands at his sides. "If you want to feel better about yourself, that's one thing. If you're doing this because some bastard told you you're overweight, then I have a problem."

Her shoulders stiffened as she turned. The second she realized how close they were, her eyes widened, but she didn't step back. Their bodies were only a breath apart and with each inhale, the tips of her breasts brushed against his chest. He was playing with fire and damn if he could stop himself. He'd always lived for the adrenaline rush and Darcy got his blood pumping.

Being this close he noticed a sprinkling of freckles across her nose. There was so much innocence in this woman, yet in some ways she seemed too tough to be innocent. She'd gone through hard times, according to her. Even if she hadn't said so, he could tell by the way she was headstrong, determined and focused. How the hell could he not find that completely sexy?

"My weight may have been mentioned in my last relationship," she told him, keeping her eyes on his. "But he's history and I want to do this for me. Will you help me or not?"

Would he help her? Close quarters, alone without Iris as a buffer and having Darcy's body as his sole focus for hours? He may not want this attraction, but it was there nonetheless and only an idiot would turn her down.

"I'll help you," he told her. "We'll start tonight after Iris goes to bed. That work for you?"

Her smile spread across her face, lighting up those expressive eyes. "It works if you take it easy on me."

Oiktirmon. Mercy.

"Oh, I plan on giving you just what you need."

Four

What had she been thinking? Darcy had been so impressed by the gym she'd opened her mouth before she could think about what she was saying. Now she'd committed to exercising with someone who should be posing for calendars sans shirt, while she looked like the before picture on a Weight Watcher's ad.

She'd been taken with Colin and his blunt declaration of attraction. Apparently a lust-filled haze had clouded her mind and hindered her common sense. He'd called out the obvious and now they both had to deal with the tension that would no doubt envelop them every time they were together.

Dinner had been comfortable, though. Iris as the focal point certainly helped. Now she was bathed and in bed, and Darcy had pulled on her favorite yoga pants and an old Loving Hands T-shirt. After pulling on her worn tennis shoes, she headed toward the gym.

The whirring of the treadmill filtered out of the partially open doors and into the hallway. When Darcy peeked around the corner, she was so, so glad she had the advantage of being behind him. Obvious eye-candy images aside, she was thankful no one could see her because there was no way she could take in this male form, all sweaty, shirtless and in action, and not stand here with her mouth open, eyes wide.

The full view of his tattoo caught her attention. A dragon started over one shoulder blade, swirled down one biceps and disappeared over his shoulder to the front. Her fingers itched to trace the pattern, to feel all that taut skin beneath her fingertips. Surely there was some meaning behind the image. Most people had tattoos based on something personal in their lives. She couldn't help but wonder if she'd ever uncover anything beneath the surface with him.

Just as Darcy eased the door open, Colin stumbled, shouted a curse and smacked the red emergency button on the treadmill. Gripping the sides of the machine, he panted, head hanging between his shoulders.

"Are you all right?" she asked, crossing to the piece of equipment in case he needed help.

Colin jerked his head around, wincing as he caught sight of her. "I thought you'd be longer with putting Iris down."

As he turned completely and started to step down, his leg went out from under him and he collapsed, landing hard on the belt of the machine.

Darcy squatted beside him, her hands resting on his bare knee. "Colin, are you okay?" she repeated.

Stupid question, as he'd obviously hurt himself and was trying to hide the fact. Still, she couldn't just stand here and not do or say something.

"Fine," he bit out through gritted teeth. "I'm supposed

to walk every day, but the doctor says if I feel like it I can try jogging."

"Is that why you were running full speed on an incline when I came in?"

His eyes met hers. There went that click once again when this man stared at her. The intensity of his gaze couldn't even be put into words because she'd never experienced such a force in her life.

"I'm not going to be held prisoner by this injury." His tone left no room for argument. "And I don't want your pity."

Colin's eyes held hers another second before they dropped to her hands on his knee. The dark hair on his leg slid beneath her palms as she started to remove her hands. Instantly, his hand covered hers, holding her in place.

"I wasn't feeling pity," she whispered. "Attracted, intrigued, yes. Not pity."

His thumb stroked the back of her hand. "This can't be an issue."

She knew he wasn't referring to his injury or the fact that she'd found him in a state of pain.

"It's already an issue," she retorted, not even trying to pretend she had no idea what he was referring to. "We just have to take control of the tension instead of it controlling us."

His eyes held hers, the muscle ticked in his jaw. "Are you ready to get sweaty?"

Darcy swallowed, then took her own advice and tried to get a grip. Offering a smile, she said, "If you're trying to keep this attraction on the backburner, I think you probably shouldn't ask questions like that."

Laughing, Colin started to rise. "Just wanted to see the look on your face."

The man actually laughed. And there went that zing of desire shooting through her again, because a brooding Colin was sexy, but a smiling Colin was flat-out ir-resistible.

Darcy came to her feet. "I'm sure I didn't disappoint," she joked.

As Colin got his feet beneath him, Darcy took a step back. "So what are you recovering from?"

Raking a hand through his hair, Colin sighed and shook his head. "A life I've left behind," he muttered.

Curiosity heightened, she wanted to know more about this mysterious man who'd so easily and swiftly captured her attention.

"Tell me what your goal is," he said, resting a hand on the rail of the treadmill. "Are you wanting to lose weight, tone up or just work on feeling better about yourself?"

"All of the above."

A wide smile stretched across his face. The combination of those bright blue eyes and that knee-weakening smile could have any woman throwing all morals and professional behavior out the window.

"Let's get started," he said, clasping his hands together.

An hour later, Darcy was questioning her sanity and wondering why she'd let those sexy, dark-skinned muscles sway her judgment. How in the world did she think she could keep up? This man was obviously in shape and she was obviously...not.

She resisted the urge to bend over and pull in much-needed air to her overexerted lungs.

"Ready for more?" he asked, hands on his hips, devastatingly handsome smile on his face.

She sent him a glare. "I'm not a masochist."

"You're honest," he replied, using his T-shirt to wipe the sweat off his brow. "I prefer honesty."

"That makes two of us."

He moved over to the small refrigerator in the corner of the room and pulled out two bottles of water. After hand-ing her one, they both uncapped the drinks and took long pulls. Water had never tasted so good.

"So why the nanny business?" he asked, propping his foot upon a workout bench. His elbow rested on his knee, the bottle of water hung between two fingers. "Because you're an amazing cook. Dinner was pretty damn delicious. All of the meals have been great, but tonight's was my favorite."

Stunned and flattered at the compliment and his openness, Darcy screwed the lid back on her bottle. "I've never known anything other than taking care of children. I went to work with my grandmother every single day and fell in love. Cooking is a fun hobby and I love trying out new things. I guess if I weren't a nanny, I'd like to be a chef or a caterer."

She'd quickly steered the conversation to cooking. Anything to avoid talking too much about babies. The facts that children of her own weren't in her future and that anything she'd saved toward adoption had disappeared with Thad cut deep. Still, taking care of others was what she was meant to be doing, of that she was sure.

"Hey." Colin tipped his head to the side, searching her face. "You all right?"

"Oh, yeah." Darcy pushed a sweaty strand of hair that had escaped her ponytail behind her ear. "Just tired."

Pushing off the bench, Colin stalked closer, his focus solely on her. "Tomorrow we'll do weights and skip cardio."

"Tomorrow?" she asked. "You mean we're going to do this every day?"

The corner of his mouth twitched. "Only if you want to. I'm here every night after Iris goes to bed. If you want to join me, you are more than welcome. If you don't want to, no pressure. Personally, I think you're perfect the way you are."

"You haven't seen me naked," she muttered, realizing her mistake the second the words were out of her mouth. "Sorry. I'm—forget I said that."

"When a woman as sultry as you says the word *naked* it's impossible to keep certain images from flooding my mind."

Darcy held onto her bottle, thankful for the prop because her hands were shaking, as were her knees, and her entire body was responding to that low, sexy, heavily accented voice.

"Where are you from?" she asked.

"Greece."

Of course he was. Someplace beautiful and exotic, much like the man himself.

"So, dinner requests for tomorrow?" she asked. "I'll probably need to run to the store at some point, if that's okay."

"Not a problem." He turned toward the doorway, motioning her to exit ahead of him. "I have no requests. You obviously know what you're doing in the kitchen, which is more than I can say for myself."

Stepping into the hallway, she waited until Colin reached in and turned off the light. Darkness enveloped them, save for the slash of light at the end of the hallway shining down from the chandelier in the foyer.

"What's your favorite food?" she asked, trying to focus on his face in the dark, though neither of them had made a move to walk into the light.

"I haven't had too many American dishes," he replied. "I normally eat a lot of fish and vegetables."

Which would further explain why he was so buff and polished, and she had more dimples than a newborn baby's backside.

"I know just what to serve," she replied.

Her vision had adjusted to the darkness enough to see

the flare of heat in his baby blues just as he stepped in closer. "You claim I can't deliver loaded statements." His rich, low voice washed over her already heated body, ironically sending shivers all through her. "I'd say that goes both ways."

Before she could respond, Colin trailed a fingertip along the side of her face.

"Wh—what are you doing?" she asked, cursing her stammer, knowing it was a sign of weakness.

"Putting my curiosity to rest."

"Curiosity?"

That finger kept stroking, causing every pleasure point in her body to tingle.

"I needed to know if you are as silky as you appear," he murmured.

Warmth radiated from his broad body as he leaned in even closer, close enough to brush against hers and have her backing up into the wall.

Her gaze held his. "Am I?"

"Here you are," he whispered. "I wonder about here."

His lips covered hers in an instant, leaving her no choice but to reply to his demands. Okay, she could've chosen to push him away, but…why?

His tongue swept inside her mouth just as his hand curved around her chin, his thumb and forefinger on either side of her face as if to hold her in place. Darcy arched into him, wanting more and taking all he delivered. So many promises wrapped in that one kiss and all she had to do was let go.

Hadn't they both agreed to keep this professional? There was nothing professional about the spiral of arousal coursing through her or the need she so desperately wanted to cave in to.

Colin lifted only to shift his stance, pressing her further against the wall and his very hard, impressive body.

Whoever Colin Alexander was, the man possessed power and control. He demanded so much without words and his actions proved he was used to getting what he wanted.

Just like Thad.

Darcy jerked her head to the side, causing Colin's lips to slide against her jaw, his hand falling away.

She closed her eyes, trying to ignore the devil on her shoulder telling her to turn back and let Colin continue whatever it was he had in mind.

"Colin…"

He dropped his forehead to her shoulder, sighed, then took a step back. "Darcy, that was inexcusable."

Holding her hand to her moist lips, Darcy risked glancing back to Colin. "No, no. We're both to blame."

He propped his hands on his narrow hips and stared up at the ceiling. Darcy had no idea what to say, what to do.

"I've never been in this position before," she told him, clutching her water and wrapping her arms around her waist. "You need to know that I don't kiss employers and I've never, ever had a relationship with any of them beyond a professional one."

"I believe you."

When he offered no further comment, Darcy couldn't take the uncomfortable silence any longer. She turned and started walking down the hallway, when he called her name. She froze, but didn't look back.

"You need to know the last person I had a relationship with was my wife." His soft words floated down the wide hall, enveloping her. "I know we aren't taking this any further, but I didn't want you to think I made a habit of coming on to beautiful women."

Beautiful women.

Darcy threw him a look over her shoulder, nodded and carried on. She didn't stop, didn't slow down until she was in her room with the door shut behind her. Her heart still pounded just as fiercely as it had when she'd been in the darkened hall with Colin, the same as when she'd been sweating in the gym with him and the same as when he'd opened the door first thing that morning looking all rumpled and sexy.

With baby monitors in every room, there was no way she'd miss it if Iris needed something. Which was a very good thing because when Colin had been kissing her, for the briefest of moments, she'd forgotten her sole purpose for even being here. Her mind had traveled to a selfish place and all she wanted was more of that talented, demanding mouth on hers.

Dropping her head back against the door, Darcy groaned. This was the last thing she needed. If she didn't straighten up and focus, she'd have to resign and she needed the full amount of money Colin was paying her if she wanted to keep the agency afloat in any way. Not to mention if she wanted to ever get an apartment or a reliable vehicle.

The video monitor on the white nightstand showed a very peaceful Iris hugging her new doll to her chest. It was in the quiet, serene moments like this that Darcy truly felt that void in her heart. Growing up around other children and loving families, Darcy had always assumed she'd have a family of her own one day.

With the way she worked herself now, though, she didn't even have time for a date, much less a husband. Losing her entire savings had only pushed her dream of adopting further back, making her wonder if she just wasn't meant to be a mother.

There were worse things in the world than not having children…though from her perspective not many. She truly wished with all her heart that she had the ability to conceive like nearly every other woman, but that wasn't meant to be and she had to quit dwelling on it and move on. She wanted to be happy, so she had to focus on happy things and things that were in her control...infertility was certainly not one of them.

Tomorrow, she vowed, she would be one hundred percent professional. She just had to figure out a way to become immune to those striking blue eyes, that sultry accent and forget the way his lips basically assaulted hers in the best, most arousing way possible.

Hysterical laughter escaped her. Sure. No problem.

Five

The alarm chimed throughout the house, indicating that someone had triggered the gate and was coming up the drive. Colin lifted Iris in his arms and headed to the door to help Darcy with her grocery bags. She'd been gone for quite a while and he wondered if she'd run away or if she was stockpiling for the next month.

He'd just gotten off the phone with his assistant who informed Colin of some rather interesting information regarding Darcy and her financial situation. Apparently she was much worse off than he'd first thought. He wasn't sure whether to bring it up or let it slide. The last thing he wanted to do was make her uncomfortable or embarrassed, but at the same time, he wanted to do…something.

He was definitely going to have to bring up the fact her business was basically failing, but he needed to figure out the delicate matter.

Colin didn't know her personal issues, and he had no doubt she had them with her financial situation. All he knew right now was that her business had hit hard times in the last year and had fallen from one of the most sought out to an agency with only Darcy as the worker. There was definitely a story there.

When he opened the door, he didn't see her car. Instead, Darcy was walking up the drive, her arms weighted down with reusable grocery sacks bulging with food.

He sat Iris on the stoop. "Stay here, baby. Daddy needs to help Darcy."

With the gated property, Colin wasn't concerned about Iris wandering off. Worst-case scenario, she'd pluck all the vibrant flowers in the beds before he could get back to her. There was a pool around back, but he'd watch her and make sure she didn't toddle around the house.

Quickly moving toward Darcy, Colin felt his blood pressure rising. "What the hell are you doing?" he asked once he'd closed the gap. "Where's your car?"

"Broke down about a half mile back."

He pulled several bags off each arm, narrowing his eyes at the red creases on her delicate skin caused by all the weight. She wasn't some damn pack mule.

"Why didn't you call me?" he demanded as he curled his hands around the straining handles. "I would've come to get you."

Left with only two lighter bags, Darcy smiled and started up the drive. "By the time you could've gotten Iris in the car seat and gotten to me, I would've been here. Plus I didn't want to bother you guys in case you were playing or she was getting fussy and ready to lie down for a nap."

Even though Darcy's hair was pulled up into a high ponytail, Colin noted the damp tendrils clinging to her neck. The heat of the California sun could be relentless.

"Where exactly is your car?" he asked, trying to keep his voice controlled.

She explained what street she'd left it on, which really

didn't mean much to him since he knew little about the area or the street names. He'd call to have it towed and then he'd work on getting her proper transportation. No way was any employee of his going to be stranded again.

What if Iris had been with Darcy? Then what would she have done? The mishap was frustrating on so many levels.

Not only was she his employee, he refused to see any woman working herself to the point of sweaty exhaustion and that's exactly where Darcy was at. A sheen of perspiration glistened across her forehead and upper lip, her cheeks were red and she had circles beneath her eyes.

Where he was from the women would never leave their homes without full makeup, perfectly styled hair and flashy clothes…much like LA. Still, Darcy didn't seem to care that she wasn't completely made up for an outing. He actually found the quality quite refreshing and incredibly hot.

As if he needed another reason to be aroused by her. He needed to nip this sexual urge in the bud and stay focused.

Once they reached the stoop, Iris had indeed plucked up a variety of flowers, clutching them in her tight little hand.

"Pitty," she exclaimed, thrusting them toward Darcy. "You pitty."

Darcy laughed. "Oh, honey. You're so sweet."

Colin looked at Darcy and saw an alluring, determined and resilient woman. How could any man not be attracted to those qualities? And her sexuality was stealthy. You didn't see the impact coming until it hit you hard. Each day that passed made him realize just how much power she was beginning to have over him.

By the time they got all the bags inside and onto the wide center island in the kitchen, Colin had worked up quite a sweat of his own.

"I'll put these away," Darcy told him as she opened the pantry. "I need to walk back to my car after and see if it's the transmission. I've been having issues with that thing, but a transmission would cost more than the old car is worth."

Colin stood amazed. "*You* plan on looking to see if the transmission is shot?"

Over the stacks of bags, Darcy met his gaze. "Yeah, why? Who else is going to look at it?"

Iris patted his leg and Colin leaned down to lift her up. She still clutched those colorful flowers in her hand so he moved to the cabinet to get down a small glass to use as a vase.

"I'd call a mechanic," he replied, filling the glass with water.

With a soft laugh and shake of her head, Darcy turned her attention back to pulling the groceries from the sacks. "Well, mechanics charge just to come look at the car, then there's the labor to fix the problem, plus the part."

As she listed all the costs associated with getting the vehicle fixed, Colin had to remind himself he wasn't back at the palace. He wasn't talking to someone who would just pay someone else to take care of the issue and move on. Darcy was obviously a hard worker and she didn't need to tell him her funds were lacking.

Taking the flowers from Iris's hand, he sat them in the glass. "There, sweetheart."

She clapped her hands together and wiggled in an attempt to get away. Carefully, he put her back down and watched her move to Darcy. The easy way Iris had taken to the new nanny made him happy he'd allowed her to stay. The incident in the hall last night, though, had kept him up questioning his decision. They were still on a trial and he really didn't want to start the process of finding someone else. That was one thing he wouldn't do to Iris.

Even though they'd moved across the globe, he wanted Iris to have as much stability in her life as possible until he was absolutely certain of their future.

"Hey, cutie." Darcy pulled out a bag of flour and glanced down to her side, a wide smile stretching across her face. "I'm almost done and then you and I can play a little game."

"I'll take care of getting your car picked up."

Darcy's eyes flashed back to his. "That's not your job."

Crossing his arms over his chest, ready for the battle she so obviously thought was coming, Colin replied, "Cooking every single meal and going to the store isn't your job, either. I'm trying to help. We agreed on sharing these responsibilities."

"You can help by letting me do what works for me with my personal circumstances. Fixing my car wasn't included in our agreement."

As Darcy ignored him to focus on putting the last of the groceries away, Colin didn't know if he was pissed to be dismissed so easily or if he was elated that she wasn't walking on eggshells around him because he was a prince. How would she react if she knew just how wealthy he was? Would she even care about his royal status? Darcy didn't seem the type to be attracted to money or power. She seemed to be doing just fine on her own.

And that was the main problem he was having. She shouldn't have to do everything on her own.

"How about I fix lunch and you can make dinner?" he suggested.

Bundling all the reusable sacks into one neatly folded pile, Darcy raised a brow and grinned. "And what are you making for lunch, oh great chef?"

"You're mocking me," he laughed. "I know I'm not as good as you in the kitchen, but I think I can give you a run for your money. Isn't that the expression you Americans have?"

Her lips pursed as she continued to stare. "It is, but I don't think you can hold your own against me."

"Challenge accepted," he told her, ready to prove her wrong.

Damn it. Now he needed to search on the internet for something easy, quick and delicious. He'd been thinking of throwing sandwich stuff together for lunch, but given her instant doubt, Colin had to raise his game. And he would, just as soon as he took care of the car. She was getting his assistance whether she liked it or not.

The shrill alarm had Darcy jumping to her feet and pulling Iris with her. They'd been coloring on the floor in the living room when the ear-piercing noise came out of nowhere.

Darcy knew that sound and it was all she could do not to laugh. Calmly, though, she rested Iris on her hip and headed toward the kitchen where lunch was probably not going to be happening anytime soon.

Standing in the wide, arched doorway, Darcy took in the scene and had to literally bite her lips to keep from laughing.

There were dirty bowls littering the island, opened packages of random ingredients spread about and Colin was currently slapping a kitchen towel at the small flame coming from the burner. Smoke billowed through the open space as Darcy moved into the kitchen. She eased Iris into her high chair and wheeled it over near the patio door, which Darcy opened to let some fresh air in. She made her way down the wall, opening each window as she passed.

Colin turned, still holding the charred dishtowel, and shrugged. "I'm not admitting defeat."

"Of course not," she replied, not even bothering to hide her smile. "Why would you?"

"Lunch will be just a few more minutes."

"I'm sure it will be wonderful." Darcy shrugged. "No rush."

Poor guy was still trying to save his pride. She wasn't about to say more. Their easy banter seriously helped take the edge off the sexual tension. Playfulness, even a little flirting she could handle. Anything beyond that… she glanced to the tiny flame Colin was smacking. Yeah, that flame signified her life right now. If she got too close to Colin she'd get burned. The signs were literally in front of her face.

Darcy had just grabbed a handful of puffed snacks to hold Iris over until lunch was ready when another alarm sounded through the house. This one was announcing a visitor.

The darn house was wired so tight with security and monitors and alarms, Darcy's head had practically spun in circles when Colin had explained the entire system to her. Who was this man that he needed so much security?

"Are you expecting company?" she asked, laying the snacks across the highchair tray for Iris.

"Actually, I am." Colin turned off the burner, sat the pan on a cooler one and turned to her. "Don't touch anything. I've got it under control. This won't take long."

He rushed from the room and out the front door.

"Your father is one mysterious man," Darcy muttered to Iris. "And apparently not a chef."

Smoothing the dark curls away from the baby's face, Darcy really studied how much Iris looked like Colin. All bronzed skin, dark molasses eyes and striking features. Iris would be an absolute bombshell when she grew up. Darcy couldn't help but wonder if Iris's mother had been a Greek beauty as well. Most likely Colin wouldn't have married someone who was an ogre.

Moments later, Colin breezed back into the house.

"Sorry about that. Lunch will be ready in five minutes if you'd like to get some plates out."

"Are you going to tell me what we're having now?"

"You'll see," he told her before he went back into the foyer.

On a sigh, she crossed the room and pulled out two plates and one smaller plate for Iris. She resisted the urge to stroke the beautiful cabinets and the quartz counter-tops. This kitchen alone cost more money than she made in a year…during the good times. Having a home and a gourmet kitchen with a family to cook for was a dream she honestly didn't see coming true. That was okay, though. For now she was here, working and making money to save her agency, and in the end that's all that truly mattered. And the fact she was caring for a baby was a great form of forced therapy she'd desperately needed to face her fears.

Moments later, Colin came back into the kitchen wearing a mischievous grin, but he said nothing as he dished out whatever he'd managed to salvage from the burning pan. Apparently he'd removed the pot before the flames consumed their entire meal.

"I admit, after the fanfare with the smoke alarm, this actually smells delicious."

He threw her a glance over his shoulder. "I have a whole host of surprises for you."

Those words held a plethora of meanings, but when said while holding her gaze beneath heavy lids, her mind instantly traveled to the darkened hallway last night and how her body still ached after such a gloriously arousing kiss.

Could such an experience be labeled by one simple word? A kiss was something that could be given from a parent to a child, from a child to a pet, from a peasant to the hand of a diplomat. The word *kiss* blanketed a lot of ground.

"Ready?"

Darcy blinked, realizing Colin stood in front of her with two plates of…

"You made shrimp Alfredo?" she asked, more than amazed.

"You think I can't boil noodles and melt some butter?" he asked, feigning shock.

Taking her plate, inhaling the garlicky goodness, she laughed. "I had my doubts."

Darcy sat her plate on the table and went to move Iris's highchair over.

"I've got her," Colin said, holding his hand up. "You eat while it's hot."

Darcy stared as Colin wheeled Iris closer to the table. She then sat in amazement as he cut up the noodles, blew on them and offered small bites to his daughter.

"You're not eating," he commented without turning his head in her direction.

"I'm surprised." Darcy slid onto the built-in bench beneath the wide window. Grabbing her fork, she started pushing the noodles and shrimp around on her plate. "I'm the nanny, so eating a hot meal isn't something I'm used to. I'm also not used to the parent doing my job while I'm sitting right here."

He tossed her a glance. "I'm not like most parents. She's my daughter and I'm not paying you to raise her so I can prop my feet up and watch her life go by. I'm paying you to help for a few months. There's a huge difference."

Darcy swallowed, hating how her observation instantly made him defensive and how she was reminded again how little time she would actually have here.

"I apologize," she said, stabbing a plump shrimp coated in Alfredo sauce. "I should know by now that every family, every circumstance is different."

"Don't apologize," he replied. "Actually, as soon as you're finished eating, I have something for you."

Intrigued, Darcy stared across the table. "You made lunch, you're forcing me to eat instead of feeding Iris and you have something else up your sleeve? You've got to be kidding."

The muscle in his jaw ticked, his eyes held hers. "I don't joke too often."

The man was intense, she'd give him that. He went from super dad to sexy employer in the span of one quick blink. Regardless of his demeanor, Colin Alexander exuded sex appeal.

Darcy didn't ask any more questions. She didn't know Colin well, but she was positive anything she'd ask would be dodged or ignored. He was a man of absolute control, absolute power. She had no clue what he did for a living, she only knew he worked from home. However Colin made his money, Darcy was positive he dominated every facet of his life, and was even more controlled and possibly ruthless in whatever business he was in.

They finished lunch in silence, except for the cute noises and random words coming from Iris. When Darcy was finished, she took the plates to the sink, rinsed them and put them in the dishwasher.

"This is a really nice dishwasher."

Inwardly she groaned. What sane person coveted someone else's kitchen appliances? Talk about pathetic. She was showing her lower-class side...which was the only side she knew lately.

Pulling the tray out, Colin lifted Iris and carefully set her on the tile. In an instant she darted off toward the living room. Thanks to the mostly open-concept design of the house, they could still keep an eye on her through the wide, arched doorway.

The little girl picked up the doll Darcy had given her,

sat on the floor and started rocking her. That familiar ache spread through Darcy. But there were plenty more blessings in her life to count. Each day with Iris was a blessing. The child was sweet, always happy and fun-loving, when she got her naps in, and Darcy was lucky to be working under such amazing circumstances.

"Get Iris and meet me out front."

Darcy glanced back to Colin. "You're making me nervous."

One corner of his mouth kicked up. "Baby, that's the best compliment anyone has ever given me."

He strode away without another word and Darcy had a gut feeling she'd just stirred the hornet's nest of hormones.

Darcy crossed into the living room and slid her hands beneath Iris's little arms. "Come on, sweetheart. Bring your dolly and let's go see what your daddy is up to."

"Doll," Iris repeated. "Pitty."

Laughing, Darcy kissed the dark head of curls. "Yes, baby. Your dolly is pretty."

Stepping outside, Darcy immediately spotted Colin with a wide grin on his face.

"What is that?" she asked, glancing over his shoulder at the big, black SUV, all shiny and brand-new.

"Yours."

Six

Colin watched Darcy as her eyes widened, her face paled.

"You—what…"

Her stuttering and the fact she was rendered speechless had him confused. "Your car isn't worth fixing and you need viable transportation. Consider this a very late birthday present."

Her eyes darted to his and instead of gratitude he saw… anger? Seriously? He didn't know a woman that didn't fawn all over gifts, especially a new car. He didn't know where he'd gone wrong here, but he'd seriously miscalculated her response.

"You said you'd call someone about my car," she explained.

"I did. I had it removed from the road and now you have a new vehicle that you won't have to worry about."

Darcy didn't look nearly as excited as he'd figured she would. In fact, she looked downright angry.

"I can't accept this," she stated, still remaining on the

concrete stoop holding onto Iris. "I want my own car fixed, not a replacement that cost more than I could ever afford. And I don't need a birthday present from you."

"If you don't want it as a late present, then just use the vehicle while you work for me," he said slowly, moving toward her as he made sure she understood this wasn't any form of bribery or something more. "Consider it one of the incentives I mentioned on your first day. The vehicle is not up for debate. You need to have reliable transportation because you're watching my daughter and had she been in your car earlier, you both would've been stranded."

Darcy rolled her eyes. "Don't be so dramatic. I wasn't stranded. I walked here. Had Iris been with me, I would've called for help and you could've been there in no time. I was only a half mile away."

"What happens when you're ten miles away?" he countered, slipping Iris from Darcy's arms. "You can't walk that far with a toddler and you can't stay in the car in this heat."

Darcy crossed her arms over her chest and glanced away. "I can handle myself."

"Do you even want to go look at the car?" he asked.

"I can see it just fine." She brought her eyes back up to meet his. "I would like to know where my car is and I want it back."

Spinning on her heel, she went back inside, slamming the door. Colin glanced to Iris who was now chewing on the small stuffed doll's hair.

"Where did I go wrong?" he asked.

Colin knew whatever had just happened had little to do with the vehicle in his drive and everything to do with something that was personal to her. Did her old broken car hold some sentimental value?

"We better go see if she's sticking around," he told Iris as he headed toward the door.

By the time he found Darcy, she was in her room, standing at the floor-to-ceiling window looking out onto the backyard. Her room was neat and tidy. She'd plumped the pillows on her perfectly made bed and her single piece of luggage sat on the floor at the foot of it. Other than a small pair of flip-flops, there was no sign she'd even made herself at home. He knew she was orderly around the house, but he assumed in her own room, she'd be a little more laid back.

"Are you quitting?" he asked from the doorway. Even though this was his house, the bedroom was Darcy's for as long as she was here and he wasn't about to infringe on her territory.

Without turning around, Darcy let out a laugh that held no humor. "I have nowhere else to go and I need this job. I'll use the car while I'm here, but I really just want mine back. I have my reasons."

"Down," Iris said, squirming against him.

"Can we come in?" he asked.

Darcy glanced over her shoulder. "It's your house, Colin."

He stepped into the room and closed the door, confining Iris to an area where he could still watch her and talk to Darcy at the same time.

"Listen, I had no idea getting you a car would set off so much emotion." Slowly closing the space between them, he came to stand in front of her. "I'll get your car fixed and have it delivered back here. But you will still be using the new one. No arguments."

She eyed him for another minute before tipping her head to the side. "One of these days someone is going to tell you no."

"No, no, no, no," Iris chanted as she toddled around the room waving her doll in the air.

Darcy laughed and Colin couldn't stop himself from smiling. "She's the only one who can get away with it," he informed Darcy.

Truly focusing on Darcy, he crossed the room. As he neared, her eyes widened. He liked to think it was from the attraction, but that was his arrogance talking. More than likely she was trying to figure him out, same as he was doing with her.

But he would get through her defenses. He knew without a doubt her secret had everything to do with the fact that she had nowhere else to go.

As the space between them minimized, Colin kept his gaze locked on hers. The closer he got, the more she had to tip her head back to hold his stare.

"I can't help but feel you're hiding something," he started. "Your background check told me your business has hit a rough patch and you are on your own now."

Darcy nodded, her lips thinning. "There are challenges I'm facing privately, but nothing that will affect my job with you. I promise. I just don't want to be indebted to you for fixing my car."

Money wasn't the root of all evil as the old saying went. The evil was the person holding the purse strings who did nothing to help others.

"I think I'll take Iris outside for a walk." Darcy skirted around him, careful to shift her body so she didn't even brush against him. "Feel free to join us if you want."

Colin laughed as he turned to face her. "Not very subtle, the way you dodged my question."

"Subtlety wasn't what I was going for." She lifted Iris in her arms and smiled. The way she headed straight out the door as if she hadn't just put him in his place really annoyed and amused him at the same time. Damn, she was fun, yet prickly.

Darcy was perfect with Iris, independent and she turned him inside out at every move.

When his marriage had started failing, Colin blamed himself. He'd put Karina through hell with his injury, his surgeries, not being there for her as a husband should be. He'd never imagined he'd feel a desire for another woman again, but here he was, pining after his temporary nanny, of all people.

If he didn't keep his head on straight, he'd be losing focus on why he was in LA to begin with. He was no closer to deciding if staying away from Galini Isle was best for him and Iris or if returning to the secure, enclosed, yet exposed, lifestyle of the royals was the way he should go.

Here he had more freedom to take her out in public. They'd walked to the park last week and it had been so refreshing not to have guards hovering nearby. The longer he stayed in the United States, the more he worried he'd never want to leave.

There was only one right decision...he only wished he knew which one it was.

Playing outside in the yard was always so much fun for Darcy. She loved hearing Iris's squeals of delight and seeing her little carefree spirit. Darcy had been here for a full month now and had easily passed the trial period. Each second she spent with Iris only had Darcy more thankful she'd fought for this position. Holding onto Iris's tiny little hand just felt right. Everything about being with this sweet child felt right.

Not to mention that working for a man who oozed sexiness, power and control was one giant glob of icing on the proverbial cake.

Talk about landing the job of a lifetime. Still, Darcy couldn't help but wonder what happened to Colin's late wife. He didn't mention her, didn't even have any photos around the house. The man seemed as if he was running away or hiding from something, but she truly had no clue what. She could easily research him online, but she wasn't going to snoop into his life. That would be sneaky and Darcy prided herself on honesty. If he wanted to discuss his life, he would when the time was right.

Iris pulled away from Darcy and started running toward the landscaping framing the patio. Shielding her eyes with her hand, Darcy stared ahead as the little girl ran after a butterfly that had landed on one of the vibrant flowers. By the time Iris got there, the butterfly had flown away.

Iris looked around and when she realized the insect was no longer nearby, her chin started quivering. Closing the space between them, Darcy knelt down in front of the toddler and smoothed the curls away from her forehead, making a mental note to pick up some hair accessories for Iris.

"It's okay, sweetheart," Darcy consoled. "Miss Butterfly had to go home for a nap. I bet she'll be back another time. Would you like to go in and lie down? I saw a butterfly book in your room. How about we read that?"

"No," Iris cried, shaking her head. "No, no, no."

The one word kids learned early and used for nearly every reply, especially when they were in need of a nap. Darcy may have been working with older children these past several years, but certain things she would never forget.

When Darcy scooped her up and headed toward the house, the tears instantly transformed from sad to angry, and Iris's arms started flying as the instant tantrum went into full swing. Maybe Darcy shouldn't have taken Iris on that walk. Apparently the window of opportunity was missed and the nap should've come first.

Patting her back and trying to dodge the whirlwind arms, Darcy took Iris into the house. Of course, inside, the cries seemed to echo into surround sound. Colin came running from the office off the kitchen, his cell to his ear, worry etched across his face.

"What happened?" he said, holding the device away from his mouth.

"She's just tired," Darcy explained. "Sorry we disturbed you."

Colin didn't resume his call as Darcy walked by. Maybe he was waiting for them to pass because of Iris's ear-splitting screams, but the way he studied them, Darcy worried he was wondering why his daughter was so unhappy. This was the first time Iris had truly thrown a fit around Darcy, but every kid had their moments and as a nanny, one just had to learn how to adjust to that child's needs accordingly.

And right now, little Miss Iris needed her bed and a couple of hours of peace and quiet.

As she reached the top of the stairs, Darcy didn't have to glance over her shoulder to know that Colin was staring at her.

"Come on, little one," Darcy cooed.

After walking around the room, shutting the blinds, turning on the small fan for white noise and grabbing Iris's blanket and doll, Darcy settled into the cushy rocking chair and began to hum, occasionally adding in a few lyrics to "You Are My Sunshine." Iris's eyes started to grow heavy. Darcy knew the rule of thumb was to lay young children down while they were still awake, but holding and rocking a baby was a temptation she couldn't avoid. Today Darcy justified it by telling herself she was just waiting for Iris to calm down.

Darcy held onto the precious bundle in her arms and

came to her feet. Iris still clutched the silky blanket and stuffed doll as Darcy eased the sleeping beauty into her bed.

With her hands resting on the rail, Darcy stared at the spiky, damp lashes resting on Iris's reddened cheeks. Moments ago this child was throwing a fit and now she slept peacefully. When she woke she wouldn't remember she'd been upset, and that was how Darcy wanted to live her life.

Moving forward was the only way to prove there was life after the death of a dream. She couldn't allow endometriosis to define her. Discovering that the family she'd dreamed of having one day wouldn't happen had been a crushing blow, but Darcy had persevered, forcing herself to become stronger than her disappointments.

Swallowing the lump in her throat, Darcy turned from the bed and headed into the hall. She'd just pulled the door closed when she turned and ran straight into Colin's hard chest.

The instant force of colliding with him threw her off balance. Colin's hands immediately gripped her bare arms to steady her. Breath caught in her throat, her heart beat a fast, bruising rhythm against her chest. An instant flash of their heated kiss flooded her mind and all Darcy could think of was how perfectly they fit together.

Down girl.

Colin's eyes studied her face, her mouth. Tingles shot through her…tingles she shouldn't be feeling for her boss.

"We need to talk."

The statement, laced with such authority, delivered a punch to her stomach. Were they going to talk professionally? Personally? Was he upset with her for something she'd done?

Or did he want her alone for purely selfish, carnal reasons?

The second he turned and walked away, Darcy followed.

Seven

Fisting his hands at his sides, Colin cursed himself as he went downstairs and into his office. He had to keep reminding himself that the woman he'd hired to care for Iris was an employee, not an object to be lusting after. He'd never been sexually attracted to an employee—before, during or after his marriage.

Not once had his professional and personal needs ever crossed paths, but every single time he looked at Darcy he felt that kick to the gut that demanded he take notice of the all-American beauty.

Added to that, she was the only woman since Karina to have any connection to Iris. Colin would be lying to himself if he didn't admit that seeing Darcy around his daughter in all her youthful, vibrant glory had something tugging on his heart.

Damn it, he didn't want his heart tugged. He had too much on his plate right now and craving a woman, his nanny, for pity's sake, was not an option.

"You wanted me?"

Grinding his teeth to keep from saying what he really wanted, Colin turned to face Darcy. He'd assumed coming to his office would make this conversation easier, less personal.

"I want you to stop rocking Iris before you lay her down to sleep."

Darcy blanched and Colin cursed himself for the rough tone he'd taken.

"She was always used to just being laid down," he went on, trying to lighten his voice. It wasn't Darcy's fault he was fighting a losing battle with his attraction for her.

Darcy straightened her shoulders, tipped her chin and gave a quick nod. "I apologize. I'll be sure to lay her down right away next time."

Stiffly, she turned toward the door and Colin hated himself for making her feel bad about herself. Damn it. He didn't want this. He didn't want the chemistry or the awkward sexual tension, and he sure as hell didn't want to have to mask his arousal by being snippy and gruff with her. He wanted Iris to have that loving touch, to be wrapped in the arms of someone who cared for her, and it was obvious Darcy cared for his little girl.

Maybe he wasn't capable of being happy anywhere if this was any indication. He'd taken out his frustrations with himself on Darcy. If he wasn't happy here, though, did that mean he wasn't happy stepping away from his duty? Is that what all of this boiled down to?

Colin had been in a great mood moments ago as he'd been talking on the phone with his best friend, Prince Luc Silva. He hadn't spoken to him in months, other than texts or emails. As soon as they'd hung up, Darcy's soft voice had filtered through the monitor system in the home and damn if hearing all of that softness wasn't like being wrapped in her sweet embrace.

He couldn't afford to be wrapped up in anything that didn't involve his country, his loyalty and the decision he needed to make regarding his and Iris's future in the kingdom.

"Darcy," he called out before she could clear the doorway.

She froze, but didn't turn around. "Yes?"

Anything he wanted to say would be a bad idea, rocking their already shaky relationship. "Nothing," he said, shaking his head.

Regardless of the attraction, Colin was glad he'd decided to let Darcy stay on after they'd verbally battled that first day. He couldn't imagine anyone else with Iris.

Each day brought them closer to the six-month mark, closer to his staying or going. And, to be honest, he was growing too fond of having her here, in his life. He was finding an inner peace he hadn't expected. He was almost angry at himself for allowing his emotions to get the better of him, but where Darcy was concerned, he was finding he had little say in the matter.

Stefan was putting the pressure on, but Colin couldn't deal with Galini Isle and Darcy simultaneously. Both issues were overwhelming and threatened to take over his life. Right now, though, he wanted to concentrate on Darcy. Even though he knew Galini Isle should come first, he needed to see if there was more to their attraction than pure lust.

After dinner, Colin wanted to give Iris her bath so Darcy took the opportunity to sew a button back on her only dress shirt. The button right at the breast had popped off after a big inhale. In order for this top to fit properly, she either needed to lose a few pounds or stop breathing. She was thankful Colin had been nowhere around to witness the mishap.

Threading the needle, Darcy quickly fixed the shirt and was putting her small sewing kit away when a knock sounded at her door.

"Come in," she called as she wound the unused thread back around the spool.

Colin stepped in, holding Iris who was wrapped in her thick terrycloth monogrammed towel. Darcy didn't even want to know how much that plush towel cost…she'd seen the designer label.

"I need to make a phone call," Colin told her, taking in the shirt in her lap and the supplies spread over the bed. "Am I interrupting something?"

"Oh, no." Darcy scooted everything out of the way and came to her feet, smoothing down her pink T-shirt. "I was just sewing a button back on my shirt."

Colin's brows drew together. "Just buy a new shirt."

Yeah, why didn't she think of that? Between being technically homeless, nearly ready to shut the doors on the business barely keeping food in her mouth and trying to keep her car running, why hadn't she just hit the mall in her spare time for a new wardrobe?

But he didn't need her sarcasm. A man like Colin wouldn't understand because if anything in his life was broken, he could just pay to have it fixed or snap his fingers and have people at his beck and call.

Another layer of division between them, showing her just how vast their differences were.

Ignoring his question, because anything she would reply with would most definitely be snarky, she came to her feet, crossed the room and reached for Iris.

"Go on and make your call." The sweet scent of freshly bathed baby always made her heart weep just a little. "I'll take care of this sweet princess."

"Don't call her that."

Jerking her attention from the wrapped, squirming

bundle in her arms to Colin, Darcy jerked. "Call her what? Princess?"

"I don't like that term," he stated, crossing his arms and leveling her gaze.

"It's a simple term of endearment," Darcy defended herself, shifting Iris to settle her more comfortably on her hip. "I'm not sure what you think I'm implying when I say it, but—"

"No more. I don't want her to be a spoiled child and that term suggests too much."

"Colin—"

He held up a hand, cutting her off once more. "She's my daughter. She will not be called princess."

Feeling her blood pressure rise through the onslaught of confusion, Darcy took a step forward. "Yes, sir. If you'll excuse me, I need to get Iris ready for bed."

She pushed by him and exited her room, headed into the nursery next door and closed the door. What on earth had gotten into him? He was still in a mood and Darcy had no clue why. Darcy quickly dressed Iris in a pair of yellow footed pajamas with little bunnies on each of the toes. Every single baby item the toddler possessed was adorable. Darcy was getting more and more used to being surrounded by everything baby. The only thing she worried about now was how she'd leave at the end of the term they'd agreed upon. Staying away from babies for years had helped to soothe her ache somewhat, but being thrust into the world of all things tiny and pink brought Darcy's wishes back to the surface. To think all of that would be taken from her again in a few months.

She had no clue what he'd do when her term was up. Perhaps he just wanted to get his feet back on solid ground since he was a widower with a baby. Maybe he thought he could take it from there. Darcy had learned long ago not to question her clients' intentions.

She couldn't get too used to the weight of Iris in her arms, or the way Iris would clutch that ugly old doll Darcy had given her or the way she had started to reach for Darcy. But such simple things had already infiltrated Darcy's heart.

And Colin, as grouchy and moody as he'd been, had also managed to capture her attention in a way she hadn't expected. She couldn't get the image of him dominating her, kissing her, demanding more, from her mind.

As Darcy turned off the lights and clicked on the projector that danced stars across the ceiling, she knew she needed to find him and figure out what was going on. The man was a walking mystery, and if she was going to stay, and she really had no choice, she needed to clear the air. He obviously had something on his mind. Now all she had to do was let him know she was here if he wanted to talk and try to prevent anymore kissing episodes from happening.

Because kissing Colin had turned into another one of those fantasies leaving her wanting more. But Darcy was a realist by default. She may want a man to love her and a family to go right along with him in her perfect world, or the image she had of perfection, but the truth was Colin and Iris were out of reach.

Darcy had to keep reminding herself of that or she'd be severely crushed when time came to leave…alone.

Oh. My.

There was a reason Darcy had made her way through the house searching for Colin, but right at this moment she had no clue what it was. In fact, she had no thoughts whatsoever because her mind and her sight were filled with a glorious image of Colin doing one-armed pull-ups, shirtless, displaying that tattoo in a sweaty way that had her all but panting.

Dark skin wrapped around taut muscles flexing with each movement had Darcy gripping the doorframe. She wasn't about to interrupt this free show. There was no way she could miss the chance to see her boss in all his sexy glory. She wasn't dead, after all. She just couldn't think clearly when he was around…an issue she'd never had with any other man.

With a grunt, he pulled himself up one last time before dropping back to the floor. Hands resting on his hips just above his low-slung shorts, Colin's shoulders shifted up and down as he pulled in deep breaths. Then he stilled, turned his head over his shoulder and spotted her.

Busted.

He held her gaze. It was now or never.

"We need to talk," she informed him, bolstering her courage by tamping down her girlie parts and stepping into the gym.

"If you want to work out, fine. I'm not in the mood to talk."

Darcy crossed her arms over her chest. "Seems like your mood is flat-out grouchy."

Colin turned fully to face her, but continued to stare. Darcy wondered if she'd crossed a line. But, boss or not, he shouldn't take his attitude out on her.

"I came to see if you wanted to talk about whatever has you brooding," she went on, trying her hardest to keep her eyes on his and not on the sweaty pecs and the ink that had her heart racing. "This tension is something I prefer not to work around and it's not good for a child because they can sense such things even at an early age."

Colin took a step forward, eyes locked on hers. "Is that right?"

Swallowing, Darcy nodded. "Yes."

He took another step, then another, eventually closing the gap between them. Darcy inhaled that musky, male scent, took in those muscles that were within striking distance and blinked up at Colin.

"If you're trying to intimidate me, you'll have to try harder." She had to keep the upper hand here because her control was slowly slipping and she had to at least put up a strong front. "If you don't want to talk, I'll leave you to your workout so you can take out your frustrations that way."

His stunning blue eyes traveled over her face. "Go change and join me."

"I don't think that's a good idea."

"Because of my mood?"

Darcy took in a deep breath. "Among other things."

"Like the pull between us?"

Why deny the obvious? She'd never been one to play games, though she did do her best to avoid uncomfortable situations. So how did she find herself here?

"Whatever has made you all surly is the main issue," she stated. "But the attraction is something we already discussed and agreed to ignore."

The muscle in Colin's jaw ticked, his nostrils flared. "Discussing and ignoring our chemistry isn't going to make it go away. As far as my mood goes, I had a disagreement with my brother on the phone and I'm dealing with some family things. That's all you need to know and more than you're entitled to."

Shaking her head, Darcy took a step back. "Obviously it was a mistake to come down here."

She turned, set on heading up to her room and figuring out new recipes for the coming week. She'd barely taken a step out the door before one strong hand wrapped around her arm and pulled her to a stop.

"The mistake would be leaving."

His words washed over her, his breath tickled the side

of her neck, the heat from his body enveloped her. Darcy closed her eyes.

"Colin," she whispered. "I can only be here for Iris. Nothing more."

"You deny yourself too much." His thumb stroked over her bare arm. "The car, new clothes…my touch. I've tried to ignore the power you have over me. I've tried, but there's only so much a man can take. You're driving me crazy and I'm taking my frustrations out on you when it's my fault I can't deal with how much you get under my skin. I snapped at you earlier because I'm angry with myself."

Darcy gasped at his raw honesty.

"Tell me you don't want me to touch you," he whispered.

"I'm not a liar," she informed him. "But I can't let you. There's a difference."

Colin turned her around so fast she fell against him. Instantly, her hands came up to settle on that hard chest she'd been lusting after. Why did she have to have such strong feelings for this man? And why was he so forceful, so dominating and constantly arousing at every single moment of the day?

"Being alone with you is not a good idea." Her defense came out weak, and the smirk on his face told her he wasn't buying it, either. "I need this job, Colin. I can't afford to…well…whatever you have in mind."

With a low growl from deep in his throat, Colin framed her face with both hands, forcing her to look only at him.

"*Moro*, you have no idea what I have in mind."

Moro. What did that even mean? Something Greek, she assumed. Coming from his lips, though, it sounded sexy, naughty.

No, she didn't want to appreciate the seductive terms rolling off his tongue, dripping with a toe-curling accent.

With taut skin beneath her palms, Darcy was fighting the urge to dig her fingers into his heated skin, rise on her toes and take what he was so blatantly offering.

"This isn't professional." She focused on his face, wondering if he was having doubts, but all she saw staring back at her was desire.

Had a man ever looked at her in such an arousing way before? If she had to ask herself the question, the obvious answer was no.

"No, it's not," he agreed, still holding her face in his hands. "But damn it, the more I fight this, the more I crave it. Do you want to quit working for me?"

"No."

"I'm not about to fire you." His thumb stroked over her bottom lip, back and forth. "So that leaves us here, fighting an urge that's only gaining momentum. What do you want?"

Was he mocking her? What did he think she wanted to do? She wanted this ache to cease, but she didn't want to be so clichéd as to sleep with her boss.

"I think you need to keep your hands off me," she whispered. "I think we need to focus on Iris and I think we need to be adult enough to have self-control."

Colin slid his hands back through her hair, tipped her head up and inched even closer, leaving only a breath between their mouths.

"I didn't ask what you thought. I asked what you want."

With her hands trapped between their bodies, his firm grip on her and air barely passing between them, Darcy did the only thing she could think to do…she kissed him.

Instantly Colin took control, pushing her back against the wall. Her hands fell away and just as she tried to grip his shoulders, he grabbed her wrists, jerked them away from his body and had both arms pinned up over her head. She was at his total mercy, at his command. His mouth covered hers, dominated, possessed and every part of her wanted more, wanted him.

Her body arched into his. The sensation of those hard planes against her had any feeling of self-consciousness disappearing. Apparently Colin didn't seem to mind his woman a little on the curvy side. If his arousal was any indication, he actually preferred a little extra flesh.

With one hand gripping her wrists, Colin's other hand found the hem of her shirt. His fingers slid beneath the cotton and found her waist. His palm flattened against her heated skin as he brushed his thumb along the satiny barrier of her bra. Such a thin layer, yet it proved to be quite a hindrance. She wanted his hands on her, all over her.

Darcy groaned as his hips pushed against hers; his thumb glided back and forth over her breast. He utterly consumed her with the simplest yet most demanding of touches and she still burned for more.

Wait. What was she saying? He was a widower. He'd been married and his wife had passed not too long ago. So, what did that make Darcy? The rebound? A fling to help him recover from a broken heart?

Wasn't that precisely what Colin was to her? Hadn't her own heart—and apparently her common sense, too—taken a hit from her failed relationship? Were they using each other as stepping-stones to get beyond the hurt?

With her arms still locked above her head by Colin's firm grip, Darcy tore her mouth away, causing his lips to land on her jawline.

"Colin," she panted. "Wait…just…this is…stop. Please."

He froze. His hand fell from her shirt as he slowly backed away. The second he released her arms, Darcy pulled some much needed air into her lungs.

With a curse, Colin raked a hand through his damp hair and turned away. Darcy watched as he walked over and sank onto the weight bench, rested his elbows on his knees and dropped his head between his shoulders. Apparently he was at war with himself.

Unsure of what to do next, Darcy remained still, hoping he'd say something to cut through this instant strain that settled between them. "Go upstairs, Darcy."

The angst in his tone had her glued to the spot. He may want to be alone, but she didn't think he should be. How could she just walk out after what they'd experienced? Ignoring it would only create more friction.

"I'll go," she informed him, smoothing her hair away from her face. "But you need to know something first."

Darcy risked walking toward him and rounding the bench to talk face-to-face, even though he still kept his focus on the ground between his legs.

"I won't be used as someone to pass the time and I won't be anyone's rebound. Yes, I'm attracted to you, but I can work and put that aside." Pulling in a deep breath of air and straightening her shoulders, she pushed forward. "What I can't do is get wrapped up in an affair that will leave me wanting more because I've been hurt before. I'm not going to lie, I'm still recovering from that betrayal. Right now I have to look out for myself because I have no one else. And as much as I'd like to take you up on what you were offering, I can't sacrifice my heart. I'm not a fling type of girl and I know what might be temporary pleasure to you would be much more than I can handle."

Slowly, Colin lifted his head, sought her gaze and nodded. "I won't touch you again. I won't kiss you and I'll make sure not to put you in a position where we're alone. Iris will be our focus. I have enough going on in my life without adding more complications."

Darcy fisted her hands at her sides. This is what she wanted him to say, right? She wanted him to treat her as a professional and not make her choose between her morals and her desires.

Yet now that he'd pulled up this invisible wall between them, Darcy couldn't help but wonder if she'd just be on the outside looking in at what she could've had. And this incident confirmed he was looking for an emotional crutch. Trouble was, she was, too, and hadn't even realized it.

Colin came to his feet, keeping his intense gaze on her. "You need to know that I never meant to make you feel like you were passing my time. I haven't been this attracted to a woman in years and damn if this timing isn't inconvenient. You're my nanny, for pity's sake. But I need to clarify one thing before you go upstairs and we table this discussion."

Darcy swallowed. "What?"

Softly, gently, Colin eased forward and touched his lips to hers for the briefest of moments before easing back. He touched her nowhere else, but just that simple kiss packed as much of a punch as when he'd practically taken her standing up.

"You deserve more than a fling, more than a quickie against the wall." His whispered tone washed over her. "There are just some promises I can't make."

Sliding her tongue over her bottom lip, she savored him. "Why did you kiss me again?"

Bright cobalt eyes locked her in place. "Because I'm selfish and I wanted one last taste."

Heart in her throat, Darcy resisted the urge to reach up and touch her tingling lips. He'd told her he had nothing else to give but a fling and she refused to settle for a few moments of pleasure. She was worth more than that and she'd promised herself after Thad left her with nothing that she wouldn't succumb to passion and charming men again.

On shaky legs, Darcy skirted around Colin and headed out of the gym. By the time she hit the steps, she was nearly running.

What would tomorrow bring, she wondered as she closed herself into her suite. Could they truly put every kiss, every touch behind them? Could she forget the fact she'd felt proof of his desire for her? That he'd touched her breast? They'd crossed into another level of intimacy and that wasn't something Darcy took lightly.

She was just about to change into her pajamas when a piercing cry came from the monitor.

Duty called. She only hoped duty wasn't calling up Colin, as well.

Eight

"How's the nanny working out?"

Colin cringed at his brother's question. For the past three days he'd managed to keep his promise to always have Iris present if he was in the room with Darcy. On the night he'd all but consumed Darcy, right after she had left the gym and Iris had started to cry, Colin had made his way upstairs and waited for a moment to make sure Darcy went into the nursery to care for his little girl.

Being so close, inhaling her fruity scent, seeing her handle Iris in such a loving, caring way, had had him questioning his sanity. They still had months to go and he was no closer to controlling his hormones than he was the moment he opened his door to her. But how could he kick her out when she and Iris were obviously the perfect pairing?

"That good, huh?" Stefan chuckled.

Colin gripped the phone, hating how his brother was across the globe and could still hone in on the truth.

"She's amazing with Iris," Colin stated. "I'm surprised how fast she's has taken to Darcy. Most times Iris prefers Darcy over me when we're playing a game. She climbs into her lap. It's like she's already choosing sides."

"And how have you taken to Darcy?" Stefan asked.

"She's the nanny. That's all."

Stefan's mocking chuckle filled the line. "Pretty defensive. I admit, I'm happy to hear it. I worried about you after Karina's death and then the backlash and speculation from the media. You closed in on yourself for a bit, but with this nanny, you sound a bit…agitated. You're showing signs of life again. You must like her on more than a professional level."

Colin watched out his office window as Darcy and Iris splashed around in the pool. Why did he torture himself by standing in here staring at her? Why did her faded, plain black one-piece do ridiculous things to his libido?

"That doesn't mean anything is going on with my nanny," he grumbled. Maybe he was so moody because nothing *was* going on with the nanny.

Darcy lifted Iris into her arms and climbed from the pool. With each step up, water sluiced off Darcy's curvy body. Watching as she bent to retrieve Iris's towel was pure hell. For several moments Colin took note of how Darcy cared for Iris, drying her off and making sure she was warm before focusing on herself.

And those few minutes were more than enough to have his body responding. He never should've gone so far the other night because now when he saw her, he could actually *feel* her. The combination was killing him.

"The ball is less than two weeks away," Stefan went on, oblivious to Colin's state. "If you're not here, the media will only try to crucify you more. Even though they won't be inside, they'll be hovering outside the palace to see who's here. Besides, word will get out and rumors will fly."

"I'm well aware of how the media would handle my absence."

Colin turned from the window. The last thing he wanted to think about was returning to Galini Isle for a ball hosting the monarchies from surrounding countries. The only bright light was that his best friend, Luc, would be in attendance, and since the man had recently gotten engaged Colin wanted to congratulate the happy couple in person.

But right now he wanted to forget all duties, all pressing issues that demanded his attention. Still, if he didn't go, Stefan was right, it would be like throwing gasoline on the proverbial fire. He just wished he weren't so confused. He was happy here, albeit sexually frustrated. He enjoyed living in California, but he also missed his brother. And being away from his duties had Colin wondering what his late parents would've thought of his actions. Would they support his decision if he chose to walk away? Would they be disappointed?

If he ended up going to the ball, he'd have to reveal his true identity to Darcy. Traveling back for the event would be tiring and he'd want her with him to help with Iris. A small sliver of him wanted her to know, he wanted to see how she'd treat him if she knew the truth. He liked to think she'd still be the same Darcy he'd come to respect and desire.

"I'll let you know what I decide," Colin stated as he headed down the hall and upstairs to his bedroom. "I'll give you a few days' notice for security."

"They're already on standby," Stefan confirmed. "They're ready to come to LA and hover over you. I had to tell them to stand down more than once."

"Keeping my identity a secret would be kind of hard with royal guards surrounding the perimeter of my home."

"Which is why I'm honoring your wishes and letting you have some privacy. But you'll have to make some decisions soon and I'm not just referring to the ball."

Colin closed his bedroom door and toed off his shoes. "You'll be the first to know what I decide. Right now I have more pressing matters to deal with."

Stefan chuckled. "I'm sure you do."

Colin disconnected the call, cutting off Stefan's mocking laugh. Quickly changing his clothes, Colin decided he was taking charge of everything in his personal life starting now. He was torn up over the decision involving his royal status, but he refused to have his libido all out of control, too. He was going to take what he wanted… and he wanted Darcy Cooper.

How would he know if whatever they were feeling was something real? Colin had told her he couldn't give her more, but those words had been spoken out of fear. He didn't want her to think he was using her, but he ached for her in ways he hadn't known possible.

Lust was something he remembered from his bachelor days, but Darcy was worth more than that shallow emotion and damn if it wasn't complicating everything right now.

He'd given her the space he promised. He'd watched her, kept his hands to himself and had not made any innuendos whatsoever. His self-control was choking him to death.

Their connection was obvious. Why couldn't they spend these next few months enjoying each other? Surely by the time he was ready to move on they'd be tired of each other.

Seduction would be the key to winning her over and he had every intention of pulling out all stops and making her just as achy and needy as he was. This entire plan was a risk because he knew he wanted to explore more, but what would happen if they reached the point of no return?

Iris wasn't acting sleepy at all after the swim and brief snack, so Darcy slipped back into the pool. Schedules were important for babies, but so was soaking up all the fun and memories they could. Delaying Iris's nap by half an hour wouldn't hurt. The other day the nap had been put off for too long, hence the mega tantrum, but Darcy had learned what Iris's nap meltdown threshold was.

Easing Iris into her baby raft with canopy, Darcy held onto the side and swished the float around in the water. Iris squealed and clapped her hands with each twist. Her little legs were working back and forth beneath the water. Darcy couldn't help but laugh as an immeasurable amount of joy filled her heart. There truly was nothing like a baby's sweet laugh. Darcy watched Iris's face as she led her further into the pool. Those bright eyes really sparkled in the sunlight…and reminded Darcy how much Iris looked like her daddy.

Dunking down lower to get her shoulders wet, Darcy tried her hardest to keep images of Colin from her mind. Of course the harder she fought, the more he kept creeping into her thoughts. It was so, so difficult to keep her professional feelings separate from her personal ones.

Darcy loved Iris, enjoyed every moment she got to spend with her. But she also thoroughly enjoyed Colin's company on a level that she hadn't expected. Her mind and her heart were in agreement for once, telling her that feeling anything for the man was a bad idea.

A flash of him doing chin-ups with one muscular arm, the memory of how he'd stared so intently into her eyes the instant before he claimed her mouth flooded her thoughts. Then there was the other side of him that also played through her mind. The man was an amazing father, always wanting to give Iris her bath, wanting to spend so much time alone with his little girl. The smile he gave Iris was unlike anything Darcy had ever seen. The man was truly in love with his daughter.

How could Darcy not be attracted to all facets of Colin? He may still be quite mysterious, and he still had that expensive SUV in the drive waiting for her to drive it, but he had her so torn up, she had no choice but to want to know more.

For the past three days he'd stayed away from her unless they were with Iris. Part of her hated the barrier she'd placed between them, but the other part knew the separation was the best thing for her. Between focusing on her business and reminding herself she needed to guard her heart, Darcy couldn't afford to fall into a fling no matter how she desired to do just that.

Memories of how amazing his weight had felt pressed against her as his mouth consumed her would just have to suffice. Unfortunately, right now, all the memories were doing was leaving her achier.

"How can I stay inside and work when there's so much fun going on out here?"

Darcy froze the same instant Iris squealed for her daddy.

No. No. No. She didn't want to turn around because if she did she knew she'd see Colin wearing some type of swimming trunks that only showcased his impressive set of abs and all of his other magnificent muscles.

She wanted to hide, to instantly be poolside and wrapped in a towel so he didn't have to see her get out of the water with her thighs jiggling and her rounded stomach that had stretched her "miracle suit" beyond the promised miracle.

From the corner of her eye, Darcy spotted a flash of black just as Colin dove headfirst into the pool. What was he thinking coming out here with her? Yes, Iris was present as they'd discussed, but he wasn't naive. He knew exactly what coming out here half naked would do to her. What type of game was he playing?

When Colin surfaced, much closer to her than she'd anticipated, he swiped the water back from his forehead and smiled at Iris.

"Hey, baby. Are you having fun?"

With Colin's hands on the raft, Darcy eased back. No way was she going to accidentally entangle her legs with his because she'd quite possibly start to whimper, which would completely override the speech she'd given him three days ago.

"I'll just let you two have some time alone."

Darcy made her way to the steps. There was no good way to get out without Colin seeing her ancient, thread-bare suit pasted against every dip and roll. Best to just get out, fake a confidence she didn't own and run like hell for the nearest towel.

"You don't have to get out because I'm here."

Darcy knew full well the man had his eyes on her, but she didn't turn to meet his gaze until she was properly wrapped like a terrycloth sausage.

"I'm not," she told him, lying through her smile.

Colin adjusted the canopy over Iris to keep her shaded. "Are you going to run every time you get uncomfortable?"

Gripping her towel at her breasts, Darcy straightened her shoulders. "I'm not running."

"But you're uncomfortable," he said with a smirk. "Your rules, Darcy. You can cancel them at any time and take what we both want for as long as we're here."

No, she couldn't.

"She'll need a nap soon," Darcy told him, dodging the obvious topic. "Just bring her in and I'll get her all dried off and ready. If you don't object, I plan on making almond-crusted chicken and grilled veggies for dinner."

"No objections here. At least not on dinner."

The man was so confusing. One minute he was moody and kissing her so she had to put on the brakes. The next minute he was agreeing to her terms and then he tried to muddle her mind by flashing that chest that should be enshrined in gold.

Darcy marched into the house, not in the mood to play whatever game he was offering. He had issues of his own, at least he said he did, and so did she. They had a temporary working relationship. Pursuing anything beyond that agreement would be wrong and settle so much awkwardness between them they'd never find their way out.

The last time she'd fallen hard for a man, she'd let him into her life, into her business because her grandmother thought he was perfect for Darcy. Darcy had trusted her hormones and ignored common sense for too long.

She'd let business and pleasure mix once before and she'd be paying for that mistake for the rest of her life.

Nine

Darcy may want him to give up, but until he quit seeing desire in her eyes each time she looked at him, he wasn't backing down. She'd been burned before and now Colin was paying for another man's sins.

She may have asked for space, and he wasn't one to go against a woman's wishes, but that didn't mean he still couldn't get what he wanted.

True, the house was huge so giving her space wasn't necessarily a problem. But their physical connection was so intense that the walls seemed to close in on them.

At first he'd fought the attraction, then he'd resigned himself to the fact it wasn't going away. Then he'd wondered if they could both heal by seeking comfort in each other. But as that thought ran through his mind, he couldn't help but wonder if there was something more building here.

He sounded like a woman thinking through all of his feelings and emotions, but Darcy was bringing out a side he hadn't known existed and he didn't want to cheapen whatever this was to a potential fling. They both deserved more than that, yet he couldn't help but want her and there was no point in trying to fight the tension anymore.

He'd failed in his attempt at seduction at the pool earlier today. He thought for sure spending time with her in a more relaxed setting with Iris would soften her. Now Darcy was up in her room and he was once again in the gym. He couldn't even come into this room anymore without seeing her pressed against the wall, flushed from arousal and looking up at him beneath heavy lids.

There had to be a way to break down the barrier she'd encompassed herself in. There were so many layers he'd yet to peel away. He wanted to know why she only wore three outfits and rotated them. He wanted to know why she was sewing things in her spare time and why she sneaked down to the gym early in the mornings before Iris woke when she thought he was still asleep. On a rare occasion he would catch her searching the internet for more recipes. Seems that cooking wasn't just a fun hobby for her as she'd stated, but a true passion.

Still, she'd made it apparent she didn't want to be alone with him so talking to her was damn near impossible, because when Iris was around he wanted to devote his time and attention to his daughter.

Colin pushed the bar back into locked position and sat up on the bench. Swiping a hand across his forehead, he cleared away the sweat as a brilliant plan entered his mind. He was going to have to get creative, to make sure there was no way she could run from what was happening between them. And something was happening whether she wanted to admit it or not.

Sliding his cell from his shorts pocket, Colin quickly did a search for the number he'd used when he'd first contacted her and placed the call. "Colin?" she answered, confusion lacing her tone.

He chuckled. "Yeah."

"Why are you calling my cell?"

A nugget of doubt slid through his mind, but he pressed on because he'd never backed away from a challenge.

"To talk."

Silence settled over the line. Maybe this was a mistake, but it was a risk he was willing to take. Hadn't he always been a daredevil? Hence his accident and recovery. "Darcy?"

"I'm here." She let out a sigh and a faint sound of sheets rustling filtered through the line. "What do you want to talk about? We're in the same house. You *are* in the house, right?"

He came to his feet and reached for a towel hanging over a weight machine. "I'm in the gym." Colin mopped off his face and neck, and flung the towel into the bin in the corner. "Did I wake you?"

"No. I had just turned off my light and crawled into bed."

Closing his eyes, he could easily picture her spread out on his guest bed, her dark, rich hair spilling over the crisp, white sheets. What did she wear to bed? A T-shirt? Something silky, perhaps? Nothing?

"Is everything okay?" she asked. "I'm a little confused as to why you're calling me."

"I want to hear your voice."

Colin shut off the light in the gym and headed toward his office. Only a small desk lamp lit the room. He knew he had to keep control of this conversation or she'd hang up.

"Tell me about your life before you came here."

Darcy laughed. "What about it? I work with kids and love to cook—that's about as exciting as I am."

She was so much more and he'd be the man to show her. Whoever she'd been with last was a jerk who hadn't realized what a treasure he had.

"You have friends, yes?" he asked.

"Yes. I was living with my best friend before I came here. What about you? You're from Greece, you're an amazing father, you keep simple working hours, but that's all I know."

"I'm not talking about me." He sank onto the leather sofa, leaned back and shut his eyes. He wanted to hear all about her, wanted her sultry, sleepy voice to wash over him. "We're talking about you."

"This Q and A can go both ways," she replied with a hint of a challenge. "How about we take turns? I'll go first. Why are you still trying to seduce me?"

"Wow. You sure you don't want to lead in with something lighter? My favorite color is red and my favorite sport is rock climbing."

"You're dodging the question," she stated. "You are the one who started this game."

"Fine. I want you." He shifted on the couch and propped his feet up on the cushions, then leaned back on the arm. "Why are you afraid to be alone with me?"

"Because you're sneaky and I wouldn't be able to resist you."

Colin smiled, settling a hand on his bare abs. "I'm not sneaky, I'm honest."

"That's debatable." She sighed and Colin imagined her upstairs in the dark, aching for him as much as he was for her. "It's my turn. How did you injure yourself?"

"I was rock climbing and made an error in judgment. Trusted the wrong rock."

Darcy's gasp had his own gut clenching. He was actually glad for the head trauma because he didn't remember the fall in any way. A minor blessing.

"You could've been killed," she cried.

"I nearly was. The doctors weren't so sure at first, but once they knew I would live, they told my wife I would never walk again."

"You're remarkable," she whispered.

As much as his ego loved her stroking it, Colin really didn't want her pity because of his accident. He wanted her, no question. But he understood she was burned in the past and he knew she was struggling for money, so she definitely had more at stake than he did.

"Tell me about the jerk who broke your heart."

Darcy groaned. "Why don't you ask something else?"

"Because my backup question is me wanting to know how fast I can be in your room with nothing between us but the darkness."

"You're not playing fair," she muttered.

Colin gritted his teeth. "Baby, I'm not playing at all. I'm tired of playing. We've danced around this attraction for too long and I'm going insane."

"Fine. We'll discuss the ex."

He didn't know if he wanted to laugh or cry at the reply.

Darcy's deep inhale had Colin eagerly waiting, but knowing he'd probably want to hunt this guy down and make him pay. Colin had no reason to be jealous, no reason to be so territorial…yet he was.

"My ex took every single dime I had to my name. I trusted him with more than my heart, he was my new business partner after my grandmother passed, and he betrayed me. Apparently he had another girlfriend and was using my money to buy her presents. And by presents I mean trips, a car, a condo." Darcy paused and Colin wasn't sure if there was more or if she was waiting for him to reply. After another soft sigh, she continued. "He not only ruined my business, he killed my dream of adopting a child."

Colin tamped down his anger. Whoever this bastard was, Colin loathed the man and wished for about five minutes alone with him. The fact he'd stolen all of her money was a sin in itself, but to know Darcy wanted to adopt was a morsel of information he was shocked she'd revealed.

Did she have a dream of adopting because she was compassionate toward kids and wanted to save them? Did she not plan on marrying? Or was there something medical that prevented her from having her own?

She'd answered one question and triggered a multitude of others.

But now he realized why Darcy had so little with her, why she was so upset over the new car and him having hers taken away without asking first. Her ex had thrown money around, albeit hers, and had used the funds to further his own desires. This woman was a fighter and she wasn't about to take handouts from the likes of Colin. How could he not admire how strong-willed she was?

Fortunately, he'd gotten her car back, now fixed, and it sat in one of the bays of his second garage behind the house. But even though he'd smoothed things over with Darcy, Colin didn't want to stop there. He was already in deep with her, so why not keep going to satisfy his curiosity?

"What's his name?" Colin asked.

"I'm sorry?"

Colin fisted his hand over his abs. "The lowlife who stole from you. I want his name."

"It's not your turn."

Her tone left no room for argument, so he waited for her to ask her question.

"You're a man of mystery. What's your profession?"

"I'm a CEO of sorts." Okay, there was no good way to answer, but he was a leader...for now. "I manage a large group back in Greece."

There. That sounded believable, didn't it? It was his turn to ask a question, but he wasn't wasting it on her ex's name. He could find that out later and take care of things. Right now, he wanted to dig deeper, to get to the point of his call. Priorities.

"What are you wearing?" he asked.

Darcy's soft laugh enveloped him as if she stood before him. Damn, he wanted to touch her, to kiss her, to feel her beneath him. He'd only known her several weeks and she all but consumed him. Obviously she had no clue the power she held over him.

"Are we playing that game now?" she all but mocked. "I'm wearing a black, silky chemise that leaves very little to the imagination."

Colin swallowed, the image now burned in his mind. "You're lying."

"You'll never know. What are you wearing?"

"Shorts and sweat. I just finished my workout where all I could do was see you pinned against the wall with your eyes closed, your mouth on mine and my hand up your shirt."

Darcy sighed. "What are you doing to me?" she whispered. "I can't keep up with how quick you turn me inside out."

"That goes both ways, *erastis*."

"What does that mean?"

"Come down to my office and I'll tell you." More like show her.

"I can't, Colin. You're making this so difficult for me. You have to understand that just because I want something, doesn't mean I can take it. Apparently you're used to getting what you want."

"I always get what I want."

"Sounds like a threat."

Colin smiled. "It's a promise."

"Tell me about your wife."

Colin eased up and shook his head. No way was he getting into how he'd let his wife down when he'd lived his reckless lifestyle and then pushed her away when he'd truly needed her most. He totally took the blame for their failed marriage because he'd been too proud, too stubborn to let her just help him through his rough time. Which was beyond ironic since he'd hired Darcy to assist him because he'd finally come to the realization he couldn't do it all.

Maybe it was time to break the cycle. To finally let someone in and keep his stubborn pride on the back burner. But, right now he had other, more pressing matters.

"Let's table that discussion for another time."

"Count on it," she said around a yawn.

"I'll let you go," he told her. "I need to hit the shower before I head to bed."

"I'll just be lying here in my chemise, dreaming."

Colin fisted his hand and came to his feet. "You're getting too good at this. Better watch what you say, you're playing with fire."

"You lit the match."

When she hung up, Colin stood in his office with a painful arousal and a ridiculous grin on his face. Yeah, he was used to getting what he wanted and he wanted Darcy in his bed.

And he would have her there. It was only a matter of time.

Darcy hadn't slept at all. Once Colin had started with the "what are you wearing" game her mind had formed so many fantasies, leaving her restless and aroused.

She hadn't lied when she said she was lying in her bed wearing a black chemise. She actually owned two. Sleeping in something so soft, so flawless gliding over her skin always made her feel more feminine. After dealing with children all day and spending most of her waking hours dealing with various problems and parents, she had to stay in touch with her femininity even if she wasn't sleeping with anyone.

Which was why last night's little chat with Colin left her aching in ways she'd never thought possible. She'd been with one man, and even during their intimacy Darcy had never felt an inkling of what she'd felt last night on the phone with Colin.

The man wasn't just chipping away at the defensive wall she'd erected, he was blasting through it with a sledgehammer. He'd started opening up just a touch over the past several weeks and he'd become playful, flirty and flat-out blatant regarding what he wanted.

Because she hadn't slept very well, she was awake even earlier than usual and in the gym. Of course, during her entire workout all she could picture was Colin down here last night. How long had he been sweating and working out while thinking of her? Did he regret calling her? Had he assumed she'd come running to him and they'd enter into this affair without giving the consequences another thought?

When she glanced at the time on her phone, she realized she'd been working out for over an hour. A great improvement over the first day. Granted, she'd had a hard time concentrating with Colin flexing his perfectly honed muscles all over the place.

If she could keep up this regime while she was here and continue eating healthily, she just may be on the fast track to getting her life back. In such a short time she already felt better about herself and had more energy.

More energy was something she would most definitely need if she was going to continue to battle Colin and his bold advances.

Darcy headed back upstairs, careful as always to be quiet while Iris and Colin slept. Grabbing a quick shower would give her time to get her thoughts in order before facing Colin. She knew the mutual desire would not go away. And as if fighting her urges wasn't enough, he wasn't playing fair. How could she keep putting up a strong front when he'd pretty much laid his cards on the table?

Lathering up her hair, she slid the strands through her fingers beneath the spray. She'd been worried about getting entangled with Colin after her last romance debacle, but Colin was so different from her ex. She only had to look at his interactions with Iris to see how loving he was. And he wasn't out to use her for anything because at this point he knew she had nothing to give.

Maybe he wanted her for no other reason than to satisfy his curiosity…just as she felt with him.

Darcy rinsed her body and shut off the water. Quickly she toweled off. She'd just pulled her hair into a messy topknot when fussy noises blared through the monitors.

Iris was crankier in the mornings than any other baby she'd dealt with. Of course, Darcy hadn't personally worked with a vast number of children under two, but Iris was certainly special. The toddler was happiest when she got her food. Darcy could totally relate.

Darcy wrestled her sports bra back on and yanked up her shorts; she didn't have time to find something else. When she turned the corner of her room and hit the doorway of the nursery, Colin was lifting Iris from her crib. That toned back with ink scrolling over his shoulder continued to mock her, because every time she saw it, she wanted to trace it…with her tongue.

The way he gently spoke to Iris, the way he held such a delicate little girl against his hard, strong body really hit

Darcy. Even rumpled from sleep, Colin Alexander was a man who demanded attention without saying a word.

When he turned and caught her gaze, his eyes did some evaluating of their own. Darcy was reminded she stood before him in only her sweaty sports bra and shorts. Not her best look, considering she wasn't perfectly proportioned or toned in any way.

"I just got out of the shower and threw on the closest thing," Darcy stated, keeping her eyes locked on Colin as he continued to close the gap between them. "Give me one minute to change and I can take her and feed her."

Colin's limp was a bit more pronounced this morning. Most likely he'd slept wrong. How had the man slept after that call? Maybe she was more revved up with this sexual tension than he was.

"You're flushed." His eyes traveled to the scoop in her bra and back up. "Looks good on you."

"Colin—"

"Go change," he urged. "I'll feed Iris and you better be fully dressed next time you're around me."

Darcy stared at him for another minute, which was a minute too long because he reached out, trailed a fingertip across her collarbone.

"Go, *erastis,* before I take what I want."

That was the second time he'd called her that and she wanted to know what it meant. She had a feeling it was a term of endearment or something sexy because his voice took on a whole other tone when he said it. She was drowning where this man was concerned and she knew it was just a matter of time before she succumbed to all of the desire and passion that kept swirling around them.

Darcy turned and all but ran into her adjoining bath. The man was killing her. She dug out a pair of jeans and her favorite pink T-shirt before heading back downstairs, praying she'd have control over her emotions. She should be praying Colin would have control over his.

She didn't see them in the kitchen, but the sound of the patio doors sliding open drew her attention. Through the wide window she spotted Colin with a banana in one hand and Iris holding onto the other as he led her out onto the stone patio. He'd just placed her on the settee when he lost his balance and went down. Darcy ran out the door and was crouched at his side in an instant.

Had he reinjured himself? Worry flooded her. How she would get him back up without hurting him further?

With a muttered curse in his native tongue, Colin pushed her away. "Don't. Just take her inside and feed her."

Darcy reached for him. "Let me help you up."

"Leave me be," he shouted, meeting and holding her gaze. "I'm not paying you to coddle me, I'm paying you to care for Iris."

Darcy jerked back and came to her feet. Iris started to climb off the chair and Darcy reached down, taking the little girl's hand.

"You're right," Darcy replied, swallowing the hurt. "I'll remember my place from now on."

Colin shifted and stood, wincing as he did so. Even though his jab sliced deep, Darcy waited until he got his bearings. Just as he opened his mouth to speak, Darcy turned.

"Come on, baby girl." Darcy swiped the banana from the ground where Colin had dropped it when he fell. "Let's get you some breakfast."

No way would Darcy make the mistake of trying to get close and help Colin again. If he wanted to run hot and cold with his emotions, he could do so with someone else. Darcy wasn't here as an outlet for his frustrations and anger over his accident.

Ten

Disgrace was a bitter, nasty pill to swallow.

After his spill that morning, Colin didn't know what he was angrier about, himself for falling and possibly hurting Iris or the fact that Darcy was there to witness his humiliation. He'd taken his anger and embarrassment out on her for no reason.

Hadn't he hired a nanny in case something like this happened? The real possibility that he would fall in the presence of, or God forbid, while holding Iris, had been his main concern. What he hadn't planned on was having his hormones thrown into the mix. And he hadn't been forthcoming with Darcy about his injury because he'd prayed there wouldn't be a mishap while she was here. He didn't want to be seen as weak or crippled.

Colin sneaked into the house through the back door after Darcy had taken Iris in for breakfast. After he'd showered and gotten his damn leg and back under control with some stretches his doctor and therapist had shown him, Colin felt somewhat human again.

This morning his goal had been to carry on the plan of seduction that he'd started on the phone last night. Then his past had come back to bite him when he'd fallen, completely erasing any impact he may have had on Darcy last night because of his inability to handle this entire situation like a mature adult. Wow, wasn't he just the king of all things sexy? Now instead of Darcy viewing him as a strong, confident man, she saw him as a cripple, as someone who couldn't even care for himself, let alone a child.

If the paparazzi back in Galini Isle ever caught a glimpse of his inability to stand on his own two feet at times, he'd be ridiculed, questioned and thrust into the limelight even more. They'd already speculated that he and Karina were falling apart, but since her death, they hadn't left him alone and he was sick of the pity, the way they portrayed him as helpless and lost.

He was an Alexander. They were strong men, determined and focused. Nothing would stand in the way of him getting everything he wanted.

Needing to get back on track and spend time with his daughter, Colin figured today would be a great day for a little outing. Darcy might not like men who threw their weight and money around, but he wanted to treat her. Out of every woman he'd ever known, Darcy most definitely deserved to be pampered, even if only for a few hours.

If she was working for him, then she was going to be treated like royalty.

Which reminded him, he needed to have a serious talk with her. He'd decided to attend the ball and he wanted Darcy to come with him. That conversation would have to take place at just the right time. He didn't want her to feel as if he'd lied to her…though he had by omission.

Just as Colin reached the bottom of the stairs, he heard

Darcy's laughter and Iris's sweet giggle. That combination slid a new emotion through him—one he wasn't sure he could identify and one he wasn't sure he wanted to.

When he found them on the floor in the living room, Colin stopped in the wide, arched doorway to take in the scene. Days ago the sight of freshly picked flowers, obviously from the landscaping, all over his floor would've had him enraged. But now, seeing those vibrant petals in Darcy's and Iris's hair had him smiling. These two were like kindred spirits and he could easily get wrapped up in watching them.

There he went again, sliding down that slippery slope even further toward Darcy. He had lost control somewhere between opening the door that first day and the first time she'd verbally matched him with her banter.

"Daddy!"

Iris squealed, scooped up all the flowers her little hands could hold and sprinkled them on top of Darcy's head.

"Deedee pitty," she exclaimed, clapping her hands.

Darcy glanced his way, but quickly darted away. "I'm Deedee. It's much easier for her to say."

Colin hated how Darcy wouldn't even look at him. He'd done that to her when he'd sworn he wouldn't hurt anyone again over this injury. Because of his inexcusable actions, he'd driven a wedge between them.

The fact his daughter had adopted a nickname for Darcy added another layer of bonding that was already wrapped so tightly around them. All part of the nanny-child relationship, nothing more—or at least that's what he needed to keep telling himself. Darcy wasn't part of this family; her presence was temporary.

"Darcy, go get yourself and Iris ready. We're going out for the day." He moved into the room and slid his hand over Iris's dark curls. "I'll work on cleaning this mess up."

Darcy came to her feet, catching the flowers as they

fell down her chest. "I'm sorry. We went for a little walk and picked some flowers from the gardens. I planned on cleaning—"

Colin held up a hand, cutting off her words, and offered a smile so she didn't think he was angry or a complete jerk after how he'd treated her earlier. "I've got it. Really. Go on."

"Okay." She bent down, lifted Iris into her arms and turned back to him. Finally, she met his eyes with a worry he didn't want. "Are you feeling all right?"

She didn't come out and ask about the fall, but he knew that's exactly what she was referring to.

He gave her a brief nod. "Do you want to know where we're going?" he asked.

Darcy's lids lowered. "My place isn't to ask questions. You're paying me to care for Iris, so I'm going to get us ready."

Colin absolutely loathed the words he'd spouted off to her earlier out of anger and humiliation. There was no taking them back now that they were out in the open. All he could do was show her he wasn't the ogre she thought he'd become.

Darcy left the room without another word. He needed to apologize, but words would only go so far. He would show her that he wasn't a terrible person. He'd make her see that she didn't have to work her butt off for nothing.

And by the time she left him at the end of her term, she'd never have to worry about her business or her finances again. If he did nothing else, he'd make damn sure of that.

He had to be kidding. That dress—as stunning as it was—cost more than an entire month's worth of groceries. Colin had talked her into shopping, but she'd had no idea he'd pull her into the most expensive store she'd ever seen in her entire life.

After working for him for several weeks now, one would think she'd have the courage to stand her ground and decline.

On the flipside, though, she'd discovered with each passing day that Colin was impossible to resist.

"At least try it on," he urged, holding up the elegant, one-shouldered, bright blue dress.

Darcy wasn't in the mood to be shopping, but Colin had claimed this was just another work incentive and he truly wanted her to have new clothes. After the morning they'd had, she really had no clue why they were here.

"I won't wear that dress," she told him, though she loved it. Being stubborn could go both ways.

On a sigh, he hung the dress back up and inched closer. "I already apologized, but I'll keep saying it until you realize I am honestly sorry for how I reacted. I know you were only trying to help, but my pride usually doesn't allow me to let others come to my rescue."

That she could understand. She, too, had her pride and he had come and apologized shortly after she'd completely ignored him.

"I just find it convenient you're getting me clothes today and calling them incentives," she shot back, talking quietly so the salesclerk didn't hear. Iris squealed and chewed on the baby doll in her stroller, oblivious to the turmoil.

"I'd planned on this anyway," he told her. "The timing is just wrong. If you're not in the mood, we can do this another day. I figured we could both use a break and to get out and do something fun."

Something fun? What man found shopping fun? Darcy chewed on her bottom lip as she considered how to approach this. She could be childish, the way he had been the other day, or she could accept the olive branch he was extending.

"Fine," she conceded.

With a wide smile, Colin lifted the dress back off the rack. "What size do you need?"

Darcy laughed, gripping the handle on the Cadillac of strollers. "Nice try, buddy. I'm not telling you my size. It's not in the single digits and I doubt that dress will look good on my frame."

His eyes scanned her body. "Your frame looks fine and you'll never know how it looks if you don't try it on."

Darcy shook her head and turned toward another rack. "Everything in here is so pricey. Why are we even here?"

Colin's hand came around, gripping hers over the handle. Darcy threw a glance over her shoulder and saw he was much closer than she'd thought.

"Pick out whatever you want." He held up a hand when she started to argue. "I'll take Iris to the toy store next door. Text me when you're done. The clerk has my credit card number."

Darcy closed her eyes. "There's nothing I need that will take me that long. Just give me a couple minutes."

"You may not need it, but you deserve it." His thumb stroked over her hand. "I'm not trying to buy you. I'm trying to put a smile on your face, to let you have whatever you want for the entire day. I'd bet my entire savings that you haven't bought anything for yourself for years."

Darcy glanced down to their hands. The contrast between his dark skin and her paleness was minor in comparison to their many differences.

"I'm not sleeping with you."

Colin jerked her around, his fingers digging into her shoulders. "I'm not offering this shopping trip as a bribe, Darcy. You going to bed with me has nothing to do with this. I'm here because I want to give you nice things while you're with me. If you want to leave everything when you go, then do that and I'll donate the clothes to charity. You were told up front you'd be getting bonuses along the way. Don't argue."

"Yet again, does anyone ever tell you no?" she asked.

A smirk flirted around the corners of his mouth. "You're the only one who keeps trying."

On a sigh, Darcy closed her eyes and nodded. "Fine. I'll pick out a couple of things. Seriously, though, we could find a cheaper store."

His eyes traveled over the racks, the displays and mannequins. "Do you not like this store?"

Darcy laughed. "Everything in here is gorgeous. I just think we could find one with smaller numbers on the price tags."

"Don't look at the price tag. Focus on how stunning you'll look, how beautiful you'll feel." Colin's intense gaze lasted a minute longer than she was comfortable with before he moved around her and gripped the stroller. "Take your time. I've got Miss Iris."

Darcy stared at his retreating back. He paused at the counter and spoke to the pretty female employee. Of course she batted her lashes and laughed at whatever Colin said before he slipped out the front door. The man seemed to have that effect on every female.

Colin was way too charming. Not only did he have that devastatingly handsome, sexy arrogance about him, he had a beautiful baby girl. All he had to do was be the loving, doting father he was and women's ovaries started weeping.

The burn in her throat had her swallowing. Colin and Iris were missing the female figure in their lives and Darcy was missing the family she'd always dreamed of having. Yet they could never mesh together because... well, just because.

She was his employee, she had goals of her own and right now she needed to get her business back up and running. Added to that, Colin made it clear he would probably be leaving in a few months to go back to Greece.

Darcy nearly laughed. She'd never have the chance to set foot on Colin's home turf. If he wanted to treat her like Cinderella today, she would let him. For once she would let someone else take care of her, do something nice for her.

By the time Darcy finished trying on clothes, she had way more in her want pile than in her "no" pile.

"Miss Cooper," the clerk called from the other side of the thick floor-to-ceiling curtain. "I have some shoes pulled and jewelry for you to look at once you're done. Can I get you any other sizes?"

Shoes? Jewelry? When had she ever purchased an entire outfit complete with head-to-toe accessories?

"My sizes are fine," she called back. "I'll be right out."

When Darcy stepped out of the dressing room, she resisted the urge to adjust her simple V-neck T-shirt. She didn't fit in this place and the clothes she'd tried on certainly wouldn't work for her daily activities relating to Iris's care. But if she left with nothing, she knew Colin would drag her somewhere else.

"What can I take to the counter for you?"

Darcy glanced to the perfectly polished clerk with her carefully applied makeup and elegantly coiffed hair. Darcy glanced back into the dressing room where she'd hung everything up.

"I'll take that blue dress for now," she told the clerk. "I need to think about everything else."

She hated to admit it, but the blue dress did hug her curves and made her feel beautiful. She didn't mind said curves or her figure so much, and with her workout sessions she was actually starting to see a difference in her body. The extra boost of confidence had her smiling.

Colin had liked the dress, so that's what she'd go with for now. And damn if he wasn't right. It had looked good on her, better than she'd ever imagined…not that she'd admit such a revelation to Colin.

"What size shoe are you? I was guessing a seven."

Amazing how the woman was dead-on, but Darcy shook her head. "Oh, I couldn't—"

"Mr. Alexander made me promise to add shoes and any jewelry you wanted to the outfits you chose." A soft smile spread across her face. "He also said not to argue and worry about the cost."

Darcy couldn't help but laugh. Colin thought he had all his bases covered. Biting her bottom lip, Darcy pondered what she should actually do versus what she wanted to do. She could go ahead and get the things Colin requested. If she didn't wear anything, he could return them and get his money back.

"I should also tell you, he also made me promise you'd leave with no less than three outfits." With her hands clasped in front of her bright pink capris and crisp white shirt, the clerk nodded toward the dress in Darcy's hand. "He also said you weren't leaving without that blue dress, so I'm glad you already chose that one."

Three outfits? The staggering cost of all that would be beyond ridiculous. Outfits, as well as accessories and shoes. What else did Colin have planned for her? Buying clothes and loaning her a brand-new car were both so personal. When he'd initially said bonuses, Darcy had assumed he'd meant the monetary kind. She really should've asked him for specifics, but she'd been too concerned about keeping her job and making it past the trial period.

"To be honest, I don't have a need for fancy clothes," she told the clerk. "I love everything in here, but I'm a nanny and caring for a child doesn't necessarily require bling and stilettos."

The clerk laughed, reached out and patted her arm. "Tell you what, let's look around and I'm sure we can find something to make you both happy. You can still be fashionable and comfortable while caring for that sweet baby."

An hour later the young worker, whom Darcy now knew as Carly, had delivered on her promise. New shorts, basic tops and adorable sandals were neatly wrapped in tissue paper and placed in two large bags…along with that blue dress Darcy would never have a use for. She had drawn the line at jewelry, though. There was no need for earrings or a necklace for Iris to tug on, not to mention Darcy wasn't preparing herself for a fashion show.

She shot Colin a text, telling him she was finished and she'd come to the toy store to meet him. After thanking Carly for all of her help, Darcy headed out the door. So much money spent for two bags worth of clothing, but he'd insisted, and to be honest she'd never let someone splurge on her before. Colin had been adamant he wanted to do this for her and she was done being stubborn.

Perhaps she was being selfish, but life had thrown so much crap at her, it was nice to have someone refreshing waltz into her life. She truly believed he wasn't buying her to get her into bed. If he'd pursued harder at home, she would have caved and they both knew it. Getting new clothes certainly didn't make her want to jump him. No, she'd wanted to do that from the second he'd opened his door and greeted her.

The bright sun warmed her face as soon as she stepped onto the sidewalk. A familiar scream of delight had Darcy turning her attention down the sidewalk to where Iris sat in her stroller, hugging a brand new elephant in one hand and a waving rather large lollipop in the other. Seeing the big, wide smile across her precious face, Darcy didn't know if she'd ever seen Iris happier.

Colin, on the other hand, looked as though he could use a stiff drink. His hair stood on end as if he'd run his fingers through it for the past hour, his lids were heavy and he appeared to be in a daze.

Darcy held back her laugh, but couldn't stop from smiling as he moved closer. "Looks like you had a good time at the toy store."

Colin's eyes snapped to hers as if he'd just realized she stood near him. "Do you know what they have in that place?"

"I'm assuming toys," Darcy stated.

"From floor to ceiling." He continued to stare as if he'd been traumatized. "But it's not just toys. There's candy. Everything lights up or sings or dances to get your attention. It's not even safe to walk through the line to check out. She was reaching for everything. It's like they don't even care about the parents."

Darcy did laugh now. "Surely this wasn't your first trip to a toy store with her."

Colin blinked, raking a hand over his face. "Actually, it was."

The statement shocked Darcy. Perhaps his late wife had always taken Iris toy shopping. Maybe they had another nanny where they'd lived before and she did all of that. Or maybe someone just delivered toys and they hadn't taken Iris to any stores yet.

"Why don't you take these bags and I'll push Iris." She didn't wait for him to answer as she thrust the sacks into his hands. "Let's head home and I'll start dinner. You look like you need to get back to safer territory. We can't have all those plush toys terrorizing you anymore."

Colin glared at her. "Now you're mocking me. We don't

need to go home. I just needed to escape that store with my life."

Darcy started pushing Iris down the sidewalk toward the SUV—the one he'd bought for her use. Yes, the man was used to getting what he wanted, in one sneaky way or another.

"I'm not mocking you," she told him. "I'm just stating a fact based on the evidence you presented to me." Colin grunted in response. Darcy smiled as she loaded Iris into the car seat. "What do you say we head over to the park and let Iris play while you recover? Then we can go home and I'll make dinner."

Colin seemed to think about the suggestion before a wide grin spread across his face. "That's a great idea. It's a beautiful day. We might as well spend it outside."

Elation pumped through Darcy. She was seriously having such an amazing day with them and it had nothing to do with her new purchases. Being out with Iris and Colin was just fun and broke up the monotony of being in the house. Darcy had been so dead set on not letting Colin buy things for her, yet here she was watching him load the new clothes he'd purchased into a vehicle that he'd also bought for her.

She was not a shallow woman and she certainly wasn't hung up on material objects. But, if she was going to be spending months with Colin and Iris, they would be leaving the house at various times and she couldn't very well keep going out in her ratty old clothes. Granted she didn't need thousands of dollars' worth of clothes, either, but she'd lost that fight. She also planned to leave them behind when her term was over because she didn't think it would be fair to keep them…not unless something deeper happened between her and Colin. And at the rate they were edging closer together emotionally, she wondered how they actually would end up at the end of the six-month term.

As they all settled into the car and Darcy climbed in behind the wheel, she realized the main problem. She was getting too comfortable with this family. Not comfortable the way she had on other nanny jobs, but comfortable as in she'd started envisioning this little family as hers. The thought alone was utterly ridiculous, but she couldn't stop the daydream any more than she could control her hormones around Colin. Everything about this family struck a chord so deep within her, she knew she'd carry them with her for the rest of her life.

Darcy was completely in love with Iris. The little girl could easily melt anyone's heart.

As for Colin…she knew she wasn't in love with the man, but she did have feelings for him. Feelings that had no place in her life or in this professional atmosphere.

Now if she could just keep telling herself that, maybe she'd believe it. But would she stop fantasizing about him?

Eleven

He had become a creature of habit at a young age, due in part to his royal status. Schedules were a normal part of his life and without them, the members of the palace's security team would not have been able to do their jobs efficiently.

And here in the United States he found he was no different. He was in the middle of his nightly workout, which meant he was sweaty, breathing hard and still aching for the woman who lately occupied his every blasted thought.

Today had been amazing and seeing Darcy's face light up was worth the sacrifice. He knew she wasn't easily bought and that was definitely not his intent.

He treated her just as he would any other employee. Colin and his brother were always quick to supply anything the members of their staff needed. Just because he was in the United States, away from the palace, didn't mean he wouldn't treat Darcy like any other member of his staff.

Except Darcy had become more than an employee the second he'd plastered her up against the wall and kissed the hell out of her.

Last night their phone conversation had stimulated him in ways he hadn't expected. Sleep had been a long time coming and he had a feeling he'd be in the same predicament tonight. For the next several months, in fact, if they didn't end up just giving in to their desires.

He needed to get his head on straight and figure out how to tell Darcy about this trip. He actually loved the thought of taking her to his home country. He could only hope she'd take the news of his royal status well and agree to go with him. Colin had just started doing squats with the weight bar across his shoulders when his cell chimed from the bench behind him. Of all his exercises, this was the one that nearly killed his back and leg so he welcomed the distraction.

Dropping the bar back into place, he turned and smiled when he saw the name on the screen. He should've expected this.

"Is this going to be a ritual?" he asked in lieu of saying hello.

Darcy's soft laugh greeted him. "I just wanted to tell you again how much I appreciate the clothes. You didn't have to do anything like that for me, and saying thanks seems so inadequate, but…thanks."

Colin gripped the phone, wishing she'd come down and thank him in person. From her soft tone, he knew she was feeling a bit insecure, most likely about the money, which meant absolutely nothing to him. He had an exorbitant amount of it, so why shouldn't he be able to spend it on people he cared about?

"You're more than welcome," he replied, playing it safe instead of telling her what he really wanted to say. "But you don't have to keep thanking me."

"Maybe I just wanted to hear your voice."

Colin froze as she tossed back the words he'd given her last night. "You hear my voice all day."

"It's not the same with Iris around."

Closing his eyes, Colin reached out and rested his arm on the cool bar. He dropped his head and contemplated how to approach this shaky ground, because each step could set off a series of events he either didn't want or wasn't ready for. "You can come to the gym if you want to hear my voice," he said, hoping she'd take him up on his offer.

"No. This is best. I just…this is so silly."

"What were you going to say?"

Her pause had him lifting his head, listening for the slightest noise in the background. Was she already in bed? Had she lain there and thought of him?

"When I talked to you on the phone last night it was as if we were alone, just without the pressure of being alone." She laughed, then let out a groan. "Forget it. I'm not making sense."

She made perfect sense. Everything about her and this crazy situation made sense to him at this point in his chaotic life.

"Maybe we should pretend we're alone and we don't have to have any boundaries," he stated, his mouth spouting off words before he could fully filter his thoughts. "What if you were here with me now? Or what if I was up there with you? If we were just two people who met and there was nothing holding us back from taking what we wanted, what would you do?"

Silence greeted him and he knew without a doubt images were flooding Darcy's mind because they sure as hell were playing through his.

"What would you do if I showed up at your bedroom door right now?" he whispered.

He knew he was torturing himself. Unfortunately, he fantasized about Darcy whether he was speaking the words aloud or keeping the thoughts to himself.

"If nothing stood in our way, I'd let you in."

Colin wasn't sure whether to be thrilled or angry at this torturous piece of information. At least she came right out and said the words, but words meant nothing without action.

"What would we do after I came in?" he asked.

Her soft laugh enveloped him. "I'm not having phone sex with you."

"I wasn't headed there." Though now that she'd put that thought in his mind, he wouldn't object to a little phone sex. "Tell me, Darcy. Once I came to your room and you let me in, what would happen?"

"Everything I've been dreaming about," she whispered. "But dreams aren't always meant to come true."

That sad tone of her voice said so much more than her actual words. He knew she'd been saving for an adoption. He wished he could be the man to give her what she wanted, but he was in no position to give anything unless it was financial or sexual. All superficial things, yes—anything involving his heart or too many emotions, hell no. He wasn't naive. He figured if things were different they may actually have a shot at something special, something more meaningful than intimacy. But how could they pursue anything beyond that when she had no idea who he was and he had no idea who he wanted to be?

A muffled sniff slid through the phone and Colin gripped the device tighter. "I'm coming up."

"No. Colin, you can't." Another sniff. "This is good, just talking. I haven't really talked about my feelings for a long time."

"You're crying."

He hated the thought of her lying up there upset, most

likely over a bad memory that had been triggered by what he'd said. Colin wanted her happy, wanted that light in her eyes he'd become familiar with and he wanted to break down every damn wall she'd erected between them.

"I'm fine," she assured him. "It's getting late and I need to get up early for my workout."

"You have a standing invitation to work out with me."

"I know."

She still wouldn't take the offer, but he had to remind her anyway. He wanted to be here for her, to give his support, and that thought scared the hell out of him. Taking on someone else's problems was not going to help him solve his own and would only push him deeper into Darcy's life…a place he couldn't allow himself to be.

"Good night, Darcy."

"'Night, Colin."

He disconnected the call and resisted the urge to throw the phone across the room. This was a dangerous game he was playing with her. Not only were her feelings obviously involved, he had a sense her heart was teetering on the brink, too. That wasn't his ego talking, either. He didn't know if he had it in him to give her his heart. He knew he wanted her on a primal level and he was fully aware that his emotional connection with her was stronger than he'd intended, but there were so many uncertainties.

On the other hand, he wasn't too keen on the idea of another man capturing her heart, either, which left him in quite a predicament.

He had some decisions to make in his personal life here and back on Galini Isle. No matter what path he chose, Colin feared he'd be making a mistake and now there were even more lives—and hearts—on the line.

Colin kicked a ball to Iris, and just as she went to raise her leg the ball rolled right by her, causing her to laugh hysterically just like the past seventeen times he'd purposely kicked it by her.

Darcy swallowed the lump in her throat. A child's laughter was the sweetest noise, and by the looks of Colin's little game, he thought so, too..

The day was too beautiful for them to eat inside so Darcy had decided to set up lunch in the outside eating area. The father-daughter duo was having so much fun, they hadn't spotted her yet and Darcy was enjoying the view. Colin epitomized what fatherhood was all about. Spending time with his child, putting work on hold and not caring if he was getting texts or emails.

Exactly what Darcy would want for the father of her child if she could've had children. But she had to wonder what profession allowed him to have such flexibility. He'd mentioned that he managed a large group back home. Maybe he delegated most of his tasks. She could totally see him in a position of power and authority.

After pouring fresh iced tea into two glasses and placing a sippy cup of juice on the table, Darcy stood back and double-checked to make sure she hadn't forgotten anything. She was trying out a new recipe on Colin and she hoped he'd like it. Finding healthy dishes that weren't an all-day task to prepare was proving to be more difficult than she'd thought.

Smoothing her hands down her new mint-green shorts, Darcy headed out into the yard. Blades of grass tickled her bare feet as she crossed the lawn. Shielding her eyes from the afternoon sun with her hand, she continued to take in the beautiful image of the sexiest man she'd ever met playing with the sweetest little girl she'd ever cared for.

To look at them right now, one would never know a piece of their life had been ripped away when his wife passed. On a positive note, Iris wouldn't remember the pain of losing her mother. But she wouldn't have any mother-daughter memories to cherish. Darcy's mother hadn't died, but she had abandoned her at a young age. Still, Darcy's grandmother had always been there and was an amazing role model.

Colin glanced up, catching her gaze and pulling her from her thoughts. "You come out to play?" he asked.

"I set up lunch on the patio," she replied, rushing to play on Iris's side. Darcy kicked the ball back to Colin. "I figured we could eat out here today."

Iris clapped as Colin sent the ball back. "Deedee kick it."

For the next couple minutes, Darcy and Colin carried on a game. Before she knew it, the competition had turned serious and she was all over the yard, rounding him with the ball, dodging any attempt he tried to get back control. Colin thought he could outmaneuver her. Wasn't he in for a surprise? She was no stranger to kicking a ball around.

Finally, Darcy had mercy on him and she kicked the ball hard, sending it soaring through the air. Colin jumped, his arms extended above his head, and caught it with his hands.

"I'm raising the white flag," he panted.

Darcy resisted the urge to bend at the waist and draw in some much-needed air. She'd gotten in her second work-out of the day, but she wasn't about to admit she was still out of shape and thrilled he'd called a halt to their impromptu game.

"How about we eat?" she suggested, reaching down to take Iris's hand. "I have fresh tea and I desperately need a drink."

Once they were all settled, Darcy sat next to Iris to help her with her food if necessary. Colin took a look at his plate and smiled.

"This looks great."

His verbal approval shouldn't have had her so excited.

She'd only grilled some pineapple and chicken and put a homemade glaze over it. Nothing too fancy.

"Were you an athlete in school?"

Darcy sipped her glass of tea, welcoming the cold, refreshing drink. "I played soccer, actually. My school was big, so we had our own girls' team."

"You were pretty quick out there."

Darcy shrugged, even though a bit of pride burst through her at his statement. "Not as quick as I used to be. After graduating and helping Gram full time, I lost most of my stamina. As I've said before, I'm pretty out of shape now."

"I've already told you, your shape is just fine."

Darcy expected to look up and find him staring at her, but he was cutting into his chicken. Apparently the comment he kept throwing her way didn't affect him the way it did her. He tossed the words out so matter-of-factly, yet they meant so much to her. More than he could ever know.

"Your new clothes look nice on you."

Iris kicked her little feet in the highchair, causing the whole thing to wiggle, sending her sippy cup to the ground. Darcy retrieved it and set it back on the tray.

"For what you spent, they better," she joked.

Silence settled in for a bit before Iris started gibbering. Darcy didn't mind the quiet meal. There was no awkwardness surrounding them, only the peaceful, bright sunshine and the beauty of the lush backyard. It was times like this that Darcy could imagine slipping into the role of something so much more than a nanny.

"Did you play any sports in school?" she asked, trying to distract herself from her wayward thoughts.

Colin's fork froze halfway to his mouth, a naughty smile flirted around his lips. "I pretty much concentrated on girls and defying my father."

Darcy could easily see that. "What about your mother?"

"She was killed in an auto accident when I was younger."

Darcy's heart ached for him. He'd lost his mother and his wife? How much could a man take in one lifetime? So much heartache, yet he still smiled, still pushed forward and created a wonderful life for his own daughter.

"I shouldn't have asked," Darcy stated, slicing into her pineapple. "That was rude."

"You can ask me anything you want," he told her. "There's no need to be sorry. You didn't do anything wrong."

"No, but I don't want to bring up bad memories."

With a slight shrug, Colin reached for his tea. "The memories are always there. Not talking about them won't make them disappear."

Once Iris was finished, Darcy tidied her up and wiped off the tray. After taking a load of dishes into the kitchen, she came back out. Colin had pretty much cleaned up the rest and had his own stack of dishes in hand.

"I would've gotten those," she told him. "Just set them inside and I'll clean up later."

He didn't say a word as he passed. Darcy pulled Iris from her highchair and took her back out into the yard to continue the game of ball before the toddler went in for her nap.

Running in the grass, laughing and playing with a little one may have been something Darcy had dodged for years, but honestly this was exactly what she needed.

But the way they'd settled in almost like a family terrified Darcy because falling for a baby was one thing, but falling for the baby's father was another problem altogether. Yet the more time she spent with Colin, the more she saw what an amazing, giving man he was and the more she wanted him.

She was done denying herself.

Twelve

For the past week, Darcy had spoken to Colin on the phone every night before bed. There was something soothing about hearing that low, sultry voice without having to look him in the eyes or be distracted by that hard body. She loved their talks, which ranged from joking to flirting to borderline naughty.

They'd also had some serious moments. Moments that probably wouldn't have happened in the light of day or face-to-face. For some reason saying personal things on the phone was relaxing—almost therapeutic. She'd shared memories of her grandmother and he'd shared stories about how he and his brother used to rock climb together.

Darcy shifted against the sheets, the satin of her chemise sliding over her heated skin. Her gaze traveled to the phone on her nightstand. They'd already hung up for the night, but she needed more.

Before she lost her nerve, Darcy picked up her phone and called him back.

"Forget something?" he answered.

Oh, the replies she could throw back.

"I wasn't ready for bed." At least not alone. "Mind talking a bit more?"

"Not at all. You're a welcome distraction from this office work."

Darcy slid from bed and padded down the hall, careful not to speak when she passed Iris's door. For once she was going to be spontaneous, she was going to take what she wanted and live for the moment because there was no way she would walk out of here with regrets when her term ended.

There was only so much a woman could take.

"Something specific on your mind?"

Easing down the stairs, guided by only the soft glow of the dimmed chandelier in the foyer, Darcy smiled. "Too many things to list."

Some shuffling and cursing in his native language had Darcy pausing, her hand on the banister at the base of the steps. "Everything okay?" she asked.

Colin laughed. "Yeah, just making a mess here."

Darcy knew that as soon as she hit the hallway he'd hear her talking, so she took a seat on the bottom step, curled her feet up onto the step below and looped her arms around her knees.

"If you wanted something more than anything in the world, but there were obstacles in your way, what would you do?"

"Are we going to pretend we aren't talking about you?" he asked.

"I'm pretending," she said with a smile, even though he couldn't see her. "You don't have to."

"Then pretend it's me," he told her. "When I want something, I find a way to claim it at any cost. I may not get it in the time frame I want, but eventually with enough patience, I make it mine."

Closing her eyes, Darcy let his strong words push through that wall of fear she'd tried so hard to hide behind.

"What if time isn't on your side?" she whispered.

"What is it you want, Darcy?"

His question, nearly a whisper, too, told her he knew exactly what she wanted...or whom she wanted.

"I started to come to you." She gripped the phone tighter as if she could somehow pull strength from him. "I'm afraid."

Admitting that really humbled her because she didn't want to be seen as weak or vulnerable. Colin was neither of those things and she didn't figure he'd find a woman who was so indecisive and fearful attractive.

"You think I'm not?"

That voice was in full surround sound. Darcy jerked her head up to see Colin standing before her, phone still to his ear. The glow from the light illuminated him, making him seem even larger than life.

Darcy laid her phone beside her on the step. "You're not scared," she countered, unsure of what else to say at this point.

Crouching down with a slight wince, Colin placed his phone next to hers before laying his hands over the arm that was still wrapped around her knee. "Just because I'm scared doesn't mean I'll let the fear control my emotions. I want you, and the second you said you were coming to me I had to meet you halfway."

The man truly didn't let anything get in his way, not fear, not worry for the unknown...absolutely nothing.

"Maybe—"

He cut her off as he claimed her mouth beneath his. His hands instantly cupped the side of her face and tipped her head for better access. Colin's body eased forward and

Darcy realized he'd placed his knees on the bottom step, so she spread her legs to accommodate him.

The moment her bare thighs slid against the side of his ribs, she groaned into his mouth. She'd never been this turned on, this ready for a man, and he'd only started kissing her. Granted, she'd only been with one man in her life, but there was absolutely no comparison between this passionate moment and anything she'd experienced before.

Breaking away, Colin peered down, stroked her bottom lip with his thumb and held her gaze. "Never hold back with me. I want it all."

At that firm command, he took her lips again. Shivers coursed through her as Colin trailed his hands down her bare arms then slid them around her waist. With only the silk of her chemise providing a barrier, the warmth of his hands seared her skin. Arching into him, she wanted more and she wanted it now.

In one swift move, Colin picked her up and changed their positions so he sat on the step and she straddled his thighs.

His eyes roamed over her body. "You really do sleep in a black chemise."

Without comment, Darcy did what she'd wanted to do since day one. She leaned forward and trailed her tongue across that ink scrolling over his shoulder and down to his pec. The muscles clenched beneath her touch and a low growl erupted from Colin. His hands came around to cup her backside, jerking her closer against his arousal.

Darcy trembled, clutching his shoulders. An ache even fiercer than before spread through her. There was nothing outside this moment. Not her financial issues, not her infertility, not the mystery surrounding Colin, because if she were honest, that only added to his allure. They were both taking what they wanted.

Colin moved one hand around, splaying it over her

upper thigh. His thumb teased just beneath the edge of the lacy trim on her panties, each stroke coming closer to the spot where she needed him the most.

Forgetting the torture of tasting his inked skin and chiseled muscles, Darcy dropped her head to his shoulder as he finally slid his thumb inside the material. Those slow strokes over her heated center were going to be the death of her. Darcy tipped her hips, silently demanding more. She'd denied herself this pleasure for so long, she simply couldn't take much more.

Her breath hitched as he eased inside her, her fingertips curled into his skin. He continued to torture her slowly, yet with so much control and power, Darcy was having a hard time getting her mind around the emotions tugging her in all different directions. But what if she wasn't enough for him? What if she disappointed him once they really got down to it?

She froze, not wanting this moment of blissful perfection to end, because it felt too good, too perfect. Too right.

"I told you not to hold back with me again," he growled in her ear. "Stop tensing up and let go."

With one hand still stroking her, he used the other to jerk down the top of her chemise. The strap snapped apart as his mouth settled over her breast. Darcy arched back, crying out as the full-on sexual encounter washed over her, sending her spiraling into the most intense climax of her entire life.

Before her tremors could cease, Colin was shifting beneath her and she realized he was working his shorts from side to side to get them down. Quickly she assisted him and found herself hovering right above a very naked, very aroused Colin. Then he slid his other hand between them and gave her chemise a tug, tearing apart the seam in the middle.

"I owe you another shopping trip," he muttered against her lips. "This time I'll be in the dressing room."

Oh, mercy. Shopping for lingerie with this man would be...heaven. They'd never make it out alive.

"I have protection in my office and in my room."

Darcy held his gaze, her mind trying to process the words because she was still in a euphoric state.

"I've been anticipating this moment so I was prepared." He nipped her lips, shifted his hips so his erection nudged her. "You have about two seconds to decide where this will happen."

"Whichever one we get to fastest."

Colin came to his feet, causing Darcy to stand on her not-so-steady legs. She didn't have to worry, though, because Colin lifted her once more, not in the romantic scoop she'd always read about or seen in movies, but hooking her legs around his waist, forcing her to wrap her entire body around him. Oh, yeah. This was the experience she wanted. Nothing mushy here, but full-out want, need and the snapping of the control they'd both been barely holding onto.

He moved down the wide, darkened hall toward his office. Only a small bronze desk lamp cast any light on the room. Still, with her wrapped all around him, Colin jerked open a drawer and tossed a foil package onto the glossy surface of the desk. Darcy nipped at his shoulder, earlobe and jawline. With protection taken care of, she wanted him. Now.

When he sat her on top of his desk, he eased back, taking her face in his hands. "You're sure?"

Darcy nodded. The intensity of his gaze and the way he held his lips firm told her he may have more to say, but instead he tore open the wrapper and covered himself before pulling her to the edge of the desk.

Darcy leaned back on her elbows, staring up at him

and watching as he gazed back down at her. Colin's hands gripped her hips as he slid into her. When he caught her gaze, a tick visible in his jaw, she smiled. "Don't worry about going slow."

Something must have snapped because the next thing she knew he wasn't holding back…in any way.

Darcy's head fell back as pleasure engulfed her, as Colin claimed her. She'd never experienced anything so perfect, so all-consuming in her entire life.

Their frantic pace sent something from the desk crashing to the floor, but she didn't care and the commotion didn't slow Colin down, either. She barely noticed papers shifting beneath her. With the way Colin's eyes were locked on hers, the way he held her waist with his strong hands and took her as if he owned her, Darcy didn't think she'd ever care about anything else again. He was completely ruining her for any other man.

Another wave crested over her and Darcy cried out, her legs tightening around Colin's waist. He jerked once more and stilled, his fingertips bruising her sides.

After they stopped trembling, Colin leaned over, his forehead resting against her shoulder.

"I haven't done that since before my accident," he muttered. "I was afraid I'd hurt you if I carried you and fell, but I had to try. I wanted you in my arms. I want to be the man you need."

He was that man and so much more. Darcy had wondered if her heart would get swept away with Colin because of his single-father status, but what she felt for him had nothing to do with his child, his finances or anything other than the fact that he alone turned her inside out and made her feel things she'd only ever fantasized about. He made her come alive in ways she never had before.

"If you give me a few minutes, I'll take you up to my

room." His lips cruised over her damp skin, causing her to already want him again. "I need you in my bed."

Darcy didn't say a word. She would follow him to his bed. She'd follow him anywhere he asked.

Darcy's hair tickled the side of his face, but there was no way he was moving. She fit perfectly against his side, tucked snugly into him, as if she was made to be there. But right now, after taking her on his desk, and pleasuring her again once they'd arrived in his room, Colin didn't want to think any deeper than this blissful, sated feeling. He couldn't, wouldn't dive into that black hole of thoughts where all of his worries and fears about committing to another woman lived.

For the first time in months, he let loose and enjoyed his time with a refreshing woman who pulled him back to basic life...exactly what he'd been searching for.

With Darcy's arm across his abdomen and her leg across his thigh, the woman was staking her own claim and he had to admit, he liked it. He liked her. To know she wasn't into one-night stands completely humbled him. She'd been brave to initiate the encounter.

"I have a trip I need to take in a few days." His words cut through the darkened silence. "I'd like you to accompany me."

Sliding her fingertips up and down his abs, she asked, "Where are we going?"

"I need to go back home for an event," he told her, unable to reveal the rest of the details. "We will only be gone a few days."

Darcy shifted, easing up on one elbow to look down at him. His eyes had adjusted to the dark, plus the soft glow from the security monitors offered a dim light.

"Do I need to pack anything in particular?" she asked with a smile. "I've never been out of the country before."

She'd need a passport if she didn't have one and that could be problematic unless his assistant pulled some strings. They'd be flying in the palace jet, but still there was customs. He'd have his staff figure out the details.

"That blue dress would be a nice start," he told her. "But just be yourself. That's all you need to do."

She didn't have to go, she could stay behind, but he wanted her there. Granted he had a whole host of people who could care for Iris—maids, butlers, assistants, his sister-in-law. The list truly was endless.

But he wanted Darcy on his turf, he wanted to see how she fit into his life.

Colin nearly gasped as a realization dawned on him. He was falling for this woman in his arms. He was falling so hard, so fast, but he couldn't admit it fully, because what if she rejected him?

"You mentioned your parents had passed. Do you have siblings other than the brother you've mentioned?"

Her question pulled him from his thoughts.

Being here with Darcy, going into public without guards or paparazzi snapping photos was so different, so refreshing and so damn freeing. But he still felt as if he was letting down not only his country but Stefan. His brother was all Colin had left and putting the entire future of Galini Isle on Stefan's shoulders wasn't fair.

"Just Stefan and his wife Victoria."

"And they live in Greece?"

"Yes," he replied, fully enjoying the way her fingers continued to travel over his exposed torso. "What about you? No siblings, I assume."

"No. It was just my Gram and me after my parents split town. Apparently they weren't into the whole parenting thing and my Gram wasn't about to let me go into the foster system. I lived with her, worked with her and learned everything I know from the most amazing woman in the world."

No wonder Darcy was such a fighter. She'd had one person to depend on her entire life...a life spent caring for others. Colin had a whole army of people he depended on back home and he was running from them.

"Did you once mention wanting to adopt a baby of your own?" he asked.

A soft sigh escaped her, tickling his shoulder. "I would love to adopt, but it's expensive and my business needs to get back on track again. I'm afraid by the time I get all settled financially and go through the process, I'll be too old."

"You're young enough."

Her fingertips traced his tattoo the same way her tongue had earlier. She'd damn near had his eyes rolling back in his head.

"I know, but given the experience I had with my ex... it just hurts." She settled her head back in the crook of his arm, but continued to run her hand over his chest and abs as if she couldn't get enough...which suited him just fine. "To know you share your dreams, open your heart to someone and have them lie and betray you like that. I'm not sure I'll ever get over that pain. My dreams were put on hold and I'm not sure I'll ever get them back."

Colin swallowed. He wasn't the same as this ex, so he shouldn't feel guilty about lying.

Still, he wanted to clear the air about something.

"The last woman I was with was my wife," he told her, hating this topic in bed, but needing to get it out. "I know I mentioned that before, but I wanted you to know I may have been reckless as a teen and into my early twenties, but between marrying, the accident and then Iris, I've calmed down. I didn't want you to think I was using you because you were here and convenient."

"I know you're not," she murmured. "I've only been with one man before you. I just don't take the time to date and a fling is not something I can do."

Colin laughed, earning him a smack. "Sorry," he chuckled.

"You know what I mean," she defended. "I'm going to be here several months, so I hope tonight wasn't a one-time thing. I mean, I guess that should've been discussed, but I assumed—"

Colin rolled over, pinning her beneath him and cutting off her words.

"I plan on having you as often as you'll allow me to," he told her. As he looked into her bright eyes, he knew he had to tell her the rest. "I need to tell you why we're going back home."

She stared up at him, her eyes locking directly onto his. "Let's not talk right now." She spread her legs so he could settle firmly between them. "I only want to think about right now, with you, in your bed."

The trip could wait.

Colin smoothed her hair away from her face, nipped at her lips. "Maybe I want you to just lay back, think of absolutely nothing but how good everything feels."

He didn't wait for her reply as he started kissing his way down her body. When Darcy clutched the sheets, he smiled as he continued his path.

The next few months were going to be amazing.

Thirteen

Darcy wore only Colin's T-shirt as she maneuvered around the kitchen getting breakfast ready. She'd skipped her early morning workout and opted to stay snuggled next to Colin's warm, strong body. Of course she'd gotten enough of a calorie burn last night, in the middle of the night and again this morning.

Not only had he ruined her for any other man, he'd ruined her for any other workout. Why exercise with some cold piece of machinery when she could get a thorough workout with a hunky man ready to meet her every need?

Iris sat in her high chair, tapping her spoon against the tray and babbling. Every now and then a coherent word would slip out, but she was mostly just entertaining herself while Darcy cooked up some pancakes.

Colin had wanted to shower early, so he should be joining them soon. Everything about the morning after wasn't at all uncomfortable the way she'd heard people say. If anything it was very…domestic and normal.

The chime at the gate jerked Darcy from stirring the pancake batter. Who on earth was trying to visit this early in the morning? As long as no one on the inside of the house buzzed the guest in, they wouldn't get beyond the gate, unless they had the code. Darcy wasn't allowing anyone to pass through because Colin hadn't mentioned he was expecting a guest and this wasn't her house.

A moment later Colin came down the steps wearing a pair of running shorts and nothing else but a tan and the tat. She'd explored that body, tasted and touched it, yet the sight of him still had her knees weakening. How had her life gone from being so bleak, so depressing, to something that sparked hope and new life?

"Was that the gate alarm?" he asked as he bent down to give Iris a kiss and ruffle her curly bedhead.

"Yeah. I didn't answer the call because I didn't know if you were expecting anybody or not."

Darcy went back to mixing, wondering how she should act this morning. The entire scene seemed so family-like, so perfect, and she feared she'd make a mistake and this dream would be over.

"I'm not. Wonder who wanted in this early in the morning?" he mumbled. "I take it you weren't expecting anyone."

Darcy laughed as she poured the batter for several pancakes onto the warm griddle. "Do you honestly think I've invited friends to come over?"

"You can, you know."

She glanced his way and rolled her eyes. "I may take you up on that. I've texted my friends, but I've just been too busy to entertain."

"You can entertain me anytime." He crossed the spacious kitchen, rounded the island and slid a hand up beneath the T-shirt she wore. "You look better in this shirt than I ever did."

How could she not get swept into the fantasy this whole scene represented? She had to keep everything separate—her attraction for Colin in one part of her heart, her love for Iris in another. And there was no room for this family bonding. Colin and Iris weren't her family no matter how much she wished they were. Being swept into a love affair was already uncharted territory, but allowing her heart to get caught up in this fantasy was only going to crush her in the end when she walked away alone.

The doorbell chimed, causing Darcy and Colin to freeze. His hand slid out of the shirt, leaving her cold where his warmth had been.

"Stay here. There's only one person who has this code besides us."

Colin didn't look happy. Who would have the code? They'd been here for two months and nobody had used it yet, so why now?

As soon as the front door opened, another male voice filled the home. She pulled the pancakes off the griddle and set them aside on a spare plate. After flicking the griddle off, Darcy cut up a half of a pancake for Iris. Raised voices from the foyer had Darcy plucking Iris from her highchair.

Who was here? Should she try to go out the back and get to a neighbor for help? Darcy cursed herself for only wearing a T-shirt. She scooted closer to the side of the kitchen that was closest to the foyer to see if she could hear better but not be seen since she was hardly dressed for company.

"Are you going to let me in?" an unfamiliar male voice asked. Whoever this man was, he had the same sexy accent as Colin.

Colin spoke vehemently, again in Greek—what sounded like a curse. Moments later the door closed. Whoever was here, Colin knew him but he was a stranger to Darcy.

Great. Her attire screamed that she'd just gotten out of bed...her lover's bed.

"Nice place," the other man commented. "But are you ready to come back and forget this notion of living in the States?"

"You should've called," Colin replied, his tone implying the guest still wouldn't have been welcome.

"We've talked nearly every single day. I wanted to surprise you."

Footsteps echoed, growing louder. Darcy moved toward the island and put Iris back into her high chair. She'd just taken her seat when a man who could be Colin's twin stepped into the room, Colin right on his heels.

"Stefan, this is Darcy."

She hadn't been able to hide behind the island in time and the man's eyes traveled over her, taking in her oversized T-shirt, the hem of the boxers peeking out from beneath it and her bare legs before going to Iris and then back to Colin.

"I'm sorry," he said, turning back toward Colin. "I didn't know...wait, is this your nanny?"

Darcy cringed and turned to concentrate on cutting up Iris's food. Whatever was going on with these two, she wanted no part of it. Clearly they had issues that didn't involve her. Well, maybe they did now.

"Stefan," Colin growled. "Not a word."

"I'm just trying to figure things out." Stefan shook his head and propped his hands on his hips. "Are you giving up your title, turning your back on your country and the throne for someone you barely know?"

Darcy froze. *Title? Throne?*

Slowly, she lifted her gaze to Colin. He stared back at her as if he was waiting to see her reaction, too.

"Shut the hell up, Stefan," Colin nearly shouted. "Apologize to Darcy. She has nothing to do with my decision and you know I'm taking the full six months to think this through."

"My apologies," Stefan said, turning and tipping his head toward Darcy. The worried look etched across his face told Darcy he was sincere. "I mean no disrespect to you. I was just taken aback. I've been waiting for my brother to come home, and I knew he'd found a reason to stay for now. I certainly didn't mean to take my shocked state out on you. Actually, Mikos has told me quite a bit about you and I want to thank you for being so kind to my niece."

"There's nothing to worry about with me," Colin cut in before Darcy could respond. "I'm still unclear on my decision."

"Mikos." The other man stepped closer to Colin. "Are you seriously that happy here that you're still confused? Have you not missed anything about Galini Isle or the people who love you?"

Darcy swallowed, terrified to ask, but needing to know. "Why is he calling you Mikos and what does he mean by throne and title?"

Colin's eyes closed on a sigh, but before he could answer, the other man turned to face her completely. "I'm calling him Mikos because that's his name and he's a prince from Galini Isle, a small country off the coast of Greece."

Darcy had no idea what to say, what to do. All those times they'd talked, every single day they'd shared together over the last two months and he couldn't find it in his heart to tell her any of that? Not even his real name?

Tears blurred her vision, but even through the hurt and confusion, she had a baby to care for. That was what he was paying her for, right?

Whatever game he was playing by seducing her, it was clear that she was pretty much just hired help. Had he ever seen her as anything more or had he been laughing at her this entire time?

"Darcy—"

With a jerk of her head and a glare, Darcy cut off whatever Colin, Mikos…whoever, had been about to say.

"You haven't told her?" the other man asked. "Classy, Mikos. Real classy."

Colin was seriously fighting the urge to punch his brother in the face. First of all, to show up unannounced was rude even for Stefan. Second, how the hell did he fix this with Darcy now? The last thing he wanted was for her to be hurt, for her to feel as though she'd been betrayed again.

But he'd lied because been so dead set on keeping his identities separate. He'd gotten so wrapped up in her, in this life, that he hadn't given much thought to consequences. He'd been thinking only of himself. Just as he had with Karina, and look how that had turned out.

"Let me feed her," Colin offered, stepping forward. "You go change."

Her hands shook with each bite she put in Iris's mouth, but Darcy didn't even turn to answer him.

"Darcy." Stefan also stepped forward. "I apologize for coming in like this and dropping a bomb on you. I'd assumed my brother would've told you about his status. Why don't you go change and I'll feed my niece? I haven't seen her for a long time."

Now Darcy lifted her head, gave a slight nod and headed out of the room, careful to go around the island to avoid getting too close Stefan and Colin. She didn't say a word, didn't look either of them in the eye.

Her pain lingered after she was gone. Colin would never forget the angst that had washed over her face right before she slid up that invisible wall and avoided looking at him. Good God, what had he done?

"I could kill you for that," Colin muttered.

Stefan leaned his hip against the island and forked up another bite for Iris. He made an airplane motion and some ridiculous noise to get her to open for him. Of course she clapped and kicked her feet, oblivious to the turmoil going on.

"Don't be angry with me that you kept the truth hidden. If you like the woman, and I have to assume you do because you're still here, then she deserved the truth."

Colin slammed his fist onto the counter. "You have no idea what has happened so don't even think about assuming you do." But Stefan was absolutely right. Why hadn't he seen this coming?

"It's about time you're showing emotion for someone else." A smile spread across Stefan's face. "I'm glad to see you're living again. Are you and Darcy serious?"

Colin rolled his eyes. This wasn't up for debate. He went to get a plate, but suddenly he wasn't hungry anymore. Right now Darcy was upstairs, most likely angry, hurt, maybe even crying, because he thought he could keep all the balls in the air and have control over every facet of his life.

"I don't know what we are," Colin defended himself. He thought he knew what he wanted, but would Darcy ever speak to him again? Did his wants even matter at this point?

Stefan paused, bite in midair. "She's wearing your shirt and whisker burn, cooking your breakfast and caring for your child. I'd say that's pretty serious. Yet you still lied to her. It makes me wonder why."

"I'm paying her to care for Iris."

Stefan glanced around the island, found a sippy cup and passed it to Iris before turning his focus back to Colin.

"And the rest? I know you're not paying her for that, and this is the first woman you've shown interest in since Karina."

"I don't give a damn what you think right now. I was planning on coming home for the ball, you didn't have to show up unannounced."

Stefan shrugged. "Last time we spoke you told me you weren't sure if you were coming back. I merely came to talk some sense into you. Victoria had to stay behind to get last minute things prepared for the event or she would've been right here with me."

Colin raked a hand over his still damp hair. "Watch Iris for me. I need to go upstairs and talk to Darcy. Stay down here and shut the hell up next time you see her. You've done enough damage."

Colin didn't wait for Stefan to confirm anything, he just turned and stormed from the room. His back was killing him, as was his leg after all the extra activities he'd participated in last night, but he was determined to march right into Darcy's room and set things straight.

He had nothing planned to say, had no clue what state he'd find her in or what was even going through her mind. He was about to enter unstable territory and it terrified him because he realized that what she thought was important.

Not only did he not want to be the one to hurt her, but he also wanted to be the one she counted on. So many people had turned away from her, betrayed her in one form or another.

And he'd just added his name to the list. Surely he could make this up to her somehow.

Yet he stood outside her bedroom door, staring at the barrier as if the inanimate object could offer insight. What a mess he'd made, all because he'd been too self-absorbed, too wrapped up in Darcy and his hormones to truly see the big picture. Not that he saw any clearer now, but he did know one thing, he still wanted Darcy and he'd make damn sure he would fix this disaster he'd caused.

Colin tapped his knuckles on the door. It hadn't latched completely so the weight of his hand eased it open just enough for him to see her standing across the room, her back to him, as she looked out onto the backyard.

"I know you want to be alone," he started, staying in her doorway. "But we need to talk."

Darcy's shoulders stiffened, the only sign she'd even heard him. Silence settled heavily between them, when only an hour ago they were lying side by side in his bed. At least she'd thrown on some pants so he didn't have to be tortured further by the sight of her bare legs. He could still feel them wrapped around him, entwined with his.

"I didn't set out to lie to you, even though that's how it looks." He had to keep talking. If she wasn't ordering him out, then he knew she was listening. "I have a lot going on back home, so much that I didn't want to talk about it with anyone. I wanted to separate myself from that part of my life for a while to get my head on straight. I had to put Iris's needs first and keeping our identity a secret was one of my top priorities."

He paused, giving her a chance to speak if she wanted. When she remained silent, he pushed on.

"I wish I could blame my brother for barging in here and dropping that bomb like that, but it's my fault you didn't know." Taking a risk, Colin stepped further into the room, raking a hand down his face as he carefully chose the right words. "You matter to me, Darcy. More than I want to admit and more than I thought someone could after Karina. I don't want this to come between us."

Darcy whirled around. The tear tracks on her cheeks crippling him in ways words never could.

"You mean you don't want your lies to keep me out

of your bed?" she threw back. "Because isn't that all we have between us? Our arrangement was never meant to be more than temporary. So, for once since I've known you, be honest."

Colin swallowed the fear, the anger. He'd brought it all upon himself. He had to stand here and take it like a man. He deserved every word, every bit of rage she wanted to fling at him.

"You're only up here because you want to continue what we started last night." Darcy shook her head and laughed, swiping at her damp face. "I was such a fool. You were probably laughing at me the entire—"

She gasped, her eyes darting to her closet before her face crumbled. Turning away, she let out a low moan as she hugged her arms around her midsection.

"You knew I had nothing and there you were, throwing your money around," she whispered.

Colin started to cross to her because he couldn't stand the anguish lacing her voice, but she spun to face him, holding him with her hurt-filled stare. He stopped only a few feet from her.

"Did you get a kick out of giving to the needy?" she asked, her tone nothing but mocking. "Did you enjoy knowing you had everything, while I had absolutely nothing? Money, power, control. You literally played me, never once thinking how this would affect me."

"I never played you," he corrected. "I wouldn't have told anyone I employed here about my life on Galini Isle. And I damn well did worry about you. Every single day we grew closer I worried how this would affect you, but I didn't know what to say or how to even approach it."

Her eyes narrowed. "Because you're a coward. Apparently running from the truth is what you do. You fled your home when you obviously didn't want to face responsibilities there."

How could she ever understand that he hadn't been strong enough to face his royal duties as a widowed father, trying to bring up a duchess? How could she ever grasp how much was involved in being a prince raising a child in the kingdom? What if Iris didn't want the title that came along with her prestigious family name?

At some point this getaway had turned from him finding himself to him deciding what was going to be best for the future of his daughter.

"I have to go back in a couple days," he told her, forcing himself to put up a strong front because the sight of her so broken was damn near crippling. "I still want you to come with me."

Pain-filled laughter erupted from Darcy. "You're insane. I'm not going anywhere with you. This isn't some fairy tale, Colin or Mikos or whatever the hell you want to be called. This is my life and I'm not just running to some island in Greece because you snap your fingers and expect me to."

"I want you to go to be with Iris," he explained, hoping she'd cave because he didn't realize how much he needed her to be there on his turf until this moment. "She's used to you, she's comfortable with you and I'd rather have you caring for her than any of my assistants."

Throwing her arms in the air, Darcy pivoted and moved around him to stand on the other side of the room. "You're something else. You probably have multiple people at your disposal, yet you continue to want to torture me. Why? Are you enjoying this power trip?"

Clenching his fists at his sides, he watched as she began to pace. "I'm not enjoying any part of this."

"You're using Iris as a bargaining tool." She stopped and propped her hands on her hips. "You're using her to get me to come with you."

"I'm being honest," he told her. "You wanted honesty,

I'm laying it out there. I tried to tell you this morning. I know that's a convenient thing to say considering the timing, but it's the truth. I want you to see my country. I want you to be the one to care for Iris while I'm home because I will be facing many challenges there."

He didn't want to get too far into everything that he was running away from. Darcy wasn't in the right frame of mind to hear it and he wasn't ready to admit how weak and vulnerable he truly was.

Darcy pursed her lips together, then nodded. "Fine, but if you want to throw that money around so much, then I want double my original pay for the entire six months. If I'm traveling, then I deserve to be compensated accordingly."

This was probably not the time to say he was proud of her for standing up for herself, for playing hardball and fighting for what she wanted. Most women would've packed their bags and left. He'd always known she was a fighter and she was coming back at him full force.

She was the only woman who'd ever challenged him. What would he do on Galini Isle without her by his side? He wasn't about to find out.

"Done," he said without second thought. "On one condition."

She quirked a brow. "What?"

"When we're at the palace, you have to do what I say. No questions."

"I don't think—"

"Do you want the money?"

Darcy stilled, and her nostrils flared as her cheeks reddened. "You're despicable."

No, he was desperate, but he'd never admit that aloud. "We'll leave Sunday evening and sleep on my jet."

"Of course you have a jet," she muttered before moving toward her door. "We're done here. I'll take care of

Iris, I'll do everything a hired nanny does and she will be my number one priority. That doesn't include sleeping with my boss. From now on our relationship is strictly professional."

Crossing the room, Colin kept his gaze locked onto hers. As he neared, her eyes widened but she never looked away. He stopped only a breath from her, then leaned down to whisper in her ear.

"I never set out to lie to you, Darcy. You have to believe me."

As he spoke, his lips caressed the side of her cheek. Just as she shivered, Colin eased back. Her hand came up to slap him, but he quickly gripped her wrist in midair.

"You're angry. Don't do something you'll regret later." Although he knew he deserved it.

Her eyes flared, filling with unshed tears. "I hate you."

He yanked her forward to fall against his chest. With one hand still holding onto her wrist, Colin hooked an arm around her waist. "There's a fine line between hate and passion," he said with a confidence he didn't quite feel.

Unable to resist temptation, Colin captured her lips, but let the brief kiss end for fear she'd bite him. He smiled down at her.

"Make sure to pack the blue dress for our trip."

He'd barely made it out her door before it slammed at his back.

Damn it. He had to do something. Somehow he had to make this up to her. Losing Darcy was not an option, but he'd messed up. He didn't deserve her forgiveness, but that wouldn't stop him from doing everything in his power to earn it.

Fourteen

Darcy could dwell on the fact that her parents had abandoned her at a young age. She could also hone in the fact that the man she'd thought she loved had stolen every last penny she had to her name. She could even focus on her most recent betrayal: Colin keeping the colossal truth that he was a freaking prince from her. But Darcy opted to go a different route.

From now on, she would choose anger, because if she even attempted to shut it out, all she'd have left to face would be soul-crushing hurt. There was no time for that because there was an innocent child in all of this...a child Darcy had been hired to care for.

As much as Darcy wanted to take the initial half of her pay and leave Colin, she wouldn't abandon Iris. Darcy couldn't walk away, not when she knew all too well the feeling of rejection. But what would Colin do at the end of the six months? Did he have other arrangements set up or was he going back home? Did he even know himself?

Darcy continued to stare out the window of the car that had been waiting for them when they'd arrived at the private airstrip on Galini Isle. Iris had been sitting, securely strapped in, between her and Colin, and since they'd left LA Darcy had barely spoken a word to him unless it involved the baby. Nothing else needed to be said at this point, the damage was done.

Iris continued to sleep, which was a blessing because the poor thing had cried a good bit of the flight. Most likely the pressure in her ears had been getting to her. Even though exhaustion threatened to consume Darcy, too, she was too angry to be tired.

Beyond the obvious anger toward Colin, she was furious with herself because of her reaction to his parting shot in her room about still wanting her. He'd known just what to say, exactly the right way to deliver the words for the most impact.

Colin may have been a different man when he was with her, a man he'd made up, yet she still wanted him. Nobody had ever made her feel more beautiful, more wanted than he did. He'd wrapped his arms around her and kissed her as if he had every right in the world.

But that was all part of his game. He'd created a new life in America and she was just another prop. More than anything she wished she could switch her emotions off to avoid the hurt, but she simply wasn't wired that way.

The chauffeur pulled into a drive. Darcy noted the gate, guards and white columns as the car made its way onto the estate grounds. What was she doing here? She was going to spend the next few days in a palace. *A palace.* Only a few months ago she'd had to sleep in her car because she'd lost her condo, and now she was going to be staying in a freaking mansion in another country. She'd never even set foot outside of California before.

When they came to a stop, Darcy started to open her

door, but Colin leaned a hand across where Iris slept and laid his other hand over Darcy's arm.

"They'll get your door," he told her.

Rolling her eyes, Darcy jerked from his grasp and opened her own damn door. Once she stepped out, she turned and reached in to gently unfasten and pull Iris from her seat. She slept on as Darcy cradled her against her shoulder.

"Ma'am." The driver held her door, tipping his head toward her. "I'll make sure your bags are brought in."

She nearly laughed. Her bag, singular, was still her ratty old suitcase that didn't suit palace living at all. Of course the clothes inside certainly did, considering they were purchased with royal money.

Ignoring Colin's attempt to put his hand on her and guide her, she stepped to the side and shot him a glare. "Just have someone show me where the nursery is and I'll take her in."

"I'll show you."

His tone left no room for argument. Whatever. She wasn't going to fight, not with sweet Iris in her arms. Darcy truly wanted the best for Iris, even if her father was a lying jerk.

The three-story mansion stretched along the grounds farther than any "home" Darcy had ever seen. Lush plants and vibrant flowers surrounded the palace, edged along the circular drive and flanked the steps leading up to the entrance. Guards in full military-looking uniforms stood at attention on either side of the door.

This world was definitely not hers. Everything about her life had been transformed the moment she'd met Colin. From the new clothes, her emotional state, her sexual experiences…every single aspect of her personal and professional life would never be the same.

Passing by guards, entering a grand home with a tiered

fountain inside the entryway—*inside* the entryway—was stunning. Darcy shook her head as she followed Colin closely. As they passed random people…maids, men in suits, servants? Darcy noted that Colin would nod in greeting while the others would slightly bow. People actually bowed to the man.

Yes, they were worlds apart in every sense of the term because Darcy was on the same level as these people bowing to the man she wanted to throttle.

Colin led her toward a grand staircase that would make the iconic home from *Gone with the Wind* seem miniscule.

Colin turned before ascending the steps. "Why don't you let me carry her up?"

"I've got her and your back has been bothering you."

The corner of his mouth tipped as if he were holding back a smile. "You know me so well. And you care."

Darcy moved around him, refusing to even look at that handsome, sexy grin, those mocking, alluring blue eyes. "I saw you cringe when you stepped off the plane and again getting out of the car. And I only care about Iris."

As she started up, she knew he was behind her, most likely eyeing her rear end. That was fine, she couldn't stop him from looking, but she could prevent him from touching.

She had to prevent him from touching because if the man even tried to come on to her, she'd have a hard time holding it together. She couldn't ignore her emotions or hormones, no matter how much she wished her body would stop betraying her.

Once she reached the second floor, she turned back to see Colin gripping the banister, taking the steps more slowly than she'd thought he would. An unwelcome tug on her heart revealed the anger still rolling through her.

With one arm securing the sleeping baby, Darcy eased down a step and reached out her free hand. Colin froze, glancing from her hand to her face. She thought for sure his stubborn pride would have him swatting her away, but he put his hand in hers and squeezed. He climbed the last few steps with her support, without comment.

Once he righted himself, he moved down the hallway and Darcy was relieved they weren't heading up to the next floor because she highly doubted Colin could make it. Being on the plane for so long had most likely agitated his injury. His limp was a bit more prominent as he moved down the wide hallway. She wanted to reach for him again, but…she couldn't. Focusing on following him, she took in the luxurious surroundings.

Gold sconces adorned each section of wall between each door. The ceiling had scrolling artwork that she would have to admire later because Colin had neared the end of the hall and was going into a bedroom.

Bedroom was seriously too loose a term. The area she entered was a condo all its own with a formal sitting area, open bedroom tucked away in the far corner and two sets of French doors that opened onto a balcony offering a breathtaking view of the ocean.

"This is the nursery?"

"This is your room. I've asked for Iris's stuff to be put in here so you can stay close to her and you won't have to be near me or anyone else."

The crib was nestled in the opposite corner along the same wall as the king-sized bed. Moving across the wide room, Darcy gently laid Iris in the crib, surprised when the little one nestled deeper into the mattress and let out a soft sigh.

Once Darcy was sure Iris was going to stay asleep, she turned and moved back to where Colin remained standing. His eyes were fixed on hers and, try as she might, she couldn't look away. She both hated this man and found herself drawn to him for unexplainable reasons.

"We'll be fine now." She hoped he'd take the hint and leave. "I'm assuming someone will bring our things to this room."

Colin stepped closer to her, closing the gap between them. Darcy had to tip her head back to look up and hold his gaze.

"The formal ball is tomorrow night," he told her. "I want you there. With me."

This fairy tale was really starting to get out of control. She only wanted to be here with Iris. Getting dressed up and playing any other role wouldn't be a smart move.

"I'm your child's nanny," she informed him, forcing herself to ignore the thread of arousal winding though her at his intense stare. "I'm not your date for hire or one of your assistants you can order around. Everything changed when you opted to keep the truth from me."

A smile spread across his face, showcasing that dimple she'd once found sexy.... His palms slid up her bare arms, curved over her shoulders and glided on up to frame her face.

"You forget you agreed to do what I want while we're here."

The reminder was the equivalent of cold water being thrown in her face.

"You can't use me like this," she whispered.

"I'm not using you," he replied, his face now hovering just above hers. "I'm simply taking what I want and I want you on my arm during the ball."

Another layer of anger slid through her. "Is that why you told me to pack the blue dress?"

"No. I don't want anyone else to see you in that dress." His thumb stroked her bottom lips, his gaze honed in on her mouth. "That dress is for my eyes only. You'll wear it for dinner tonight."

"I don't want dinner with you," she threw back, though

her voice wasn't as strong as she'd hoped it would be. "You said I didn't have to leave my room if I didn't want to."

That thumb kept sliding back and forth with just enough pressure to have Darcy nearly begging him to kiss her. Darn hormones betraying her common sense.

"You're not leaving your room," he stated. "Dinner will be delivered."

He stepped away, leaving her aching, wanting more and all he'd done was use that low, sultry voice and fondled her lips. How pathetic could she be?

"Be ready by seven."

With that he turned and walked out of the room. Darcy continued to stare at the door long after he'd left. How dare that man expect her to just be at his beck and call? If he wanted to have dinner with her, fine, but she had a surprise of her own for him and it sure as hell didn't involve that sexy blue dress.

Darcy was playing hide-and-seek with Iris—which was quite easy in a room of this size with the adjoining bath and colossal walk-in closet—when someone knocked on her door.

Iris squealed and ran to the door, standing on her tiptoes to try to reach the knob. Darcy laughed and eased Iris back so she could open the door.

Darcy was greeted by one of the most beautiful women she'd ever seen in her life. The stranger was holding a long, white garment bag.

"Hi, Darcy," the woman said with a wide, radiant smile. "I'm Victoria Alexander. I'm Stefan's wife. Would you mind if I came in for just a moment?"

Iris sneaked around Darcy and started reaching for Victoria.

"Hi, sweetheart." Victoria bent slightly, shifting the

bag to the side so she could give Iris a kiss on her head. "How's my big girl? I missed you so much."

Darcy stepped aside and let Victoria pass through. Victoria crossed the room and hung the garment bag over the door leading into the closet area.

When she turned back around, she scooped Iris into her arms and squeezed her. The instant burn to Darcy's eyes was unexpected. Iris obviously had so many people who loved her, who needed her. Darcy had to face the harsh reality that she was just a random employee of the prince passing through. The impact on Darcy was huge, life-altering, but Iris would never even remember her.

"First of all, let me tell you how sorry I am about this whole thing." Iris wiggled in Victoria's arms until she was let free. "Stefan explained everything to me and I am embarrassed that he dropped what I'm sure was shocking news when he visited. I'm even more embarrassed that my brother-in-law took it upon himself to lie to you by omission. The Alexander men can be infuriating and you were dealt a double dose."

Darcy clasped her hands in front of her, not quite sure how to take this woman, but from the looks of things, she could be an ally.

"I'm from LA, too, so I know this whole royalty thing can be overwhelming at times," Victoria went on, offering a sweet smile. "I just want you to know that while you're here, please feel free to let me know if you need anything. Stefan and Mikos can be quite…difficult to communicate with at times. They seem to have their minds set on certain agendas and tend to let nothing stand in their way."

Darcy laughed. "That's one way of putting it."

"Mikos really is an amazing man." Victoria's eyes darted to where Iris was running around the spacious room, dodging the chaise longue, weaving through the sheers by the patio doors. "He's a wonderful father and he's been through so much. Don't be so quick to judge him when he's clearly made a drastic mistake."

Darcy shook her head and sighed. "I'm just the nanny. It's not my place to judge."

"If you were just the nanny, I wouldn't have spent the last two days making a dress for you to wear at the ball tomorrow." Victoria pointed to the garment bag. "Once you try it on, let me know if it needs to be altered. Mikos was pretty specific in his instructions."

Darcy stared at Victoria, then to the bag. "What? You made a dress?"

"I'm a designer. It's what I do." Victoria shrugged. "Sounds silly, I know, considering I'm also the queen, but that's just a title. I was designing dresses before I ever married into the Alexander family and I didn't want to lose my identity."

A bit taken aback, Darcy made her way to the garment bag and slid the zipper down. Peeling away the protective plastic, she gasped at the shimmering, pale blue formal gown. With one shoulder open and the other covered in clear crystals that were heavy at the top and tapered off toward the ruched waistline, Darcy didn't know if she'd ever seen a more beautiful dress.

"You made this?" she asked as she stared over at Victoria. "In two days?"

Laughing, Victoria nodded. "I did and I have to say, I think you'll look stunning in it."

Darcy's eyes locked onto the dress. Colin had requested this for her? He'd not only requested it, he'd been specific about what he'd wanted.

Darcy swallowed, unable to even comprehend this world she was temporarily living in.

"Would you mind if I took Iris out for a walk?" Victoria asked. "Stefan and I were going to go down to the beach before the guests start arriving and things get crazy around here."

Still in a daze, Darcy turned back to Victoria. "Oh, sure. Of course."

Victoria lifted Iris into her arms and kissed her neck until the baby giggled. "Let's go get some sand between our toes."

"Thank you," Darcy said before Victoria cleared the doorway. "The dress is spectacular, so 'thank you' seems so inadequate."

Victoria nodded and grinned. "It was my pleasure. I'll bring Iris back shortly. You look like you could use some time to let all of this sink in."

Just as Victoria reached the doorway, she turned and glanced over her shoulder. "I know it isn't my place, but I can't let this go. Mikos left here because he couldn't face being a widowed father. Between all of the responsibilities and losing his wife, he was severely broken. He was only looking out for Iris when he left. She's always been his number one priority, so whatever he said or didn't say to you, was only to protect her in the long run."

Victoria slipped out the door, shutting it with a soft click. Iris's squeals could still be heard, but Darcy was stuck on Victoria's parting words.

A new plan started to form. Colin was coming for dinner and he expected her to wear the other blue dress.

What was it with him and blue? Apparently that was his favorite color.

She shook her head and focused on her plan. She'd wear the blue dress, but she was going to make him suffer. He might think he had control here, but they both knew she carried the power right now. She'd seen the vulnerability in him when she'd helped him up the steps and she'd seen how much he fought the weakness that continued to plague him.

But as far as their relationship went, she knew he still wanted her and most likely he'd planned dinner in her room as a way to seduce her. He may have started off lying to her, he may not have meant to hurt her, but he'd had ample opportunities to tell her the truth before taking her to bed.

If he wanted her for more than a romp, she wasn't going to give in so easily. She'd make him beg if she had to, because she was worth it.

Tonight she'd see what they both were made of.

Fifteen

Colin wanted to get to the room before the dinner arrived. He'd also asked Stefan and Victoria to keep Iris for a few hours this evening. He hated incorporating them into his plan, but he had to call for reinforcements because time was not on his side.

Taking a deep breath and willing his damn nerves to settle, Colin knocked on her door. He wanted time alone with Darcy, wanted to be able to let her into his life, his world because he'd come to realize she mattered more than he'd ever thought possible. At first the instant physical attraction had eaten at him, but he'd soon come to the conclusion that she was much more than someone he wanted to sleep with. Darcy was honest, invigorating and perfectly suited to him…someone he could spend the rest of his life with. The woman had woven her way into his world just when he wanted to be left alone the most. She'd awakened something fresh, something new inside of him he'd thought was long dead and gone.

When the knob turned and the door eased open, Colin's breath caught in his throat as his eyes traveled over the stunning image before him.

"I didn't think you'd actually wear it."

His eyes raked over the bright blue dress that wrapped over Darcy's breasts, dipping low enough for him to see the swell, then securing at her waist where her classy figure dipped in just above the flare of those hips that drove him insane with want and need.

She'd left her hair down, silky and straight. The barest of makeup made her seem so natural, so beautiful and so seamlessly matched to what he wanted but hadn't known he was looking for.

"Why wouldn't I?" she asked, gesturing for him to come on in. "You requested it. You are paying me, after all."

Cringing as he walked in, Colin hated that he'd thrown money in her face once again. He'd been so low as to dangle the very thing she needed and then relished his delight when he got his way.

He was no better than her ex and deserved nothing at all from the woman he'd found himself falling for.

Before he could say more, another knock sounded on the door and a member of the waitstaff rolled in a covered cart. He took it on out to the patio, bid them a good evening and was gone.

"Shall we?" she asked.

Not giving him a chance to answer, she headed toward the open doors that lead to the terrace. The ocean breeze slid through her room, bringing that familiar saltwater scent he'd taken for granted as a kid, but positively loved now. And he realized how much he'd missed the island now that he was back.

White table linens, gold candlesticks and a cluster of white roses adorned the table set for two. Darcy went to take the cover off of one of the dishes on the cart, but Colin stepped in front of her, blocking her action.

"You look beautiful," he told her, needing her to know how he felt, that he believed what he was saying. "You're more than I deserve right now."

She tipped her chin, leveling his gaze. "I'm your nanny, Colin. Or would you prefer Mikos? Perhaps Your Highness. What do your other servants call you?"

"You're not my damn servant." Colin gritted his teeth. She was mocking him. "You can call me Mikos or Colin. Either would be fine."

She bowed and something in him snapped. He gripped her shoulders and gave her a slight shake.

"Don't bow to me. Ever."

Her eyes widened as she ran her tongue over her plump, glossy lips. "I'm your employee, am I not?"

"You're more, damn it, and you know it."

She stiffened beneath his touch. "Do I? Because I assumed even friends were up front with each other. Employees and employers keep their private lives separate, so excuse me if I'm a little confused."

He needed some space to cool off and she needed to get used to the fact that he wasn't going to give up so easily.

Releasing her, he pulled out a chair. "Sit. I'll get your dinner."

Surprisingly, she obliged. Once he'd served the meal, they ate in strained silence. Thoughts, possible conversations played over and over in his mind. There was so much he wanted to say, needed to say. But would she hear him, would the words penetrate into her heart where he needed them to go?

Pushing away from the table, Colin came to his feet and moved to the rail of the terrace. Watching the water ebb and flow against the shoreline calmed him. He absolutely loved his home, loved this view he was blessed to wake up to every day. It was all the hype around his name, his title that he could live without. He wanted a simple family life and the ability to live without the media snapping photos of him and his daughter, splashing whatever headlines they chose.

Stefan and Victoria had managed to attain such a life. They were making it work with their titles and they always managed to find time to themselves, away from all the hype and press. Could he have that, too? Could he attend to his duties and actually have a family?

His heart clenched. He hadn't known how much he wanted a family…a family with Darcy and Iris.

"I stared at this view for hours after I came home from the hospital," he started as he kept his back to her.

He hadn't counted on talking, but he couldn't keep her shut out of his world…not if he truly wanted her to be a part of it. And now more than ever he knew what he wanted.

"I'd sit out on the balcony off the master suite and curse that damn wheelchair. Karina was pregnant and all I could think was what type of father I could be to our child when I couldn't even stand or put on my own pants."

Darcy's chair scooted against the tile, but Colin kept his back to her. He couldn't turn and look her in the eye, didn't want to see pity staring back at him.

"I gradually got stronger, but I was too busy working on myself to realize I had to keep working on my marriage. Karina went through the pregnancy pretty much alone because I devoted all of my time to my recovery. I was determined to be on my feet when our baby came."

From the corner of his eye he saw Darcy step up to the rail, but far enough away that she was just out of reach. Probably for the best. With his emotional state, if she touched him, if she offered compassion right now, he'd break down, and baring his heart was about all the vulnerability he could handle. No way in hell did he want to be that man who clung to a woman, sobbing…which is exactly what he feared would happen if he didn't concentrate on the words and not the feelings of the past.

"When Iris came my whole outlook on life changed," he went on as he watched a palace guard pass by below. "The media wanted pictures of her, wanted photos of the happy family. It was then I realized we weren't a family. Karina had started sleeping in another room, she started distancing herself more and more from me and I can't blame her."

"It takes two to make a marriage work," Darcy added, her soft voice hitting him square in the heart. "You can't take all the blame."

Risking a glance over his shoulder, Colin met her intense gaze. No pity lingered in her eyes, if anything he saw understanding.

"I abandoned her long before she decided to leave," he replied. "After she suddenly passed away, I couldn't handle the strain of my life here any longer. It's no secret to my family that I've never wanted to be Prince of Galini Isle. I didn't want that weight on my shoulders. Stefan took the lead as king, which was fine with me, but if anything happens to him, I have no choice as long as I retain my title."

The familiar twinge in his back started out dull, the way it always did before blowing up into something major, so Colin pushed off the rail and stood straight, twisting at the waist to keep the muscles warm.

"Are you okay?" she asked.

"Fine. Just needed to move."

She stared at him another minute before looking back out to the water. "I have no clue about the life you were running from. I see this place and I think you have it all. But then I hear the pain in your voice and I know you are torn. I know you don't take this for granted and you're seriously worried about what step to take next."

Turning to fully face her, Colin took a step closer. "I'm not only worried about the title, Darcy. I'm worried about us."

Shaking her head, her lids lowered as she bit her lip for a moment before speaking. "How can *us* even exist? There was one night. One amazing night, but it was built on lies."

He started forward again, but halted when she held out her hand. With a deep breath, she turned to face him. "You don't understand how deeply you hurt me. You can't imagine what it cost me to come to you that night. I kept avoiding you because you had everything I always thought I was looking for and I was terrified if I let my guard down, I would want too much. I would love too much."

Breath caught in Colin's throat. "Darcy—"

"No." She shifted, backing up a step as if she feared he'd reach for her. "Whatever I felt wasn't real because I developed feelings for a man who doesn't exist."

Swallowing hard, damning any risk he was about to take, he closed the distance between them and gripped her arms. She fell against his chest, her mouth opening in a gasp.

"Does this feel fake to you?" he demanded, holding on to her a little too tightly. "Every time I kissed you, touched you, did all of that feel like a lie?"

Her intense gaze held his as he continued to loom over her. She'd cracked open something deep within him, something he hadn't even known he was holding back. His heart was wide open for her and she just needed to walk through. Damn it, he needed her to.

"You were so brave, calling me, wanting to come to me." He softened his voice. "You realized what we had was worth putting yourself out there for and you were ready to take a chance. Don't back away now, Darcy. Don't make judgment calls until you really see the big picture."

With the way he stood over her, her body arched against his, Colin couldn't avoid temptation another second. Nipping his lips against hers, testing to see if she'd let him continue, he nearly wept with relief when she didn't pull away.

As he wrapped his arms around her, pulling her hips flush against his own, he covered her mouth completely and deepened the kiss. Darcy's hands remained at her sides, though her mouth opened, inviting him in. For a split second, she froze, as if her mind were starting to override her emotions.

"No," he murmured against her lips. "Don't think. Feel. I never lied about how I feel and you know that. Everything we shared with our bodies was real. Everything I ever told you about how I felt was real."

With her eyes closed, she licked her swollen lips. "I can't do this, Colin. I'm here for Iris."

"Well I'm here for you," he whispered.

Not giving her another chance to speak, he claimed her mouth once again and ran his hands around to the front of her dress. He gave each side of the material a yank to expose her lace-covered breasts. On a gasp, Darcy tore her mouth from his and he feared he'd gone too far, but she tipped her head back and groaned. Colin stole the chance to trail a path of kisses down her silky skin until he reached the edge of the lace bra.

Darcy's hands fisted in his hair as he turned and backed her up against the smooth stone next to the patio doors. The last thing he wanted was to stay close to the rail and have one of the guards look up. Darcy was his and sharing even a glimpse of her was not an option.

Colin reached down, bunched up the bottom of her dress and slid his hand over her heated center. She adjusted her stance as he tore away her lacy panties and he had no doubt they matched the bra he was about to remove.

With a flick of his fingers, the front closure sprang open. Colin feasted on her while his hand continued to pleasure her. Her heavy panting quickened as her body arched against the stone. This is how he wanted Darcy, delirious with passion, aching with a need only he could provide because he was the only man for her.

"I pictured this the moment I saw the dress," he murmured against her heated skin. "It was made for you, made to drive me insane with wanting you."

Her hands went from his hair to his shoulders. Fingertips dug into him, but he continued, ready to feel her release, to watch her come apart in his arms.

As her hips bucked against him, Colin lifted his head to see her face. When he glanced up, her eyes were on him. The intensity of her gaze flooded him with a hope he wasn't sure she even knew she was offering.

Within seconds she was flying apart, calling his name. Colin gritted his teeth, concentrating on making this moment all about Darcy, no matter the cost.

As her trembling ceased, Colin slid his lips against hers. "You're mine for the ball tomorrow."

When she started to speak, Colin laid a finger against her lips. His other hand smoothed down her skirt as he kept his eyes on hers.

"Whatever you may think of me, know that I want you and I don't just mean physically. Yes, I lied. I did it to protect Iris because in the beginning she was all that mattered. But now you matter, too, more than you could ever know, and I'm giving you the chance to see everything about me without any guard on my heart. I want you to take it all in before you decide anything."

With shaky hands, she refastened her bra, pulled her

dress back into place. "What about...you're not leaving now, are you?"

He smiled. "You mean why aren't we having sex? Is that what you want right now, Darcy?"

Her eyes held so much heat, so much desire. "I don't know what I want," she whispered. "I thought I did."

As much as it cost him, he took a step back. "I'm not staying and I'm not making love with you. Tonight was all about you. I wanted you in that blue dress because I knew you'd feel beautiful. I wanted you out here on the balcony for dinner because I know you normally eat fast to get back to taking care of children. And I wanted you to come apart in my arms without giving anything in return to me. From here on out, everything in my life will be centered around my daughter and you. Take all the time you need to think about what that means because I'm not going anywhere."

Her chin quivered. If she started crying, he'd have to hold her and he wasn't sure he was strong enough to wrap his arms around her and not take more than she was ready for at this point. Never in his life had he been this scared of losing it all. Even when he'd battled with his duties or being confined to a wheelchair, nothing had put fear in him as much as the thought of losing Darcy.

"Not all guys take everything, Darcy. Don't compare me with the jerk who shattered your dreams." He started toward the open French doors, but stopped at the threshold to look back at her. "I may just be the guy who can make your dreams come true if you'd take the time to look beyond the anger."

Oh, how he hoped she would do just that. Living without Darcy was simply a life that was unthinkable.

Sixteen

Colin swirled the amber liquid around in his glass, resisting the urge to throw it across the room. He hadn't heard a word from Darcy since leaving her room last night. The ball was in a few hours and he honestly had no idea if she was going to be there with him or not.

But right now he couldn't care less about the ball. He wanted to know where he stood with Darcy. He'd bared his soul to her, he'd passed all power over to her and now he had to wait. This was not how he lived his life…ever. Power and control were staples in his life, ingrained in him at a young age. But Darcy was worth giving all of that up for. She was worth every sacrifice.

"You're going to drive yourself mad and drinking won't help."

Colin didn't turn at the sound of his brother's useless advice. "If I want to drink, I will."

Standing on the balcony off his suite, Colin wasn't calmed by the water rushing the shore. For the first time in his life, he was consumed by emotions he had no control over: fear, frustration, worry.

"Luc just arrived." Stefan's shoes scuffed over the tile as he leaned against the rail beside Colin. "I told him you'd be down shortly."

Colin wanted to see his best friend, especially since he hadn't met Luc's fiancée yet. But he had to get his head on straight first. He couldn't go down to the ball with this much emotional baggage. Even if the media had not been permitted inside, he didn't want fellow dignitaries to see him so vulnerable.

"What have you decided?" Stefan asked.

Tilting back his glass, Colin welcomed the burn of the whiskey. "I haven't decided anything."

"Because of Darcy?"

Colin shifted, leaning one elbow on the rail as he stared at his brother. "You were a mess on your coronation day, if I recall. I know I was fresh from the hospital and in a wheelchair, but I remember how you were torn up over Victoria leaving you."

Stefan nodded. "She was my wife."

"Only because you needed her to be," Colin corrected. "You married her for one reason and fell in love with her later. It's no different with Darcy and me. She started out as Iris's nanny, but…"

Stefan's eyes widened. "Are you saying you're in love with her?"

Colin swallowed, afraid to say the words aloud. He merely nodded because the first time he admitted the truth verbally, it would be to Darcy, not his brother.

"And you're waiting to see what happens with you two before deciding whether to keep your title or not?"

Colin glanced out to the ocean, contemplating his next decision because no matter what he chose, the outcome would be life-altering.

"I'll remain on Galini Isle if Darcy stays with me."
Colin pushed off the rail, began to pace in an attempt to
release some tension. "I can't do this alone, Stefan. Raising Iris, helping you reign over this country. I won't leave
Iris to be raised by staff, not when I have a woman I can't
live without, and Iris loves her. I've realized that Iris is
happy here or in LA but she is really attached to Darcy.
And so am I."

Stefan smiled. "Then maybe you should tell her how
you feel. I'm not the one you need to be selling this to."

Colin stopped in front of his brother. "You think she's
a good fit for me?"

"I think Victoria is crazy about her and it's obvious
Iris is, too." Stefan slapped a hand on Colin's shoulder.
"And I've never seen you this torn up over a woman. I've
also seen you face cliffs that would make even the most
experienced climber cringe. Even after your accident you
wanted to get back out there. You were angry the doctors wouldn't allow it. So the fact this woman has you in
knots, yeah, I think she's a perfect fit."

"Then I need your help."

Colin laid out his plan, ready to fight for the woman he
loved…the woman who completed his family.

The risk he was taking was huge, but the payoff would
be substantial if every part of his plan fell into place.

Victoria had delivered Colin's message to Darcy that
he wanted to meet her in the south hall, just outside the
private entrance into the ballroom. Now he paced as Iris
sat on the gleaming marble floor, playing with the simple
doll Darcy had given her that first day.

He'd battled over whether or not to have Iris present
for this moment; he didn't want Darcy to think he was
using his child. But he needed Iris here because they were
a package deal, they were a family.

The soft click of heels echoed behind him. Colin took in a deep breath, willed himself to be strong and prepared to fight for what he wanted.

"Deedee pitty!" Iris exclaimed before she jumped to her feet.

"You are beautiful." Darcy's upbeat voice gave him hope that she wasn't miserable, that she wasn't dreading tonight. "Your gold gown is so pretty, Iris. What a big girl you are tonight."

Pulling up a courage he'd never had to use before, Colin turned and was nearly brought to his knees. Darcy stared across the open space. She wore the gown he'd asked his sister-in-law to make, she'd pulled her hair back into something sleek and fit for a princess and she wore the diamond earrings that had been his mother's. Obviously Victoria had delivered those along with his message, but Colin hadn't expected her to wear them, though he was so glad she had.

Yet, as breathtaking as Darcy was right at this moment, it was the sight of her holding Iris's hand that stole his breath away. The two most important women in his life stared back at him, waiting for him to say something, but he was utterly speechless.

"Thank you for the dress." Darcy took a step forward, and Iris, still holding onto her hand moved with her. "I've never felt so…I don't know what the word is."

"Breathtaking," he murmured. "You're positively breathtaking."

Her eyes widened. "I could say the same for you. I've never seen you in something so formal."

The standard royal uniform of a black double-breasted jacket with gold buttons, his medals for various works and services and his signature blue sash meant nothing to him. His entire life on Galini Isle meant nothing without this woman by his side.

"Are you ready to go in?" she asked, smoothing her hand down her gown as if nerves were getting to her, too.

"Not just yet. I wanted a minute alone with you before we go inside."

Darcy glanced down at Iris before meeting his gaze again. "I actually wanted to talk to you, too."

No. He refused to hear her say she couldn't do this anymore. He needed to tell her everything he'd planned before she made any decisions.

"Let me start," he told her.

"Me, me, me." Iris let go of Darcy's hand and extended both arms up. "Deedee hold me."

Laughing, Darcy swung Iris up into her arms. Colin wanted to capture this mental picture of Darcy in that pale blue gown and Darcy in her gold dress with matching gold headband, both of them laughing and smiling at each other. The bond those two had formed had been instant.

Colin zeroed in on the doll Iris clutched. He'd frowned upon it at first, but realized now how much it represented. Life could be simple, he could still have a normal existence, as long as Darcy shared it with him. Every relationship took work and he was ready to put forth every effort to make sure Darcy was in his life and happier than she'd ever been…if she would have him.

"Colin." Her eyes held his as she stepped forward. "What did you want to say?"

"I love you."

Darcy jerked, her gasp audible in the nearly empty hall.

He cursed beneath his breath. "That's not how I wanted to tell you. I wanted to lead into it by telling you how you've changed my life, how you've brought out something in me I thought was dead."

Colin closed the last bit of space between them, placing a hand on her arm and another on Iris's back. "I wanted to tell you how being without you all day has nearly killed me and how going to sleep at night without hearing your voice has left me feeling empty. I needed you to know how much you mean to me, how much you mean to Iris before I told you how deeply I've fallen in love with you."

Unshed tears swam in Darcy's eyes. "You're going to make me ruin my makeup."

He gently swiped the moisture just beneath her lashes. "I want to be the man who ruins your makeup for all the right reasons. I want to bring tears of joy to your life, I want to lie by your side every night, knowing you're happy and that I've done everything in my power to give you all the love you deserve, all the happiness you can handle."

Darcy bit her lip and lowered her lids as Iris laid her head on Darcy's shoulder and cuddled in closer.

"I can't give you any more children," she whispered. "I know you'll want more heirs."

He shut her up with a soft kiss to her lips. "The only thing I want is you and Iris. You both will complete my family."

She glanced up at him, one tear trickling down her cheek. Colin swiped it away with the pad of his thumb and cupped the side of her face.

"We can adopt, too." He watched as her eyes widened, her breath hitched. "I'll adopt as many babies or children or teenagers as you want. I'm not above giving children a home. I love that you have such a strong will to help others and I know you'll make an amazing princess of Galini Isle."

"Colin," she whispered on a gasp. "What—"

"I want you to marry me."

Darcy wrapped her other arm around Iris and continued to hold his stare. Iris's eyes were slowly drifting closed, as this was her bedtime, but between the ball and Colin wanting her to be part of this monumental moment, he couldn't just leave her to sleep in her room.

"Have you thought about this?" she asked. "Have you thought about what having someone like me will do to the media you tried so hard to dodge so you could find the life you wanted?"

"I found the life I wanted," he told her, stroking her damp cheek. "I found you. I wasn't even sure what I was looking for, Darcy. I wanted to be alone, I wanted to figure things out, but you kept working your way deeper into my heart and I can't be without you now. No matter where we live, I want to be with you. Facing this country, standing by my brother's side is what I'm supposed to do. I just don't want to do it without you."

"I have a life in America, Colin. I have a business I'm trying to save because of a promise I made to my grandmother. I can't ignore who I am, I can't lose my identity."

Colin nodded. "I understand. You will restore Loving Hands to its former glory. I don't want you to lose your identity, either, because it's what made me fall in love with you to begin with. See what staff you can hire back and have someone manage the office while we are here. So much can be done online, but I'm assuming you have someone you'd trust to run the office?"

Darcy nodded, her eyes darting away as if she were already thinking through the plans that would need to be made.

"Tell me we can make this work," he pleaded. "We can even keep the home in LA to use when we go back."

"You'd come with me when I go to check in on Loving Hands?" she asked, her eyes wide, brimming anew with unshed tears.

Colin wrapped his arm around her waist, tucking her side against his so he didn't squeeze Iris too much now that she was sound asleep. So much for her taking part in his epic moment.

"I have to admit, I'm quite fond of those steps," he muttered against her mouth before he slid his lips across hers. "I think keeping that house is a great idea."

"I'm still under contract, you know. What happens at the end of my six-month term?"

"We can make it our wedding date, if you'll have me."

Darcy sighed into him, opening her mouth beneath his. Everything about her felt right, perfect. How did someone from a completely different world fit so effortlessly into his?

He eased back. "I should tell you, I allowed a trusted media source into the ballroom. If you agreed to stay with me, I wanted to be in control of who revealed our good news first."

She froze, her eyes searching his. "I thought you hated the media."

"I hate the stories they make up and how they were portraying Iris and me as broken. We're a strong force, and with you by our side we are even stronger."

Darcy smiled. "You're an amazing father. I love you, Colin."

He'd never tire of hearing those words. "What was it you wanted to talk to me about?"

Her smile widened. "I was going to tell you I wanted to give us another chance."

Shocked, Colin eased back. "You mean you let me go through all of that knowing you were giving me another chance?"

With a shrug, she shifted Iris a bit higher in her arms. "I wanted to know how far you'd go. I needed to see you grovel, just a bit."

Sliding a hand around her waist, Colin leaned in to whisper in her ear. "You want to see groveling? I still owe you a shopping trip and I plan on helping you in the dressing room. We'll see who's groveling then."

Before she could utter a word, Colin wrapped his arms

around his girls and ushered them out. After putting Iris in her bed with a staff member close by the nursery, Colin whisked his future princess into her first royal ball. The first of many royal gatherings they'd be attending as a family.

* * * * *

THE DESERT KING'S
SECRET HEIR

ANNIE WEST

This book is dedicated to the wonderful men
in my family across three generations:
all heroic in their own way.
What excellent role models for my heroes!

CHAPTER ONE

'LET ME BE the first to congratulate you, Cousin. May you and your Princess be happy all your days.'

Hamid beamed with such goodwill Idris felt his own mouth kick up in a rare smile. They might not be close but Idris had missed his older cousin as they'd carved separate lives for themselves, Idris in Zahrat and Hamid as a UK-based academic.

'Not my Princess yet, Hamid.' He kept his voice soft, aware that, despite the chatter of a few hundred VIPs, there were plenty of ears eager for news of his impending nuptials.

Hamid's eyes widened behind rimless glasses. 'Have I put my foot in it? I'd heard—'

'You heard correctly.' Idris paused, tugging in a breath before it lengthened into a sigh. He had to conquer this sense of constraint whenever he thought of his upcoming marriage.

No one forced his hand. He was Sheikh Idris Baddour, supreme ruler of Zahrat, protector of the weak, defender of his nation. His word was law in his own country and, for that matter, here in his opulent London embassy.

Yet he hadn't chosen marriage. It had chosen him—a necessary arrangement. To cement stability in his region. To ensure the line of succession. To prove that, despite his modern reformist ways, he respected the traditions of his people. So much rode on his wedding.

Change had been hard won in Zahrat. A willingness to conform in the matter of a suitable, dynastically necessary marriage would win over the last of the old guard who'd fretted over his reforms. They'd viewed him as an unseasoned pup when he'd taken over at just twenty-six. After four years they knew better. But there was no escaping the fact this wedding would achieve what strong leadership and diplomacy hadn't.

'It's not official yet,' he murmured to Hamid. 'You know how slowly such negotiations proceed.'

'You're a lucky man. Princess Ghizlan is beautiful and intelligent. She'll make you a perfect wife.'

Idris glanced to the woman holding court nearby. Resplendent in a blood-red evening gown that clung to a perfect hourglass figure, she was the stuff of male fantasy. Add her bred-in-the-bone understanding of Middle Eastern politics and her charming yet assured manner and he knew he was a lucky man.

Pity he didn't feel like one.

Even the thought of acquainting himself with that lush body didn't excite him.

What did that say about his libido?

Too many hours brokering peace negotiations with not one but two difficult neighbouring countries. Too many evenings strategising to push reform in a nation still catching up with the twenty-first century.

And before that too many shallow sexual encounters with women who were accommodating but unimportant.

'Thank you, Hamid. I'm sure she will.' As the daughter of a neighbouring ruler and a means to ensure long-term peace, Ghizlan would be invaluable. As the prospective mother of a brood of children she'd be priceless. Those children would ensure his sheikhdom wasn't racked by the disruption it had faced when his uncle died without a son.

Idris told himself his lack of enthusiasm would evaporate once he and Ghizlan shared a bed. He tried to picture her there, her ebony hair spread on the pillow. But to his chagrin his mind inserted an image of hair the colour of a sunburst. Of curling locks soft as down.

'You'll have to come home for the ceremony. It will be good to have you there for a while instead of buried in this cold, grey place.'

Hamid smiled. 'You're biased. There's much to be said for England.'

'Of course there is. It's an admirable country.' Idris glanced around, reminding himself they might be overheard.

Hamid's smile became a chuckle. 'It's got a lot going for it.' He leaned even closer, his voice dropping further. 'Including a very special woman. Someone I want you to meet.'

Idris felt his eyes widen. Hamid with a serious girlfriend? 'She must be out of the ordinary.'

One thing the men in his family excelled at was avoiding commitment to women. He'd been a case in point until political necessity forced his hand. His father had been famous for sowing his wild oats, even after marriage. And their uncle, the previous Sheikh, had been too busy enjoying the charms of his mistresses to father a child with his long-suffering spouse.

'She is. Enough to make me rethink my life.'

'Another academic?'

'Nothing so dull.'

Idris stared. Hamid lived for his research. That was why he'd been passed over for the throne when their uncle died. Everyone, Hamid included, acknowledged he was too absorbed in history to excel at running a nation.

'Will I meet this paragon tonight?'

Hamid nodded, his eyes alight. 'She's just gone to freshen up before—ah, there she is.' He gestured to the far end of the room. 'Isn't she lovely?'

Only a man besotted would expect him to identify an unknown woman in that crowd. Idris followed Hamid's eager gaze. Was it the tall brunette in black? The svelte blonde in beads and diamonds? Surely not the woman with the braying laugh and the oversized rings flashing like beacons beneath the chandelier?

The crowd shifted and he caught a sliver of silk in softest green, skin as pale as milk and hair that shone like the sky at dawn, rose and gold together.

His pulse thudded once, hard enough to stall his breath. Low in his belly an unfamiliar sensation eddied. A sensation that made his nape prickle.

Then his view was blocked by a couple of men in dinner jackets.

'Which one is she?' His voice echoed strangely, no doubt due to the acoustics of the filled-to-capacity ballroom.

For a second he'd experienced something he hadn't felt in years. A tug of attraction so strong he'd convinced himself it hadn't been real, that imagination had turned a brief interlude into something almost…significant. No doubt because of the dark, relentlessly tough days that had followed. She'd been the one lover he'd had to put aside before his passion was spent. That explained the illusion she was different from the rest.

But the woman he'd known had had a cloud of vibrant curls, not that sleek, conformist chignon.

'I can't see her now. I'll go and fetch her. Unless—' Hamid's smile turned conspiratorial '—you'd like a break from the formalities.'

Tradition decreed that the ruler received his guests on the raised royal dais, complete with a gilded, velvet-cushioned throne for formal audiences. Idris was about to say he'd wait here when something made him pause. How long since he'd allowed himself the luxury of doing something he wanted, not because it was his duty?

Idris's eyes flicked to Ghizlan, easily holding her own with a minor royal and some politicians. As if sensing his regard she looked up, smiled slightly then turned back to her companions.

No doubt about it, she'd make a suitable queen—capable and helpful. Not clinging or needy. Not demanding his attention as too many ex-lovers had done.

Idris turned to Hamid. 'Lead on, Cousin. I'm agog to meet this woman who's captured your heart.'

They wove through the crowd till Hamid halted beside the woman in green. The woman with creamy skin and strawberry-blonde hair and a supple, delicate figure. Idris's attention caught on the lustre of her dress, clinging to her hips and pert bottom.

He stilled, struck by a sensation of déjà vu so strong it eclipsed all else. She said something to his cousin in a soft, lilting voice.

A voice Idris knew.

He frowned, watching Hamid bend his head towards her, seeing her turn a little more so she was in profile.

The conversations around them became white noise, a buzz like swarming insects.

His vision telescoped.

Her lush lips.

Her neat nose.

Her slender, delicate throat.

Two facts hammered into his brain. He knew her, remembered her better than any of the multitude of women who'd once paraded in and out of his life.

And that strange feeling surging up from his gullet and choking his throat with bile was more than surprise or disbelief at the coincidence of meeting her again.

It was fury at the idea she belonged to Hamid.

'Here he is at last. Arden, I'd like to present you to my cousin Idris, Sheikh of Zahrat.'

Arden widened her smile, determined not to be overawed by meeting her very first and no doubt last sheikh. Coming to this formal reception, surrounded by VIPs who oozed money and privilege, had already tested her nerves.

She turned, tilting her head to look up, and felt the world drop away.

His face was severely sculpted as if scored by desert winds. Yet there was beauty in those high cheekbones and his firm yet sensual mouth. His nose and jaw were honed and strong. The harsh angle of those beetling black brows intimidated. So did the wide flare of his nostrils, as if the Sheikh scented something unexpected.

Shock dragged at her, loosening her knees till her legs felt like rubber.

His eyes…

Dark as a midnight storm, those eyes fixed on her instinctive movement as she clutched at Hamid for support. Slowly they lifted again to clash with hers, disdain clear in that haughty stare.

A shuddering wave of disquiet rolled through her as she blinked up, telling herself it wasn't possible. It couldn't be.

Despite the frantic messages her body was sending her, she *couldn't* know this man.

Yet her brain wouldn't listen to reason. It told her it was *him*. The man who'd changed her life.

Heat seared from scalp to toe. Then just as quickly it vanished, leaving her so cold she wouldn't be surprised to hear the crackle of ice forming along her bones, weighing her down.

Her grip on Hamid's arm grew desperate as tiny spots formed and blurred before her eyes. She felt as if she'd slipped out of the real world and into an alternate reality. One where dreams did come true, but so distorted as to be almost unrecognisable.

It wasn't him. It couldn't be. Yet her gaze dropped to his collarbone. Did he have a scar there?

Of course he didn't. This man was tougher, far more daunting than Shakil. She'd bet he didn't do easy, charming smiles. Instead he wore royal authority like a cloak.

Yet she could almost hear herself asking, *Excuse me, Your Highness, would you mind undoing that exquisitely tailored suit and tie so I can check if you have a scar from a riding accident?*

'Arden, are you okay?' Hamid's voice was concerned, his hand warm as it closed over hers.

His touch jerked her back to reality. She slipped her hand from his arm and locked her wobbly knees.

Tonight had revealed, to her astonishment, that Hamid now thought of himself as more than a friend. She couldn't let him labour under that illusion, no matter how grateful she was to him.

'I'm...' She cleared her throat, hesitating. What could she say? *I'm reeling with shock?* 'I'll be all right.'

Yet her gaze clung to that of the man towering before her as if he was some sort of miracle.

It was that realisation that snapped her back to reality. He wasn't Shakil. If he *had* been Shakil, he'd be no miracle, just another of life's tough lessons. A man who'd used her and tossed her aside.

'It's a pleasure to meet you, Your Highness.' Her voice sounded wispy but she persevered. 'I hope you're enjoying your stay in London.'

Belatedly she wondered if she was supposed to curtsey. Had she offended him? His flesh looked drawn too tight and she glimpsed the rigid line of a tendon standing proud in his neck. He looked ready for battle, not a society meet and greet.

For long seconds silence stretched, as if he didn't want to acknowledge her. She felt her eyebrows pucker into a frown. Beside her Hamid's head swung sharply towards the Sheikh.

'Welcome to my embassy, Ms…'

That voice. He had the same voice.

'Wills, Arden Wills.' Hamid spoke since Arden's voice had disappeared, sucked away by the tidal wave of horror that seized her lungs and stopped her breath.

'Ms Wills.' The Sheikh paused and she glimpsed what almost looked like confusion in those dark eyes, as if he wasn't used to pronouncing such a commonplace name.

But Arden was too busy grappling with her own response to Hamid's cousin. He looked and sounded exactly like Shakil. Or as Shakil would if he'd sloughed off his laid-back, live-for-the-moment attitude and aged a few years.

This man had a thinner face, which accentuated his superb bone structure. And his expression was grim, far harder than anything Shakil had ever worn. Shakil had been a lover not a fighter and this man looked, despite his western tailoring, as if he'd be at home on a warhorse, a scimitar in his hand as he galloped into battle.

Arden shivered, clammy palms skimmed her bare arms as she tried to ease the tension drawing gooseflesh there.

He said something. She saw his lips move, but there was a weird echoing in her head and she couldn't make out his words.

She blinked, swaying forwards, stumbling and steadying herself, drawn unwillingly by his dark velvet gaze.

Hamid pulled her against his side. 'I'm sorry. I shouldn't have insisted you come tonight. Your condition is too delicate.'

Arden stiffened in his hold, dimly noting the Sheikh's sharply indrawn breath. Hamid was a dear friend but he had no right to feel proprietorial. Besides, it was a long time since she'd craved any man's touch.

'I'm perfectly healthy,' she murmured, trying to inject power into the words. The flu had knocked her but she was almost back to normal. Yet her recent illness provided a perfect explanation for her woozy head and unsteady legs.

She moved a half step away so he had to drop his arm. Gathering the shreds of her composure, she met the Sheikh's midnight eyes again, instinctively fighting the awareness thundering through her, and the crazy idea she knew him. That wasn't possible. Shakil had been a student, not a sheikh.

'Thank you for the welcome, Your Highness. It's a beautiful party.' Yet she'd never wanted to leave anywhere with such urgency.

It felt as if he delved right into her thoughts with that unblinking regard. It took all her control not to shift under his scrutiny.

'Are you sure you're well, Ms Wills? You look unsteady on your feet.'

Her smile grew strained and she felt the tug of it as her face stiffened.

'Thank you for your concern. It's only tiredness after a long week.' Heat flushed her cheeks at the realisation she'd actually come close to collapsing for the first time in her life. 'I'm very sorry but I think it best if I leave. No, really, Hamid, I'm okay by myself.'

But Hamid would have none of that. Nothing would satisfy him but to see her home.

'Idris doesn't mind, do you, Cousin?' He didn't wait for an answer but went on. 'I'll at least see you back to the house then return.'

From the corner of her vision Arden registered the sharp lift of the Sheikh's eyebrows, but she had more to worry about than whether she offended by leaving his party early.

Like how she could kindly but effectively stave off Hamid's sudden romantic interest without straining their friendship.

Like how Sheikh Idris could be so uncannily like the man who'd torn her world apart.

And, most important of all, why it was that even after four years she felt sick with longing for the man who'd all but destroyed her.

A night without sleep did nothing for Arden's equilibrium. The fact it was Sunday, the one day of the week she could sleep in instead of heading in to work at the florist's shop, should have been a welcome pleasure. Instead she longed for the organised chaos of her workday race to get out the door.

Anything to distract from the worries that had descended last night. And worse, the memories, the longings that had haunted each sleepless hour.

Life had taught her the dangers of sexual desire, and worse, of falling in love. Of believing she was special to someone.

For four years she'd known she'd been a naïve fool. Brutal reality had proven it. Yet that hadn't stopped the restlessness, the yearning that slammed into her like a runaway truck the moment she'd looked up into the eyes of Sheikh Idris of Zahrat.

Even now, in the thin light of morning, part of her was convinced he was Shakil. A Shakil who'd perhaps suffered a head injury and forgotten her, like a hero in an old movie with convenient amnesia. A Shakil who'd spent years searching desperately for her, ignoring all other women in his quest to find her.

Sure. And her fairy godmother was due any minute, complete with magic wand and a pumpkin carriage.

Shakil could have found her if he'd wanted. *She* hadn't lied about her identity.

He'd taken pleasure in seducing a gullible young Englishwoman, starry-eyed and innocent, on her first overseas vacation.

Arden shivered and hunched her shoulders, rubbing her hands up her arms.

She was *not* giving in to fantasy. She'd done with that years ago. As for the Sheikh looking like Shakil—it was wishful thinking. Wasn't it Hamid's almost familiar looks that had drawn her to him that day at the British Museum? That and his kind smile and the earnest, self-effacing way he spoke to her about the elaborately beautiful perfume bottles and jewellery at the special exhibition of Zahrati antiquities.

He'd reminded her of Shakil. A quieter, more reserved Shakil. So was it any wonder his cousin the Sheikh had a similar effect? Maybe crisp dark hair, chiselled features and broad shoulders were common traits among the men of their country.

Right now she'd had enough of Zahrati men to last a lifetime. Even Hamid, who'd suddenly turned from friend and landlord to would-be boyfriend. When had that happened? How had she not seen it coming?

Setting her jaw, Arden grabbed an old pullover and shrugged it on, then cautiously opened the cleaning cupboard, careful not to make too much noise. At least, as the only one awake, she had time to ponder what to do about Hamid and his sudden possessiveness.

Grabbing a cloth and the brass polish, she unlatched the front door and stepped outside, pulling it to behind her. She always thought better when she worked. Rubbing the brass door knocker and letter box would be a start.

But she hadn't begun when she heard footsteps descend to the pavement from the main house door above her basement flat. A man's steps. Arden took the lid off the polish and concentrated on swiping some across the door knocker. She should have waited till she was sure Hamid had left. But she'd felt claustrophobic, cooped up inside with her whirling thoughts.

'Arden.' The voice, low and soft as smoke, wafted around her, encircling like an embrace.

She blinked and stared at the glossy black paint on the door a few inches from her nose. She was imagining it. She'd been thinking of Shakil all night and—

Footsteps sounded on the steps leading down to the tiny courtyard in front of her basement home.

She stiffened, her shoulders inching high. This wasn't imagination. This was real.

Arden swung around and the tin of polish clattered to the flagstones.

CHAPTER TWO

HUGE EYES FIXED on him. Eyes as bright as the precious aquamarines in his royal treasury. Eyes the clear green-blue of the sea off the coast of Zahrat.

How often through the years had he dreamed of those remarkable eyes? Of hair like spun rose gold, falling in silken waves across creamy shoulders.

For a second Idris could only stare. He'd been prepared for this meeting. He'd cancelled breakfast with Ghizlan and their respective ambassadors to come here. Yet the abrupt surge of hunger as he watched Arden Wills mocked the belief he was in command of this situation.

Where was his self-control? How could he lust after a woman who belonged to someone else?

To his own cousin?

Where was his sense, coming here when he should be with the woman to whom he was about to pledge his life?

Idris didn't do impulsive any more. Or self-centred. Not for years. Yet he'd been both, seeking out this woman to confirm for himself what Hamid had implied last night—that they lived together.

A ripple of anger snaked through him, growing to gut-wrenching revulsion at the idea of her with his cousin.

'What are you doing here?' Her voice was husky, evoking long ago memories of her crying out his name in ecstasy. Of her beguiling, artless passion. Of how she'd made him feel for a short time, like someone other than the carefree, self-absorbed youth he'd been.

How could such ancient memories feel so fresh? So appallingly seductive?

It had only been a holiday romance, short-term fun such as he'd had numerous times. Why did it feel different?

Because it *had* been different. For the first time ever he'd planned to extend a casual affair. He hadn't been ready to leave her.

'Hamid's away.' Was that provocative tilt of her jaw deliberate, or as unconscious as the way her fingers threaded together?

Satisfaction stirred. It was beneath him perhaps, but reassuring to discover he wasn't the only one on edge. Idris was used to being sure of his direction, always in command. Doubt was foreign to him.

'I didn't come here to see Hamid.'

Those eyes grew huge in a face that looked even milkier than before. Hamid had talked of her being *delicate*. Was that code for pregnant? Was that why she looked like a puff of wind would knock her over?

Jealousy, a growling caged beast, circled in his belly. It didn't matter that he had no right to feel it. Idris had stopped, somewhere around four this morning, trying to tell himself he felt nothing for Arden Wills. He was a pragmatist. The fact was he did *feel*. He was here to sort out why and then, with clinical precision, to put an end to it.

'You should sit. You don't look well.'

'I'm perfectly fine.' She crossed her arms, making Idris aware of the swell of plump breasts under her shapeless pullover. Had her breasts always been like that? He remembered them as delectable, but—

'I'm up here.' A palm waved in front of his eyes and, for the first time he could recall, Idris felt embarrassment at being caught ogling. Heat flushed his face. It wasn't a sensation to which he was accustomed.

When he lifted his gaze he saw a matching bright pink stain on her cheeks. Annoyance? Embarrassment? Or something akin to the untimely, unwanted attraction he couldn't quash?

'I came to see you.' His voice dropped to a primal, darkly possessive note he couldn't hide.

'Me?' Now she was on the back foot and, ridiculously, it pleased Idris. He hated the sensation, since last night, that he careered out of control.

'You. Shall we go inside?'

Her folded arms dropped, spreading out a little from her body, almost as if she'd bar his entry to the house. 'No. We can speak here.'

Idris scowled. 'Surely even in Britain one invites guests inside?'

Her mouth tightened but she remained defiant. 'I prefer to stay outside. It's...better.' She took a step back. To prevent him hauling the door open?

Idris felt his head snap back as if he'd been slapped. Did she have so little faith in his chivalry? Was she really afraid to be alone with him?

He was torn between delight at the idea he wasn't the only one feeling the burn of rekindled lust and horror that his feelings were reciprocated and therefore harder to quell.

'I have a key to Hamid's house, if you'd like me to let you in upstairs. Since you're his cousin, I'm sure he wouldn't mind.'

Idris jerked his gaze up to the glossy black door a level above them, and then to the one behind Arden, noting for the first time the brass street number with a small but significant letter A beside it. The relief washing through him was palpable.

'You live in a basement flat? You don't live together?'

She drew herself up till she almost topped his shoulder. Idris told himself the movement wasn't endearing, yet he felt a little corkscrewing twist of pleasure that punctured his satisfaction in an instant.

'We don't live together. Hamid is my landlord.'

Yet that didn't mean they weren't lovers. For all Hamid's devotion to history and old books, he, like every other male in their family, had a penchant for a pretty face and a delectable female body. Besides, there'd been no mistaking Hamid's proprietorial attitude last night, or his meaning when he'd spoken about a *special* woman in his life.

'It's you I came to see.'

She shook her head and a froth of hair swung around her, the colour of the desert at sunrise. Last night he'd been thrown by the smoothly conventional way she'd worn it. This was the woman he recalled, with a riot of loose curls that made his palms itch to feel all that silken softness.

'Why?'

Was she being deliberately obtuse?

'Perhaps to talk over old times?'

There was a thud as she fell back against the solid door, her face a study in shock.

'It *is* you! You were at Santorini.'

Idris stared. 'You thought I was someone else? You didn't remember me?'

It was impossible. He might have had more lovers than he could remember, but the idea Arden Wills had forgotten him was inconceivable.

Especially when his recall of her was disturbingly detailed. After four years he still remembered the little snuffling sigh she made in her sleep as she snuggled, naked, against him. The feel of her slick, untried body when they'd made love the first time returned to him time and again in his dreams. He'd almost exploded disgracefully early at the sheer erotic enticement of her delicate, tight body and the knowledge he was the first man to introduce her to ecstasy. Doing his duty and walking away from her had been amazingly difficult.

'I thought...' She shook her head, frowning. 'How can you be a sheikh? You were a student.'

'Ex-student—I'd just finished a graduate degree in the States when we met. As for becoming Sheikh—' he shrugged '—my uncle died. It was his wish that I succeed him and that wish was ratified soon after his death.'

It sounded easy, but the reality had been anything but. He was a different man to the one he'd been four years ago. Responsibility for a country that had suffered so long because of its ruler's neglect had transformed him. He carried the burden of changing his homeland into one ready to face the future instead of dwelling on the past. This morning was the first time in years he'd carved time to do something simply because he wished it. His secretary's disbelieving look when he'd altered his schedule had spoken volumes.

Idris took a step closer, his nostrils flaring at the astringent smell of metal polish and something more delicate that tickled his memory—the scent of orange blossom.

'Come, let's take this conversation indoors where we can—'

'No!' Her eyes were round as saucers and if it weren't ridiculous he'd say she was shaking.

That brought him up short. He might be supreme ruler of his kingdom and an emerging force in regional politics, but he wasn't the sort of man who deliberately intimidated women.

'I have nothing to say to you, *Your Highness*.' She all but sneered his title and Idris scowled. It hit him suddenly that, for all they'd shared, there was a lot he'd never learned about her.

'You have a problem with royalty?'

She tossed her head back. He couldn't remember her being feisty before, just warm and eager for him. 'I have a problem with men who lie about who they are.'

Idris's hands clenched and his jaw hardened. He wasn't used to having his will crossed, much less his honour impugned. The fact they were having this conversation metres from a public footpath, albeit in a quiet square, incensed him.

His fingers itched with the urge to haul this spitfire of a woman into his arms and barge through the door into her private domain.

Except he knew in the most primitive, instinctive part of his brain that if he touched her he was in danger of unleashing something far better left alone.

He'd come here to satisfy his curiosity and put an end, somehow, to the nagging sense of unfinished business between them.

He was about to become betrothed to a beautiful, diplomatically desirable princess. Their match was eagerly awaited by both nations. Getting involved in any way with Arden Wills would be a mistake of enormous proportions. Giving in to the dark urge to lay hands on her and remind her how it had been between them with a short, satisfying lesson in physical compatibility would be madness.

And so tempting.

'I never lied,' he said through gritted teeth.

Dark gold eyebrows rose in a deliberately offensive show of disbelief that stirred the anger in his belly.

'No? So you're telling me you're not Sheikh Idris? Your name is actually Shakil?'

'Ah.' He'd forgotten that.

'Yes, ah!' She made it an accusation, looking down that little nose of hers as if he were some lowlife instead of a paragon of duty and honour. No one had ever looked at him that way.

'I used Shakil when we met because—'

'Because you didn't want me finding you again.' The words spat out like poisoned darts. 'You had no intention of following through on that promise to meet again, did you? You'd already wiped your hands of me.'

'You accuse me of lying?' No man, or woman, for that matter, had ever doubted his word.

Arden crossed her arms over her chest and tipped her chin up in a supercilious expression as full of hauteur as that of any blue-blooded princess. 'If the shoe fits.'

Idris took a step closer before his brain kicked into gear and screamed a warning. Ire overcame the seductive tug of that orange blossom scent. Caution disappeared on the crisp breeze eddying down from street level.

'Shakil was my family nickname. Ask Hamid.' It meant *handsome* and was one he discouraged, but back then it had been a handy pseudonym. He heaved a deep breath, telling himself he didn't care that the movement reduced the distance between them. Or that his nostrils flared as the scent of warm female flesh mingled with the fragrance of orange blossom. 'I used Shakil on vacation to avoid being recognised. There'd been a lot of media speculation about me and I wanted to be incognito for a while. I was Shakil to everyone I met on that trip. Not just you.'

He'd grown tired of people clamouring for attention because of his royal ties and wealth. Merging into the holiday throng in Greece as Shakil had been a delicious freedom. And it had been a heady delight knowing that when pretty little Arden had smiled at him in that bar on Santorini there'd been stars, not dollar signs in her eyes. She saw simply the man, not the shadow of his family connections and how she might benefit from them.

Was it any wonder he remembered their affair as special?

Still she didn't look convinced.

'As for not turning up at the rendezvous that last afternoon—you can hardly hold me to account. You didn't show.'

A phone call had hauled him out of Arden's bed and back to the upmarket hotel room where he hadn't spent a single night for the week since he'd met her. All he'd known at first was something important had happened and he needed privacy to talk with his uncle's closest advisers. It was only when he was alone in his hotel that he'd learned about his uncle's heart attack, the fact his life hung by a thread, and that he'd named Idris his heir.

There'd been no question of returning to the rendezvous with Arden—three o'clock by the church—even if she had decided to accept his invitation to an extended vacation in Paris. There'd been no question of Paris or a lover, not when he was urgently needed at home.

And if he'd been fleetingly disappointed that she'd thought better of accepting his offer, he'd known it made things easier given the enormity of what he faced. He had enough experience of clinging women to know severing ties could be tiresome.

'You went to the church to meet me?' Her words held a breathless quality and there was something in her eyes he couldn't read.

'I had to fly home urgently. I sent someone instead.'

There was a tiny thud as her head rocked back against the door. Her eyes closed and her mouth twisted. Idris frowned at what looked like pain on her features.

'Are you okay?'

'Fine.' Finally she opened her eyes. 'Absolutely fine.'

She didn't look it. She looked... He couldn't put a name to that expression, yet he felt an echo of it slap him hard in the chest.

'He didn't wait long.'

'Sorry?'

'Your friend. He didn't stay long.'

'You're saying you *did* go to the rendezvous?' To say goodbye or accept his offer of a longer affair? For a moment Idris wondered, until he reminded himself it was history, done and dusted.

'I was late.'

It was on the tip of his tongue to ask why. Second thoughts? A last-minute dash? He pictured her running through the narrow streets of Thera, between the white-washed buildings she'd so enjoyed exploring. Her hair would be down like now, and her summer skirt floating around those lissom legs.

He chose to say nothing. What was there to say now, after four years? What was done was done.

Except, remarkably, it seemed that what they'd shared in that sultry week in Santorini hadn't quite ended.

Arden Wills wasn't dressed to seduce. Her dark green pullover swam on her, just hinting at the curves beneath. Her old jeans were frayed and there was a patch on one knee. Her face was free of make-up. Yet her hair rippled around her like a halo on a Pre-Raphaelite model, beguiling and exotic. She made him want to forget duty, forget necessity, and tug her to him so she fitted between his thighs, cradling him with her hips.

'So, what is it you want?'

'Pardon?' Idris shoved his hands deep into his trouser pockets as he realised the direction his thoughts wandered. To whether she wore a bra beneath that bulky pullover and whether her pale skin was as petal-soft as he recalled.

'Why did you come here, if not to see your cousin?' She paused, her lips tightening. 'Surely not to catch up on old times.' Her breathing altered, drew short and jerky, as if she, too, remembered how it had been between them all those years ago.

'Why not?' Idris lifted his shoulders in a show of insouciance he was far from feeling. 'I was…curious about you. It's been, what? Four years?' As if he didn't know precisely how long it had been. His reign as Sheikh of

Zahrat dated from that week. 'There have been changes in both our lives.'

Her face stilled, her eyes darting to the side almost furtively, as if tempted to look behind her but thinking better of it.

Instantly Idris was on alert.

He couldn't read that look but instinct warned him something was afoot. Something she hid from him. His gaze lifted to the gleaming paint of the door behind her. What could she possibly feel the need to hide? She wasn't living in squalor, not here. Something sordid? A lover?

Adrenalin surged, coiling his tension tighter. He took another half step forward, only stopping when a small palm flattened against his chest. He felt the imprint of it through the fine wool of his suit. His skin tingled where she touched as if abraded. As if she'd scraped sharp nails over his bare flesh.

Idris sucked in oxygen and forced himself not to react.

'I don't want you here.' Those eyes were so huge in her face he felt he could dive into them.

His hand covered hers and fire danced across his skin before burrowing deep inside. A judder of potent sexual hunger tightened his groin.

'You need to say that as if you mean it.'

The scent of her was so vivid he could almost taste her on his tongue. Sweet with a telltale hint of warm musk. No woman before or since had smelled like Arden Wills. How had he forgotten that?

'I do mean it.' Yet her voice had a soft, wondering quality that reminded him of the night they'd shared their bodies that first time. Her eyes had shone with something like awe. She'd looked at him as if he were a glorious deity opening the secrets of the heavens, until her eyes clouded in ecstasy and she'd shattered in a climax so powerful it had hauled him over the edge.

His thumb stroked the back of her hand and she quivered. Her hand was small but strong. He recalled how, as her confidence grew, she'd been as demanding as he, exploring, stroking, driving him to the brink with her generous passion.

She'd driven him to flout his self-imposed rules and invite her to France on holiday with him, because a week together hadn't been enough.

Idris hauled himself back to the present. To the slant of sunlight burnishing her hair and the distant sound of a car. London. His betrothal. The peace treaty between his nation and Ghizlan's.

He shouldn't be here. His life was about duty, control and careful, deliberate decision-making. There was no room for spur-of-the-moment distractions.

In another second he'd step away.

But first he needed her to acknowledge what was between them. Even after all this time. Idris couldn't countenance the idea that he alone burned. Pride demanded proof that she felt this undercurrent of hunger. This electricity simmering and snapping in the air. The charge of heat where they touched.

'You need to leave. Don't make me scream for help.' Her head tipped back against the door, as if to increase the distance between them, yet her touch betrayed her. Her hand had slipped under his jacket lapel, fingers clutching his shirt. Heat poured into him from her touch, spreading to fill his chest.

He forced his hand to his side, conquering the impulse to haul her close.

'I said, leave me alone.' Her breath was warm on his chin and his thoughts whirled as he imagined her sweet breath on other parts of his body. He needed a moment to curb his arousal.

Here, on a London street!

Anger flared. At this woman. At his unruly body that for the first time in memory didn't obey.

'It's obviously escaped your notice, but I'm not touching you. *You're* the one touching *me.*'

His voice, crisp with challenge, nevertheless held that once heard and never forgotten deep note that resonated right to her core.

Arden blinked, dragging her gaze from his mouth and solid, scrupulously shaved jaw to his chest.

Heat scorched her cheeks at the sight of her hand clutching him, as if she couldn't bear to let him go. As if, even now, his desertion couldn't kill the slavish passion she'd felt for him.

Though, if he told the truth, he hadn't deserted her.

It was too much to take in.

Too terrible to think that perhaps he hadn't betrayed her as she'd believed.

Words trembled on her tongue, the truth she hadn't been able to share with this man for four years. But caution held her back.

She needed time alone to sort out what it meant if he *hadn't* deserted her. Time away from his piercing dark gaze and hot body that reduced her hard won defences to ash.

Arden dragged her hand away, pressing it against the solid door behind her. That was what she needed. To remember where they were and how much was at stake. She couldn't risk revealing too much.

'You need to go. This isn't right.' A weight lodged on her chest, making her breathless so she could only manage short sentences.

Something that might have been anger flickered across his face. Yet still he didn't shift.

Desperation coiled tight in her belly. A desperation

fuelled by the urge to spill everything to him, here and now, as if by doing so all her burdens would be lifted.

But Arden had spent a lifetime learning self-reliance. The last years had reinforced that. She carried her burdens alone.

'We've both moved on, Shakil.' It was as if she evoked the past with that one single word. 'Idris,' she amended quickly.

'Moved on where? To Hamid?' His voice was a low growl that sent fear feathering her skin. His head lowered and she felt tension come off his big frame in waves. 'You're afraid your lover will see us together?'

'Don't be ridiculous.' It came out as a hiss of distress. It had been bad enough realising last night that Hamid now saw himself as far more than a friend.

'Ridiculous?' Idris's eyes narrowed to ebony slits. Those carved cheekbones loomed threateningly high as his face drew taut. 'You call me ridiculous?'

Fire branded her neck as hard fingers closed around her nape, moulding to skin turned feverish at his touch.

Arden swiped her suddenly arid mouth with her tongue, searching for words to stop the fury in that glittering gaze.

But his touch didn't feel like anger. That was the problem. She could have withstood it if it did.

Arden trembled as the hand at her neck shifted and long fingers speared her hair, spreading over her scalp, massaging. Shivers of delight rippled through her and her eyelids hovered, weighted, at half mast. Tendrils of fire cascaded from her scalp down her spine and around to her breasts where her nipples peaked.

She swallowed convulsively and forced herself to straighten away from the door, even though it meant brushing against him.

'I didn't mean—'

'Of course you did.' His mouth twisted. 'You're right.

It *is* ridiculous. Impossible and inconvenient…and inevitable.'

Then, while Arden was still absorbing his words, his head lowered.

His mouth on hers was just as she remembered. A huge, tearing fullness welled in her chest as his lips shaped hers, not hard and punishing as she'd expected from the glint in his eyes, but gentle, questing. As if seeking an answer to a question she hadn't heard.

Shakil. The taste of him burst on her, rich and delicious. It was the one sense memory she hadn't been able to recall in the years since he'd left her. Now it filled her, evocative, masculine and, she feared, potently addictive. For her head was lolling back, lips open to allow him access.

Somehow her hands had crept up to brace on his chest. The steady thrum of his heart was a reassuring counterpoint to her sense of disorientation.

His other hand slipped around her waist, pulling her against a body that was all hard power, making her feel soft and feminine in ways she'd almost forgotten.

And still that kiss. No longer quite as gentle. Arden heard a guttural sound of approval as her tongue met his in a foray into pure pleasure.

He shifted and delight filled her as her nipples grazed his torso. She moved closer, absorbed in heady, oh-so-familiar delight, till a long hard ridge pressed against her belly.

Arden's eyes snapped open and she saw his eyes had narrowed to slits of dark fire. Then, over his shoulder, high up at street level, came a burst of light, a glint of sunlight off something. It was enough, just, to bring her back to reality.

'No.' No one heard her protest since their lips were locked.

She had to shove with all her might for him to lift his

head, blinking as if unable to focus. That might have made her feel better but for the realisation that just five minutes in this man's company had obliterated every defence she'd spent years constructing.

'No,' she gasped. That full feeling behind her breastbone turned to pain. 'This is wrong. We can't…'

She didn't need to go on. Sheikh Idris of Zahrat agreed completely. It was there in the dawning horror sharpening his features and the unsteady hand that swiped his face. He shook his head as if wondering what he was doing.

Nor did Arden need to shove him again. One swift pace backwards on those long legs took him almost to the base of the area steps and left her feeling appallingly alone.

Chest pumping, Arden stared at the dark-gold face of the man she'd once adored. The man who now looked at her as if she were his personal nightmare.

Desperate, she put her palms to the door behind her, needing its support.

Despite it all, the anger, hurt and betrayal that had shaped her life for four years, she'd harboured a hope that if they met again he'd admit he'd made a terrible mistake in leaving. That he'd missed her, wanted her, as she'd missed and wanted him.

In her dreams he'd never looked at her with horror.

Pain lanced her chest and kept going right down through her womb.

With a choking gasp of distress she whirled around, hauled the door open and slipped into her sanctuary. Her hands shook so much it took for ever to bolt and latch the door. When it was done Arden put her back to it and slid down to sit on the floor, arms wrapped around her knees as silent sobs filled her.

CHAPTER THREE

'Your Highness, if I may?'

Idris looked up from the papers on the ambassador's desk. His aide, Ashar, stood in the doorway, expression wooden. That, Idris had learned in the turbulent first few years of his rule, was a sure sign of trouble.

Please, not another delay with the combined peace and trade treaty. Ghizlan's father might be eager to cement a dynastic bond with Idris but he wasn't past trying to wheedle more concessions before the betrothal was announced.

Idris turned to the ambassador, who, ever the diplomat, was already standing. 'If you'll excuse me, Highness, I'll leave you to check for news on that US investment project.'

Idris nodded. 'That would be useful, thank you.'

When the ambassador had left, Ashar entered the room, closing the door behind him. Silently he passed a computer tablet across the desk. Bold black lettering filled the screen.

Off the Leash in London, Sheikh Tastes Local Delicacies.

Beneath the headline was a photo. A close-up of Idris locked in an embrace with Arden Wills, her hair a riot of curls against the black of her front door.

The air rushed from his lungs as an unseen punch slammed a sickening blow into his midsection.

Damn it. Hadn't he known it was a mistake, going to her house? Hadn't it defied logic? Yet when she'd told him to leave, what had he done? Had he behaved like the sane, prudent man he was and returned to his embassy? No, he'd reacted like…like…

Words failed.

Worse was the fact that, facing a nightmare public debacle, he had total recall of her sweet mouth and her soft body moulding to his.

'There's more.'

Of course there was. It was the way of the world that you slaved twenty hours a day for your country and the first time in four years you did something utterly selfish, utterly incomprehensible, the press was there to turn a molehill into a mountain.

He sighed and forked his hand through his hair. 'Let me guess. Princess Ghizlan.'

He scrolled to the next page and the next headline.

Two-Timing Sheikh Keeps Fiancée and Lover in Same City.

Idris swore long and low. There was a photo of him and Ghizlan at the embassy reception. Beside it was one of him with Arden. His hand wrapped around her neck, pulling her to him, and her eyes were closed, those plump lips open, as if eager for his kiss. As if she hadn't just told him to take a hike.

Fire shot from his belly to his groin. Even now, with all hell about to break loose, his body was in thrall to the Englishwoman he should have forgotten four years ago. Instead he remembered it all. She'd been ardent, so deliciously honest and real. Her desire had been for *him*, not his wealth or connections. Together they'd created a magic he'd craved more of, though brutal logic said it must eventually burn out. Passion always did. That was how it always was for the men in his family, how it was for him—lust and desire, never anything more permanent.

He shoved the tablet across the table and shot to his feet, stalking away from the desk.

Of all the impossible timing. This was the worst. For his country, and for Ghizlan's.

Ghizlan! He'd put her in an appalling situation.

'Get me the Princess on the phone.' He spun around. 'No. Contact her aide and ask for a meeting. I'll come to her hotel immediately.'

Ashar didn't move. 'There's more.'

'More? How could there be more? There *was* nothing else. That—' he gestured to the photo of him hauling Arden into his arms '—is the sum total of what happened.'

His jaw was so rigid it felt as if it might shatter. Self-contempt swamped him.

How often had he told himself he was better than his uncle, the old Sheikh, who'd frittered his time and energy on endless lovers instead of governing? Or Idris's father, whose philandering destroyed his family and any respect he might have garnered from the people?

Idris had taken pride in devoting himself to his people, putting duty before pleasure. His planned marriage to Ghizlan was for the good of both nations. He'd modelled himself on the one completely honourable man in his family, his grandfather. The old man had been the sole exception in six generations to the rule that men in his family couldn't love. Idris didn't expect a miracle—to love one woman all his life like his grandfather had. But he aimed at least to be loyal to his wife. A great start he'd made on that!

'There's something you should see before you talk to the Princess.'

Ashar's expression was as grave as on the day Idris had returned home to find his uncle on his deathbed.

Idris put out his hand for the tablet. 'Show me.'

Ashar scrolled to another page, then passed it to him, half turning away as he did so.

Idris frowned. It felt almost as if Ashar was trying to give him privacy. The notion was laughable. His aide knew as many diplomatic and royal secrets as he did. More probably.

Then Idris looked down and felt the floor buckle beneath his feet.

Royal Baby Secret. Which Cousin Did Arden Seduce?

This time there were three photos. One of his cousin Hamid entering college with a briefcase in his hand. One of Idris in traditional robes, taken at some public event.

And one of Arden Wills holding a toddler in her arms.

Idris felt his eyes bulge as he took in the details. Arden's attention was on the child throwing bread to some ducks. A child whose face was golden, in contrast with her ivory and rose features. A child with glossy black hair and dark eyes.

A child with a remarkable resemblance to Idris at that age.

Or his cousin.

Idris tried to read the words beneath the photos but they blurred into lines of swarming black ants. He blinked and ordered himself to focus, but his eyes were drawn to that telling photo. Arden smiling radiantly at a child who, Idris would bet his sword arm, belonged to the royal family of Zahrat.

Sensation bombarded him and he had to brace his feet so as not to collapse back into the leather chair.

How old was the child? He knew nothing of babies. Two? Three?

Could it be his?

Shock scattered his thoughts. He should be planning an appropriate public response, deliberating on the fallout and talking to his almost-fiancée.

Instead he stared at the photo with something like possessiveness.

He was marrying partly to secure an heir but becoming a father was a political necessity, not a heartfelt desire. His own father had been distant and Idris knew little about good father-child relationships. He'd assumed his wife would take the lead in child-rearing.

Yet, looking into the laughing face of a child that might be his, Idris was gripped by a surge of protectiveness he'd never before experienced. This could be his son or daughter. The idea slammed into him like a physical blow, stealing his breath and obliterating any illusion of disinterest.

'Boy or girl?'

'A boy. She named him Dawud.' Not an English name then. There was obvious significance in that.

'Dawud.' An unseen cord tugged at his heart, making it thud faster.

Why hadn't she contacted Idris? Why keep his existence a secret? Anger stirred amidst the glowing embers of softer emotion.

Unless he's not yours.

Remember Hamid last night, his 'someone special'. Arden was living under his roof.

Yet if Hamid was the father, why not claim the child as his own? Hamid might have inherited the family practice of sowing his wild oats, but he had a serious side. He wouldn't shirk responsibility, especially if he cared for Arden as he seemed to.

Idris stared at the photo, trying to read the truth in the curve of the child's chubby cheek and wide smile.

That was when he realised his hand was shaking. And the feeling snaking through his belly wasn't mere curiosity but something perilously close to jealousy. At the thought of Hamid and Arden.

Idris dropped the tablet onto the desk and scrubbed a hand over his face.

Did he *want* the scandal of an illegitimate child? A child whose first, vital years he'd missed?

He'd have to be crazy.

His phone was in his hand before he realised. He called Hamid's number and looked up, surprised, to see the sun still streaming through the high sash windows. It felt as if time had galloped since Ashar had entered the room.

No answer from Hamid, just the message bank. It took far too long for Idris to remember his cousin mentioning an early flight to an academic conference in Canada. He was probably in the air, absorbed in one of his beloved journal articles.

Idris swung around to Ashar. 'Anything else?'

Ashar's lips twitched in what might in another man have edged towards a smile. 'That's not enough?'

'More than enough.' Scandal in London and no doubt at home, as well as in Ghizlan's country. A betrothal contract about to be signed, a peace treaty on the table and a child who might be his.

And, simmering beneath it all, the taste he hadn't been able to banish from his memory. The sweet taste of Arden Wills, sabotaging his ability to concentrate.

'Get me the Princess's suite on the line. And send a security detail to my cousin's house.'

'To keep the press back? They'll already be there in droves.'

'To observe and report back. I want to know what's going on.'

Whether the child was his cousin's or his own, Idris had a responsibility to protect mother and child from the notoriously intrusive paparazzi. At least till he sorted out the truth.

'And find out what time my cousin's flight touches

down in Canada. I want to talk to him as soon as he lands. Get someone to meet the flight.'

Arden ignored the pounding on the front door, turning up the television so Dawud could hear the music of his favourite children's programme. He sat enthralled, bouncing while he clapped his hands in time with the music.

When the reporters had descended on the house he'd cried, awakened from his nap by the hubbub of voices and the constant noise of the phone and knocking at the front door. Arden felt wobbly with frustrated outrage because even now they hadn't left.

She'd been more than reasonable. She'd gone to the door and asked politely for some privacy. She'd given a 'no comment' response to their frenzy of questions and faced their clicking cameras, giving them the pictures they wanted.

But it hadn't been enough. They'd clamoured to see Dawud. They'd even known his name. That was when anger had turned ice-cold, freezing her from the inside out.

She wouldn't let those vultures near her precious boy. They'd mobbed her, trying to follow her into her basement flat. Terror had grabbed her as she slammed the door shut, her hands slick with sweat.

She'd turned to find Dawud watching, eyes huge and bottom lip trembling, as the noise echoed through their little home.

There had to be a way out of this. Somewhere to escape. But Hamid was overseas and her friends had no more resources than she did. Certainly not enough to spirit her and Dawud away.

A shudder racked her. She needed to find somewhere safe till this died down. How she was going to do that when she was due at work tomorrow she had no idea. Would the reporters hound her at the shop, or mob Dawud's nursery?

Probably both. Her stomach roiled and nausea stirred.

She'd known she shouldn't have gone to that embassy reception. Not because she'd suspected for a moment she'd see Shakil… Idris as he now was. But because it was pure weakness to give in to her curiosity about his country. Look where it had got her.

It's not your fault, it's his. He was the one who kissed you. He was the one who wouldn't leave.

Yet, if she were truthful, those moments in his arms had been magic, as if—

A sharp knock sounded on the front door. That was when Arden suddenly realised how quiet it had grown. As if the crowd of reporters had left.

She didn't believe it for an instant. It was a trick to lure her out, preferably with Dawud.

Arden smiled at her son as he looked up at her, singing the simple lyrics they often sang together. She hunkered down and cuddled him, joining in.

But the rapping on the door started again. Peremptory. Unavoidable.

Kissing Dawud's head, she got up and walked softly into the tiny entrance hall, closing the door behind her. The letter box flap opened. She hadn't thought of that. She was just wondering what she could use to stick it closed when she heard a man's voice. A deep, assured voice that had featured in her dreams far too often in the last four years.

'Arden. Open the door. I'm here to help.'

Her feet glued to the floor. She was torn between the offer of help and the knowledge that this was the man who'd brought disaster crashing down on them.

And the fact that, despite a sleepless night, she was no closer to knowing if she wanted him in Dawud's life.

As if you've got a choice now.

In the background she heard a rising murmur of voices, presumably from the paparazzi. Yet he didn't speak again. Perhaps because he was used to minions running to obey his every whim. Yet she understood how much courage it took to stand there alone, with a mob of press recording his every move.

And he'd come to help.

She reached out and unlatched the door, staying behind it as she swung it open just wide enough for him to enter.

Swiftly he bolted the door then turned.

Idris. He was definitely Sheikh Idris now. There was no hint of Shakil, the laughing, passionate lover she'd known in Santorini. This man's face was a symphony in sombre beauty, lines carving the corners of his mouth, ebony eyebrows straight and serious.

'You're all right? Both of you?'

Arden nodded. To her dismay her mouth crumpled. Until now she'd been buoyed by fury and indignation. But one hint of concern and she felt a great shudder pass through her. She hadn't realised before how her anger had masked terror.

'Arden.' He reached out as if to take her arm then stopped. His mouth flattened and he dropped his hand.

'We're okay.' Her voice was husky. She told herself she'd react this way to sympathy from anyone after facing the press onslaught. It had nothing to do with the concern in his dark eyes. Yet that look ignited a new warmth in her frozen body.

Finally her brain engaged and she frowned.

'You shouldn't have come. You've made it a hundred times worse. What were you thinking?'

His eyebrows rose in astonishment. Clearly he wasn't used to anyone questioning his actions.

'It can't get any worse. Not after the photos they've already got.' He folded his arms over his dark suit, for all the world like a corporate raider contemplating a run on his stocks, not a Middle Eastern potentate. Surely sheikhs wore long robes and headscarves?

'But now they've seen you here they'll think—'

'They already *know*.' His tone was so grim it made the tiny hairs at her nape stand up. 'In fact—' he paused, his voice dropping to a silky, dangerous note that made her think of an unexploded bomb '—some would say they know more than I do.'

Arden wanted to say the press didn't know anything. They assumed. But it was splitting hairs.

'Couldn't you have sent someone instead?' She crossed her arms tight across her chest, where her heart catapulted like a mad thing against her ribs. Grateful as she was for assistance, she refused to feel guilty about what had happened. This wasn't down to her. *He* was the one who'd attracted press attention. She was a nonentity.

'I did send someone. But they reported you were surrounded. Your phone is switched off and I assumed that if a stranger knocked on your door, claiming to represent me, you'd think it was a ruse to get you out to face the cameras.' Ebony eyes held hers, challenging.

Reluctantly Arden nodded. He was right. She'd never have opened the door to anyone she didn't know.

'I had to come. There was no other choice.'

How did he sound so calm when they were in this mess? Arden couldn't begin to imagine how she and Dawud could go back to their normal, anonymous lives. She wanted to rant, to point the finger of blame at him, but what would that achieve? She had to protect Dawud. There was no time for the luxury of hysteria.

Besides, despite her fine words, she hadn't been forced into that telltale kiss.

Shame filled her. She'd clung to his broad-shouldered frame, losing herself in his sensuality, in the pull of an attraction that was as powerful as it had always been.

Despite the way he'd abandoned her years ago.

Despite the fact he had a fiancée.

Arden hated herself for that. She should be immune to him now. Her stomach dropped and she stepped away, her back colliding with the wall. Determination filled her. She would *not* fall under his spell again.

'What?' His voice was sharp.

'Your fiancée.' The word rasped out, rough-edged.

'Not my fiancée.'

'But Hamid said—'

'Hamid doesn't know everything.' That twist of his mobile mouth looked cruel. As if the words he held back would flay someone alive.

Slivers of ice pricked her all over.

In that instant he morphed from saviour to threat.

She'd been almost relieved to see him but suddenly, as if scales fell from her eyes, she saw him not as the man she'd once loved, or as Hamid's cousin and a potential safe harbour in this press storm, but as an absolute monarch, accustomed to getting whatever he wanted.

Arden licked her lips. 'What do you want?'

Her gaze flicked to the closed sitting room door before she could stop herself. He noticed. Of course he noticed. How could he not hear the muffled children's ditty and guess who was in there?

The fact he hadn't even turned his head towards the other room only scared her more.

Thinking he'd washed his hands of her once their affair was over, even covering his tracks with a false name, she'd believed herself a sole parent in every sense. But Idris was here now, and she realised in dawning horror that she had no idea how he felt about a child. A male child. A child he might consider his heir. A child he might try to take.

Terror dug razored claws into her belly and her stomach cramped so hard she doubled up, gasping. Surely he didn't plan to steal her baby!

'Arden? What is it?' This time he did reach out, long

fingers branding her upper arm and sending flames licking through her.

'Don't *touch* me!' It was a hoarse whisper, the best she could do. But it was enough. He reared back as if scalded.

She straightened, forcing herself to stand tall, jutting her chin to lessen the distance between them.

'Tell me what you want.'

Had she just made the biggest mistake of her life, letting Dawud's father into her home? A father who had the power, physically and financially, to take her baby away?

'Tell me!' Heat glazed her eyes. If he thought he was taking Dawud from her, he understood nothing about a mother's love.

Something she couldn't decipher glowed in those narrowed eyes. 'I want to get you and your son to safety, where you won't be bothered by the press. Then, we need to talk.'

Her stomach did that roller coaster dip again. *Talk* didn't sound at all appealing.

But she was out of choices. She and Dawud couldn't stay holed up, hoping the press would leave. They had to go out some time. Idris was her only lifeline. No one else could get them away from the press. She *had* to trust him, for now at least.

'Pack what the pair of you will need for a couple of days. There's a car outside to take you away and one of my men will be posted nearby to make sure none of the paparazzi break in here to get more fodder for a story.'

Arden's jaw dropped. She hadn't thought of that. Of some stranger pawing through their belongings, sullying their home.

'Don't worry. It won't happen. I won't let it.'

Arden snapped her mouth closed, reeling at his absolute conviction. Never in her life had she been able to rely on anyone. Every time she'd begun to trust she'd been let down. Her parents, foster parents, even Hamid, pretending there was more to their friendship than existed.

There was something inherently appealing about Idris's assurance. Just as well she knew better than to depend on him. But, for the moment, she and Dawud needed help.

'Give me ten minutes.' She started down the hall then stopped, hesitating outside the sitting room door.

'Don't worry. I'll wait here.' It was as if he read her mind, her worry about Dawud.

She hesitated, unable to dismiss the thought of him simply striding in, picking up Dawud and carrying him out of the door.

'You are both safe with me.' That deep voice mesmerised—so grave, so measured. She badly wanted to trust him. He took a single step nearer. 'You have my word, Arden.'

She caught the velvet brown of his eyes that from a distance looked pure black. She read determination in his jaw, strength in his proud stance and honesty in his direct gaze. For a second longer she wavered. Then she spun on her heel and darted into the bedroom.

She'd hear if he tried to scoop up Dawud and take him. Dawud would yell and it would be impossible to exit quickly with that mob outside.

Yet relief hit when she emerged to find him still in the hall. He stood, head bent as if listening to Dawud's high voice carolling enthusiastically. Arden dropped the two bags, a bulky one full of Dawud's toys and clothes and a small one for her.

Idris's head jerked up. 'Ready?'

Arden nodded, trying and failing to read his expression. 'I'll need a child's car seat and—'

'No need. Arrangements have been made for a car seat. All you need is your bags and your son.'

Your son. Not Dawud. As if Idris was trying to distance himself. Pain turned like a twisting stiletto in her chest. Arden told herself she was pathetic. Seconds ago she'd worried Idris might try to kidnap Dawud. Now she was disappointed he wasn't more enthusiastic about him.

He hasn't even asked if he's the father.

Because this whole situation was a mighty inconvenience for him. More than an inconvenience. Coming just before his marriage to Princess Ghizlan it must be a headache of massive proportions.

She made herself nod and put down the bags. 'I'll get him.'

'You can introduce me.' When she hesitated Idris continued. 'It will make things easier. It will be scary enough for him facing the crowd outside, even with my security men keeping them back.'

Arden hadn't thought of that. It was odd, and unsettling, having someone else point out what her son needed before she did. She couldn't get her brain past the immediate. Right now that was overwhelming. Introducing Dawud to his father. The man she'd thought he'd never know.

The doorknob felt slippery in her clammy hand and she breathed deep, securing a smile for her son. This had to be done and it was up to her to ensure he felt none of the tension crawling up her spine and along her hunching shoulders. Deliberately she pushed back her shoulder blades and walked into the room.

'Mama!' He swung round as the song ended, a huge smile on his face.

Reaction hit her square in the chest as she met his laughing gaze. Eyes of dark brown velvet, so like his father's. When he'd been born they'd been a constant, difficult reminder of the man who'd duped and deserted her. But over the years they'd become simply Dawud's eyes.

Now, seeing the similarities, not just in his eyes but in his whole face, from his jet dark hair to his determined chin, a powerful tide of emotion rose. Arden wobbled to a halt.

'Mama?' Dawud scrambled to his feet and came towards her, arms outstretched. But before he reached her he halted, head turning, eyes growing.

Arden sensed rather than saw Idris beside her. It was as if he generated his own force field, one that made her flesh prickle and tighten whenever he got close.

Was he as nervous as she? As if this were an irrevocable step beyond which the future could never be the same?

She fell to her knees and held her arms out for Dawud. 'Hello, darling.' Dawud's eyes remained fixed on the man looming over the pair of them, his head craning high to take him in.

Arden was just about to scoop him up when she felt a brush of air beside her as, in a single movement, Idris sank to the floor, settling cross-legged. His knee touched hers but he didn't seem to notice. His attention was fixed on Dawud.

Idris leaned forward a fraction and said something in his own language. Something melodic yet strangely husky, and made a fluid, graceful movement with one powerful hand from his face to his chest.

For a second Dawud stood motionless, then a smile creased his features. 'That!' He pointed at Idris, first his head then his chest.

Idris made the gesture again, slower this time, a courtly gesture of greeting, she realised. Dawud clapped his hands and chuckled, then waved one hand in front of his face, trying to emulate the gesture.

Again that unseen cord tugged at her insides. To watch Dawud smiling at his father, trying to copy him…it was something she'd never expected to see. Not after the hell she'd gone through trying to locate Shakil and finally acknowledging defeat. She didn't even know if she *wanted* to see them together, yet the shining joy in her son's face was hard to resist.

Unwillingly, as if forced by an unseen hand, she turned her head for a better view. The forbidding majesty who wore hand-made clothes worth more than she earned in six months smiled at Dawud the way Shakil used to smile at her.

Her heart knocked her ribs and dislodged the last of the air in her lungs.

She was still reeling when he turned. Was it imagination or did his eyes glow brighter?

'It's time we left. I can carry Dawud if you like. But my men will keep the paparazzi back so they can't jostle you and Dawud might be happier in your arms than mine.'

Arden nodded. Again he was thinking ahead to the logistics of getting them out of here. Of keeping them safe. She suspected this big man would protect Dawud from all comers. More, he was thinking of Dawud's feelings and his reaction to the stress of change.

A squiggle of heat channelled through her belly and she looked away before he could see how his consideration affected her.

She leaned forward and scooped Dawud into her arms, relishing his scent and the way he snuggled into her. 'Come on, Dimples. We're going out.'

'Man come too.' His gaze was still fixed on Idris.

'Yes, darling. The man will come too.'

The man in question was already on his feet, holding his hand out to help her up. More proof of his thoughtfulness.

But Arden pretended not to notice, scrambling to her feet without assistance.

Touching him was just too unsettling.

Already she feared she was about to walk out of the frying pan and straight into the fire.

CHAPTER FOUR

'WHAT IS THIS PLACE?' Arden had spent most of the trip focused on Dawud, in the car seat between her and Idris. Now she looked around the underground garage with its security door to the street already closing.

'My embassy. You'll be safe here. We approached from the back entrance and weren't followed. My staff ran interference along the route so the press can't be sure exactly where we've gone.' He turned and unclipped Dawud's safety harness as easily as if he'd been doing it for years.

Perhaps he had. The Internet search she'd done on him after the reception didn't mention a wife or children but—

Her thoughts frayed as Dawud leaned forward, reaching for Idris instead of her.

He was a friendly, confident child, but at the moment, selfishly, she felt a pang at his fascination with the big man looking down at him so intently.

Then it struck her that though his attention was fixed on Dawud, Idris hadn't reached out to take him. Because he felt her qualms? Or because he didn't want to?

Arden lifted her son into her arms, reassured by his warm weight and clean little boy scent.

'I'd prefer a hotel.' She was indebted enough to Idris. More, she knew a foreign embassy was like foreign soil. While here she was in his territory, under his control. Her nerves prickled with foreboding. A spectre of doubt rose. Had she walked into a trap?

Dark eyebrows rose speculatively. 'You'd prefer to run the gauntlet of the press? To hope no hotel employee sells photos of you both to the media?'

Arden gathered Dawud closer, instinctively drawing into the corner of the wide back seat.

'I hadn't thought.' Shock hammered anew and to her horror she began to tremble. It had been a terrible day that got worse by the moment. The picture he painted was as disturbing as the pack of jackals who'd howled questions at them when they got into the car, then tried to follow them down the street.

'It's all right, Arden. There's private accommodation here. You won't be disturbed while we sort out a solution. I can guarantee the discretion of every member of staff.'

Because he was an absolute monarch and he'd have their heads if they betrayed him?

The proud jut of his jaw and the fierce light in his eyes spoke of certainty.

Looking up into a face as hard and beautiful as that of some carved ancient god, Arden felt the terrible imbalance of power between them. He had only to snap his fingers and his staff would obey.

Had she felt this vulnerable facing the paparazzi?

'I need your word first. I want a promise that when I want to leave, with my son, you won't stop us. That we're both free to go.'

For a heartbeat fire pulsed between them. Then his gaze dropped to Dawud. Reflexively her hands tightened and Dawud wriggled, protesting, till she eased her grip. She didn't take her eyes off Idris. Nothing in the world was more important than her son. She'd never let him go.

'You have my word. You're not a prisoner but a guest.' He lifted his gaze to mesh with hers and heat consumed her.

'Come. Let's get the boy settled somewhere more comfortable so we can talk.'

Still Arden hesitated. She was wary of entering his territory. But it was worse than that. Her fear was sparked as much by the way the scent of sandalwood and hot male flesh filled her nostrils, stirring a longing she'd believed herself immunised against. Her body betrayed her with its yearning for a man who'd never be right for her. Even if he'd cared for her, which he hadn't, he was a royal sheikh, a monarch, and she was a single mum from a less than impressive family tree. She didn't belong here.

Frantic thoughts raced. Of her escaping with Dawud in her arms. But to where? Idris and the press would find them.

Idris didn't speak, just sat, watching her as Dawud shifted impatiently and demanded to be put down.

They both knew she was out of options.

Finally, heart heavy, Arden turned towards the door.

Arden had thought the embassy magnificent the night of the reception, with its soaring double storey ceilings topped by intricately glazed domes, its radiant chandeliers and of course the dais with the gilded throne. But she'd assumed the rest of the building would be a little more ordinary.

She'd assumed wrong.

For a start it was even bigger than she'd expected, not one building but several, with a private garden at their centre. Somewhere, she guessed, were offices where staff went about diplomatic duties, but she found herself in a town house, several storeys high and furnished in the luxury she'd seen only in lifestyle magazines.

Yet it wasn't the expensive fittings or exclusive address that impressed; it was the blessed quiet. Peace after the ruckus she'd left behind on her street. Arden hadn't realised how high her anxiety had been till her heartbeat finally eased into something like a normal rhythm.

She settled Dawud into a bright bedroom, spreading out his favourite toys where he could see them. To her surprise Idris didn't insist on that talk to 'sort out a solution'. Instead he left them to relax and explore. Then a young woman with a gentle smile brought a meal for Dawud, explaining the ambassador employed her to care for his children and that she'd been asked to assist, if that was acceptable.

Again Arden was given no cause for complaint. Her consent was sought, though Idris or some super-efficient underling had thought of and provided everything before she even asked.

It was ungrateful to feel *managed*. It was just that she was used to making her own decisions. She was dependent on no one, a lesson learned in childhood. Arden told herself she should learn to accept assistance gratefully, for Dawud's sake. But it was tough.

They had been treated with courtesy and respect. Yet she remembered the fire in Idris's eyes when he spoke of the press knowing more than he about Dawud, and again when he spoke of his cousin, as if there was a rift between the pair. None of that anger had been directed at her.

So far.

No matter how plush the surroundings, she couldn't forget they were in Idris's domain. Were they prisoners despite his promise? Arden shivered, vowing to leave as soon as possible.

Misha, the nanny, offered to sit with Dawud while Arden met 'His Majesty'. Arden was trying to find a reason to put off that meeting when Dawud's drooping eyelids opened wide.

'Man! Hello, man!' He sat up in bed, dimpling as he grinned, and Arden felt a familiar trickle of awareness course from her nape all the way down her spine.

Her breath snagged and her nostrils widened. She told herself she couldn't possibly detect the tang of sandalwood on the air, but her nerves rioted anyway. She swallowed, trying to banish the memory of how Idris had tasted, hot and delicious on her tongue. Not an ancient memory this time but one that was raw and new and all too disturbing.

Reluctantly she turned. Idris leaned in the doorway, immaculate in a dark suit that emphasised his height and hinted at hard-packed strength beneath. His stance was relaxed but there was nothing casual about his expression.

Arden's chest squeezed. He hadn't even noticed her. His attention was fixed on Dawud as if utterly absorbed. The stark intensity of that scrutiny made her stomach churn, as if the squirrels in their local park had invaded her body, leaping and circling faster and faster till she felt nauseous.

He turned, spearing her with that dark gaze, catching her unprepared. Fire licked inside and she pressed her palm to her belly, only to let it fall, knowing she gave away too much when he followed the movement.

'Everything is satisfactory?'

His calm riled her. She'd been through hell today, and was still scared of what the future held for her son. Yet Idris took it in his stride.

'If you call being hounded by the press satisfactory.' Her lip curled. 'Being forced to hole up here instead of...'

Silence descended as Arden ran out of energy, the air rushing from tight lungs. 'I'm sorry. That's ungrateful.' Even if it *was* his fault, manhandling her like that, especially in public. 'The room is lovely. And Misha—' she turned to smile at the young woman putting away some toys '—has been such a help.'

'Good. Then you have no qualms about leaving Dawud here while we share a meal?'

Of course she had qualms! Arden wanted to go back to the way things had been, just her and her precious boy, safe and secure.

Except then he'd never have a chance to know his father. Despite feeling she teetered on the edge of a very high, very dangerous cliff, Arden knew how important it was for Dawud to grow up supported by both parents. Even the fiasco with the press was worth it if they found a way for him to have a constructive connection with his father.

Apart from anything else, it would be far safer—if anything happened to her, Dawud wouldn't be adrift in the world as she had been.

She recalled the night she'd given birth in a bare hospital room, terrified and alone but for a midwife. She had friends but none close enough to share the intimacy of birth. It had struck her how utterly dependent her baby was on her. She'd vowed to do everything she could to give him love and the sense of belonging she'd been denied as a kid.

'Arden?' Idris took a step closer, frowning.

She blinked. 'Thank you. Dinner would be good.'

'Man!' called an imperious voice. 'I want man.'

'Please,' Arden said automatically.

'Peeze.'

Was that a twitch of Idris's precisely sculpted lips? Before she had a chance to decide, he crossed the room and sat on the edge of Dawud's bed.

Seeing them together, dark heads inclined towards each other, surveying each other with grave interest, Arden's heart gave a silly little flutter. Once, years ago, she'd longed for this, had spent so many hours fruitlessly searching for the man who'd left her pregnant and alone, refusing to believe he'd callously misled her. Until there'd been no alternative.

A hiccupping sigh rose as her little boy brought his hand up to his forehead then swiped it down to his chest, all the while watching the big man before him.

When Idris repeated the gracious gesture of greeting he'd used earlier, Dawud beamed. He swiped his little hand back down from his head in mimicry, this time all the way to his tummy. 'More.'

'Please.' That deep voice was gentle and Arden blinked, feeling foolishly emotional. It had been a long, difficult day. That was all.

'Peeze.'

Idris's mouth hitched up at the corner in a smile Arden had never seen before. A smile that melted a layer of the brittle protection she'd placed around her heart. He repeated the gesture yet again, this time accompanying it with a lilting flow of words in his own language.

His words wove like an exotic, alluring current around the room, mesmerising her, and she wasn't surprised when Dawud leaned closer, obviously rapt.

How long Arden would have sat there, enthralled, she didn't know. But Misha got up, excusing herself to go and tidy up the bathroom after Dawud's enthusiastic splashes.

Suddenly, with her departure, the atmosphere changed. Idris didn't turn but his words this time were clipped.

'I spoke to Hamid. He says the child isn't his.'

Arden blinked and found herself sinking into a nearby armchair.

'Of course he's not Hamid's!' What a crazy idea.

'Is he mine?' Idris asked before she could continue. Again, he didn't face her, but kept his gaze on Dawud. Trying to read her son's parentage in his face?

The sight of Idris's broad back felt like an insult.

'Let me get this straight. You think I went from your bed to your cousin's? What sort of woman do you think I am?'

This time Idris did turn. Unreadable sable eyes pinioned her to her seat. 'I don't know. That's why I ask.'

Arden sagged against the upholstery. Well, that summed up their situation. At twenty she'd spent a week with a man called Shakil and believed she'd met her soulmate, her one true love, and that she knew everything she needed to trust him utterly.

That week had changed her life. Would have changed

it even if it hadn't left her pregnant with her precious son. For the first time in years she'd dared to hope, dared to put her trust in someone.

But that life-altering week had clearly been something far...*less* for him. All those passionate words, the promise in his eyes and his touch, his desire to have her with him after Santorini...they'd meant nothing. Nothing except they were physically attracted.

Arden kept her head up as she met his gaze. 'Dawud is your son.'

She waited for some reaction but saw none. Did he feel so little? She'd have sworn she'd read at least a hint of deep emotion when he looked at their little boy. But maybe it was wishful thinking because she so wanted Dawud to be loved by both his parents.

And if he wasn't? She'd give her son so much love and support he'd never notice the lack from his father. Except she, of all people, knew it didn't work like that. Nothing made up for the absence of parents.

Her lip curled. 'I suppose you want a DNA test?'

'It would be sensible, since we're talking about the heir to a kingdom.'

Arden's fingers dug into the padded arms of her chair, biting hard. She told herself he was right. Of course he'd need unassailable proof Dawud was his. Yet it all boiled down to the fact he didn't trust her word.

It took a moment for the rest of his words to hit her. *The heir to a kingdom.* Did Idris intend to acknowledge his son publicly?

Arden was torn between relief that Dawud would have access to both his father and mother and burgeoning fear at what that acknowledgement might mean for their cosy life. Did Idris envisage sharing their son, half the time in the UK and half in Zahrat? The idea of being separated from her baby plunged a dagger through her heart. Until she told herself she was getting ahead of herself.

She looked across to see Idris again talking to Dawud in his own language, even teaching him to say something. Dawud's smile grew and grew as he parroted the simple sounds. Despite her fears, Arden knew that, however difficult this would be for her and Idris, for Dawud, having a family was immeasurably precious.

Misha returned and Idris stood.

'Nigh'-nigh', man.' Dawud opened and closed his hand in his three-year-old's version of a wave.

In response Idris said something first in Arabic, then followed it with, 'Goodnight.'

Arden crossed to the bed and kissed her boy, pushing back his silky dark hair. 'Night-night, sweetie.'

'Nigh'-nigh', Mama.' He pressed his hand to his mouth then flung out his arm in an exuberant kiss that made her smile despite the tension dragging at her belly.

She made herself turn away, reminded Misha to call her if Dawud had trouble settling and followed Idris from the room.

'What was that word you taught Dawud?' Arden asked him across the table laid for two in an intimate dining room.

She looked tired and tense but that didn't staunch the need dragging low through his body. She hadn't dressed up for dinner with him, wearing jeans and a T-shirt, not even any jewellery. Her only trace of make-up was a clear lipgloss and something to darken her lashes. Yet Idris struggled against the need to touch her.

'*Baba?*' Idris passed her a platter of slow-roasted lamb before taking some.

'That's it. What does it mean?'

She wasn't looking at him as she helped herself to a

salad. She hadn't looked at him directly since she'd left the bedroom. As if the sight of him offended.

Was she blind to the fire of attraction crackling between them? Or pretending? Were her plain clothes an attempt to show she wasn't trying to impress? Or that she disdained him?

He didn't know what angered him more, her pretence or that she'd had his child in secret.

The soft lighting turned her hair to spun gold and the tantalising scent of orange blossom drifted to his nostrils. Idris felt his lower body jerk hard.

The fact Arden Wills got under his skin so easily made her dangerous. Idris had no intention of ceding power of any sort to anyone. Not after he'd spent years working day and night to cement his position as the youngest Sheikh in two hundred years. Too much effort had gone into stabilising his nation and building its future.

'*Baba* means Daddy.'

As expected, that got her attention. Her head shot up and once more he felt that jolt as their eyes met. Their kiss had been explosive. It made him wonder what a more intimate touch would be like.

'You don't even know he's yours. Not till you get your paternity test done.' Was that indignation? Certainly there was fire sparking in those extraordinary aquamarine eyes.

The jangling tension inside spread, his blood pumping faster.

Idris shrugged, adopting insouciance to hide his reaction. He wasn't ready to admit he didn't need a scientific test to know Dawud was his son. He couldn't explain his certainty because it defied logic. It wasn't wish fulfilment because, while he'd expected children with Ghizlan, he'd seen that simply as his duty.

Yet he'd looked at the boy and felt something he couldn't explain and had never expected. Certainty was part of it.

Happiness, a bright burst of pleasure and protectiveness was another. And relief. Because the idea he'd harboured since seeing the press reports, of Arden and Hamid as lovers, had made him feel wild, out of control.

Idris didn't do out of control. He did planned, logical, well-executed.

'You had no right.'

'Pardon?' He'd lost the thread of her conversation.

'You had no right to tell him you were his father.' Her small, lush mouth was set in a pout that would have been inviting, if not for her abrasive words.

He didn't bother to remind her he'd been speaking his own language, not English, and that the child hadn't understood. But he would soon. Idris would make sure of it.

'*No right?*' He planted his palms on the table and saw her lean back, away from him. 'I have every right. He's, what, three years old? All that time you kept him from me.'

That knowledge had battered him since the moment he'd walked into that basement sitting room and seen his son, a complete stranger yet still his son, sitting on the floor, clapping his hands. It was as if someone had scraped his heart bare, leaving it open and unprotected.

Even when some inner voice had taunted him with the idea the boy could be Hamid's.

'Not by choice. You lied to me about who you were.'

Idris shook his head. 'I told you—I didn't lie. I used an old nickname while I travelled to avoid publicity. I'd been under the microscope because of my family connections and wanted a break, to relax and be like everyone else. I had every intention of explaining who I was if you came with me to Paris.'

It still amazed him that he'd made that offer. But he hadn't been able to get enough of her. Arden's unstinting warmth and zest for life, the way she'd looked at him as

if he made the sun shine and the moon rise, had been ir-
resistible.

She didn't look at him that way now.

His jaw set. 'Everything else I told you was true.'
Though he'd steered clear of his connection to royalty.
'There was no cause to deny me my son.' He stiffened as
he fought the bubbling anger he'd repressed all day.

He flexed his fingers, resisting the urge to reach for her.
To shake her into an apology? To kiss her till she stopped
hissing at him as if *he* were at fault, not her?

'I didn't keep him from you!' Arden threw her napkin
on the table and shoved her seat back.

Idris was on his feet before she was, ready to block the
door, determined to have this out. He'd contained himself
earlier, knowing the needs of the child had to come first.
Patience was a hard won quality. One he'd mastered after
assuming the throne, for implementing reform in Zahrat was a slow business. But his patience wore thin. This
woman pressed all his buttons.

'Then why not tell me? What did I do on Santorini that
convinced you it was better to raise our son alone? How
can you justify keeping him from me?' Idris heard the
harsh resonance in his voice and hauled in a deep breath.
He hated revealing his feelings.

Arden planted her hands on her hips in a provocative
stance. Her round chin angled up, her eyes sparked and
through her white T-shirt he saw her nipples stand out as
hard little points.

He flexed his hands again, resisting the need to reach
out and touch. Abruptly he shoved his hands in his pockets.

'How was I supposed to contact you? Tell me that? You
hid your tracks too well.'

'I did not—'

'No?' She stalked forward, her face tilted up to meet
his. 'I never knew your family name.' She ticked off a fin-

ger. 'The one name you gave me was false.' Another finger ticked. 'When I found I was pregnant and contacted the hotel you said you'd booked on Santorini, they refused to confirm you'd been there, much less give me contact details.'

Idris scowled into her angry face. Those security arrangements were normal procedure to protect the privacy of the royal family. It had never occurred that they might have kept Arden from contacting him.

'I had no idea,' he said slowly.

'Sure you didn't.' Her lip curled and she rubbed her arms as if chilled.

About to bite out that hiding from women wasn't his way, Idris paused. If she *had* tried to contact him, how desperate must she have been when she couldn't locate him?

'When you didn't show at the rendezvous I assumed you were happy to walk away.' At the time, he'd had other things on his mind, like suddenly assuming the throne and responsibility for a nation.

'I told you, I did go. Just a little late. At the last minute I couldn't find my passport' Her chin hiked up and those aquamarine eyes held his. 'When the hotel refused to help me contact you I called the Zahrati embassy here in London.' Her mouth twisted and Idris felt a dart of discomfort.

'Do you have any idea how horrible it was, trying to locate you through official channels? All I could tell them was that your name was Shakil, you were twenty-six and spoke excellent English, that you'd studied in the US and you'd once broken your collarbone. I didn't even have photos of you since you were so camera shy.' Her mouth pursed, her nostrils thinning. 'Oh, they were very polite, very kind. I think they felt sorry for me because they guessed why I needed to find you so urgently.'

Heat washed her pale features but her gaze didn't waver.

Idris read hurt and defiance there and, if he wasn't mistaken, remembered embarrassment.

What had it been like to discover at twenty that she was pregnant to a stranger? To a man whose real name she didn't even know?

Guilt smote him. It reminded him of the blow he'd received at fourteen, learning traditional battle skills, when he'd been knocked, winded, from his horse and cracked a couple of bones.

Except that had been a clean blow in fair combat. This felt different, tainted with shame, though he hadn't intentionally misled her.

'I'm sorry.' He paused, knowing it wasn't enough. 'I apologise, Arden. What you went through—it must have been devastating. I really do regret that you felt deserted.' Idris stilled. She'd been so young. So bright and innocent. His lungs squeezed hard at the thought of her, scared and alone.

'I never meant to dupe you or hurt you. I only wanted a chance to enjoy myself without attracting public attention.' How selfish and irresponsible that sounded now. 'As for pregnancy, I assumed the precautions we took would be enough.' He felt his shoulders rise. 'I was thoughtless, not even considering repercussions, and for that I apologise again. But believe me, I wasn't trying to hide. Within a week of leaving Santorini I became Sheikh of Zahrat. It never occurred to me you couldn't find me if you needed to.'

Arden stared, her gaze raking as if sifting fact from the lies she'd imagined. 'I had other things on my mind than current affairs. Even if I'd read about it I wouldn't have made the connection between the Shakil I knew and a royal sheikh.'

Idris nodded. How could she have known? How could either of them? It was no one's fault, just an unfortunate series of circumstances.

Yet that edgy feeling of guilt still lined his gut. He remembered her telling him she had no family. Her parents had died years ago.

'You were okay? Through the pregnancy and birth?' It didn't matter what logic said. Honour dictated he should have been there to provide for her.

Her eyes rounded. 'As you can see, I'm fine.'

Which didn't answer his question. Instead it made him wonder what she hid. Had there been anyone by her side through that ordeal?

'You were well looked after?'

Her gaze hardened. 'I looked after myself. At least I had a steady job to go back to. That supported us both.'

Idris felt her stare like a slap, knowing it was what she didn't say that damned him. He knew next to nothing about childbirth but even he understood women needed support and rest, not just during delivery but after. How soon had she been forced back to work?

'I don't shirk my responsibilities,' Idris said slowly, watching the flash of fire in her eyes. 'If I'd known I would have helped, as I intend to help you now.'

The girl he'd known had been sweet, affectionate and easy-going whereas the woman before him was complicated, feisty and obstinate. Yet her passion and her determination to keep him at a distance only made his hunger for her more acute.

It was inexplicable.

'Good. I always wanted Dawud to know his father. It's important for a child to have a positive relationship with both parents.' She crossed her arms and surveyed him as if considering whether he measured up to her high standards.

Idris paced forward, closing the gap between them.. 'I agree. Which is why we'll marry as soon as possible.'

CHAPTER FIVE

ARDEN STARED UP into dark velvet eyes that glowed in a way she didn't like at all.

It made her think of how he'd hemmed her in against her front door and wrapped his big hand around the base of her skull, holding her captive as he kissed her senseless. And how she'd let him.

Of the heat that shimmered through her every time their eyes met, as if the smallest spark would ignite a conflagration she couldn't douse.

Of the way she'd melted at his touch, his kiss, even his voice.

She didn't want to melt. She wanted to cling to fury at his desertion, believing he'd deliberately dumped her. But, despite her anger and fear, Arden found herself believing the regret in his eyes, the honesty in his voice, the steadfastness in his body language. He hadn't intentionally left her high and dry. He'd sent someone to meet her and she hadn't been there.

An ache opened up in the pit of her belly. The fact it was random circumstance not deliberate intent that had kept them apart somehow seemed almost worse. And now this!

'Marry?' Her voice stretched and splintered.

'Of course. It's the logical solution.'

'Solution? I'm not a problem to be solved!' Easier to let anger hide her curious disappointment.

After all this time did she still pine for the fantasy she'd once harboured? Of him saying he loved her and wanted to spend his life with her?

Surely she was stronger than that.

Arden pushed by him to pace the room, passing the

exquisitely polished dining table with its crystal glasses, silverware and fine porcelain.

A table fit for a king. A king who'd planned to marry a princess. If anything was needed to highlight the differences between them that was it.

'What about your fiancée?' She swung to face him. Even from the far side of the room he was too close.

'I was never engaged. The betrothal wasn't finalised.'

Something in his voice told her he glossed over a difficult situation. Or maybe it was the hard line of his jaw. She could only guess at the diplomatic furore caused by those press reports.

'You don't just call off a royal marriage.'

'You expect me to wed Princess Ghizlan when I've discovered you're the mother of my son?' He grew before her eyes, his face taking on an implacable expression that made her think uneasily of his desert warrior heritage.

'I've been the mother of your son for years.' She folded her arms. 'We've survived quite well without you.'

It was the wrong thing to say. She knew it as soon as the words spilled out. The gleam in his eyes turned positively dangerous.

'I've been robbed of three years of my son's life.' He spoke quietly yet the lethal precision of those words sent her nerves into jangling alarm. 'I won't be robbed of more.'

'*I* didn't rob you of anything!' Her voice was overloud.

'Perhaps not.' She opened her mouth to speak again but the thoughtful, patient man who'd put Dawud's needs first all day had disappeared, replaced by a forbidding figure whose aggressive stance spoke of steely resolve. 'But the fact remains he's mine.'

'And mine!' Arden shot forward a step.

'Precisely. You said yourself it's best if a child has a positive relationship with both parents. Marriage will ensure that.'

'Marriage isn't required.' Arden stifled hollow laughter that she was rejecting him. Once the idea of marrying this man would have been a fantasy come true.

Because once she'd loved him with all the desperate, optimistic yearning of her young, innocent heart. She'd been drawn not just by his looks and charisma but by the way he *noticed* her. Shakil had made her feel special, as if she wasn't ordinary but remarkable. He'd shared new experiences with her, laughed with her, worked to please her with a generosity and charm that had seduced her completely. Now she realised she'd never really known him.

He tilted his head as if assessing her.

What did he see? An ordinary—too ordinary—young woman. Arden wasn't in the same league as Princess Ghizlan—beautiful, gracious and glamorous. Arden was a working class mum. She'd never owned a couture dress or mixed with the rich and famous.

Nor was she beautiful. Beneath the bright but untameable hair lurked an ordinary face, a short nose and mouth that, while well shaped, wasn't wide enough for current tastes. She juggled work and motherhood, was more at home singing nursery rhymes and cooking eggs with toast soldiers than dining in an elegant room like this.

'You're not thinking straight.' His jet eyebrows lifted and his eyes narrowed to gleaming slits, but Arden refused to be intimidated. 'This is a knee-jerk reaction. When you consider you'll realise the idea of us marrying is...'

'Logical? Long overdue? The best thing for Dawud?'

Arden shoved her hands on her hips, whipping up outrage. 'I was thinking more ludicrous, unnecessary and painful.'

'You think marriage to me would be painful?'

Arden couldn't tell if it was shock or fury tightening his face but he morphed from broodingly aggressive to fearsome in the blink of an eye. Idris looked like a marauder planning a raid on some unprotected outpost.

A shiver ripped through her but she stood her ground. 'You'd find it painful. I'm not cut out to be a royal wife.'

And it would be painful for her, living a parody of the life she'd once imagined with the man she'd loved.

A slashing gesture, like the downward slice of a sword, dismissed her argument. 'You can learn.'

'I'm not interested in learning.' Why couldn't he see they were mismatched?

He stepped forward, not stopping till she felt his warm breath on her upturned face. Arden swallowed as a frisson of fear skated down her backbone.

'It may have escaped your notice, Arden.' He lingered on her name and the frisson became something else. Something that made a mockery of her antipathy. 'But it doesn't matter what you're interested in. What you and I want no longer counts. What matters is what's best for Dawud.'

Stupidly, her breath caught. He'd touched a nerve. She'd do anything for her son, anything to ensure he had a bright, stable, happy future.

Except what Idris suggested was a recipe for disaster.

She folded her arms. 'Dawud doesn't need us to be married. It's far better if he has parents on friendly terms than ones making each other miserable because they married the wrong person.'

'Who do you want to marry?' It was out like a shot. 'My cousin?'

Arden backed a step and found her way blocked by a chair. 'No! Hamid is a friend, that's all.'

'Then who do you want to marry?' Idris stalked closer and Arden wondered how she'd ever considered him easygoing.

'No one. I was speaking in general terms. But that does raise the question of love.'

'Love?' He said it as if it was an alien concept.

'Of course.' Was he being deliberately difficult? 'If one of us fell in love with someone later...'

Idris shook his head. 'There's no danger of me falling in love with anyone else.'

For a split second the old Arden, the one she thought she'd left behind years ago, waited for him to declare he'd fallen for her all those years ago on Santorini.

It couldn't be true. That dream was ancient history. Yet her voice was husky. 'Why not?'

'I've never been in love and nor will I be. No one in my family marries for love.' He shrugged. 'We're renowned for being impervious to romance. Call it an inherited failing.'

'I see.' Stupid to feel disappointment. She'd known she'd only been a holiday fling. She'd long ago acknowledged her feelings for him were the product of girlish romanticism in the face of her first real crush.

'Unless you're afraid *you'll* fall in love?'

Arden's laugh was short and cynical. 'Definitely not.' The reality of becoming a single mother a week before her twenty-first birthday had shredded her romantic fantasies, even if seeing Idris again evoked shadowy memories of what she'd called love. She was too tired just getting through each day to think about romance.

'Good. Then that's not a problem.'

Arden shook her head. 'But there are plenty more.'

'Such as?'

Was he serious? The whole idea was laughable.

'Your people won't accept me as Queen.'

'My people will accept any woman I marry.' It was said with a conviction that told her it was the absolute truth.

'I couldn't accept the restrictions of being a woman in your country. Your traditions are different to mine.'

That pulled him up short. Arden watched his brow crinkle.

'It's true our traditions aren't the same,' he said slowly, 'but change is happening. My country is very different to the way it was four years ago. Besides, as my wife, you'd be able to model change for other women, to lead the way.'

'Princess Ghizlan would do that far better.'

He shook his head, his lips flattening. 'How many times do I have to tell you she's out of the picture? I can't ask her to marry me in the face of this scandal. The only decent thing I can do, for everyone, is marry you.'

That put her in her place. She was nothing but an albatross around his neck.

She heaved in a deep breath. 'I'm sorry for the trouble the news has caused. To *all* of us. My life's not going to be easy either, at least for a while. But it's not my fault. Nor do I think jumping into marriage is a solution. All I want is what's best for Dawud.'

'At last we agree on something.'

His words gave her hope. Maybe he could be persuaded. She hadn't exactly been tactful in rejecting his proposal. If you could call his statement that they'd marry a proposal!

Arden lifted her lips in a small, conciliatory smile. 'You're right. That's a starting point, isn't it?'

He gave no answering smile and Arden wondered how often people argued with the Sheikh of Zahrat. Was he so used to having his own way he couldn't concede there were other options?

'Look. Why don't we sit down and discuss some possibilities?'

To her relief he stepped back, allowing her to slip into her vacated seat. Just in time. Stress and weariness had taken their toll. Her legs shook as if she'd run all the way to the top of St Paul's Cathedral.

Idris settled beside her. 'You were saying?'

'Well…' She slid a fork across the tablecloth, watching

grooves appear then disappear in the fine linen. 'Perhaps he could spend part of the year with you.'

Just saying it stabbed pain through her chest. She couldn't imagine a day without Dawud. Her breath snared in an audible hiss.

But she had to be realistic. Dawud should have a chance to know his father.

'As a part-time prince, you mean? Living sometimes in my palace and sometimes in your basement flat?'

Arden's head jerked up. His voice was cool, almost detached, but surely that was anger she heard?

'It makes more sense than pretending the three of us can be the perfect family.'

'I'm not asking for perfection, Arden.'

She bit down her retort that he hadn't *asked* anything. But bickering would get them nowhere. She had to put aside resentment and fear and think of what was best for Dawud. Even if being with Idris made her feel trapped. 'Sharing him is a workable compromise.'

'You really think Dawud can go back to the life he used to lead now I know he's mine?'

Arden stiffened. The heavy silver fork thudded to the table. She worked hard to provide for her boy. 'Why not? A dose of working class reality to compare with palace life might be a good thing.'

Idris shook his head. 'You misunderstand. The damage is done now the world knows Dawud is my son. It's my duty, as well as my wish, to have him live with me. If I don't I'd be remiss and I'd be thought weak by my people. It would be an insult to you too, if I didn't marry you. And an insult to Ghizlan if I rejected her then didn't marry the mother of my son.'

Arden gritted her teeth. 'I'm a person in my own right.' She didn't care what his people or his Princess thought. All she cared about was Dawud.

'You would let your personal preferences stand in the way of Dawud's happiness and safety?'

'You're exaggerating. I've cared for him perfectly well up till now.'

'That was before.' A large hand covered hers, clamping it to the table. She was surprised how reassuring that touch felt. 'You've only had one day's taste of what the press can do. Do you want to put Dawud through that again and again?'

A chill invaded her bones. 'Surely once the novelty wears off...'

'Arden, this won't go away. Ever. Whenever there's an item of news about my country, or a slow media day, or a significant event for you or Dawud—a birthday, his first day at school, even weekend sports—the press will be there, snapping candid photos. They'll rehash the story— the difference between my life in the palace and his in London. Every step he takes will be pored over, particularly since he's so photogenic. Every decision you make as a mother will be scrutinised and judged.'

She was almost grateful for the warmth of his hand as her skin crawled at the picture he painted.

'Dawud won't have anywhere to hide. He'll be hounded, a freak for the press to exploit.'

Arden ripped her hand away and pressed it to her pounding chest. 'Dawud isn't a freak!'

'Of course not. He's a perfectly normal little boy.' Idris's voice curled comfortingly around her. 'I want him to stay that way.'

'By making him live in a palace!'

Idris's chuckle was rich and far too appealing. It reminded her of Shakil, the man who could make her heart turn over with just a smile. 'You make it sound like a prison. Believe me, Dawud can live a more normal life there than in London. In Zahrat I can protect you both.'

Arden swallowed a clot of apprehension. It was too extreme to contemplate. Yet in her heart of hearts she knew Idris was right. She and Dawud couldn't go back.

A great shudder racked her.

'I suppose we could try living in Zahrat, if you helped find us a house.' Could she work there? Did they even have florists? She put her hand to her temple, where a dull thudding headache had taken root.

'You would live in the palace. As my wife. It's the only sensible option. Together we can give him a stable home, no end-of-week handovers and complicated custody.' Idris didn't look aggressive now, just coolly composed. As if he knew he held all the aces.

Arden slumped in her seat. She felt cornered, her mind whirling fruitlessly as she sought alternatives to the one Idris presented.

'This is about Dawud,' he murmured. 'About what's best for our boy.'

Our boy. Not his son, or her son. *Our boy.*

That one small phrase bridged the gaping chasm between them. It made her feel less alone.

That shouldn't matter. She was used to shouldering responsibility. Yet there was a disarming allure to the idea of sharing this load.

'I need to think.' She slid her hand out from beneath his. 'I need time.'

'Of course. I'll come for your decision at nine tomorrow morning.'

At four the next afternoon, and after a night of soul-searching, Arden became betrothed to Idris, Sheikh of Zahrat in front of a throng of witnesses.

She'd planned to reject him. The idea of tying herself to the man who, accidentally or not, had left her floundering four years before, rankled. She wanted to walk away, defiant, independent and dismissive.

But she, more than most, understood what it was to be utterly alone and unprotected. If anything happened to her… No, Dawud had the right to grow up secure and loved, free from press intrusion, free to accept his birthright if he wished. And from all she'd been able to discover from the Internet, Idris would work as hard at being a good father as he did every other responsibility. He had a reputation for honest dealing and care for his subjects.

Yet her signature on the contract was shaky, like a child's just learning to write, because she trembled all over, her stomach twisting in knots. Beside her on his throne Idris signed with a slashing flourish that reflected complete ease.

No doubt he was used to signing important papers. But as she stared at the massive parchment with its gilt edging and beautiful decorative calligraphy border, Arden felt she'd signed her life away. Hers and her son's.

A chill clamped her neck and shoulders and her heart pounded so hard she was surprised no one heard it. She'd had no real choice, yet still she worried—

'Let me be the first to congratulate you.'

She looked up to see Princess Ghizlan. In an amber silk suit and a fortune in pearls around her throat, she looked every inch the glamorous, aristocratic princess. Everything Arden would never be, despite the costly outfit Idris had provided as an alternative to her ancient jeans.

Surprisingly the other woman's smile was warm and Arden felt grateful. She'd been alarmed when she'd spied the Princess amidst the serious men in the throne room. After all, she'd been all but jilted because of Arden.

'Thank you, Your—'

'Ghizlan, please.' She turned to Idris. 'Congratulations

on your betrothal, Your Highness. I hope you'll both be very happy.'

There was nothing in her face or his to indicate anything between them but calm goodwill. No tension, no fraught looks. Were they superb actors, Arden wondered, or was it true the match between them had been nothing but a formality? Arden's head spun. This royal world she'd entered was confusing and unnatural.

'Thank you.' His voice was deep and grave, a reminder that this ceremony was about securing his son's future, not anything as joyous or natural as a love match. He hadn't smiled once today.

Because this is about duty and respectability. Nothing more.

Arden's heart gave another heavy thump, rising up against her throat.

'I wondered if I might steal you away to take some refreshment.'

Arden was on her feet instantly then paused, wavering. Was she supposed to sit beside Idris to accept congratulations? But he was getting up and, frankly, she'd had enough formality.

'That sounds lovely.' As she followed the other woman to the lavish buffet her stomach growled. She'd been too nervous to eat.

'I'm the same,' said Ghizlan softly. 'I don't eat before official engagements then I regret it. They go on far too long.'

Arden cast a sideways look at the statuesque woman now filling a fine porcelain plate with delicacies.

'You really don't mind about…me?' she blurted out, then silently cursed her crassness. This wasn't the time or place. But she was curious about this poised, beautiful woman who'd so nearly married Idris.

The Princess cut her a swift look. 'Let's go somewhere

more comfortable.' She nodded to lounges in a corner Arden hadn't even seen.

All she'd noticed on entering the room was the crowd and Idris, tall and unsmiling. Her pulse had tumbled out of kilter as she drank in his spare, handsome features. It horrified her that just looking at him left her breathless.

'Arden? I may call you Arden?'

'Of course… Ghizlan. I'm sorry, I'm a little distracted.' She sank into a seat, carefully holding her plate of delicious-smelling food.

'I'm not surprised. If you're not used to these formal ceremonies they can be daunting.' The other woman leaned close. 'The trick is to have something else to think of during the boring bits. I do my best planning then.'

A smile tugged Arden's lips and some of that horrible, wound-too-tight feeling in her stomach settled. 'It's good of you to be so nice to me. I didn't expect—I mean, thank you. I didn't mean—'

Ghizlan's lustrous kohl-lined eyes widened, then she laughed, the sound rich and appealing. Male heads turned.

'You're absolutely welcome. I suspect I'm going to like you very much.'

Arden plonked her plate on a table and leaned closer. 'I didn't mean it to come out that way.'

Ghizlan waved away her words. 'It's good to hear someone so frank. You'll understand once you're hemmed in by diplomats and courtiers. And you're right.' She paused. 'This is tough for all of us.'

'I'm truly sorry about that.'

'It's not your fault. None of us had a choice once the news came out about your boy.'

Arden searched the beautiful face for signs of hurt but read nothing. 'It must be especially difficult for you.'

Ghizlan looked away. 'A diplomatic storm, that's for

sure. But it will pass. Our betrothal hadn't been formalised, and now, if you and I are seen together on friendly terms things will ease a little.'

Slowly Arden nodded. *That* was why Ghizlan was here. It wasn't simple goodwill behind this *tête-à-tête*. Disappointment stirred. 'I see. You think this—' her gesture encompassed the pair of them in the intimate cluster of seats '—will help stave off gossip?'

'Now *you're* offended. I'm sorry. I told Idris you mightn't want me here, but he assured me there was no sentimental attachment between you. Please forgive me.'

She made to rise but Arden's out-thrust hand stopped her. 'No, please.'

A roiling wave of emotion surged through her. Idris's words shouldn't hurt. They were true. Anything they'd once felt for each other was long dead. And what had Ghizlan done but try to ameliorate a disaster?

'I'm sorry.' Arden swallowed hard. 'I do appreciate you being here. It must have been difficult for you and it's nice to have another woman here.'

'I thought it might help. Plus it will take some of the fuel from the fire if it looks like I'm in London to support you instead of being on approval for Idris.'

'On approval?'

Ghizlan's face took on that smooth, unruffled expression that Arden now realised masked other feelings. 'Our marriage was to build a bridge between our two countries that have feuded for generations. It was tied to a peace treaty and a trade agreement but still, we needed a little time in each other's company to…test the waters.'

Arden blinked as something hot and jagged, something almost like jealousy, bit into her. But she jammed a stop on her imagination before she could wonder how far *testing the waters* went.

'There'll be hell to pay when I return home but meanwhile supporting you helps us both by deflecting the worst of the gossip.'

Arden looked into that beautiful face, so still and poised, and realised how much courage it took for the other woman to be here, smiling as if her hopes of marriage hadn't been dashed so scandalously. If she...*cared* for Idris...

To her amazement, fellow feeling rose. She'd loved and lost him once and it had soured her on the idea of love ever since. But she'd never forgotten the pain. It still sideswiped her when she least expected it.

'I like your thinking, Ghizlan.' Arden hesitated then plunged on. 'Maybe you could advise me a little about what to expect? I know nothing about protocol and ceremony, or even what I should wear.'

She looked down at the pretty pale blue dress that shimmered under the brilliant lights. It had appeared in her room this morning and she'd accepted it gratefully rather than face this ceremony in old denims.

If she let herself dwell on how unprepared she was, she'd hide away and never come out. Or work herself into a fury at how she was being railroaded. But it was too late for second thoughts.

'You like the dress?'

'It's gorgeous. But I have no experience in buying expensive clothes and I have no idea what's required for...' Arden's words faded as she saw the smile on the other woman's face. '*You* picked this?'

Ghizlan shrugged. 'Just gave a couple of suggestions. I thought, given how quickly this all happened you mightn't have anything suitable for today.'

Arden blinked as gratitude welled. 'You really are a nice woman, aren't you?'

Before she could feel self-conscious about blurting out her thoughts again, Ghizlan gave a delighted laugh.

* * *

Idris followed the muted sound of laughter to see both women with their heads together. One dark, one golden, both beautiful, his rejected bride and his affianced bride.

His belly tightened at the thought of the frantic work he had still to do to salvage something from the debacle caused by Arden and Dawud. Relations with Ghizlan's royal father were in tatters, as were the treaties they'd negotiated. Conservative elements in his own country were up in arms about his illegitimate son and his plans to marry an Englishwoman. Yet what alternative did he have?

Any other course would be ruinous.

Any other course would deprive him of his son and make Dawud an object of ridicule and gossip.

Any other course would deprive him of Arden.

He watched her lean in to talk with Ghizlan. The movement tugged her silk dress tight, outlining that slim, delicious figure he'd fantasised about all night.

With half an ear he listened to the conversation around him, the first steps in building a new rapport with representatives of Ghizlan's father. Yet his attention was fixed on Arden. The woman he would marry.

For the first time since he'd agreed to consider taking a bride, he felt a sharp tug of eagerness.

Arden might be trouble on two beautiful, sexy legs. She had no pedigree, no dowry or influence in his region. Worse, she had no training for a royal role, no knowledge of diplomacy or the arcane ceremonies and rituals which still persisted at court.

Yet she was the mother of his son and for that alone would be accorded respect.

Except that wasn't the only reason he would marry her, was it? Last night he'd confronted the uncomfortable truth that he couldn't in all honesty marry Ghizlan when it was Arden he wanted in his bed.

Want was such a weak word for the hunger simmering within him. It might be just sex, but it felt alarmingly like a compulsion. Like the weakness all the men of his family shared, a weakness he'd thought he'd put aside when he took on the sheikhdom.

He must learn to conquer this weakness or master it. He intended to approach this marriage like any other contract. With a cool head and in total control.

CHAPTER SIX

'AN AIR-CONDITIONED LIMOUSINE will drive you and your son to the palace, Ms Wills.' Ashar, the Sheikh's aide, smiled reassuringly from the seat beside her on the plane. 'It's a short drive and it won't be long before you're settling into your rooms to rest.'

'Thank you.' A rest sounded wonderful. Even here in the comfort of Idris's private jet Arden hadn't been able to relax.

Perhaps because she wasn't used to people waiting on her. Misha, their temporary nanny, had taken Dawud to another cabin in the luxurious aircraft so Arden didn't have the distraction of a toddler who'd crush her new designer suit. Yet instead of revelling in the luxury of some quiet time Arden felt deprived. Of course she could have gone to him, but deep down she realised her stress wasn't about Dawud, it was about her fears for the future.

What had she done, agreeing to leave London and marry Idris? Could she marry him and trust him to do what was best for Dawud?

Logic reminded her Idris wasn't the carefree, careless young man who'd left her bereft and struggling. She'd seen the change in him. Yet she couldn't stifle unease.

Everything had happened so fast, the betrothal ceremony, the blur of new faces as Idris's personal staff were introduced. The shopping trip with Ghizlan to a famous couturier who'd opened his doors just for them while stony-faced security men kept the press at a distance.

Resigning from her job by phone had been a surreal experience. Her boss had read about her 'adventure' and had been agog for news. Arden was left with the unsettling suspicion she'd be more valuable to the business now she was an almost-VIP and potential drawcard than ever before. As for closing up the flat—it had been done for her. Idris had spoken to Hamid before she could, explaining she wouldn't be returning.

Of everything that had happened in the last few days, that was the worst. It felt as if her life had been ripped away. She'd poured in hours of work and what little cash she had, turning it into a warm, bright home, full of treasured memories.

It didn't matter that everything was done efficiently and with exquisite politeness by the royal staff. Beneath every courteous query about her preferences lay a stark, terrifying truth.

She had no choice in anything that mattered now. She'd agreed to marry Dawud's father and their lives would be dominated by that from now on.

'I'm sorry.' She blinked and focused on the royal aide. 'You were saying?'

'I asked if you'd like some water or anything else. You look pale and we're about to land. If you're ill…?'

Arden shook her head. 'I'm okay, thanks. Just tired.'

'Then I'll leave you alone for now.' Ashar nodded and melted away.

Arden's lips twisted. Wasn't that the perfect indicator of what this royal marriage would be like? It wasn't her soon-to-be husband asking about her well-being. Idris had excused himself as soon as they boarded and headed into a study off the main cabin. She'd barely seen him since she'd agreed to marry him. It was left to his ever-watchful staff to be concerned for her.

Arden straightened her shoulders. She didn't need their concern. She could do this. She *had* to do this.

No matter how tough, no matter how challenging her

new life, she'd face it like she'd faced everything else life threw at her.

After a lifetime solo, one important thing had changed. She was no longer alone. She had Dawud. He was more precious to her than anything, even phantom memories of first love and heartbreak.

She did this for her son.

Arden turned to look out of the window, staring at the misty blue mountains that rose in the distance, jagged and forbidding. Below her a broad, tawny plain sprawled to the coast where white sand edged a turquoise sea.

Zahrat. Legendary for its fiercely independent people and its arid vastness of desert and rugged mountains.

Despite her determination to be strong, Arden couldn't repress a fervent wish that she and Dawud were safely back in London, leading their familiar, ordinary lives.

From astride his horse Idris surveyed the people lining the streets that wound through the capital. Every man, woman and child, it seemed, had come out to see their Sheikh make his traditional entry to the city.

And to see his son, and the Englishwoman who'd soon be their Sheikha.

As decreed by custom, there was no applause, no shouting, merely bowed heads as he passed. Yet that didn't stop the crowd craning for a view of the vehicle following him, the car carrying Arden and Dawud.

He'd wondered how the news of his ready-made family would be taken. Not that anything would deter him from his duty to marry.

His people were proud and traditional. No doubt the older, more conservative ones would frown about a foreign bride. Yet he noticed a few silken banners, a customary sign of rejoicing, flying in the street. Turquoise for the sea that bordered Zahrat and scarlet for the desert at sunset, or, as popular belief had it, for the blood of their enemies, shed whenever the Zahrati defended their land.

Idris was musing on this sign of welcome when the Captain of the Royal Guard rode close.

'Highness. The car. It's stopped.'

Instantly alert, Idris whipped around, pulling his horse to a halt.

There was no sign of a problem yet his heartbeat quickened, his body tense, ready for action as he scanned the street for signs of an ambush. Security was a necessity these days, yet in his homeland Idris had always felt his bodyguard was more to satisfy tradition than because of any threat.

But if anyone were to threaten Dawud and Arden—

The rear door of the limousine opened and she emerged, the afternoon sun turning her hair to spun rose gold. The quiet crowd seemed to still completely. The silence grew complete so the thud of his horse's hooves as it pranced towards the car filled the void. That and the rough pulse of blood in his ears.

What was she doing? No stop had been scheduled. Was she ill? Was his son ill?

Idris vaulted from his horse, thrusting the reins into the hand of a nearby guard, then slammed to a halt.

That was why the cavalcade had stopped?

Arden crossed to the side of the street where the onlookers crowded in the shade of an ancient shop awning. Near the front of the packed group one single person had ignored tradition. A girl, no more than six or seven by the look of her skinny frame. She sat in a wheelchair, gripping a straggly bouquet of flowers, her eyes huge as Arden approached.

In her slim-fitting straw-coloured suit that gleamed subtly under the fierce sun, Arden probably looked like a creature from another world to the girl.

The sight of Arden, cool and sophisticated with her high

heels and her hair up, had stolen his breath when he'd seen her earlier. The air had punched from his lungs as desire surged, as fresh and strong as it had been years ago. Desire and admiration and something else, some emotion that was tangled up in the fact she'd borne his child. *His responsibility to protect. His.*

His visceral reaction had been possessiveness. The desire to claim her, and with far more than words, had sent him into retreat. He'd taken a separate vehicle to the airport and on the plane had immersed himself in work. Keeping his distance meant keeping control.

Arden stopped before the girl and crouched down, saying something he couldn't make out. He strode across, his steps decisive on the ancient cobbles.

The girl whispered something, shyly smiling, and held out the flowers which, he saw now, were no more than a collection of wildflowers such as grew in the rare fertile areas near the city. One of them, yellow as the sun, looked like a dandelion.

But Arden held them carefully, as if they were the most precious bouquet.

'*Shukran jazīlan,* Leila.'

The little girl's face lit up and from the clustering crowd murmurs rose.

Idris stopped, stunned. Arden spoke his language? He listened, amazed, as she went on, haltingly but competently, to ask where the girl lived.

The conversation was short, for soon the child noticed him and grew too shy to speak.

Idris repressed a frown. The girl's reaction wasn't surprising. People didn't address the royal Sheikh unless invited, yet he couldn't help but feel like a big, black thundercloud, blotting out the sun and marring their rapport. Especially when Arden looked over her shoulder, her mouth compressing when she saw him.

He didn't want her to look at him like that. He wanted her to look at him with the dazed longing he'd seen too briefly the day he'd kissed her at her front door. Or, better yet, with that expression of awe and bliss he remembered from years ago, when she'd been eager for him, especially in bed.

His thoughts horrified. Here, on the main street of his capital, under the gaze of thousands of his subjects, he was fretting over a woman. He was caught in a morass of political and diplomatic difficulties because of the current scandal—every waking moment he was busy negotiating a minefield of trouble and trying to salvage the peace treaty—and he let himself be distracted.

Arden stood and turned, her expression this time blank. Which, absurdly, made Idris clamp his jaw tighter as he took her arm and escorted her to the car.

She felt surprisingly fragile beneath the fine fabric of her new clothes, making him even more aware of the imbalance of power between them. He told himself they were both victims of circumstance. He did only what he must for the sake of his child and his country. But he disliked the reminder of Arden's fragility, the fact she'd given up everything she knew to come here, an unwilling bride.

He paused, breathing deep, searching for the sense of calm and control that had eluded him since Arden had burst back into his life.

With careful courtesy he helped her into the car, gave a few instructions to waiting staff, then stalked around the car and got in.

Arden's eyes widened as Idris took the far corner of the back seat. Even with Dawud's child seat between them Idris dominated the rear of the huge limo.

He'd looked larger than life astride his gleaming horse and to her dismay her heart had done crazy flip flops as she watched him through the windscreen. She'd never seen him in traditional dress and was amazed how the horseman's outfit with loose trousers tucked into long boots, a white headdress and light cloak had turned the most attractive man she'd ever seen into the stuff of pure fantasy.

The fantasy had died when she'd turned to find him looming over her like a disgruntled bear. He couldn't have made it clearer that she'd broken some taboo by getting out of the car and talking to little Leila.

Arden refused to apologise. Her heart had caught at the sight of the little girl and that one tiny token of welcome after kilometres of staring, silent, obviously disapproving people.

'Are you going to tell me off now or wait till we get to the palace?' She glanced at the closed window shutting them off from the driver and bodyguard in the front.

'Tell you off?' His words were abrupt, as if jerked from him.

Arden rolled her eyes and turned. He looked as forbidding as he had out on the street but stupidly some weak, utterly female part of her found him compellingly handsome. Her gaze dropped to his sculpted lips, now in a flat line, and she had the crazy impulse to lean over and kiss him till his pent-up fury disappeared.

That was one impulse she would *not* give in to!

She opened her mouth to speak but a sound stopped her. She whipped her head around to stare at the people crowding the street. The noise, a high-pitched, rhythmic trill, swelled, surrounding them, making the hairs on her arms prickle upright.

'What's that?' Reflexively one arm shot protectively across the front of the seat where Dawud slept.

'It's all right. It's nothing to worry about.' Idris's deep voice reassured. 'Quite the opposite. It's a sign of approval.'

'Approval?' Her head jerked around as the car slid forward.

Idris's lips quirked at one corner. Not quite a smile but the closest she'd seen to one in days, and even that had been directed at Dawud, not her.

'Don't look so worried. Approval of you.'

'Me?' She turned back to look out of the window, watching the faces slide by. 'Why? Because I spoke to that little girl? Surely it's not such a big deal.' In the UK it wasn't unusual for VIPs to talk with people who'd waited patiently to see them. Besides, Arden was a long way from being a VIP. She felt like an imposter in this procession.

'It *is* a big deal in Zahrat. Where the royal family is concerned tradition is slow to change. And tradition has it that when the Sheikh enters the city his people will greet him in silence, bowing to show their loyalty.'

Arden's heart sank. She hadn't even arrived at the palace and already she'd broken some important rule.

'So I shouldn't have stopped and got out?' She frowned. 'Leila won't get into trouble, will she? I spoke to her before she spoke to me, you know.'

He shook his head, that elusive hint of a smile rippling further along his mouth. She felt an answering pang deep inside. Once his smile had made her glow all over, when she'd believed he loved her.

'Far from it. She'll be the centre of attention. She'll probably dine out on the story when she's old and grey.'

'So it's just me who's broken the unwritten law.'

'More a guideline than a law.' Lustrous dark eyes held hers and Arden felt her heart thump against her ribcage. 'And I told you, that's approval you hear. You'll hear it again the day we celebrate our wedding.'

She'd got this far by not thinking about their marriage. It was a travesty of all she held dear. To marry not for love but for show went against all the hopes she'd once cherished.

'They were impressed too that you spoke our language.' He paused. '*I* was impressed. Why didn't you tell me?'

'Why should I? Clearly it made no difference to my suitability as your wife.' Was it imagination or did she truly taste bitterness on the word *wife*? 'Besides, I don't really speak it. I started learning but didn't get far. I was too busy with Dawud and work.' She thought grimly how those words glossed over her constant exhaustion as she'd struggled to provide for her son. Lucky she was good at her job so her boss had been understanding. 'I only know some very basic phrases but Hamid helped me practice the pronunciation.'

Idris's eyebrows slanted down in what could only be described as a scowl. What was his problem? That she only knew a few phrases after all? Or was it something to do with Hamid? Surely he wasn't still convinced she and Hamid were lovers? He'd spoken to his cousin. He must know now that wasn't true, even if Hamid had begun to see their relationship leading further than she wanted it to go.

'Nevertheless, it's a valuable bonus that you know as much as you do, and that you've demonstrated it to my people. That's one more thing in your favour when it comes to them accepting this marriage.'

'In addition to my son, you mean?'

Idris had made it clear their relationship, if you could call it that, was a necessary evil.

'*Our* son, Arden.'

For long seconds he held her gaze, till she felt heat rise in her cheeks and turned away. It was fantasy to imagine she read something intimate in those black velvet eyes.

The road was rising and above the rooftops a citadel rose, amber in the sunlight, on sheer cliffs. A massive palace grew there, apparently out of the very rock. Its roof glittered, dazzling her eyes even from this distance.

Idris must have followed her gaze.

'The Palace of Gold,' he murmured. 'Your new home.'

CHAPTER SEVEN

ARDEN HAD BEEN dumbfounded by the palace when she'd seen it from the limousine. But the interior was even more stunning. The older parts of the building featured walls studded with semi-precious jewels, while the modernised sections were unlike anything she'd ever seen.

She knew Idris was a man with a deeply sensual side but she was shocked at the luxury of his home. Until Ashar, her guide when Idris excused himself and disappeared down another corridor, mentioned it had been Idris's uncle, the previous Sheikh, who'd lavishly updated the royal accommodation.

Arden's suite was vast, comprising a bedroom for Dawud with a bathroom and playroom that linked to accommodation for the nanny. For Arden there was a sitting room, study and bedroom. The bedroom had three walls of pale sea-green silk which on one side hid a walk-in wardrobe and a bathroom almost as big as her old flat.

Scallop-edged arched windows gave an unrivalled view of the city and the coast beyond. Her bed, the biggest she'd ever seen, sat on a raised platform with ornamental drapes of silver tissue pulled back from the head. Exquisite raised plasterwork on the wall behind it gave the impression of a vast silvery tree with delicate curling shoots and leaves inlaid with mother-of-pearl.

She couldn't begin to imagine how many hours of craftsmanship had gone into decorating the room, much less the cost.

As for sleeping here...

Arden shook her head. She'd feel like an imposter,

curled up in that vast luxurious bed. The room was a breathtaking fantasy, designed for a princess.

She looked down at the silver-embroidered bedspread, noticing intricately stitched figures of horsemen in procession, banners streaming, riding across the spread. Horsemen with the proud warrior demeanour of Idris as he'd sat astride his stallion today. Until she'd stopped the cavalcade to talk with Leila.

Arden stared at her hand on the fine embroidery. Pale skin instead of the lovely golden colour of the locals and of Princess Ghizlan. Short, sensible nails. Hands that were nimble and strong after years working as a florist, wiring bouquets, lifting heavy buckets of water, snipping and arranging and making deliveries. *Not* the delicate, pampered hands of a princess, despite her recent manicure.

What on earth was she doing here?

Arden's knees gave way and she collapsed onto the edge of the mattress, chest tight and breath unsteady.

Just as well she'd left Dawud in his playroom under Misha's watchful eye while she explored the suite. Arden didn't want him to see her anything but calm. She couldn't afford to let her doubts and fears mar his acceptance of their new surroundings. Not if they were to stay here.

Anxiety gnawed at her belly.

She firmed her lips. She'd already faced this doubt and decided she was doing the right thing for Dawud. Yet that didn't stop the horrible sensation of being trapped. Losing control of her future scared her, as much as the unwanted emotions Idris stirred. The longing for what could never be. What she needed now was something familiar, something normal. Someone on her side.

Hamid. She hadn't spoken to him since the night of the embassy reception. The night her life went off the rails.

Arden reached for her phone, then hesitated. She'd

wanted to talk with Hamid about the change in him—from friend to would-be lover. But so much had happened that she hadn't picked up the phone. Now, thanks to Idris, Hamid knew she was betrothed to his cousin.

She drew in a slow breath. This wouldn't be easy. But no matter what false hopes Hamid had begun to harbour, he'd been a good friend when she needed him and she owed him an explanation. She'd never told him who Dawud's father was, because by then she'd given up trying to find him, believing Shakil had unceremoniously duped and dumped her. Hamid must be reeling too.

She punched in his number and lifted the phone.

Idris found her in the bedroom. She still wore the pale gold suit that emphasised her slenderness, but she'd kicked off her shoes. The sight of her bare feet on the intricate mosaic floor conjured images of the rest of her naked. Naked and willing in his bed. Once her fresh enthusiasm, sweet honesty and sexy body had made her more alluring than any woman he'd known. It seemed that hadn't changed.

His heart gave a now familiar thump—a symptom of the weakness he hadn't been able to eradicate. Even now when, because of her, he faced a diplomatic nightmare in his homeland and more especially with their regional neighbours.

Relations with Ghizlan's country had been tinder-dry for generations and the prospect of a dynastic marriage to seal their new-found peace was a huge win for his people's well-being. Now that was in tatters.

He should be dealing with the fallout, ensuring peace and prosperity, especially now he had a family to care for as well as a nation. Instead he'd taken a break from crisis talks that would go on all night to check on Arden. Idris raised a hand to knock but let it fall as she spoke.

'I understand, Hamid.' She leaned against the window

frame, her posture defeated—head bowed and shoulders slumped. 'Of course.' She swiped at her cheek. 'Goodbye, then.'

The sight of her dejection hit Idris a hammer blow. There was a crammed full feeling in his chest, the suspicion of an ache there at odds with the fire of anger in his belly. Was she really so cut up about leaving Hamid? Had she been in love with him?

Idris considered himself a civilised man, far removed from the tyrants who'd ruled this country long ago. Yet at the moment he'd happily have slammed his fist into his cousin before throwing him into a dungeon.

He stepped into the room, the riding boots he still wore loud on the fine tiles.

Arden's head whipped up and he had a swift impression of tear-glazed eyes and burning cheeks before she pivoted away to place her phone on a bedside table.

When she turned back her colour was high but she was completely composed.

'I'd prefer you to knock before coming into my room.' She folded her arms. Did she know how provocative she looked? Her hair was coming down in sensual waves around her shoulders and her touch-me-not air was an incitement to tip her back onto the bed and put an end to the pretence she didn't want him as he wanted her.

Except she'd been crying over his cousin. The thought was an icy douche to desire.

'You'll need to get used to my presence in the suite.' When she opened her mouth he continued. 'I intend to see my son regularly and establish a relationship with him. I've got three years to catch up on, remember?'

Slowly Arden nodded. 'Of course.' Her voice was croaky. 'But not in my bedroom.'

Idris was tempted to inform her this was the royal bedroom, to be shared by the Sheikh and Sheikha. But she looked so damnably vulnerable with her stiff spine and sad eyes. It made him feel, yet again, that *he* were in the wrong. When he was the one putting things right!

Besides, he'd promised himself he'd keep out of Arden's bed. There was enough scandal already. He would honour tradition and his bride-to-be by keeping his distance temporarily.

'Then come into the sitting room. We need to talk.'

Arden watched him disappear with a swish of his long cloak from spectacular shoulders and fought the squiggle of feminine heat swirling through her.

Would it always be this way? Would she always go weak at the knees around Idris?

She flattened her lips and told herself it was just memory—the fact he'd been her first and only lover. In time she'd look at him and feel nothing.

The enormity of that lie almost undid her. If anything, her yearning for the warmth they'd once shared, the crazy but potent sense of belonging, was stronger than in all the years since they'd parted.

She didn't want to face him. But she had no choice.

He stood near the window, feet wide, hands on hips, face set in stern lines. He looked as if he ruled everything he surveyed.

Arden bit down rueful laughter, realising it was true. He *did* rule it all.

'You wanted to talk?' She sank onto a chair, repressing a flutter of foreboding. His mouth looked stern, as if something displeased him.

That would be her. Already defying protocol on her first day as well as upsetting his plans for a grand marriage.

The idea of becoming Sheikha was as appealing as walking a tightrope. She hated the certainty she'd fail ignominiously.

'I do. We need to set some ground rules.'

'Ground rules?' Her brow puckered.

His wide shoulders lifted. 'We've had no discussion about our expectations of each other.'

Arden sank back. 'You mean like not coming into my room uninvited?'

His lips flattened but he nodded. 'That sort of thing.'

Arden racked her tired brain. This wasn't the best time to talk, when she was exhausted and stressed. But she owed it to herself and Dawud to take the opportunity.

'I want an equal say in all decisions affecting Dawud, his education and how he lives.'

Idris's black eyebrows slanted down. 'There are traditions around how a crown prince is raised.'

'And I'll try to respect as many of those as I can. But I insist on the right to decide, with you.' It was an enormous concession. She'd always made every decision for her son. Learning to share would be tough—relinquishing any control over him scared her. But she'd agreed living here was best for Dawud. Now, reluctantly, she had to make that work, no matter the personal sacrifices, like pretending to be something she wasn't and consulting Idris on important issues.

'If I don't like the traditional ways, I expect full consultation. I expect us to negotiate an agreed solution. And I need that agreement in writing.' Arden laced her fingers tightly. Idris had the weight of royal authority but she refused to budge. She couldn't gamble on Dawud's well-being. 'If you can't agree to that the deal is off.'

Those expressive eyebrows rose. 'You'd try to back out of the marriage?'

Arden lifted her chin. 'Not *try*. I *would*. I'm accepting your terms by coming to live here, and by agreeing to marry. But I won't give up the right to decide what's best for my son.'

For long seconds Idris surveyed her silently, then abruptly he nodded. 'That's fair. I agree.'

Arden sank back, her heart racing. She'd been prepared for a fight.

'What else?'

What else mattered as much as her son?

'I'll try not to flout too many traditions in Zahrat, but I'd prefer to wear my own clothes, western clothes, most of the time. I wouldn't be comfortable wearing a veil.'

His sculpted lips lifted at the corners. 'You may not have noticed, but veils are optional. A lot of women, at least in the cities, opt for western dress. Zahrat is traditional in many ways but very few would expect a European woman to dress in Zahrati costume.' He paused. 'Anything more?'

There were probably lots of things but that was all she could think of at the moment. Except for one thing.

'Even though this isn't an ordinary marriage, I'd prefer it if you kept any…liaisons private. I don't want to know about them and I don't want Dawud to hear about them when he's older.' It would be enough trying to make this marriage of convenience work without Idris flaunting his lovers. The idea of those faceless, but no doubt gorgeous, women made her feel nauseous.

'My liaisons?' The hint of a smile vanished from his face.

'Your lovers.' She dragged in a tight breath. 'I'd appreciate you being discreet.'

His nostrils flared as if he repressed annoyance, but he gave a curt nod. 'Agreed.'

Arden tried to feel relieved but instead felt absurdly wobbly. Her husband-to-be had just promised to keep his lovers out of sight. It wasn't as if this were a love match. It was a paper marriage for purely practical reasons, but it seemed plain wrong to go into it making arrangements for other women to share her husband's bed.

Especially when, to her dismay, he still made her crave intimacies she'd never shared with anyone but him. Not just sex but the warm feeling of being appreciated, being special.

'Arden?'

'Sorry?'

'I asked if there was anything else.'

She shook her head. 'That's all I can think of at the moment. Now, if you'll excuse me...' She made to get up from her seat.

'Not so fast. You haven't heard my expectations.' Gleaming eyes held hers and suddenly Arden found herself breathless.

'It's not enough that I move here and agree to marry you? I'm the one making all the concessions.' Her voice was strident, masking nerves.

'Believe it or not, we're both making compromises, Arden.' He said no more but she knew he was thinking of Princess Ghizlan, beautiful, charming, no doubt with a pedigree a mile long and an innate knowledge of diplomacy and protocol and royal ceremony and all those things Arden was totally lacking.

'Okay.' She knotted her fingers in her lap. 'What else?'

'Since you raise it, no lovers. Not even in secret. Once you marry me I expect complete loyalty.' His face had that stark look again, nostrils flared and jaw taut.

Arden stared. What difference could that make when this wasn't a real marriage? Then she realised she was about to protest just for the sake of it. She'd had no interest in men since Shakil/Idris, especially since Dawud's birth and her almost constant state of exhaustion. As for the frisson of erotic energy she felt when she was with Idris, she knew it was only a hangover from the past. She couldn't imagine herself ever having the time or inclination to fancy herself in love with anyone else.

'Okay.'

His eyebrows slanted up as if he'd expected an argument. 'And I'd rather you kept contact with my cousin to a minimum. Friendships between men and women aren't the norm in Zahrat and your friendship would be misinterpreted.'

'You don't ask much, do you?'

Idris said nothing, just waited for her response.

Once more she felt like refusing him, because surely what he asked was unreasonable. Except she'd already just said goodbye to one of her closest friends. Hamid had told her it didn't feel right to maintain their friendship once she married his cousin. Reading between the lines Arden knew he was hurt she'd chosen Idris. Whichever way she looked at it, her friendship with Hamid was in the past.

'Very well,' she muttered, 'I'll avoid contact with Hamid.' She paused, waiting for more. Except suddenly she couldn't take any more. Arden shot to her feet. 'If that's all, I'd like to be alone now. I'm tired from the trip.'

She was already heading for the door when his words pulled her up short.

'That's not quite all.'

'Yes?' She tried to guess what other condition he'd put on their arrangement. Limiting contact with her other friends perhaps? Or her freedom of movement? Wearily Arden pushed her shoulders back and turned, ready to fight for her rights.

'The wedding.'

'Yes?' *The wedding.* Not *our* wedding. The formal ceremony that would seal her fate and Dawud's. A tremor shot from her nape to the soles of her feet.

'It will be held in ten days.' His tone was even and unemotional. Everything Arden didn't feel at the prospect of marriage.

'So soon?' She pressed a palm to her chest where her heart nosedived.

He shrugged. 'There's no point waiting. The sooner this situation is settled the better.'

Situation being code for *scandal*. For an unwanted wife and an illegitimate son.

'Don't worry, all the arrangements will be taken care of.'

In other words she'd have no say in her own wedding.

Arden told herself that suited her perfectly. 'And if I want to invite anyone?'

'Let Ashar know and he'll organise the invitations.'

'I will.' She paused. 'That's all now?'

A tiny frown settled on Idris's brow. Why? Had he expected her to make demands about the size of the cake or the colour scheme? As far as Arden was concerned it was far better someone else organised the nuptial extravaganza. She didn't have the stomach for it.

'No, that's all.'

'Good. Then I'll see you later.'

She needn't have worried about Idris coming to her room. For ten days she never saw him alone.

So much for the rogue idea he might want her in his bed.

At least he was serious about building a relationship with his son. He'd breakfast with them then stop by after Dawud's bath to play a game or read a story in his own language. The gleam in Idris's eyes when he was with Dawud, the rich, enveloping sound of his laughter, tugged her back to those halcyon days on Santorini. Except, unlike *their* affair, this would last. For, to her surprise, she saw something like love in Idris's expression when he looked at their son, not duty. Their connection was real and growing. It brought a lump to her throat, seeing them together. She'd done the right thing—Dawud needed his dad too.

Inevitably though, Ashar waited in the wings, reminding Idris of his next meeting, making her wonder when he ever stopped.

Arden told herself she was grateful. She didn't *want* to see Idris alone. She had enough to do.

There were the language classes, classes on Zahrati customs and history, plus an increasing number of appointments and requests. Would she wear a gift of exquisite ivory silk from the silk weavers' guild at her wedding? Would she permit a women's embroidery group the honour of decorating the cloth with traditional bridal designs? Would she visit the school Leila, the girl she'd met during the procession, attended?

Her days were crammed and she lived on tenterhooks, knowing and hating the fact she'd inevitably make mistakes. It seemed impossible she'd ever succeed in this new role Idris expected of her. But if she failed would Dawud be accepted? That worry kept her trying, despite her reservations. Despite her exhaustion, she was too wired to sleep. Instead, each night she'd watch the shadows wheel across the vaulted ceiling above her bed.

Tonight, though, she'd sleep. Wedding preparations had begun at dawn and there would be not one but two ceremonies, one English and one Zahrati, followed by feasting and celebrations.

Butterflies, or perhaps a huge Zahrati eagle, emblem of the royal house, swooped and swirled in Arden's stomach as her attendants led her through the palace. As they approached the state rooms the exquisite furnishings became even more lavish, the scale of the interior growing till the cluster of twenty women were dwarfed.

With each step Arden felt the swish of fine fabric around her legs, the weight of heavy antique pearl necklaces so fabulous she hadn't believed they could be real. That was until her golden wedding coronet was placed on her head. Delicately made, it had flowers of ruby and sapphire, each with lustrous pearl petals.

Arden's neck was tight, her shoulders stiff and achy. She told herself it was fear that if she bent her head the coronet would slip off, despite the pins securing it.

But deep down she knew it was the thought of marriage to Idris knotting tension within her. Her heart raced as she halted before vast gilded doors.

Was she doing the right thing?

She was doing the only thing that seemed right for her son.

Still she was more nervous even than when she'd gone into labour.

Her retinue fussed and fiddled, tweaking her long skirts, adjusting her necklaces and bracelets. One elegant lady took Arden's hand in both of hers and said something earnestly in a lilting voice. The other women murmured the same words, smiling, and she guessed it was a blessing.

She was about to ask what they'd said when the doors swung open and sound assaulted her. Laughter, music, voices. Her eyes widened. She'd seen the Hall of a Thousand Pillars before. It was one of the most spectacular rooms in the palace, but never had she seen it filled to capacity. It looked and sounded as if the whole city had crowded in.

Arden stood, dazed. She swallowed hard and told herself she would not flee.

Abruptly all sound ceased as if someone had switched off a soundtrack. Every head turned towards her. She breathed deep, telling herself to enter, but her feet stuck to the floor.

She heard a noise—the steady pace of the man approaching her, tall and magnificent in traditional robes, dazzling in white and gold.

Arden's heart stuttered as he filled her vision, so imposing, so attractive. She reminded herself this was a sham marriage, perpetrated to protect their son. But as Idris smiled and took her hand, heat poured through her. Her pulse leapt and she leaned towards him, as naturally as years ago when she'd loved him with all her youthful heart.

'You are beautiful, Arden. Breathtaking.' The words were for her alone as his lips brushed her temple.

That was when she realised how dangerous this was. How easy it would be to believe the fantasy that she and Idris shared something more than the need to protect their boy.

It was as if she *wanted* to believe Idris desired her, respected her, loved her.

Arden closed her eyes, summoning the courage she'd built over the years when she needed to face down the odds and be strong for Dawud.

When she opened them Idris was still there, still looking like the answer to every woman's prayer.

But he was her partner in a contract, not her lover. Together they would protect Dawud and give him the future he deserved.

'Thank you for the compliment.' It was only encouragement to see her through a difficult day. 'And you look spectacular too.' She let him lead her into the vast room, head up, spine straight and a smile fixed on her lips.

Arden swayed with tiredness as her attendants stripped the exquisite ivory and gold wedding gown away and led her to the bathroom. Steam curled invitingly from the bath in the centre of the room and blush-pink rose petals covered the surface of the water.

A bath fit for a royal bride.

Suddenly all the pomp, glamour and luxury of the day mocked her.

She needed to be alone.

She'd done her best to play her part, smiling through the endless speeches and ceremonies. Not flinching when Idris took her hand and led her to a fabulous gilded throne. Nor when he fed her delicacies from his plate, his eyes shining with a look anyone who didn't know the truth would interpret as desire. Only Arden knew it was satisfaction that they'd got through the day without a hitch.

But enough was enough.

'Thanks very much, but no.' She shook her head as a servant approached, ready to attend her in the bath. 'I prefer to bathe alone.'

Still it took a few moments to convince them she was serious. When they'd gone she stripped off her lace underwear, pinned her hair and sank into the bath.

A sigh escaped. Or was it a groan? The warm water did marvellous things to muscles twisted with tension. For the first time in hours she began to relax in the bliss of the fragrant bath.

She was dozing, her head lolling against the cushioned headrest when she heard the door open.

'I'm fine,' she murmured drowsily. 'I don't need any help.'

'Not even to scrub your back?' The voice, deep and soft like a ribbon of plush velvet, stroked her bare skin.

CHAPTER EIGHT

WATER SPLASHED AS she sat up, twisting towards the door.

'Idris!' It was the barest wisp of sound. Her voice disintegrated as she took him in.

Gone were the white robes he'd worn for their wedding. Now there were only loose trousers of fine cotton, slung low across his hips. His torso was bare, a muscled, glorious expanse of dark gold with a smattering of ebony hair across his pectorals, resolving into a thin, dark line bisecting his abdomen. Arden remembered being fascinated by that line, and where it led, in the week they'd once spent together.

She swallowed hard.

As she watched, muscles rippled across his chest and abdomen, as if stirred by her stare.

Instantly she dragged her gaze up. It collided with a bright, intense look that reminded her she was naked.

Arden drew her knees up to her breasts, looping an arm tight around her legs.

'What are you doing here?'

His mouth curled in a smile that drove a sexy groove down one cheek and made her aware of a sudden ache of emptiness high between her legs.

It was the first genuine smile he'd given her in four years and it made her feel like the lovestruck innocent she'd been on Santorini, all breathless anticipation and hammering heart.

She hated that he had such power over her.

'Why are you here, Idris?' Her voice was sharp.

'I thought that was obvious.' He walked closer and

crouched down so his breath feathered her face. 'I'm here to help my wife bathe.'

'Wife in name only. And I'm perfectly able to take a bath alone.'

'But why should you when you have a husband willing and able to assist?'

'Husband in name only.' Arden gritted her teeth, annoyed at the way her body reacted to the rich, clean scent of sandalwood and man. As if four years hadn't passed. As if she were still besotted with him.

'On the contrary, our marriage is as real as two wedding ceremonies can make it.'

She shook her head, not in the mood for semantics. 'You agreed not to come into my room without permission.' It was a struggle to keep her voice even. All those years he'd visited her in her dreams, taunting her with the knowledge that, despite being an exhausted single mum, she was also a woman with needs. Now here he was in the too tempting flesh.

He braced his forearm on the edge of the bath, inches from her bare shoulder, and she shivered as if he'd touched her. 'Ah. That's where you're wrong. You mentioned that, but if you think back you'll remember it was one condition I never agreed to.'

He lifted his other hand and trailed the tips of his fingers in the water near her knees. He didn't touch her but the ripples he made were like tiny caresses teasing her flesh.

'Stop that!' He stilled and Arden dragged in a shuddery breath. 'Stop playing word games. You're not welcome here and you know it.'

Yet as she spoke Arden felt excitement rip through her at his heavy-lidded look. It stirred her body to tingling anticipation for his touch and, despite everything, for the unique sense of belonging and well-being she'd known in his arms. She reminded herself that was illusory but still her body trembled, igniting anger.

'We married for pragmatic reasons. Don't try to pretend this is about love.' She wasn't foolish enough to fall for that.

Idris shook his head, his expression too close to smug for her liking. 'That doesn't mean we need to keep our distance. Why should we when we want each other?'

'I don't—' Her voice cut out when his hand swirled through the water to caress her knee. Instantly a powerful judder of response racked her.

From a touch to her knee! That should be impossible. But so too should the avid look on Idris's face, as if he wanted to lean in and gobble her up, or maybe taste her slowly. Another quiver coursed through her and she pulled sideways, away from his touch, wrapping her arms tighter round her folded legs.

'Why don't you amuse yourself with one of your lovers and leave me alone?'

'One of my...?' For the first time Idris seemed lost for words.

'I don't want you in my suite.' Even though her body cried out for him. It was a shocking realisation but she'd get over it, just as she'd got over so much in the past.

'First—' he leaned in, all trace of a smile gone '—this is *our* suite. My bathroom and dressing room are on the other side of the bedroom.' Behind what she'd thought were blank walls? 'Rather than have you and Dawud settle into guest rooms then move after the wedding, I thought it would be less disruptive for Dawud in particular not to have to move twice. I've been sleeping elsewhere till the wedding.'

Dimly, part of her applauded his concern for their son. But mainly she was stunned by the revelation he'd expected her to share his bed all this time.

'Second, I don't have lovers waiting in the wings. I haven't had a lover in…' he shook his head '…a long time. I've been busy with other things.' He drew in a deep breath that expanded his chest mightily, reminding her of his sheer physical strength and beauty.

'Do you really think I'd go to another woman on my wedding night?' He looked angry, as if she'd insulted him.

'Why not? Unless you think because I'm conveniently close I'm available. If so, you're completely wrong.' Old bitterness welled. She understood now that Idris hadn't deliberately avoided her all those years ago but it was hard to erase the pain of rejection. 'You can't ignore me for weeks then swan in here, expecting intimacy.'

'Ignore you! I've seen you every day.' His face drew tight in that dangerous expression she'd privately dubbed his bronzed warrior look. 'I've spent every waking hour trying to smooth the way so that our marriage is viewed positively instead of as a hole-and-corner affair. So you and Dawud are accepted and welcomed. So we can live in peace and safety if I manage to salvage this treaty.'

Idris looked proud and forbidding. Yet Arden's heart leapt. There was something incredibly invigorating about being at the epicentre of all that furious energy.

But it wasn't enough.

'I'm not some *duty*.' She tipped back her head and glared. 'I'm a *person*. You can't treat me like a stranger then expect me to have sex with you.'

The harsh words jarred. Once she'd thought of it as making love. Glorious, heaven-touching love. But she'd learned a lot since those days of innocence. Idris had never loved her, though she'd been besotted enough to throw in her job and follow him to Paris.

His nostrils flared as he bent closer.

There was something incredibly intimate about the fact he was inhaling the scent of her skin and the exotic cinnamon and pomegranate wash they'd used on her hair this morning. He was drawing her in and, despite her anger, her body was eager for him to devour her.

'You think I treated you as a stranger?' His voice dropped to a deep note that wove its way into every sense receptor in her body. 'You think I ignored you?'

Idris tilted his head from side to side in a slow, emphatic negative. His hand closed around her knee in a deliberate, possessive hold that stilled her breath.

She'd never been attuned to any man as she was to Idris. Even wanting to break free, she couldn't deny the connection between them.

'For ten days I've worked myself into a stupor rather than come to your bed.' His voice grated, harsh and low. 'For ten days I've done the right thing, honouring you as a bride should be honoured. For ten days I've tortured myself with the sight and sound and scent of you.' He paused, inhaling again, and another of those erotic quivers coursed through her. 'But I didn't touch because I respected you. And I wanted everyone to know that.'

Idris leaned in, so close his dark eyes and golden skin filled her vision.

Arden was drowning in a sea of sensation. His touch on her bare skin, the intoxicating promise of sensual pleasure in his velvety eyes, the scent of him, potent male with a hint of sandalwood, even the sound of his breathing, steady and strong, dragged her down into a well of desire.

'And because you want me I'm supposed to welcome you with open arms?' Fear spiked. She suspected surrendering herself physically to Idris would be more complete, more irrevocable even than marrying him. A piece of paper, however important, was nothing compared with the intimacy of sharing herself.

'No, *habibti*. You'll welcome me because you want me

too. That hasn't changed, has it? The desire is as strong as ever.'

Arden opened her mouth to deny it when she realised he'd taken his hand from her knee. She felt it now underwater. Deep underwater.

Unerringly his big hand stroked between her legs, insinuating itself between her thighs and finding the spot where the heavy, sensual pulse of arousal struck hard and fast at the core of her.

Arden gasped and stiffened, clamping her thighs tight. It was too late. He was already there, stroking that most secret place with a sure yet delicate touch that sent whorls of excitement spiralling through her.

'Stop that!' She made a grab for his forearm underwater but couldn't shift him. Instead she felt the fine movement of tendons as his fingers flexed and stroked.

The sensation was too unsettling, as if she contributed to her own weakness, and she ripped her hand away, clutching the side of the tub instead, gasping.

She made herself stare up into his gleaming eyes. 'I don't want this.' But it wasn't true. Torn pride demanded she reject him. But the lonely, needy woman who'd once found magic with this man stirred to life.

'If I believed that for a second I'd walk out the door.' Abruptly the stroking fingers stopped, ending the addictive pressure on that sensitive nub, and to her dismay Arden realised her hips were tilting, lifting up towards his touch, pressing herself against him.

The tiny movement was utterly telling.

She stifled a sob of distress, of shame laced with despair. *She wanted him again...still.* As if those four lonely years had never been.

Yet instead of gloating over it, Idris said gently, 'Let me do this for you. You've been wound so tight all day I thought you'd break.'

Arden prised open tight lips, though what she'd have said she never discovered because he touched her again. This time he delved while his thumb circled, and sensation shot through her, making her jump and her breath snatch.

Instinctively she grabbed for support, one hand on the rim of the bath, the other on a hot, bony shoulder, padded with muscle.

'That's it,' he whispered, his voice at the same time soothing and incredibly sensual. 'Hold on tight.'

Eyes like the midnight sky held hers. This close she saw soft dark brown against black pupils. If it weren't for the fierce intensity of that stare she'd call it tender. Tender enough to soothe her lacerated, confused soul.

Then there was no time for thought as, with one deft stroke, Idris toppled her over the edge. Delight exploded, razing her defences and her self-protecting lies.

Dark eyes held hers as she rode wave after wave of pleasure till, at the end, she had no place left to hide. And no energy to maintain the fiction that she didn't want him every bit as much as she had four years ago.

Triumph warred with tenderness as Arden came apart at his touch. He felt each juddering spasm, heard each snatched gasp, her sweet breath was warm on his face, her hand clawing at his shoulder so hard she probably scored his flesh. And through it all those remarkable aquamarine eyes locked with his, drawing him into ecstasy till he feared he might explode, just watching her come.

It felt as if he'd waited a lifetime to possess her, not a mere couple of weeks. It was a miracle he hadn't simply stripped off and taken her where she lay in the water.

Except, even now on their wedding day, Arden didn't make anything easy. Accusing him of having a lover tonight of all nights! What sort of man did she think he was?

It infuriated him and slashed at his pride that she'd believe such a thing. He'd done nothing but treat her with courtesy and respect and still she...

She blinked and to his amazement moisture welled, drowning her lovely eyes. The sight jabbed something sharp and hard through his gut, skewering him. Her mouth twisted as if in anguish and she swung her head away so all he saw were damp wisps of rose gold hair clinging to her pinkened shoulder and throat.

She regretted this?

Idris slowly drew his hand back, feeling a final, needy clench of her muscles. Despite the bliss he'd given her, he hadn't broken down Arden's resistance. He knew he'd hurt her terribly, that she'd suffered because of his unintentional desertion. But he'd been sure she was ready to start afresh. Sure she wanted him as he craved her.

Had he really expected this to be so easy?

Somewhere Fate laughed at him and his foolish ego.

He looked at her ripe mouth, caught at one corner by white teeth as if even now she fought the bliss he'd bestowed. Her body might be ready for him, but emotionally Arden wasn't.

Memory slammed into him, of her bent head and defeated voice as she spoke to his cousin on the phone. She'd said he wasn't her lover, but clearly there was something between them, or had been, till Idris entered her life again.

He got to his feet, towering above her. In the sunken bath her milky pale body, flushed here and there with the rose blush of sexual satiation, was too much like the erotic fantasies he endured night after night.

Breathing quickly, trying to ignore the fragrance of sweet woman, he pivoted away, wrenching his mind from the need to possess her.

'Idris?' Her voice, husky and soft, tantalised. 'Where are you going?'

His shoulders set like granite.

'I won't force myself on an unwilling woman.' The knowledge she didn't want him scalded his pride and something else, something unnamed that hurt far more than he'd believed possible.

Idris heard the rush of sluicing water and felt warm drops splash the backs of his legs, sticking thin cotton trousers to steamy hot skin.

'*Unwilling* would be an exaggeration.' She was breathless. 'I was so sure I didn't want this. Now I don't know what to think.' The pain in her voice tore at him.

He closed his eyes, seeking strength. His groin was rock-hard, throbbing with the need, not just for release, but for *Arden*. He wanted to be inside her, feeling her come again, grabbing him tight with the undulating waves of her next climax. He wanted her complete surrender. He wanted her screaming his name—*his* name and no one else's.

He didn't think he had the stamina for any more celibate nights with her under his roof.

Hands clenched, he spun round.

Everything, his thoughts, his determination, even his pride, melted. Only his body grew impossibly harder at the sight of her, standing up to her thighs in water. Her hair glowed, framing her flushed face. Her beautiful Cupid's bow lips parted as if eager to taste him. Her eyes shone brighter than any gems in the royal treasury and her body was a symphony of delicate femininity. Between her thighs was that V of rose gold, hiding the gate to Paradise.

His gaze swept back up, pausing, fascinated by the delicate, shimmery striations just visible on her belly—marks where her satin-soft skin had stretched to carry his child.

A bolt of lightning struck down, welding his feet to the floor.

He'd never seen a more desirable woman, never felt such primitive possessiveness.

'Don't toy with me, Arden.' His voice was strangled.

She took a slow breath that lifted her tip-tilted breasts towards him. 'I'm not.' She swallowed and he watched the convulsive movement of her throat. 'I thought I could keep my distance. Keep separate. But I can't.' Her mouth crumpled at the edges and his chest squeezed. 'I was wrong. I want you, *still*.'

She didn't sound happy about it. He recognised the same conflicting emotions he felt—tension, need and something akin to fear at the force of what was between them. From the first he'd felt *more* with Arden. Every need, every emotion had been more intense, more real.

Arden held out her arms, slick and shining with water. 'Take me.' Her eyes held his and power jolted through him.

He needed no second urging. In one swift movement he scooped her up, one arm at her back and the other beneath her knees. Her wet, glorious body against his was a form of perfect torture as he marched across the marble floor and into the next room.

The cover of the vast bed had been pulled back, the sheets scattered with delicate petals.

There was nothing delicate about Idris's movements. Four huge strides took him to the bed. An instant later Arden landed on the mattress, her breath expelling in a soft *oof* of air as he followed her down, pressing against her slick body, revelling in the slide of smooth flesh against his.

A groan sounded in his ears. His? Hers? It didn't matter, for now she was touching him, her hands skidding over his shoulders and down his back, so low they slipped beneath thin cotton to cup his buttocks.

Instinctively he thrust forward, hard and high, revelling in the slide of flesh against flesh, heat against silken coolness. Her fingers curled tight, grabbing, as her thighs lifted, cradling around him in a damp caress.

Idris had a momentary impression of sultry, half-lidded

eyes, the eyes of a temptress inviting a lover, then Arden's hands slipped up his back, cupping the back of his neck to pull his head down.

Their lips fused and this time it was Arden setting the pace, Arden angling her mouth against his, a delectable hum of need vibrating from her throat and filling his mouth. Her tongue seduced his, eager and sensual, and he felt the power of that erotic connection right through him. His erection pressed heavily against her belly, his hips shifting with the unbearable tension.

Dimly Idris registered his complete loss of command over his body. It was moving of its own volition, incited by this sensual woman to abandon any hope of control or expertise. Instinct and hunger drove him. Already he was fumbling at the drawstring of his trousers, shoving the material down, scrabbling to be free.

He was just lowering himself back to Arden's delicious body when ingrained habit halted him.

'What's wrong?' Her words were the faintest, muffled sound in his mouth.

'Condom.' He paused, dragging air into tight lungs. Even as he said it he knew he wanted nothing more than to be inside her, no barriers between them. The thought was so arousing he scowled, drawing on every ounce of control not to shatter prematurely.

Idris wrenched away, lunging for the bedside table. Since they hadn't had that vital conversation about future pregnancies, he'd taken the precaution of bringing a box of protection. A large box.

'You were so sure of me?' Her voice held an edge.

Idris rolled on the condom, gritting his teeth at his sensitivity, then turned to her. Deliberately he slid his knee over hers, dragging it towards him, opening her thighs. His palm settled on her soft belly.

'Sure of *us*.' His voice was gruff. Speaking grew harder

each second. 'This is mutual, Arden. You must know that. I've been burning for you since I saw you again in London.'

Veiled eyes held his, as if she sifted the truth of his words. Then he lifted his hand to capture her breast and her breath hissed in.

She was so soft, so delicate, so perfectly made for him. How could he have gone all these years without finding her again and inviting her into his bed?

Idris lowered his head to capture her nipple between his teeth, grazing it gently, and she almost catapulted from the bed. He leaned over her, covering her, enjoying the slide of his body against her slick flesh.

This time he flicked her nipple with his tongue, cupping her satiny breast, overwhelmed by the familiarity of her. Beneath the fruit and flower aromas of Zahrat from the bath, it was the scent of Arden that befuddled his brain. The feel of her—familiar as if they'd shared a bed just days, not years, before, the tiny growl of arousal at the back of her throat that made his erection pulse eagerly against her thigh.

His hand tightened around her breast, his teeth nipped harder. Delicacy was beyond him. What he felt was too primal, too urgent to be contained.

Yet she welcomed him, grabbing his shoulders and urging him higher. He caught a flash of aquamarine between slitted eyelids, felt her restless bucking, heard those urgent mews of pleasure and knew she couldn't wait either.

Idris shifted to lie within her cradling hips, the bulk of his weight on his arms. His eyes rolled closed when she tilted her pelvis, grinding herself against him.

Then there was nothing but instinct and pleasure, pure pleasure, as he nudged her entrance and thrust home with one sure stroke.

She cried out, a husky sound of welcome that he tasted

as he took her lips, possessing her mouth in mimicry of the way he took her body.

Arden wrapped her arms behind his back, pulling him in. He slid further still when she lifted her legs and locked them around his buttocks.

The feel of her surrounding him everywhere was too much. He withdrew a fraction then surged high and hard and the ripples of pleasure began.

Fire caught his throat and chest, flames flickered in his blood at the tightness, the slick heat, the absolute perfection of her taking him in.

Another thrust and the ripples became shudders racking them both, making them jerk and shake together, turning fire into an explosion of white-hot ecstasy. Idris swallowed her shout of elation as he pulsed within her then disintegrated into tiny splinters of being. His world shattered in the exquisite pleasure-pain of sensation stronger than anything he could remember.

CHAPTER NINE

ARDEN WAS OUT for the count, limp with satiation, yet Idris couldn't keep his hands off her. She'd slept at least an hour and he was only human. He'd already fumbled on the bed-side table for another condom and sheathed himself, yet still she hadn't stirred.

Idris ran his palm over the sinuous curve from her shoulder down her ribcage to her narrow waist then up to her hip. Lying on her side, that intoxicating female outline was even more pronounced.

His hand drifted from her hip to her belly, feathering the soft down between her legs, and she sighed in her sleep, shifting and stretching. He smiled, closing the gap be-tween them. Immediately he felt her buttocks press back, cushioning his erection.

His breath stalled. His heart pounded so hard she must feel it hammering against her back.

'Shakil?' Her voice was a drowsy mumble that made him smile, though he registered chagrin that she'd used his boyish nickname.

Even half-awake she knew it was him. He'd hated the thought of the other men who'd no doubt been in her life. It was unreasonable, but he wanted to be the only man she'd ever had.

He remembered his soaring elation, the unexpected hu-mility of learning he was her first lover. That had to ex-plain this deeply proprietorial response he hadn't been able to conquer since London.

That and the fact she's your wife.
Your life has changed for ever.

Yet the dread voice of reason couldn't dim the sheer excitement of having her in his bed.

His.

Idris slid his fingers down, following that downy arrow to her sensitive nub. Her breath caught on a sigh and her pelvis tilted into his touch. She might be barely awake but she wanted him. He pressed his mouth to her neck, tasting the rich sweetness that was hers alone. Then her earlobe, scraping it gently with his teeth, and she shivered delicately, her back bowing again, arching that lush bottom into his groin.

But it wasn't enough. 'Tell me what you want.' He needed to hear it again.

'You. I want you.' Her voice was husky with desire and it aroused him as much as her sexy body. More. Her admission was potently exciting, even though he'd observed, as long ago as London, the attraction she tried to deny.

She wriggled, pressing herself against his groin, creating a firestorm of wanting.

In one swift movement he rose to his knees, grabbing her hips and lifting her so she knelt on the bed before him, his hands planted hard on her hips, caging her to him. Idris waited, breath bated, partly to give himself time to regain some control and partly to see Arden's reaction.

She bunched the sheet in her outstretched hands and shimmied her hips back and up into his pelvis.

Idris swallowed a groan of pain. It was exquisite torture, bliss and unbearable longing, kneeling here, with her so inviting before him. Impossible not to look down, to see her peach of a backside pushing at his erection.

Once again the firestorm hit—a blast of longing, of desperate arousal stronger than anything he could recall.

Had it always been like this? He'd thought his memories of their affair were coloured by the crises that followed, turning it into a glorious, perfect interlude because of the grimness immediately afterwards. He'd thought he'd imagined the perfection of their passion and that sense of being in the one place in the world he needed to be. But as he guided himself inside her, one hand welded to her hip, his rapt gaze on the erotic sight of their joining, he knew memory hadn't exaggerated.

Arden gave another shimmy of her hips so he lodged deeper in her welcoming warmth, and Idris knew once more the panicked delight of impending climax.

Where was his patience? His sensual prowess? His ability to savour sex and please his partner?

Gone the second Arden welcomed him into her body.

Desperately he bowed over her, one hand seeking her pouting breast, cupping it and rolling her nipple between thumb and forefinger so she jerked against him, her breath a hiss of air. His other hand arrowed down between her thighs, straight to her moist centre, pressing down on that sensitive nub as he withdrew then hammered home again, right to her core.

Her hands on the sheets were white-knuckled, her movements as she pushed back rough and urgent. He clamped his hand harder around her breast and she gasped, rolling her head back. Instantly he was there, leaning in, biting her earlobe, in time with the thrust of his body and the hard circling of his fingers.

'Yes!' Her triumphant shout filled the night. 'Yes, yes, yes. Shakil!' She grabbed his hand on her breast, pressing it to her as her body began to quiver around him. The quivers became shudders, caressing him, milking him with a sweet ferocity he couldn't resist.

With a groan of rapture he grabbed her hips and spilled himself, hard and fast into her slickness.

His last thought before he collapsed on her and rolled them both onto their sides, still joined, was that next time, surely, he'd be able to take it slow.

* * *

Arden squinted against the light. Surely it wasn't time to get up. Had they managed to sleep at all?

Heat bit her skin from her scalp to her toes and everywhere in between as she remembered the urgency with which they'd made love. With such desperation it made her think of stories she'd heard about people who'd survived some terrible life or death event and were driven by instinct to procreate.

Once she'd believed love was the reason she and Shakil had made the earth tremble on its axis. Now she realised sex and love needn't intersect. There was something about the man she'd married, something she responded to every time, that made the sex earth-shatteringly wonderful.

Sex, she reminded herself. Not lovemaking.

Disappointment eddied. With herself for not completely banishing that old yearning for love. A touch was all it had taken for Idris to smash through her caution. She'd acted as if the last four years had never been!

She opened her eyes wider, taking in the rumpled bed, the sun streaming in the arched windows and the complete absence of her husband.

There might have been rose petals strewn on the bed but this wasn't a hearts and flowers marriage. It was a cold-hearted convenience for the sake of their son and her husband's reputation.

'You look pensive this morning.'

Idris strode towards the bed, damp hair slicked back, buttoning his shirt.

Instantly Arden's heart fluttered and her stomach gave that little quiver of anticipation she despised. No matter how often she told herself she felt nothing for Idris, her body betrayed her.

She needed to conquer or at least control her response.

If she didn't she feared it would make her completely vulnerable.

'I need more sleep.'

Except one glance at him and it wasn't sleep on her mind. A pulse twitched between her legs and she shifted beneath the sheets, drawing his gaze. When his eyes met hers they gleamed hot and hungry and Arden found herself wondering at his stamina. How he found the energy even to walk she didn't know.

'Then sleep. I need to farewell those guests who stayed overnight.'

Reluctantly Arden dragged herself up against the pillows, drawing the cotton sheet around her, ignoring his raised eyebrow that reminded her he was intimately acquainted with every bare inch of her.

'If you wait fifteen minutes I'll come too.' Arden felt imprisoned in this new world that had been foisted on her, and by last night's proof of weakness. She didn't want to stay here, brooding, with the bedroom walls closing in. Besides, she had to start as she meant to go on. For Dawud's sake she'd fulfil her new royal role, as far as she could.

'No need.' His mouth widened into a smile that could only be described as smug. 'No one expects to see you today.'

Arden frowned. 'Yet they expect to see you?'

He grabbed his watch from the small table covered in condom wrappers, smiling at her as he strapped it on. The sight was ordinary yet intimate, reminding her they really were tied in marriage, husband and wife, come what may.

'As a vigorous man in the prime of life I'm supposed to take a wedding night in my stride.' His eyes flickered and Arden wondered what he was thinking.

'And the bride isn't?'

He shrugged and there was no mistaking the satisfaction in his tone. 'A new bride might be a little...tender, and need rest.'

'After a *vigorous* night with her new husband?' By a miracle Arden didn't blush. She was more than a little tender. She felt exhausted but also dangerously exhilarated, which disturbed even more.

'Precisely.' His high wattage smile rocked her back against the pillows. 'There'd be dismay if you appeared. People would think I hadn't done my husbandly duty.'

His words pummelled her. It had been husbandly *duty*, nothing more. Except, she guessed, surveying his lazy satisfaction, pride and the masculine ability to take pleasure wherever it was offered.

And she'd offered. She'd been as eager for Idris as he was for her. The difference was that to him she was just an available body. For her there still lingered shreds of the sentiment she'd once felt for him.

She had to change that fast, before she fell for that old romantic daydream.

'You never told me about that day in Santorini. What message you passed on.' The words blurted out before she realised she'd formed them. Suddenly it was vital she knew the whole truth.

'Sorry?' Idris was halfway to the door but turned at her words. 'What message?'

'You said you'd arranged for someone to meet me four years ago. At the rendezvous that last day when you couldn't meet me.'

'That's right.' Slowly he nodded.

'But you never told me what you'd instructed him to say.'

Dark eyes bored into hers. 'It hardly matters now. What matters is our future.'

Oh, it matters. From his sudden stillness, she guessed it mattered very much.

'Humour me. Was he going to take me to meet you in Paris or…?'

Idris breathed deep, his chest expanding as he took his time answering.

'I didn't go to Paris. My uncle was dangerously ill so I returned here.' He swung towards the door. But Arden wasn't letting him off. She'd spent years wondering about that day.

'So what was your message for me?'

He paused. For the first time Arden felt Idris was at a loss. Yet this was the man who took international scandals in his stride, even the discovery of a son and a forced wedding.

His gaze settled at a point beyond her head. 'To give my regrets and say we couldn't be together after all.'

Arden told herself she wasn't surprised, despite the chill clinging to her bones. 'To say goodbye.'

He nodded, his eyes briefly meeting hers. Then he exited the room.

It was what she'd expected—that, despite her girlish dreams, he'd planned to reject her that day. She, in her innocence, had fallen in love with the handsome stranger who'd swept her off her feet. But to him she'd been a mere holiday amusement. There'd never been any question of him taking her to his home. Her grand romance had been a fantasy.

Arden watched him leave and told herself she was grateful she'd finally unearthed the truth. What better time than now when, in the afterglow of Idris's lovemaking, she was in danger of reading too much into their intimacy?

He'd never wanted her as she'd wanted him. Never needed her.

Something inside her chest crumpled but she breathed through the pain.

It reinforced the lessons life had taught her. Those she

cared about always ended up leaving her to fend for herself. First her parents. Then the foster parents who'd changed their mind about adopting her when they discovered they were expecting a child of their own.

Then Shakil.

Just as well she wasn't in love with him any more. She'd moved on, even if Idris could still make her feel more than she should.

The only person she loved, who loved her back, was her son. That, she reminded herself as she shoved the sheet aside and headed for the bathroom, was all she needed.

At least Idris was honest about his feelings, or lack of them. She was grateful for that. He made it clear their marriage was solely to scotch scandal and provide a solid future for Dawud.

In the bathroom she wrenched on the taps in the shower, spurning the idea of a languorous soak in the tub. The decadence of that sunken tub, and what had happened there last night, was too dangerous. She needed to ground herself. A shower, fresh clothes and time with Dawud. Then she'd apply herself to the long, daunting process of learning what was expected of a royal sheikha.

It didn't matter that she felt doomed to fail and completely overwhelmed. She bit back a silent scream of hurt and helplessness, refusing to let tears well. She had to find strength. She *had* to make this work. Dawud's future depended on it.

Idris found her, not in bed but playing with their son in a private courtyard.

He forced down disappointment. He'd returned as soon as he could, the image of her waiting for him in bed, her hair a golden cloud around bare milk-white breasts, had distracted him through the protracted farewells, leaving him aroused and edgy. Never had the tedium of official duties weighed so heavily. He'd all but thrust the last guests through the palace portals.

He squashed annoyance that she hadn't waited for him, naked. He should be grateful she was a caring mother. Right? Wasn't that what this marriage was all about?

But as he stepped from the shadows of the portico it wasn't their necessary marriage consuming his thoughts. It was sex, hot and urgent, with the woman who diverted him from all thoughts of duty.

'Baba!' He heard the cry as Dawud's beaming smile caught him full-on. There was a curious thud in the region of his chest, as if his heart had missed a beat then pounded out of rhythm. Then he was crouching, arms open, as his son hurried over, his dark hair tousled into the beginnings of curls—just like Idris's own hair if he let it grow.

'Watch out, he's wet!'

But Idris didn't mind. He closed his son in his embrace, ignoring the way the little wet body saturated his clothes.

His son.

Idris had been surprised from the first at the feelings the boy evoked. They grew every day. And they made everything, the hassle of organising a royal wedding in record time, the frowning disapproval of the old guard, even the strained relations with Ghizlan's father, fade to nothing. He was more determined than ever to secure peace, now it meant protecting his son.

'Baba.' Dawud lifted a hand to Idris's face, tiny fingers patting at his cheek and nose.

Idris laughed and caught Arden's surprise. It made him realise how rarely he laughed. Until Arden and Dawud arrived he'd spent all his time working. Yet he'd enjoyed the last weeks with them, despite the enormous strain of dealing with crises.

He greeted Dawud in Arabic and was amazed when

Dawud answered in kind, lisping a little on the unfamiliar words.

'He remembered what I taught him!'

'He's a quick learner.'

Idris nodded, taken aback by the swell of pride at his boy's cleverness. Did all fathers feel this way? His father had never doted on him, caught up instead in his schemes for personal pleasure. Idris had been closer to his tutors, including the hard men who'd taught him the ancient arts of warfare.

'He likes to please you too.'

Arden's voice made him look up. She stood, hands clasped tight as if to stop from reaching out to grab their son. The twist of her lips told him it wasn't simple pride she felt. Didn't she trust him with Dawud?

Idris had worried he'd get this fathering thing wrong with no role model to guide him. So far he seemed to be doing okay but would instinct be enough as Dawud grew?

Yet even as the familiar doubt surfaced he noticed the way Arden's wet blouse had turned transparent, giving him a tantalising view of luscious breasts in a lacy half cup bra. She took his breath away every time.

Idris stood, lifting Dawud into his arms, but the boy wriggled to be let go. That was when Idris noticed the plastic toy boats floating in the shallow pools inlaid with tiny tiles of lapis lazuli, marble and gold.

His lips quirked as he put Dawud down and watched him plump with a splash into the couple of inches of water, immediately absorbed in his game with the boats.

'You don't mind him playing here?' Arden's expression was guarded. 'There's no playground but I thought he couldn't hurt anything here, if he's supervised.'

Idris thought of the painstaking, delicate work that had gone into creating the ornamental pools with their exquisite sixteenth century mosaics. They were national treasures, one of the reasons for the palace's heritage status.

'I think it's a perfect place to play with toy boats. I wish I'd thought of it when I was young.' When he was a kid there was no way any of his royal uncle's entourage would dream of letting a small boy enjoy such freedoms. 'We must see about a proper playground. Perhaps with a sandpit and a climbing frame?'

He watched with pleasure as some of the tension bled from Arden's stiff frame. 'That would be perfect. Thank you.'

That confirmed what he'd known from the first—the way to Arden's good graces was through their son. Even after a night spent in Idris's arms, she'd looked anything but relaxed until he started talking about plans for Dawud.

Regret stabbed. Was that really their only connection? Their boy? It should please him that Dawud was so important to her, yet pride demanded she acknowledge his own place in her life.

Then he saw the tension in her twined hands. Of course she wanted him. He couldn't have asked for a more willing, generous lover. But they were strangers still. He needed to give her time to adjust to her new life.

Idris settled himself on the warm flagstones behind their son, reaching forward to propel a tiny sailboat forward. Dawud crowed with delight, splashing his appreciation and chattering. Idris joined in, enjoying the game, heedless of the water drenching his formal robes. Dawud's excitement, the laughter, the spray of water in the sunlight, created a sense of well-being, as if for once there weren't a million tasks clamouring for Idris's attention. As if this simple joy was all that mattered.

Arden dragged a chair into the shade of an ornamental tree and sat on the other side of the pool, watching. It struck Idris that, no matter what the law said about his rights as a father, she was working hard to allow him access to his son. Not every woman would make it so easy.

'It must be hard, sharing Dawud after all this time.'

Her eyes widened, their pale depths glittering in surprise. 'I…' She shrugged. 'It takes a little getting used to. In the past I was the only one he'd run to. Me and his nursery teacher.'

'Not Hamid?'

The question was a mistake. Arden tensed and the easy atmosphere fractured.

'Hamid was always kind to Dawud but he never got down on the ground to play with him.'

Her words pleased Idris. It was petty to compare the relationship he'd begun to build with his son against his cousin's. Yet he couldn't fully excise that sliver of jealousy over the time Hamid had spent with Arden and Dawud in London.

'Hamid was a friend. He never acted like Dawud's father—'

'And he wasn't your lover?' Snaking distrust wound through him.

'I've said it before and won't say it again. You'll have to take my word for it.' Her chin lifted and her eyes flashed and Idris had never wanted her more.

Her stare might spit fire but, aware of their son playing between them, she kept her voice low. It struck him that his hunger for her wasn't purely physical. There was something about the way she protected Dawud that got to him at a level every bit as primal as sex.

The mother of his son. A woman who'd do anything for their boy, even marry a stranger in a strange land.

Pride throbbed through Idris. Pride and admiration. And, as ever, that undertow of desire.

'I apologise, Arden. I should have taken your word from the first.' Despite the remnants of jealousy, he believed her. What did she have to gain by lying? Even Hamid had made it clear they hadn't been lovers. Idris had to conquer this dog-in-the-manger jealousy. It was completely out of character.

Arden provoked emotions that were unique—both positive and negative. He wanted to understand why. Understand her.

'Why did you call him Dawud? A name from my country, not yours?' She'd believed he'd abandoned her, so it was odd she'd given their son a name that linked him to Idris's homeland.

She lifted her shoulders, her gaze veering away. 'I went to an exhibition of beautiful antique artefacts from Zahrat and discovered one of your rulers had been King Dawud. I liked the name and wanted our boy to have some connection to your country. To own a link to his father's heritage as well as mine.'

'That's very generous, given what you thought of me.' Idris frowned. 'It surprised me.' And it was one of the reasons he'd thought Hamid her lover.

'Wouldn't you have accepted him with an English name?'

Idris stared her down till her cheeks flushed pink. Surely she couldn't believe he'd ever deny his son? 'I would have accepted him no matter what. But it makes it easier for our people when he has a name they recognise.'

Again that little shrug. 'It's close enough to the English name David if he wanted to change it later. But I thought he'd appreciate some link to his father's culture.'

'That's why you began learning Arabic? To teach our boy?' Idris should have made the connection. Now it struck him how significant her actions had been. Even believing herself deserted, Arden had tried to build a bridge between their son and a cultural inheritance to which she was an outsider. Idris leaned closer, fascinated by such generosity of spirit.

'I wanted Dawud to feel he belonged, to feel a sense of connection, even if he never knew his father. I believe it's vital for a child.'

The way she spoke, the determined glint in her eyes, suggested this wasn't just about Dawud. Idris raked his memory for what he knew of Arden's history. All he knew was that she had no family. But maybe that explained her fierce purpose in giving Dawud links to his paternal as well as maternal cultures.

He was about to ask when Dawud set up a grizzling cry. Instantly Arden was on her feet.

'It's past nap time. I'd better dry him off and let him rest.'

'I'll carry him.' Idris scooped up Dawud and tucked him close. Despite the wetness and the jarring kick of one small heel against his ribs, he enjoyed holding his boy.

They walked together into Dawud's room where Idris reluctantly handed him over. The interlude of intimate communication was over. He should return to his office. It might be their honeymoon but securing peace took precedence, especially now he had a family as well as a nation to protect.

Yet Idris paused, watching mother and son. Again that hard thud resonated through his chest as if his heart beat out of sync.

'Thank you, Arden.'

Her head shot up, her brows furrowing in puzzlement.

'King Dawud was my grandfather. A great leader and revered among my people.' It was a shame his son, Idris's uncle, hadn't ruled in the same mould. 'I'm honoured you named our boy after him, and pleased that you thought to give Dawud such a gift. You could as easily have severed any connection with my country. I appreciate what you've done for him.'

Her eyes rounded, her mouth opening a little before she snapped it shut. 'It seemed only right.'

Idris knew that for many women doing what Arden had would have been a step too far. He admired her for that.

He was discovering Arden was far more than a sexy bed mate and the mother of his son. She might even have the strength and generosity to prove the naysayers wrong and become the Sheikha his kingdom needed. The wife he hadn't realised he wanted till now.

Perhaps marriage wouldn't be nearly the trial he'd imagined.

CHAPTER TEN

ARDEN SMOOTHED THE skirt of her full-length dress. The silvery material was soft as gossamer, the cut amazing. Only the best for the Sheikh's wife.

She stared at the intricately inscribed wedding band on her left hand, proof she really was the Sheikha.

Her mouth quirked. Her life was full of such proofs. She hadn't slept alone since the wedding and had grown used to curling up against Idris's hot, muscled body through the night. She'd almost become accustomed to the hum of arousal that filled her when he looked at her with that particular gleam in his dark eyes.

She'd stopped fretting over the fact she enjoyed the sex, enjoyed being with him. Surely it made sense to accept the perks in this marriage of convenience. Especially when increasingly she caught glimpses of the charming, engaging man she'd known before duty took over Idris's world. That man made her smile even when her day had been exhausting.

A pity she found it far more difficult being royal.

The sight of people bowing before her made her feel a fraud. Even on her visits to schools where the children seemed fascinated by their ruler's foreign wife, Arden felt like an interloper. She enjoyed being with the kids, sharing their smiles and enthusiasm, but all the time she knew they believed her to be someone special when really she was utterly ordinary.

Except for the fact she'd married Idris.

Daily she struggled with the simplest of royal protocols. As for understanding who was who in the complicated hierarchy of regional politics... Arden had given up trying to follow the complex behind-the-scenes machinations and treated everyone with the same courtesy she would have in London. She'd seen raised eyebrows at several gaffes but it was the best she could do. She wasn't bred to this role like Princess Ghizlan.

The thought of Ghizlan made her eyes dart to her dressing room's full length mirror. Arden didn't have Ghizlan's panache but she had to admit that tonight she looked different. With her hair up and wearing a stunning silver couture dress, she looked a far cry from the frazzled single mum who'd attended the royal reception in London in a borrowed dress.

Different enough that Idris would notice?

Of course he'll notice. He doesn't miss anything.

What you mean is, will he appreciate you as he would someone like Princess Ghizlan?

The snide voice made her stiffen. Was she really that pathetic? Idris noticed her. And he was attracted. Their passionate lovemaking proved that.

But Idris made the best of circumstances, as she did. He hadn't chosen her because he loved her, or because she met the qualifications of a well-bred princess. He hadn't really chosen her. She'd been foisted on him by circumstance and scandal.

And still she craved—not his approval—but his admiration. She wanted to be more than an encumbrance or a convenient partner.

Arden stared into the shadowed eyes in the mirror and knew that was bad. She shouldn't need any man's admiration to feel good about herself. This…craving was a weakness. A sign she felt far more than she should for the man she'd married.

Or perhaps, she thought with relief, it was just that things were so different here. She was out of her depth so surely it was natural to crave a sense of belonging, of being appreciated.

A glance out of the window at Zahrat's capital city, a mix of ultra-modern and traditional architecture, reminded her how far she was from home. Everything here, though fascinating and often surprisingly modern and easy, was foreign. Her experience of the world beyond the UK was limited to the single week in Santorini when she'd met and fallen for Idris.

She had so much to learn. No wonder she was floundering, despite the intensive lessons. She hated feeling so out of her depth. It ate at her self-respect.

'Sorry I'm late.' The deep voice made her spin round.

Idris stood in the doorway, in his tailored tuxedo looking scrumptious enough to eat.

Heat radiated across Arden's throat and cheeks as she remembered the way she'd nibbled her way along his body this morning. She'd paused to savour the taste of him till he'd growled impatiently and flung her onto the mattress, imprisoning her with his bulk and driving them both to completion with a series of quick, perfect lunges that reminded her again how very good he was at sex, how experienced, especially compared with her.

'Are you okay?' His brow knitted and he stepped closer. 'I'll be by your side all evening. There's nothing to worry about.'

Arden forced her mind away from the delights of his naked body. 'Of course there isn't. Who'd get nervous about a royal reception for several hundred VIPs?'

Idris smiled and her heart gave that little shivery beat. The man had too much charisma, especially with that hint of a laugh in his eyes. 'Most of them will be more nervous than you. Besides, all you need to do is smile and be yourself. They'll be charmed.'

Sure. As if the local glitterati were interested in the

ramblings of a London florist whose passions, apart from her son and her sexy husband, were gardening, tennis and curling up with a good book.

'I've brought you this. I thought you might like to wear it tonight.' He held up a box of royal-blue leather, stamped with ornate gilt work. Arden recognised it. The diamond and pearl necklaces she'd worn at their wedding had been lifted reverentially from similar boxes.

'That treasury of yours must be enormous,' she murmured, forcing a smile to cover her nerves. The value of the pieces she'd worn at the wedding had only added to her tension. What if she'd damaged them?

'It's big enough. Remind me to take you to look. You could pick out some pieces you like.'

Arden couldn't imagine it. She wasn't the sort to wear pigeon's egg rubies to show off her newly manicured hands.

'Aren't you going to open it?'

Her eyes snapped to his. She thought she read excitement there. But she must have imagined it—a second later and the impression was gone as he glanced at his watch. It was time they made their appearance.

Taking a deep breath, Arden lifted the tiny gold latch then raised the lid. Whatever she'd been about to say disintegrated as she gasped, barely able to take in what she saw.

'You like it?'

Arden shook her head. Surely it couldn't be real.

'Of course it's real.' Had she spoken aloud?

A large, square hand plucked the exquisite choker necklace from its nest of oyster satin and lifted it, dazzling her.

The piece was about two inches wide, diamonds and platinum creating a delicate tracery of leaves that sparkled outrageously. Above and below it was edged with what looked like ribbon but was actually square cut green stones she guessed were emeralds. The necklace secured at the back and at the front it dipped gracefully towards a single huge faceted emerald drop.

'I've never seen anything like it,' she croaked. It should belong to an empress.

'Here, let me.' Idris stepped behind her and she felt the cool weight of it around her throat, the pendant heavy against her skin while his fingers deftly closed the clasp at her nape. 'Take a look. It goes perfectly with what you're wearing.'

Arden was still in shock and it affected her hearing. To her ears Idris's voice sounded strangely hoarse. And the grip of his hands as he turned her towards the mirror seemed to dig in too hard.

She lifted her head and stared.

'Well?' Idris cleared his throat over unfamiliar tightness. 'Do you like it?'

'I don't know what to say.' In the mirror Arden's eyes were huge, but she didn't smile.

Why didn't she react? In the past generous gifts to lovers had been received with enthusiasm.

But this was different. *She* was different. He'd never had a lover so unconcerned with his prestige and wealth. Arden tried hard to fit in with life at court but he suspected she wasn't impressed by its pomp.

Which made him wonder how she felt about *him*. It niggled that, except when they were naked, he found it hard to read her thoughts.

He'd commissioned this personally with her in mind. He'd seen some preliminary work by a renowned jeweller and immediately imagined it gracing Arden's slender throat. He'd never before had something made specifically for any woman. Was that why he was eager for her reaction?

It looked superb. Regal but feminine. Elegant but incredibly sexy. So sexy he wanted to see her wear it and nothing else. He wanted to ignore the guests waiting in the Hall of a Thousand Pillars and make urgent love to her.

Then make slow, thorough love to her all over again.

He was on fire and not just because she looked spectacular in silk and emeralds. He always burned for her. Even when she wore old clothes to finger paint with Dawud. Especially when she wore those tight jeans...

Idris forced his hands from her bare arms, looking over her shoulder at her reflection in the glass.

His wife. His queen.

She was beautiful.

'Say you like it.' The words jerked out, appallingly needy, as if he craved approval. It was an unfamiliar feeling, one that disturbed him.

'I like it.' Their eyes met in the mirror and his doubts fled. What he read in her face, the softening warmth and wonder, were everything he could want.

It reminded him of her ardent passion. Every time they had sex she made him feel more than the man he'd been before. He was rapidly becoming addicted to that radiant pleasure.

This was the first time Arden had regarded him with that glowing wonder when they weren't having sex. Idris wrapped an arm around her waist, tugging her back against him, revelling in the way she fitted so perfectly.

'Though I'm not sure it's really me,' she whispered. 'I'm more a noodle sort of girl.' Her mouth twisted wryly in that self-effacing way and Idris recognised the reference to the bangle she and Dawud had made one day out of dry pasta.

'Believe me, it's you.' She mightn't be the most classically beautiful woman in the world, but Arden had a vibrant loveliness all her own. 'You look spectacular.'

Soft colour washed her cheeks. 'Not as spectacular as you.'

'Even without diamonds?' He pretended to preen and was delighted when she giggled.

Two months of marriage and he'd discovered her smiles could change his mood in an instant. Each one felt like a gift to be savoured. More and more he found himself responding, teasing and laughing, living in the moment instead of always focused on work.

Why was Arden's warmth and enthusiasm so potent? He put it down to the fact it was easier to live with a woman who was upbeat and practical, ready to meet him halfway. He'd discovered marriage far less difficult than expected, if he didn't count the continuing fallout over his choice of bride. Though even that was fading as diplomacy, frantic hard work and his bride's refreshing ways worked their magic.

'Diamonds would be overkill with that dinner jacket.' Her smooth brow furrowed. Her fingers went tentatively to the emerald resting just below her collarbone. 'You're sure about this? I can't help feeling nervous wearing something so expensive and beautiful.'

Idris had never heard any woman express such a sentiment. Arden continued to surprise him.

'I'm sure. You can pretend it's made of pasta if that makes it easier.'

She grinned and a shaft of warmth shot straight through him. 'I might just do that.'

'Come on, Princess.' He turned and held out his arm.

He couldn't describe the feeling inside when she smiled up at him and slipped her arm through his. Satisfaction, triumph, pride. None quite captured the unfamiliar blast of delight he experienced as he swept out of the room with Arden on his arm.

Arden was flagging after the initial round of introductions but gamely kept her chin up. How Idris managed so many handshakes, so many bows and introductions from people all eager to make an impression, she didn't know. Her muscles ached from fatigue, even though she'd taken Ghizlan's advice and worn beautiful shoes that were still comfortable and not skyscraper tall.

She wished Ghizlan was here. It would have been comforting to have a friend on her side. People were generally pleasant, except for those few older men who always regarded her stonily as if her presence was a catastrophe. Arden drew in a slow breath, reminding herself acceptance would take time.

Nevertheless it was tough keeping up the image of royal correctness. Formality didn't come naturally to Arden.

Ghizlan had understood her total inexperience. There'd been no need to pretend with her and that had been liberating. Against the odds they'd bonded over the fiasco in London. Ghizlan had texted answers to questions about dress codes and etiquette, along with scurrilously funny anecdotes about ceremonial disasters, for months now. But in the last few days there'd been nothing. Not since her initial response to Arden's sympathy on her father's unexpected death.

Ghizlan had returned home and it was no surprise she had no time for messages. Idris said there was some question over who would succeed Ghizlan's father as Sheikh. Ghizlan would be busy with that and—

'Excuse me, Sire. I must talk with you.'

Arden blinked, stirred from distraction by the voice of the palace steward. The line of people being presented had petered out so she and Idris stood a little apart from the throng, on the royal dais. Two thrones inlaid with gold and precious stones dominated the area and she'd deliberately turned her back on them. Silly to be overawed by some furniture but they, like the eye-watering perfection of the necklace she felt every time she swallowed, reminded her she was an imposter here.

'Can't it wait?' Idris matched his voice to the steward's low tone.

'I'm afraid not, Your Highness. I would have done something about it before but you asked me to leave tonight's arrangements to my staff—'

'Because I entrusted you with the celebrations to open the new city hall and convention centre next week. I value your expertise to bring it off in style.'

'I pride myself it will be a success, sir. But in my absence there's been a...regrettable error of judgement. A problem with the banqueting hall I've just discovered.'

'A problem? It was in perfect condition yesterday. Has it been damaged?'

A tingling began between Arden's shoulder blades. A tingling that skittered down her spine and wound into her belly, unsettling her already nervous stomach. She swung around to meet the palace steward's eyes just before he dragged his gaze back to Idris.

The tingling became a wash of foreboding, stirring nausea. Had she erred again? And tonight of all nights, when she'd been at such pains to complete her royal duties with grace and decorum?

'Not damage as such, Your Highness. If I'd been here it would have been rectified immediately. Unfortunately my second in charge, though competent, isn't as familiar with the way things must be done.'

The old man's eyes flickered but didn't meet hers. Yet Arden knew instantly he was remembering the times they'd clashed. The day when, thin-lipped, he'd warned her that using an ancient mosaic-floored corridor for games with Dawud was inadvisable. And that allowing a group of visiting schoolchildren into one of the palace courtyards might not only damage national treasures but show disrespect for royal tradition.

His manner intimated that disregard for the riches surrounding them was only what he'd expect of an outsider who had no concept of Zahrati custom and sensibilities.

'I'm afraid it's probably my fault,' Arden said, her voice defensively brusque. She was tired of being on the back foot, continually reminded of the many ways she didn't measure up as a royal spouse. Not that Idris ever said a word. But others, like the steward, were always sure to tell her.

'Your fault?' Idris smiled and heat danced through her, reminding her of the strange intimacy between them when he'd given her the necklace. Of the sense, for a second or two, that maybe she was wrong and there was more to their marriage than convenience and necessity.

The steward shuffled his feet and the idea shattered.

'I suspect the problem relates to today's visitors. Am I right?'

She met the steward's guarded stare with outward confidence. She mightn't like the man, might even believe he was deliberately difficult, but she had no intention of showing her horror that once more she was in the wrong. First there'd been the contretemps when an elderly lady had curtsied to her and Arden had impulsively helped her rise when it seemed her knees had locked. How was she to know that touching a stranger at court without invitation was a shocking misdemeanour?

Since then there'd been several *faux pas*. The night she'd used a fruit spoon instead of the purpose-designed sorbet spoon from the vast array of gold cutlery was the least of her dining mistakes. The reception where palace staff, eager in the knowledge their new Sheikha had a reputation for liking flowers, had installed numerous floral arrangements complete with trailing jasmine. Sadly Arden hadn't thought to warn them she was allergic to the scent and she'd spent the evening sneezing through every speech.

'I met with some school groups today.' She turned to Idris, her smile perfunctory. 'You said it was all right to have them here.'

Since her visit to Leila, the girl who'd offered her a bouquet in the street, Arden had been invited to several schools. Seeing the enthusiasm of both children and adults, Arden had sought Idris's approval to invite some school groups to the palace. Today goggle-eyed children had taken in the grandeur of the reception rooms while teachers expounded on the palace's historic treasures.

Another reason the steward disapproved of her. Previously only VIPs saw the palace interior. In Zahrat there was traditionally little direct contact between the royal family and their subjects.

'I'm sorry,' Idris murmured. 'I didn't ask you how the visits went.'

'Excellent. I thought it a success, and so did the teachers. The children were excited but very well behaved.' Arden glimpsed the steward's impatience and felt her heart sink. Obviously something had gone wrong. She hoped some priceless ornament hadn't been damaged.

'So what's the problem?' Idris turned to the steward.

'It's the banqueting hall, Sire. I just returned to the palace and saw the room had been *decorated* in a way that made it unfit for tonight's formal dinner.' He almost groaned his horror. 'I told the staff to fix it immediately but was informed the Sheikha had said the…decorations were to remain until she directed otherwise.' His glare said what he thought of that.

Over the steward's shoulder she saw staff opening the doors into the adjoining banqueting room. Arden's pulse fluttered as she remembered how that room had looked today when the children visited. Laughter bubbled inside but it died as she watched the first of the exquisitely dressed VIPs pass through the open doors. They all looked so suave and important.

'I'm sorry.' She swung around to Idris. 'It's my fault. The younger children brought gifts as a thank you for their visit and I said we should display them. Some of the staff seemed eager to remove the decorations as soon as possible but I didn't want to disappoint the kids by taking them down while they were in the building. I told the staff to leave them till I instructed they be removed.' Except later she'd forgotten.

'That's the problem?' Idris frowned. 'Gifts from children in the banqueting hall?'

The steward stepped closer. 'No fault attaches to the children or teachers. The gifts were a sign of appreciation. But sadly they are inappropriate in such a majestic setting. Especially given tonight's formal diplomatic dinner.'

The man didn't look at Arden, but something inside her shrank. Clearly if fault lay anywhere it was with her.

Once she'd have thought the old man overreacted, but she knew Idris had faced a firestorm because of their marriage. He'd worked tirelessly to rectify damage from the scandal. Tonight was a major part of his campaign to have his nobody of a foreign wife accepted. The place was filled with diplomats and VIPs.

Had she sabotaged it? Arden felt sick at the thought.

'Thank you, Selim, for the warning. We'll manage from here. I'm sure it will be all right.' Idris took her arm, holding it high as he led her off the dais and towards the crowd disappearing into the banqueting room.

Arden's stomach felt like lead but she had no choice but to tilt her head up, fix on a smile and follow his lead.

Idris paused in the doorway to the vast banqueting room and tightened his lips to repress a broad grin. Elegant guests milled around tables laid for a seven course banquet. Surrounding them were pillared walls of shell-pink marble carved by master craftsmen generations ago. And blooming on the priceless marble was a lopsided, improbable field of bright blossom.

Huge paper flowers in purple, orange, sunburst-yellow and even sky-blue crowded the surfaces in ragged, enthusiastic abandon. He spied names written in crayon on the leaves.

Idris paced further into the room, Arden with him, her hand cold in his. Was she so nervous of the official reception? She'd done marvellously through the lengthy introductions, greeting people with a charm and warmth that came naturally to her. She was a people person and a welcome breath of fresh air.

'It's fine,' he said under his breath, pressing her hand reassuringly. 'Nothing to worry about.'

Her fingers twitched in his hold and she nodded, but her smile looked fixed. Damn Selim for bustling in, making a fuss and upsetting Arden.

That was why Idris had put the steward in charge of the city hall opening. It was an excuse to get him out of the palace. Idris knew he took any chance to show her up.

He led Arden towards a cluster of lopsided sunflowers. 'I've never seen the place so festive.'

She looked up, eyes wide. 'Not even at our wedding banquet?' she murmured.

Idris remembered the cloth of gold swags at each entrance, the garlands of exotic lilies intertwined with crystal and pearls on each table. 'These are simple but they're gifts from the heart.' He preferred them to the formal opulence of the wedding.

He turned, smiling and raising his voice so the guests could hear. 'I hope you enjoy the decorations for our meal tonight. You all know my wife's interest in our children and her visits to local schools. These are gifts brought by students from those schools. I think you'll agree they show great enthusiasm and creativity.'

There was a murmur of voices and a few nods though some of the guests still looked bemused.

Idris caught the eye of the Minister of Education, one of the government leaders who'd actually been eager for the modernisation Idris had been leading.

The Minister inclined his head. 'Encouraging our children in art as well as the sciences is traditional in Zahrat. It's good to see that continuing with the personal support of our new Sheikha.' He smiled and Idris heard Arden's snatched breath. She hadn't expected the compliment.

The realisation angered Idris.

He'd been so frantic dealing with the fallout from his sudden marriage and its impact on both the peace treaty and his own position. Becoming a husband and father had distracted him too. He'd known Arden faced difficulties but hadn't realised she felt so vulnerable. Guilt hit.

He pulled her close, abandoning any pretence of royal dignity as he wrapped his arm around her waist, ignoring the way she stiffened.

'Come,' he ordered, his voice rough with barely concealed annoyance at himself. He should have done more, he saw now, to ease her into her new responsibilities. He should never have left it to his staff. 'Tell me about these flowers. Particularly this one.' He injected a light-hearted note. 'It seems, intriguingly, to resemble a camel.'

Tense she might be, but Arden was quick. 'That's because it's a camel, despite the petals. The little boy...'

'Ali?' Idris tilted his head to read the name written on one knobbly camel's leg.

'That's it.' Her smile looked almost natural now. 'Ali confessed he didn't like flowers. He likes camels so that's the shape he cut out. But when he heard the class had been asked to make flowers for me because I liked them, he compromised by putting petals on his camel. That's why the hump droops.'

Idris chuckled, imagining the scene, and there was a ripple of laughter as guests moved to inspect the work.

By the time they sat down to dinner, Arden, sitting opposite him with an ambassador on one side and the Minister for Education on the other, looked almost relaxed. Her smile wasn't radiant, but as the meal progressed the horrible tension he'd felt in her dissipated and she charmed her companions with her ability to listen and her direct questions.

Idris had been right. Arden would make an excellent sheikha. Just as she was a superb mother. And as a wife—

She lifted her head abruptly, catching him staring. Pink stained her cheeks as their eyes met. By the time she looked away Idris found himself impatiently counting the time till they could be alone together.

CHAPTER ELEVEN

IT WAS WELL past midnight when they reached their private apartment. Arden was exhausted. Every muscle groaned from being held taut so long. Her jaw ached from smiling and a stress headache throbbed in time with the beat of her pulse.

Idris had handled the situation suavely, turning what could have been embarrassing into an opportunity to promote his agenda for improved education.

Yet the fact remained he'd had to cover for her slip up. Again.

Everyone made mistakes. It was just that hers were always in a glaring spotlight of public disapproval. And after months of marriage she was making as many as ever.

Arden had known she wasn't suited for the role of royal wife. How long before her shortcomings created a rift between Idris and those who supported him?

She knew he was popular—he'd gathered support through sheer hard work and the positive results of every hard-won reform. But she also knew there were traditionalists in high places horrified at the scandal surrounding his marriage. And her unsuitability as his wife. People who could make trouble, not just for her but for Idris and all he was trying to do.

She'd been on tenterhooks tonight, trying to remember the correct forms of address and so many other minutiae of Zahrati custom. She'd been congratulating herself on getting through the first part of her trial by etiquette when the steward brought his news.

Nor had she missed her husband's set expression when he'd entered the banqueting hall and discovered its elegance marred by wonky paper flowers. Idris hadn't been impressed.

'I'm really sorry about tonight.' She crossed to the dressing table, pulling out hairpins, stifling a sigh as the tight, elegant coiffure disintegrated into waves around her shoulders.

'Sorry?'

Arden put the hairpins down, hating that her fingers shook. Keeping up the appearance of ease all evening, while her stomach roiled with nerves, had taken its toll.

Abruptly she turned, only to find Idris right behind her. He grabbed her shoulders before she could walk into him, his dark eyes peering straight into her soul.

Arden's heart kicked. Even weary and despondent, desire shivered through her. Her need for him was constant, unrelenting. He didn't love her and her love for Idris had died in the years she'd believed he'd abandoned her, yet her yearning for him only seemed to grow.

If she wasn't careful he'd take over her life even more than he had already. She'd lost her home, her job, her independence. She couldn't afford to lose any more. She needed to be able to stand up for herself and her son.

Arden sidestepped, dragging in a quick, relieved breath when he dropped his hands.

'I'm sorry about the banqueting hall. That was my fault. I should have had the artwork taken down hours ago.'

She just hadn't thought of it. Straight after the school visits she'd met a delegation of women who'd travelled two days to present their new Sheikha with gifts they'd prepared themselves: delicious attar of rose scent and exquisitely woven stoles. Then there'd been an afternoon crammed with language lessons and appointments, including one with a stylist who'd clearly been challenged by Arden's riotous hair. There had been barely enough time to see Dawud before his bed time.

'Don't fret, Arden. It's not a problem.' Idris's soothing voice only stirred her guilt. She knew tonight could have been a disaster. 'Our guests loved the decorations.'

He stepped into her line of vision but didn't touch her. Arden was glad. She wanted distance, didn't she?

Except, stupidly, she also wanted to lean her tired head on her husband's broad shoulder.

'Only because you turned it into something they could relate to. If not for that...' She shook her head, remembering the initially stunned looks from their guests and the palace steward's outrage.

'You're worrying too much. You saw the reaction Ali's camel got.' Idris's chuckle wrapped around her like balm on a wound and the gleam in his eyes tugged at her. 'Maybe we should add Dawud's finger painting to the display. What do you say? I think the boy's got real talent.'

Despite herself Arden grinned, thinking of Dawud's latest picture of the three of them, all heads and spindly legs. And how Idris had joined in the painting, teasingly threatening to daub her nose with red paint when she dared to critique his efforts.

'Our guests were delighted by the art. It's exactly the down-to-earth touch I want. The palace has been cut off from the people too long. Maybe we should expand those school visits into a regular programme.'

'Your steward will love that,' she murmured, trying and failing to picture the old man smiling as children invaded the Hall of a Thousand Pillars.

Instantly Idris sobered. 'He won't be here. Tomorrow he'll be relieved of his duties.'

Arden gazed, stunned at Idris's stern expression. It gave the lie to his assurance that tonight had been a storm in a teacup.

'I told you—' she stepped near, inhaling the scent of

sandalwood and spicy male '—that was down to me. It wasn't his fault.'

Idris shook his head. 'I'm not worried about the banqueting hall. What concerns me is that Selim made a ridiculous fuss about it in front of you. I know he's a stickler for the old ways and he makes you nervous with his fussing. That's why he's been working outside the palace.'

Arden's jaw dropped. 'Because of *me*?' She was torn between dismay that her discomfort had led to such drastic action and glowing warmth because Idris had tried to make things easy for her.

His mouth tightened, his expression austere. 'You are my wife and his queen. If he makes you uneasy he goes. Permanently.'

Arden blinked. Before her eyes her husband had morphed into the proud autocrat she remembered from London. It struck her that she hadn't glimpsed that man lately.

Idris might get distracted by politics but she enjoyed being with him. He was patient and gentle with Dawud, passionate with her. Good company, she realised, sometimes teasing but never dismissing her concerns. Never aloof.

The autocratic warrior King hadn't made an appearance in ages. To her surprise she wasn't fazed by him any more. Now she understood that expression was Idris determined to do what he believed was right, even if difficult. He'd moved on from the carefree, thoughtless man she'd once known. She discovered she actually liked this man better—the complex mix of strength and honesty, of decency as well as passion and humour.

'You can't dismiss him.'

'I won't have him making you nervous. He undermines your confidence.'

Arden stared, flummoxed that Idris had noticed what

she'd taken care to hide. 'How do you know? Most of the time you're not around when I'm with him.'

One sleek jet-black brow tilted high. 'I notice everything about you, Arden.' She had the strangest sensation of his words echoing endlessly within her. His stare was intense, as if he read her deepest secrets. He lifted a hand, stroking her cheek in a butterfly touch that resonated right to her core.

Arden felt the weight of something powerful between them, something she couldn't name. Then he spoke and the instant shattered.

'He unsettles you. He'll leave tomorrow.'

She caught Idris's wrist. 'No. Don't do it.'

'I won't have you undermined.'

Arden's lips curved in a tight smile as she recognised that her husband's support bolstered her flagging determination. It was *she* who'd made a mountain out of a molehill tonight. She'd let herself be led by Selim, fretting over something that, now she considered properly, was a minor glitch.

'He works hard and he's good at what he does. He doesn't deserve to lose his job.' Still Idris looked unconvinced. 'I can cope. I *prefer* to.'

'There's no need. Let me do this for you.' The look in his eyes made her chest tighten as she forgot to breathe. She dropped her hand from his. She wasn't used to being looked after. It was nice but scary too…unfamiliar.

'I know you're trying to help but it would be wrong. He *does* fuss and make me feel like an uneducated barbarian—' Idris's breath hissed. 'But he's retiring soon.'

'In thirteen months.' Idris must have checked. For some reason that lightened her mood. He really had given this thought, and not just tonight.

'That will give him time to train his replacement. Besides, I can learn a lot from him.'

Still Idris frowned.

'Did I ever tell you about my first boss, when I began as a florist?'

He shook his head.

'She must have liked something about me since she hired me but to begin with I never did anything right, even sweeping the cuttings off the floor.'

'She sounds like a tartar.'

'She was. But she was also passionate about what she did and expected the best. She insisted everything I did was the best it could be.' Arden shook her head. 'I remember rewiring the first bridal bouquet I did for her until I got it just right. But in the end I was glad she was so picky because I acquired the skills and confidence to cope, no matter how demanding the work.'

Something like a smile danced in Idris's eyes. 'That's why you'd rather keep our palace perfectionist?'

Arden lifted her hands, palm up. 'He's here and has an encyclopaedic knowledge of royal ritual and custom. I might as well make the most of him, even if he does make me want to gnash my teeth sometimes.'

Idris's laugh curled round her like tendrils of silk, caressing tight muscles. Even the dull headache diminished a fraction.

'On one condition.' The laughter faded. 'If you change your mind, or if I catch a hint of disapproval from him, he's out.'

'Agreed.' Yet still Idris didn't look totally sold.

'I'll be fine, really.' Surprisingly, after the doubts that had dogged her so long, she actually believed it. Something had changed tonight and it made her more than ever determined to make a go of this official side of their marriage.

The private part was already working well.

Well? She'd never imagined anything so good. Dawud was thriving. Idris was a caring, involved father and as a husband…she couldn't ask for more. He was considerate, passionate and respectful of her needs.

It would be too easy to believe their union was real, a marriage of hearts as well as minds. Alarms sounded in Arden's head. This was no match made in heaven.

She shifted back a fraction, making her point. 'I appreciate you supporting me. But it's important that I stand on my own two feet. It's the only way I know.'

Freshly showered, Idris flicked off all the lights except a bedside lamp and slipped naked between the sheets. Arden was in her bathroom and he'd been tempted to seduce her there. Except he remembered how she'd trembled with tiredness as they talked. He'd seen her tension and guessed her head ached. She'd slitted her eyes against the light and more than once lifted her hand to her forehead, massaging absently.

When her bathroom door opened, predictably his body tightened with desire. Her hair was a frothing, rich gleam around pale shoulders and her lacy nightgown clung to that delicious body the way his hands itched to.

Day after day, night after night, he couldn't get enough of Arden. A heavy schedule, the burden of renegotiating a new agreement with neighbouring kingdoms, all the concerns of a ruler for his country, couldn't distract from this hunger. It puzzled him how passion kept growing, intensifying rather than diminishing with familiarity.

She slipped into bed and he saw the shadows beneath her eyes, the furrow of pain on her brow. Regret rose. He could convince her into sex. She'd enjoy it—he'd make sure of it. But Arden had had enough for one night.

'Here, move closer.' He lifted the sheet, encouraging her to his side of the bed.

'I'm tired, Idris.' Even so, he saw the way her gaze dipped down his bare body.

'I know, *habibti*. You can just sleep.'

He'd never been fond of sleeping tangled up against anyone. The exception had always been Arden. When they'd first met he'd put it down to exhaustion, after wearing themselves to the point of oblivion with sex. These past months, though, Idris had discovered he *liked* holding her as they rested. It felt…satisfying.

'It doesn't look like it's sleep you have in mind.'

His erection throbbed in response to her stare and Idris hauled her close. Instantly his body hardened still further, eager for intimacy. The wriggle of her hip then her buttocks against his arousal as she turned to spoon against him, tore the air from his lungs.

'Stop twitching,' he growled.

Was that a tiny, breathless laugh? He slid his arm around her and cupped her breast, his thumb moving in a deliberate, slow caress of her peaking nipple.

'Idris!' The sibilant was soft and drawn out, just the way he liked her saying his name. A grim smile tightened his features as he tried to ignore the pleas of his body.

He distracted himself with the fact she'd called him Idris. In the first weeks of marriage Shakil had been the name on her lips when she urged him on in the throes of passion, or when she cried out in climax. It had felt oddly as if she betrayed him with another man. Shakil might only have been his younger self but Idris had wanted Arden in the present, making love to *him*, not a memory.

He hadn't heard the name Shakil for more than a month. That pleased him, satisfying a proprietorial side to his nature he'd never before recognised.

'Shh. Relax.'

'How can I relax when you do that?'

Sighing, Idris released her breast, sliding his hand down lace and silk to splay over her belly.

He focused on controlling his breathing and found his thoughts turning to the idea of Arden carrying his baby. He'd missed so much—her pregnancy and Dawud's early years. The idea of sharing such experiences appealed, the idea of her pregnant again stirring impulses he was trying to stifle.

'You're twitching,' she murmured.

'You're distracting me.' He only had to catch her light orange blossom scent and he was distracted. 'You said you were used to looking after yourself. Why is that?' Talking would take his mind off his body's torture. Besides, he wanted to know.

'I'm used to being alone.'

Idris found that hard to believe. But then he'd been stunned all those years ago in Greece to discover Arden was a virgin. 'Are all the men in England blind?'

She huffed out a laugh and the movement made him grit his teeth. He was sensitive—too sensitive.

'You're such a smooth talker.'

'Only stating the truth. Surely in all these years there was someone…with you.' Idris chose his words carefully.

'I *told* you; your cousin was just a friend. A good friend and, after a time, my landlord. But that's all.'

'No need to get het up. I believe you. But in four years there must have been someone.'

'Must there?' She paused and Idris realised he had second thoughts. He didn't want to know about her love life after all. 'Well, you're wrong. There was no one.'

'No one?' It barely seemed possible. Yet elation rose in a soaring wave. It shouldn't matter. She'd been a free agent, like him. Yet the idea of Arden with other men—

'Don't sound so surprised. I was pregnant to start with and later…' Later, what? Surely he didn't expect her to say she'd pined for him. Not when she'd thought he'd dumped her. 'Later there were barely enough hours in the day for everything that had to be done, looking after Dawud, working, scrimping to make ends meet.'

Guilt tightened his gut. His splayed hand pressed her close. 'You don't have to worry about being alone ever again.' He'd take care of them both. They were his responsibility. More, he *wanted* to look after Arden and Dawud.

Instead of easing in his embrace, Arden stiffened as if she might pull free of his hold.

'What is it?' Sixth sense told him he'd hit a nerve.

'Nothing. I'd like to sleep now.' But she held herself rigid, her breathing short. She was hiding something or, he amended, protecting herself. From him? The idea was like biting down on a crisp apple, only to taste the sourness of decay.

'I mean it, Arden. You have me now, as well as Dawud.' Surely she didn't think he'd abandon them? Not after he'd gone to such lengths to marry her?

'Yes.' Yet her voice didn't convince.

'Why did you make such a point earlier about the fact you were used to standing up for yourself?' She'd made similar comments in London.

'I told you; it's what I've always done.'

Silence. Not the companionable silence of a few minutes ago, but an edgy wariness. He'd bet her eyes were wide open. He felt tension hum through her.

'Me too,' he said slowly, deciding against another direct query. 'I was an only child. That makes a difference, don't you think?'

She shrugged. 'I suppose so.'

'I wasn't close to my parents. Well,' he amended, 'to my mother when I was very young. But she died when I was just a kid.'

'Really? How old were you?'

'Four.'

'I'm sorry.'

'It was a long time ago. I had my father and aunts and uncles, plus my cousin, Hamid.'

'Your father brought you up?'

Idris felt his lips tighten. 'My father wasn't a hands-on dad. He had other interests.' Like seducing other men's wives. His father's relentless pursuit of pleasure and string of conquests hadn't made him warm or contented.

Idris had started out the same. Not seducing other men's wives, but sowing plenty of wild oats.

'I was brought up by tutors and members of my uncle's court. There was a focus on honour and duty.' Probably to counteract the wayward tendencies of the males in his family. 'How about you?'

'Sorry?'

'Who brought you up? I know your parents died but I have no idea when.'

Seconds stretched before she answered. 'They died when I was six.'

'Both?' His voice was sharp with surprise.

'It was a car accident. They died at the scene of the crash.'

Something about her tone made his nape prickle. 'You were there?'

'In the back seat.'

'Oh, Arden.' He wrapped himself tighter around her, tugging her back against him. 'I'm so sorry.'

'Like in your case, it was a long time ago.'

'But still tragic.' And difficult for her even now. It was there in her too flat voice and the way she held herself. 'It's young to lose your family.'

'Yes,' she said dully. 'I was losing them anyway but death is so final.' She drew a deep breath, her ribs expanding against his chest. 'They used to argue a lot. That night in the car, they thought I was asleep and they were at it again. Dad said he was getting a divorce and they were fighting over who'd have me. Dad didn't want to take me and Mum was upset, saying she couldn't manage alone. In the end they didn't have to worry.'

What could he say to that? Idris didn't try. He pressed his lips to her hair, gently reminding her of his presence.

'Did you have any family at all? Aunts and uncles?' He, at least, had had extended family when he'd lost his mother.

Arden shook her head. 'I went into foster care.'

'I'm sorry.' Idris couldn't believe he'd never thought to learn her history. Surely it had shaped Arden. Shame was a hot blade in his belly. He'd been too busy with other things to try understanding the woman he'd married.

'Don't be. It was okay most of the time.'

'And the rest of the time?' He'd heard appalling stories about defenceless, vulnerable children.

'Truly, it was okay. I was with one family for years. They treated me like their own little girl and I was happy. They were very kind.' Yet sadness lingered in her voice.

'But you left them?' he guessed.

'They planned to adopt me. They couldn't have children and wanted to keep me as theirs. But right at the end, before everything could be finalised, a miracle happened.' Her voice was matter-of-fact, as if she recited words supplied by someone else. It made his chest clench. 'They discovered they were expecting, not just one baby but twins.'

Arden drew a deep breath. 'They were nice people and upset they'd led me on only to disappoint me. They just couldn't afford three children or find space for that many. It wasn't anything personal.'

'Of course not.' Yet he wanted to find them and screw their necks for the pain they'd caused her.

Now he had some inkling of why Arden was so adamant about standing up for herself. Had there ever been anyone she could rely on long term?

She'd witnessed her parents squabbling about who'd

have to take her as they tore their family apart. Then she'd lost them both in horrific circumstances. Years later she'd lost the second secure home she'd known in a way guaranteed to break any child's heart.

And don't forget your part in her life. You seduced her and walked away without a backward glance. She thought you'd deliberately dumped her, abandoned her without a thought that she might be pregnant.

It hadn't been deliberate but he hadn't considered possible consequences. He hadn't made sure she was okay. He'd been too wrapped up in Zahrat and his own concerns.

He tightened his arms about her but now there was nothing sexual about his embrace. 'I'm here and I'm not leaving,' he whispered against her hair, shutting his eyes as her sweet fragrance filled his senses. 'I'm not walking away from this marriage. You and Dawud are safe with me.'

He'd make her happy. Make sure she never regretted marrying him.

CHAPTER TWELVE

A SHARP RAP on his open office door made Idris look up from his computer. Ashar, his aide, was already crossing the room, his expression shadowed. Foreboding streaked through Idris at that look.

'What is it?' Some new disaster. The treaty?

'Everything's under control; they're both safe.' Which meant it was Arden and Dawud.

Idris surged to his feet. 'Define *under control*. What's happened now?' It wasn't that Arden attracted trouble. It was more that her limited knowledge of Zahrat and her enthusiasm sometimes led her into unexpected situations.

Not just her. The palace was awash with children's artwork: flowers, animals, even a few dragons and a sea monster. Since news of the decorated banqueting hall got out, schools across the country had sent contributions for display. The Ministry of Education had quickly brought forward reforms to encourage creativity and innovation in schools to take advantage of public interest. A display of the art was planned for the new city hall, along with awards for teaching innovation—all part of the agenda to increase school attendance.

'You're sure they're both safe?' Idris leaned forward on fisted hands.

'They're fine. Their bodyguard is following them.'

The steely grip of tension in Idris's shoulders and spine didn't ease. 'Following? That implies they don't know where they're going.'

'That's why I came to see you. To check if you know of the Sheikha's plans for the afternoon.'

Idris shook his head. 'A visit to a community playgroup

with Dawud then back here.' Idris had thought long and hard about letting his son accompany Arden on the visit, but she'd been so eager and so persuasive. He'd wondered if Arden was lonely for the company of women her own age, young mothers with children. Her life was so different here from what it had been in London.

'They went to the playgroup, then they walked to the covered market where they bought food.'

Food? When they had a galley of chefs busy in the palace? It didn't make sense. There'd been no mention of a trip to the market this morning. 'Where are they now?'

'Driving the inland highway. The Sheikha is driving herself.'

Idris frowned. It was usual for Arden to have a driver as well as bodyguards. Mainly as a symbol of her status, since the threat level in Zahrat was virtually non-existent. But there was still the possibility of danger.

A new thought struck. That highway led to Zahrat's interior mountain range and to the airport. Arden wouldn't head to the mountains so late in the day. But the airport?

He rounded his desk, heading for the door. 'Get me the chopper *now*, and a line to the head of security.'

The *whoomp, whoomp, whoomp* of a helicopter split the late-afternoon quiet. Arden looked up, wondering where it was heading, but the endless blue sky was clear and the sound ceased. It must have landed nearby. She recalled Idris saying they used helicopters for mercy hospital flights. Perhaps someone had been injured on the highway.

'Mama. Look at fiss.' Dawud dragged her attention back to the pond where ornamental fish darted, glinting in the sunlight.

'Yes, darling. Lovely fish.' She grinned at her son's fascination with water—an unexpected trait in the son of a desert sheikh. Back at the palace he loved nothing better than paddling in the reflection pools. It was time she taught him to swim. She'd feel better when she knew he could keep himself afloat.

'Come on, our picnic's ready.' She patted the soft grass beside her in the dappled shade.

'Bye-bye, fiss.' He waved solemnly to the fish then trotted over to plop down beside her.

In the same instant swift movement in her peripheral vision made her twist around.

'Idris!' He strode across the garden courtyard, his expression harsh. Behind him she saw two men in black, her security detail, melting back behind the golden stone arches of this ancient palace. 'What are you doing here?'

'I could ask you the same thing.' He sounded different, his accent pronounced, his tone terse.

He looked different too.

Almost, she realised in shock, like the arrogant man she remembered from London. The autocratic warrior prince who expected instant obedience. His expression was stern, almost harsh.

'Baba!' Dawud was on his feet in a moment, hurrying towards his father, arms upstretched. Idris scooped him up in one easy movement, swinging him so high he giggled.

Arden watched the carved lines of Idris's face ease, his face creasing into a smile as Dawud wrapped his arms around his neck, burrowing close. Her heart leapt hard against her breastbone, seeing her son's unquestioning love for the big man who'd been a stranger till a few months ago, and such tenderness in Idris's expression. She'd done the right thing for Dawud, marrying Idris.

His gaze caught hers again and something hot and potent shivered through her.

'What are you doing here?'

'Having a picnic.' She waved to the packets she was unwrapping—dates and apricots, flat bread, soft goat's cheese, nuts and her favourite tiny pastries filled with pistachios and drenched in sweet syrup. 'Would you like to join us? I wasn't expecting to see you till tonight. Did your plans change?'

'You could say that.' He moved closer, Dawud tucked in his arms.

'You look tense. Is something wrong?' She frowned. The way he looked at her began to make her nervous.

'A slight crisis, caused by the fact neither your security detail nor the palace staff had any idea where you were going this afternoon. You gave your bodyguards the slip.'

'I did no such thing! I told them I wanted time alone with Dawud. I didn't see them after that.'

Idris shook his head. 'You thought they'd return to the palace without you? That's more than their jobs are worth, or their honour. They withdrew to give you space but they couldn't let you walk off alone. You gave them the fright of their lives when they lost you in the covered bazaar.'

Arden scrambled to her feet, shock hitting.

'You told me Dawud and I were safe in Zahrat. Everyone was friendly in the markets, and you said yourself it would be a good thing for us to get about more with the people, rather than being surrounded by courtiers.'

Idris shut his eyes for a second and Arden knew he was gathering his patience. She hated this feeling that, again, she'd inadvertently done the wrong thing. Nor was she used to explaining her every move.

'Is it so wrong to want to spend time doing something normal?'

'Normal?' He looked as if he'd never heard the word.

Arden gestured wide. Even her choice of picnic spot was dictated by the fact royals didn't simply set themselves down to eat in public parks. Weeks ago Idris had shown her this little palace on its own rocky outcrop just beyond the city. It had been the dower residence of his grandmother and Arden loved its tranquillity and beauty. Today she hadn't been ready to return to the palace and, after just over three months in Zahrat, this was the only other private place she knew.

'Yes, normal. Doing a little shopping. Passing the time of day. Spending time with other mothers and children.'

It wasn't till she'd visited the playgroup that she'd realised how much she missed those small freedoms. She'd been invited in her role as Sheikha, but in reality it had been plain Arden, mother of an inquisitive, busy toddler, who'd chattered with the other mums. 'I need some freedom, Idris. You must understand that.'

With a sigh, Idris lowered Dawud to the ground then wrapped his palm around the back of his neck as if easing an ache. It made her want to massage his knotted muscles, and wish she'd never even thought of a picnic.

Dawud plonked down at their feet and reached for some dried apricots.

'Idris?'

'I understand. You weren't born to this world. It takes a lot of adjustment. But next time let the staff know what you intend. You caused a security scare going off grid like that.' The corners of his mouth tucked down and he rolled his shoulders.

Seeing his tension, Arden felt a familiar wriggle of guilt in her belly. She got it every time she said the wrong thing at a royal event or broke some unwritten tradition.

'How much of a security scare?' Her eyes rounded. 'That helicopter?' At his nod she squeezed her eyes shut. Had they mobilised the army too? She felt about an inch tall. 'I'm so sorry. I didn't realise.'

Idris was right. She didn't understand all the rules. His life would have been easier if he'd married a real princess who knew how to behave and didn't disrupt the smooth workings of the royal machine.

Arden shook her head. She refused to go there again. She was doing her best.

'Hey.' An arm wrapped around her, tugging her against him. She opened her eyes to find herself fixed by his dark, velvety gaze. 'It's all right. There's no harm done.'

Her mouth crumpled in a travesty of a smile. 'I'm sure it's not but thanks for pretending. Just tell me, my bodyguards won't get into trouble, will they?'

He shook his head. 'Chastened but fine. Think of it as keeping them on their toes.' A sudden grin lit his face. 'You're good for them. They have no chance to get complacent.'

This time her smile felt real, but still distress lurked. She'd so enjoyed this afternoon. Hadn't dreamed it could hurt.

'What are you thinking?' His breath warmed her forehead as his arm slipped around her waist.

'That next time I want to go on a picnic I'll probably have three chefs and a dozen attendants with me. After filling out a security form detailing my intended movements down to the minute.'

'It's not that bad.' When she raised her eyebrows his lips twisted. 'Not *quite* that bad. And I'll see what I can do about making things easier. Starting right now.'

'Now?' Surely her little escape had ended.

'Now.' His voice deepened and a slow smile lightened his features. 'You've got me away from the office and I intend to make the most of it. I vote we play hooky together.'

Abruptly he sank to the ground, pulling her with him so she fell across his lap. She had an impression of midnight eyes and gleaming golden skin then his lips were on hers, not softly but with a pent-up hunger she recognised. Arden grabbed his shoulders, fire igniting instantly at her feminine core.

She was just going under for the third time when a strident voice piped up. 'Mama.' A little, warm body pushed against her, one sticky hand touching her cheek. 'Dawud kiss too.'

She heard Idris's chuckle, felt him shift to tug Dawud close and for one exquisite moment let herself believe in the perfection of the three of them together, like a real family.

Idris made the most of his unscheduled escape from royal duties, turning the afternoon into an idyllic family adventure exploring the tiny but lovely old palace. Tiny by Zahrati standards. It was still a mansion, filled with gorgeous furnishings and with an unrivalled view to the coast, the city and the mountains beyond.

With Dawud they investigated, admiring splendid mosaics, bedrooms and grand salons. The palace was furnished with beautiful antiques but somehow felt more like a sprawling home than a royal estate.

Evening came and with it a grander picnic than anything Arden had imagined. White coated servants from the Palace of Gold spread turquoise and scarlet rugs on the grass. Braziers were lit around the garden, glowing and scented. The array of delicious food was a feast for the senses.

Later the servants disappeared and Dawud's nanny carried him, sleeping, to the car for the drive back to the citadel.

Finally alone, Idris insisted on feeding Arden dessert with his own hands. Ripe peaches, bursting with rich juice, dark red grapes still with the bloom of the vine on them and sweet oranges.

Then he licked up the spills where juice had dripped. She laughed, buoyed by the delight of this special time alone, by the hungry look in her husband's eyes and the eager yet tender touch of his hands as he stripped her clothes away. It was no surprise when Idris carried her inside to find that one of the beds had been made up with fine linen sheets scented with cinnamon and rose petals. Candles glowed around the room, turning it into a romantic bower.

'The honeymoon we never had,' Idris said when she exclaimed at the beauty of the scene. Then he laid her on the bed and she stopped thinking about her surroundings.

Arden gasped for air, her lungs tight. Her blood pounded as bliss shuddered through her in aftershocks so intense she thought they'd never end.

She didn't want them to end. Not when Idris was there, above her, inside her, surrounding her with his big body and powerful shoulders, quaking like her as his climax slowly faded. She felt the throb of his life force, the sensation that together they touched heaven, and she didn't want to let go.

She loved him coming apart in her arms, his weight hemming her in, his breath jagged in her ear, his formidable control shattered. In this they were equals and she revelled in it.

He groaned against her shoulder, sending fresh waves of pleasure juddering through her. Then Idris rolled onto his back, pulling her with him to sprawl naked across his steaming body.

Arden squinted one eye open, seeing the pink flush of dawn streaming in the open window. Soon Idris would get up to begin work.

But she didn't want to leave the Dower Palace. The spell of the place enveloped her. She wanted to hold Idris here, make him stay so she could enjoy the luxury of being alone with him, away from royal responsibilities. Here she'd felt not only happy but cherished.

Was she reading too much into last night's bliss? Into

their sexual compatibility? Was she mistaking the after-glow of orgasm for a tenderness centred on mutual feeling?

'I was thinking,' he murmured, his lips moving against her hair, one arm wrapped around her waist.

'Hmm?'

'About another baby.'

Arden stilled, her finger poised where it had been strok-ing light circles across his ribs.

'A baby?'

'A brother or sister for Dawud. What do you think?' Did she imagine a thread of excitement in his voice? No. She'd been wrong. Idris sounded as calm as ever.

'You want another child?'

'Don't you?'

Yes. The answer slammed into her. She didn't need to think about it. Something deep down, something intrinsic to the woman she was, knew the answer as if she'd pon-dered it long and hard.

Arden blinked, stunned by the excitement she felt bub-bling up. She'd got pregnant so young she hadn't really had time to think about having kids and since having Dawud she'd been too busy even to consider a relationship and another child.

'Arden?' Idris crooked a finger under her chin, lifting her face. He was propped up a little, his arm folded be-hind his head. The way he lay emphasised the impressive muscles of his arm and shoulder. Instantly heat drilled through her tight chest to her pelvis. Exhausted from sex and still she craved this man!

'Yes? I…' She refocused on his question. 'I don't know,' she prevaricated, for reasons she didn't understand. 'Why do you want another?'

Those jet eyebrows crunched together as if he didn't like her question. Had he expected her to jump at the idea? That was intriguing.

'Don't you think a sibling would be good for Dawud?'

'Possibly.' Actually, she thought it would be wonderful but she reminded herself she owed it to her son and herself to do more than act impulsively. She'd done that when she fell for Idris years ago and it had turned her life on its head.

'Neither of us had siblings. We know how lonely that can be, especially when tragedy strikes.'

Grimly Arden nodded, her stomach cramping, not at the memory of those lonely childhood years bereft of family but at the idea of anything happening to Idris.

Horror filled her. A deep-down chill like the one she'd felt six months ago when for a few heart-numbing minutes she'd lost Dawud in a crowded shop.

She laid her palm flat on Idris's chest, feeling the steady thump of his heart, telling herself it was stupid to hypothesise about tragedy striking down Idris.

'Besides,' he went on, unaware of her fear, 'it sounds old-fashioned but it's a good way to ensure the security of the throne, and the nation, for the future. That's an important consideration too.'

'In case anything happens to Dawud?' Her voice was harsh.

Idris cupped a soothing palm around her bare shoulder. 'Nothing is going to happen to Dawud. But you never know—' he smiled in the way he knew made her melt '—our firstborn may want to go off and become an academic like my cousin, or a rock star. Having a brother to take the throne—'

'Or a sister,' she bit out, anger rising. As the law currently stood, only a male could inherit the throne. Unfair as she thought it, it wasn't that fuelling her temper. It was the notion she should have Idris's child to keep the throne safe and avoid political turmoil. They were talking about children! Children who deserved to be loved for themselves. Not pieces in some dynastic game!

'Or a sister.' Idris raised one eyebrow. 'Which would lead us to a discussion on exactly how many children we'd like to have.'

She recognised that lazy smile. It spoke of sexual promise. She had no complaints about making love with Idris. He made her feel not only satisfied but treasured. Which showed how skilled Idris was. To him having a child meant sex, which he clearly enjoyed. Enjoyed it enough to appear almost insatiable for her, a woman foisted on him by circumstance rather than personal preference.

But having a baby was about a lot more than that, as she knew too well.

'I'll think about it.' She pulled back, putting a little distance between them and watching his complacent smile slip. 'It's a lot to ask.'

His stare raked her. Clearly he hadn't expected that response. 'Of course.' Yet a frown rippled his broad brow and his grip on her shoulder tightened. 'There's plenty of time to think it over. Neither of us is going anywhere.'

Because he'd given his word.

Because he'd married her in front of thousands of witnesses.

Because he had no other choice but to stick with her.

Suddenly exhaustion filled her.

She hadn't married for love, other than the love of a mother for her child. She'd actually been enjoying her marriage to Idris, discovering as the months passed that their marriage suited her. *He* suited her. Even her life in Zahrat, though still challenging, brought satisfaction and a tentative sense of accomplishment. So why did the reminder that this was a purely practical union bring a bitter taint to her tongue?

Because your husband sees all this—you, your marriage, even your children—through the lens of practicality. Whereas for you...your heart is engaged.

Idris hauled her close, cupping the back of her head and drawing her against his chest. Automatically Arden fitted herself to him, one knee across his thigh, an arm round his waist.

But her mind raced, horrified by the stark truth of her discovery. That sudden, unbearable flash of insight had exploded her convenient belief that she could accept a loveless marriage.

Furtively she blinked back the haze of moisture misting her view of the dawn.

How had she deluded herself so long? It seemed impossible she'd never seen the truth before.

You didn't want the truth. You were wilfully blind because you knew the implications and didn't want to face them.

Arden bit her lip and tried not to panic, but it was almost impossible.

She'd congratulated herself on being reasonable and civilised, giving Dawud's father shared access. Accepting a sensible, convenient marriage though it meant living with a man she barely knew and embracing a whole new culture, giving up her safe, familiar world.

She'd even applauded the fact she could embark on a sexual relationship with the man she'd once loved and it wouldn't matter.

Of course it mattered.

Some sly part of herself must have realised the truth from the first. That it hadn't been so much of a sacrifice to marry him.

Because she was in love with Idris.

She had been all along. Only pride and pain had made her pretend she wasn't.

He was the only lover she'd ever had and, she realised with a hollow fear that threatened to engulf her, the only man she'd ever want.

* * *

Back at the Palace of Gold, Arden paced her sitting room, arms folded tight around her middle as if that could prevent the deep-seated ache inside.

Idris had left her with a bold kiss and a gleam in his eyes as soon as they returned from the Dower Palace. She'd clung to him, desperate to be held, though her brain said she needed to break free and decide what to do. For that she needed space and solitude.

First she'd cancelled her appointments for the day, surprising an understanding smile on one of the secretaries. Arden supposed all the palace staff knew she and Idris had spent an unscheduled belated honeymoon night.

Then she'd gone to Dawud, eager for the familiarity of his sturdy little frame and bright smile. She joined him in a game involving toy cars and a road map floor mat and lots of noise. But even as she smiled and crawled along, there was a terrifying blankness inside her where she fiercely shut out the hurt that would flood in if she let it.

Finally, when she felt calm enough to face what she must, she'd left Dawud with Misha and come here to her room. Stopping by the window she stared out beyond the city to the small Dower Palace.

She longed to recapture the magic of last evening. The thrill of being with Idris, not as a bride forced upon him by circumstance but as his lover. The woman who loved him and for a few thoughtless hours had lived as carefree and content as if he loved her too.

The wall damming the dark pain cracked and despair poured out, making her clutch at the window frame with the force of that hurt.

Desperate, she told herself nothing had changed. Idris had never pretended to love her. He was decent and caring, dependable, honourable and, yes, charming. She loved his wry humour and he was great with Dawud. The pair were building a fantastic rapport.

It was she who'd changed. Or, if her suspicions were correct, not changed, but finally realised she'd been fooling herself. Because she loved Idris with all her being. Just as she'd loved Shakil all those years ago. Loved and lost.

Arden clawed the window frame and sank, a bundle of brittle bones, onto the window seat.

Loving and losing was a constant theme in her life.

First her parents. Then her foster parents. Then Shakil. Now Idris.

No, she wouldn't lose him, not that way. He'd promised to stay with her, support her and do the right thing by Dawud. He'd do it, she knew he would. She knew him now, better than she had all that time ago. He saw this marriage as his duty and he'd stick at it no matter what.

There'd be no divorce. But Arden wasn't a naïve girl now. She knew a man like Idris would have sexual needs long after he lost interest in her. This honeymoon period, prompted she guessed by novelty and his desire for more children, would end soon enough.

What then? Arden had told him she didn't want to find out about his lovers. He hadn't demurred, simply agreed and moved on. At the time she'd been devastated at the idea of marrying a man already planning to be with other women.

That was before she realised she loved him.

How could she cope when he turned away and discreetly found with other women what he no longer wanted from her?

A tearing sound rent the air and she realised it was a groan of pain.

Idris would turn his back and she'd be left high and dry. Again.

Once more she'd got her hopes up. She hadn't consciously thought that one day her husband might come to love her but it had been there, a hidden nugget of hope, all this time.

She'd always craved love, stability, someone to value her as the most important person in their life. Every time hope had been snatched away.

Was that her fate? To seek love and always be disappointed?

She couldn't live like this, as merely a necessary wife. Idris cared about her but not enough. Loving him when he felt only mild affection, seeing him turn to other women, would destroy her. She wouldn't let that happen. She would be strong, for herself and for Dawud. It was the way life had made her.

Arden got to her feet, grimacing at her creaky movements, as if the hoary fingers of age already claimed her. Slowly she straightened, her eyes fixed on the beautiful little palace beyond the city.

She had to find a way to survive this deal they'd made, do the best for Dawud, and for Idris, but keep her self-respect. And she had an inkling how she could do it.

This time she wouldn't be the one left behind.

CHAPTER THIRTEEN

A QUICK RAP on his study door made Idris look up, his brain still grappling with the new draft of the treaty.

Ashar stood in the doorway, his features so carefully blank that unease instantly ripped up Idris's backbone. It reminded him of yesterday when his aide had come to report that Arden was driving out of town, destination unknown.

This was worse. He sensed it.

'Tell me.'

Not Arden. Not Dawud.

The ferocity of his fear for them paralysed him.

'They're both fine. Both well.' Ashar stepped over the threshold, closing the door behind him, and Idris sagged in his swivel chair, his fingers grabbing the edge of the desk too tight. His heart catapulted against his ribs, its rhythm sharp.

'But?' Idris tried to tell himself it was another small misunderstanding. It couldn't be anything major. Despite her doubts, Arden was increasingly adept at dealing with courtiers and the public. As for visiting VIPs, she charmed them with an ease that made him want to laugh. This was the woman his advisers had doubted could hold her own in public and she was proving his best asset with her unconventional, direct ways.

He wished he'd had her at his side when he'd first taken the role of Sheikh. The burdens would have been much lighter, and his life so much better.

'Tell me, Ashar.' His aide's silence was unnerving.

Idris watched him take a chair on the other side of the desk. 'The Sheikha and the little Prince are both at the Dower Palace.'

Idris let his pent-up breath surge out. For a moment he'd feared something terrible.

'Another picnic?' A smile curved his mouth. He'd toyed with the idea of shirking all his appointments today and spending time with his family. Amazing how much the idea appealed. He'd had to force himself out of Arden's arms and their bed in the little palace, telling himself this new treaty, and the meeting on improving infrastructure for remote provinces, were too vital to delay.

But he'd vowed to take Arden back there soon. Last night had felt like the honeymoon they'd never had. More, as if they'd found a new level of understanding. Their necessary marriage had blossomed in a way he'd never expected. She made him *happy*, he realised. Happy and proud. It was a revelation.

Ashar shook his head. He opened his mouth but didn't speak. Instead he cleared his throat.

Foreboding dimmed Idris's smile. 'Out with it, quickly.'

Ashar looked down at his hands. 'The Sheikha has co-opted several palace staff to help her refurbish the Dower Palace.'

'Refurbish?' Idris didn't know if he was more perplexed by the idea of it needing refurbishment or the fact Arden had directed staff to do anything. She was notoriously unwilling to issue orders, unused to having paid servants.

Ashar shrugged. 'Perhaps not refurbish. But open up the rooms ready to be lived in.' He paused, his gaze lifting to Idris. 'She gave the impression the order came from you.'

Ashar met his wary eyes. They both knew Idris had given no such order.

'Anything else?'

His secretary's expression flickered with something that might have been sympathy. 'I understand your wife and son's belongings have been packed up and moved out of the Palace of Gold.'

* * *

Idris slammed the door of his four-wheel drive and signalled his staff to remain here in the courtyard of the Dower Palace. Anger took him across the cobbled yard to the arch where ancient wooden doors, said to be as old as his family's rule on the throne of Zahrat, sat open.

A couple of strides took him to another, smaller courtyard and a maid, her arms full of bed linen. Her eyes rounded when she saw him and she stopped, curtseying.

'You're to leave here now and return to your usual duties.' His voice rasped out, harsh and unrecognisable. Like the fury he only just held in check. Fury that Arden would play such a game, trying to make a fool of him. 'Tell the other staff to stop what they're doing and get out immediately. Close the front doors behind you.'

She bobbed her head and scurried away, clasping the linen to her chest.

Idris stalked forward, through more doors, across the courtyard where just last night Arden had lain in his arms while he fed her sweet treats and seduced her into boneless compliance.

Of all the emotions that had rushed through him at Ashar's news, the strongest was hurt. Hurt that after all he and Arden had shared, after the sense of wordless understanding he'd woken to this morning, she should play such a trick. He couldn't believe she'd deliberately make him a laughing stock. Or that she was attempting some sort of blackmail, moving out to secure a better deal for herself.

When had he not given her what she desired?

When had he withheld his support? His riches?

When had he been anything but the best husband he could be? And in return he knew she'd strived to meet the demands of her new role.

So what was she playing at?

If she was unhappy she just had to say and he'd deal with the problem.

But this wasn't something she wanted him to fix. That was clear from the fact she'd moved out and taken Dawud.

This was a pre-emptive strike.

He'd trusted her! Let her become part of his life in ways he'd never imagined letting any woman, and she'd betrayed him.

He couldn't believe it. Or the excruciating ache in his heart.

Room after room passed. Some untouched, some bearing traces of recent change. Dustcovers removed. Mirrors sparkling. Mosaic floors glistening from scrubbing. He passed the room where they'd spent the night but it was deserted. Another room and there was a familiar white bed, tucked in a corner by the window. The mat he'd bought Dawud, a carpet road map for him to play on, lay beside it. Idris recognised the books and toys on top of a new dresser, and in the bed a tousled dark head, a small hand still grasping a teddy as Dawud slept.

Idris stopped, his heart skidding against his sternum as relief battered him. *Dawud was safe.*

He drew in a deep breath, then another, trying to ease the hammering of his pulse as his gaze ate up the sight of his boy.

Something, some infinitesimal sound made him turn. Seconds later he was in the doorway of another bedroom. A white sheet snapped in the air as it was flung across a bed. A bed much smaller than the one he and Arden shared. Yet it was Arden smoothing the crisp cotton down the mattress. Arden, not in her finery but wearing a simple white sleeveless dress. Arden with her hair gleaming in the sunset glow coming from the window.

Idris stepped into the room, securing the door behind

him. The snick of the lock made her look up, then her hand was at her throat, her face pale as chalk.

'Idris! You scared me!'

He folded his arms across his chest, not bothering now to keep a lid on the ire that had burned and bubbled since his aide's visit. Was Idris the last in the royal compound to hear that his wife had moved out, sneaking their son with her?

Arden's hand fell to her side and she backed a step as if the sight of him frightened her. *Good!*

'I didn't expect to see you yet.'

Yet? That implied she *had* intended to see him. He felt a trickle of relief. Till he wondered where she'd planned to meet him. In the office of a divorce lawyer? No lawyer in the country would take her on. He'd see to that.

'I suppose you're wondering what I'm doing?' Her hands twisted together till she saw him notice and hauled them behind her back like a naughty schoolgirl. But this was no teenage prank.

'Why don't you say something?' Her voice was thin, as if stretched taut by emotion. Which was all wrong. She'd planned this deliberately, with cold calculation. *He* was the one feeling.

'I'm waiting for an explanation.'

'I…' Her hand climbed her throat again, fingers splaying nervously, till she blinked and dropped her arm. Her chin tilted. 'I'm moving out.'

Idris stared, watching her lips circle the words, hearing them resonate in his ears, and yet the sound didn't seem real. It was as if she spoke from a long distance, the words muffled by the skip of his pulse and the throbbing tension wrapping him so tight he felt his skin would split and bleed.

'Explain!'

'Dawud and I—' She gestured: a quick circular motion

encompassing the room and, presumably, the one next door. 'We'll live here. It will work out better this way. I was going to tell you—'

'Really? And when were you going to impart this news?' His voice was barely above a growl, low, guttural and cold as her frigid English heart. 'Before or after the whole city heard about it?'

Her eyes widened and her mouth sagged. 'No, I—'

'No, you weren't going to tell me after all? You were going to let me find out for myself? Just as, in fact, I did?'

Fury rose to towering levels. He paced the room, planting himself between Arden and the door. She'd betrayed him, made a fool of him, stolen his son. He'd woken this morning to a sense of peace and promise unlike any he'd ever known. He'd looked forward to building a family with her and all the time she'd planned to leave.

He'd never known such pain as that tearing at his vitals. Only years of warrior training kept him upright.

If she thought he'd permit her to get away with this she was incredibly naïve.

Arden looked up into hard, fathomless eyes. She didn't recognise them. Didn't recognise the man before her. This wasn't the bronzed warrior prince she'd come to love. This was a stranger. As he uncrossed his arms and flexed his fingers she shivered.

She told herself to buck up. She'd known this wouldn't be easy. But if she was to preserve her sanity and her self-respect it had to be done.

'Why don't we go somewhere more comfortable and sit down to discuss this?' She felt trapped by his forceful presence, literally cornered.

'Stop delaying.' He widened his stance and re-crossed his arms over his powerful chest, reinforcing that potent male power battering her shredded nerves.

How was she supposed to fight him when part of her wanted to nestle against that broad shoulder and accept what he offered her, even though it wasn't enough?

Arden swallowed a tangle of emotion and forced herself to meet his glare.

'This marriage isn't working for me. I had my doubts from the start, you know that, and…' She gestured vaguely. 'Well, it turns out I was right.'

'In what way isn't it working?' His face was so flinty, his expression so fixed, his lips barely moved.

'I don't feel…' *loved.* She couldn't admit that. 'You must understand.' Another quick wave of her hand. 'Zahrat, living in a palace, marriage to a sheikh; it's all a far cry from what I'm used to. And what I'm comfortable with.'

Was it possible that his thinned lips tightened even further?

'I don't feel able to continue like I have been, so I've come up with a compromise.'

'This doesn't look like compromise to me,' he snarled. 'This looks like desertion.'

Arden jammed her hands onto her hips, summoning anger to block out the pain in her heart. 'Desertion would be me taking Dawud on the next flight out of here and filing for divorce.' Her breath came so fast she couldn't keep going.

She heaved in more air and dredged up some words before he interrupted. 'Instead I propose to live here with Dawud. Close enough that you can still see him daily. He can go to the Palace of Gold to visit you or you could come here.' She paused. Having Idris here in what would be her sanctuary would just prolong her heartache. But what alternative could she offer?

Idris opened his mouth and she raised a hand to stop him. 'Just hear me out.' She snagged another quick breath. 'This way you have the marriage you needed and the heir but without the encumbrance of…me. You know I'm not good at the whole royal thing. Everyone will understand the split. I told the staff it was your order that I move here. People will think *you've* set me aside, and they won't be surprised because everyone knows I'm an embarrassment.' Heat crept up her cheeks at the memory of so many public blunders.

But in the scale of things those mistakes meant nothing. Not compared to walking away from the man she loved. Dully she wondered how long it would be before the hurt started to ease. Or if it ever would.

'I won't embarrass you if I'm living here, out of the public eye. And you'll be free to take lovers without worrying about me being on the premises.' Something within her collapsed, crumpling at the thought, but she kept her chin up. 'It's the best solution.'

Except she didn't believe it for a moment. Living in Zahrat, so close to Idris, would be torment. Yet for Dawud's sake she'd endure it.

Idris's gaze bored into hers. 'This is the second time you've mentioned my lovers. You seem inordinately interested in them.' Something flickered in that enigmatic dark stare. 'Why is that? Are you intending to vet them yourself to see they're not a negative influence on our son when they meet?'

'You wouldn't do that! You promised to be discreet and not flaunt them in front of Dawud.' Fury rose, a fiery column, scorching her from the inside. She actually took a step closer till she read the predatory stillness in Idris's big frame, the intensity of his haughty glare, and realised he was deliberately taunting her.

That casual cruelty punctured her indignation, leaving her empty and fragile. She swayed, praying for the strength to see this through.

'It's time to admit it's not working and accept a sensible compromise. You've done everything that could be expected of you, Idris. You've married me and legitimised Dawud. You've upheld your honour.'

Idris stared at her. A nervous, defiant woman who looked like the beautiful wife he'd taken to bed last night but couldn't be. His wife had spent the evening sighing her pleasure while setting out to please him more successfully than any other woman ever had.

Then, as usual, she'd curled confidingly close. He'd grown used to her snuggling against him as if, even in sleep, she needed physical intimacy to settle.

He'd grown used to greeting the dawn making love to her. More often than not sharing a bath or shower with her. He'd even become accustomed to chatting with her after formal events, sharing observations and insights, always fascinated by the different perspective she provided. And breakfasting with her and Dawud, enjoying a growing understanding and shared purpose in caring for their boy. He'd been proud of her progress in dealing with state occasions, and her surprising aptitude at his language. He'd laughed with her over things he'd never been able to share with others and found increasing pleasure in relaxing with her.

Over the past months she'd become more than a convenient bride. She'd become his *wife*.

How had it all gone wrong?

Why had she done this?

Idris stepped closer, watching with mingled satisfaction and pain as she shrank against the wall.

'Honour! You talk to me of honour? As if that's all this marriage is about?' He was so incensed he had to work to keep his voice low enough that it didn't disturb Dawud in the next room. Fire ran in his veins, a white-hot incendiary burn that ate him up from the inside, devouring him. Or perhaps that was the anguish he was trying not to think about.

'What about *us*, Arden? You and me? And Dawud?' He leaned over her and her head tilted back against the wall. But she didn't look scared any more. She looked tired, and that tore at him.

After what she'd done, and the way she'd insulted him, he felt *concerned* for her?

'As you say,' she said softly, 'this marriage is about you and me and our son. I think it best for Dawud not to grow up watching our marriage disintegrate. Better to make an amicable break now and come to a compromise that allows him to grow up with both of us.'

Compromise. There was that word again. Idris had never hated it so much.

'You're lying. Whatever is behind your actions, this isn't about Dawud. This—' a sharp gesture encompassed the half-made bed and his errant wife '—is about you and me.'

Instinct drove that observation and he saw it confirmed when her eyelids fluttered and her gaze skated sideways, as if she were scared he'd read the truth in her expression.

What *was* the truth? She'd hurt him as surely as if she'd taken his grandfather's ceremonial sword and sliced Idris right through the chest. He'd never experienced anything like this pain he was helpless to understand or control. It made him even more determined.

Another step took him into her space. Her chin tipped high to keep him in her sights. He sensed her fight or flight response in her sharp, tremulous breaths and her air of expectation.

Just let her try to flee. He'd enjoy stopping her.

'What could it be, I wonder?' He thought over her explanation.

'All that about being an embarrassment to me is whitewash. You don't embarrass me and you never have. You know that. I'm *proud* of the way you've adapted. You've got a gift for putting people at their ease, a gift for making them feel welcome. You like people, you're interested in them and that shows.'

Her eyes grew wide. 'But I—'

'No buts. You know it's true. Don't I tell you time and again how wonderful you are? How quickly you've mastered your royal duties? You've already won the hearts of half the schoolchildren in the country and their parents. That only leaves fifty per cent to go.'

Where he found levity from Idris didn't know, but the idea of Arden hiding like some shameful secret was totally absurd.

Her reasons for moving out didn't make sense.

'Then there's the question of my lovers.' She flinched then schooled her expression into immobility. His hunter's instinct sharpened.

She cared about him having women?

Of course she cared. He'd be outraged if she didn't.

The idea of Arden and his cousin as lovers had unearthed previously unknown violent instincts in Idris, till she'd convinced him there'd been no man in her life for four years.

No man in her life but himself.

His thoughts slowed to a familiar, all-consuming satisfaction. Idris was her only lover and he intended it to stay that way. He couldn't countenance the idea of Arden with any other man. Ever.

Sudden heat bloomed in his chest as realisation smacked him.

He rocked back on his feet, actually taking a half step away as knowledge smote him.

'My lovers,' he repeated slowly, his brain, *finally*, catching up with instinct. 'You don't want to meet my lovers.'

The voice wasn't his. It was hoarse, thick and dull, stunned by what he'd blithely never considered before.

Had he really been so blind?

His heart hammered against his ribs and his breath came in sharp snatches, dragged into lungs that felt too small to cope with the enormity of the knowledge battering him.

'You promised. You agreed not to flaunt them so Dawud or I would see them.' She glared, hands on her hips, her bottom lip jutting belligerently. In her white silk dress, with her hair in gilded waves around her shoulders and her aquamarine eyes dazzling like gems, she was stunning.

How could he want another woman when he had Arden?

He shook his head, blinking at the patent absurdity of it.

She stepped forward, prodding his chest. 'A man of *honour* wouldn't go back on his word.'

Idris clapped his hand over hers, pressing it against his racing heart. He saw her still, her eyes widen from slits of anger to pools of shimmering surprise.

'Feel that?' His voice was a raw rasp. 'You do that to me, Arden.' As he said it Idris felt the power of it fill him like a shaft of sunshine streaming all the way to the bottom of an abandoned, empty well.

Except he didn't feel empty now. He felt filled to the brim with fierce, choking, glorious feeling.

She tugged at her hand, her mouth turning down, her brow knotted. 'You're angry at the inconvenience I'm causing. That's all.'

'Not angry. Furious. I was furious. But I'm not now.'

Yet his heart rate didn't ease. His temper might have dried up but what he felt now was simultaneously the most amazing, frightening thing he'd ever experienced.

He swallowed hard, his Adam's apple bobbing painfully.

'I don't care, Idris. I just want you to let me go.' Arden's voice rose in a wailing sob that cut him to the bone. Her pain was his, tenfold.

He lifted his other hand and stroked the hair from her cheek, marvelling again at the softness of her skin. He closed his eyes, trying to save this moment of absolute awareness, inhaling her light orange blossom fragrance.

'There will be no other women.'

Finally she stopped trying to free herself. 'Pardon?'

'There won't be any other women for me. I never intended to take another lover.'

'But you agreed—'

His eyes snapped open and he looked down into her stunned face. 'I agreed never to flaunt a lover. I never said there would actually *be* any lovers.' He paused, amazed at how slow-witted he'd been. He'd never questioned why that was. 'I knew even then that I'd want no one else. I haven't since I met you again.'

Her mouth tightened. 'You're saying that because you think it will make me change my mind. But it won't. It's nothing to me if you have a whole harem of lovers.'

'Isn't it?' He cupped her cheek. 'You may not care but I would. I just couldn't do it.'

He stared into her grumpy, set features and told himself he owed her the truth, even if by some ill-omened fate he was wrong about Arden's feelings for him. His pulse sprinted like a mad thing and fear tightened his belly.

'Aren't you going to ask me why I couldn't take a lover?'

She blinked then looked away. He felt her tremble and her pain made his chest seize. 'Don't do this, Idris. I don't think I—'

'I couldn't take another woman into my bed because there's only one woman I'll ever want, in my bed and in my life. That's you, Arden. I love you, *habibti*. I have from the start, though I was too slow to see it. I felt it. I hated believing there'd been other men in your life. I hated feeling that you didn't need me or want me. That's one of the reasons I acted so quickly to secure you, before you could run off again.'

'I never ran anywhere.' Her eyes were round as saucers and her tremor intensified till she shook all over.

'It felt like it.' Now, in retrospect, he realised that was exactly how it had been. 'I deserted you because I had to face my responsibilities, my *duty*.' His mouth twisted. 'But it seemed like you'd run away with my heart. I never felt for any woman what I felt for you. Not in all the years we were apart.' He shook his head. 'Why do you think I made a beeline for your house the morning after the reception? I *had* to see you again, had to be with you, even though it was total insanity if I really planned to marry someone else.'

'Idris?' Arden's voice was a tremulous whisper, her mouth working. 'Please. Are you just saying this because—?'

'I'm saying it because it's true, Arden. I love you. You make me feel whole.' He fell to his knees before her, ignoring generations of royal pride, knowing only that he *had* to make her believe. He gathered her hands in his.

'I didn't think it possible. The men in my family never lose their hearts. All except King Dawud, my grandfather, who adored my grandmother till his dying day.' Idris pressed her hands, willing her to believe. 'That's my excuse for not realising how I felt about you. It didn't even occur to me that the jealousy and lust, the pride and admiration, the liking, were all part of love.'

He lifted first one of her hands, then the other, pressing kisses to each. 'I love you, Arden, with all my heart. With all that I am. On my honour, on the honour of my family and the memory of my grandfather, it's true.' He paused, emotions surging so high speech was difficult.

'But if you don't believe me yet, don't worry, you will. I intend to convince you every day for the rest of our lives.'

If she let him.

Tears glistened in her eyes and his heart cramped. Dismay filled him and dread that perhaps he'd been wrong to imagine she cared for him.

But before he could conjure a protest she'd sunk to her knees before him, her hands gripping his strongly.

Heart in mouth, he watched her raise his hand, then press her delicate lips to it. A ripple ran up his arm, across his shoulder to splinter to spread through his body. Slowly she kissed his other hand and his heart sang.

'I love you, Idris.' Those stunning eyes, washed, he realised, with tears of happiness, were the most beautiful in the whole world. 'I loved you in Santorini. I even loved you in the years we were apart though I told myself it wasn't so.' Her mouth curved in a secretive smile that melted his soul. 'I'll always love you.'

A huge sigh escaped him, shuddering out the pent-up breath he'd held too long. His whole being felt renewed, stronger, better. 'Then we're perfectly matched. For I will love you till the last breath in my body, and beyond.'

He watched the stars shine in her eyes, the sun rise in her smile and knew he'd come home.

'I have a suggestion.'

Her gaze slid to the bed beside them and he laughed, the sound of pure joy ringing around them. 'Soon, Arden.' Already he was strung taut and eager for her. 'But I wanted to suggest we move in here together, you, me and Dawud.'

'Really? But you need to be at the Palace of Gold. All your official responsibilities...'

'*Our* official responsibilities,' he amended. 'I propose that during the week we stay there, and do what's expected of a royal sheikh and sheikha. And on weekends we live here, out of the limelight, just being a family.'

'You could do that? Really?'

'*We* can do it. With some planning I don't see why not. In fact, I insist.'

Her smile said everything he could have wanted as he pulled her to him.

'It sounds just perfect.' Whatever else she intended to say was lost against his lips as he bestowed the first kiss of the rest of their lives. A kiss of love, offered and received. A kiss of promise.

* * * * *